Frion Farrell

GW00391588

The Au
by
Frion Farrell

Third and Final Book of the Myriar Series

Best Wishes

Frion Farrell .

PLATFORM ONE 2017
SECOND EDITION 2022

First Edition 2017
Second Edition 2022

Other books in the Myriar series:

The Round Spear
First Edition 2013-Wordbranch
Second Edition 2017-Platform One
Third Edition 2021-Platform One
ISBN9781549569593

The Stone Of Mesa
First Edition 2014-Wordbranch
Second Edition 2017-Platform One
Third Edition 2021-Platform One
ISBN9781549566158

Email:platformonewriting@gmail.com

DEDICATION

For Thomas Fanning, Rosemary Breen and in memory of Fiona Stuart

Teachers of Kindness

GLOSSARY

Alleator- music maker

Amron Cloch – Song Stone

Arwres – Myriar stone of the Inscriptor

Chalycion- Myriar stone of the Creta

Chimera- Part lion, part goat, part serpent

Creta- A seed of the Myriar- artist

Devouril- Once Mourangils, followers of Belluvour

Fossilia – tiny, butterfly-like light beings that facilitate movement between space and time.

Frindy- shortened version of Pont y Ffrindiau

Galinir – female Devouril

Irresythe- a giant winged creature

Iridice– the Myriar stone of the Reeder

Inscriptor-Seed of the Myriar – translates ancient and modern language

Kejambuck - eel-like creature that directs the energy of the Undercreature

Lute- A Seed of the Myriar that hears the melody of all things, manipulates sound

Mesa - mankind's origin and Moura's sister-planet

Mensira- mind control used for evil

Magluck Bawah – the Undercreature- malevolent energy

Mourangil- one of the bejewelled race

Ordovicia – the first human habitation on the planet

Perfidium- obsidian stone that has been refashioned to disguise a powerful evil weapon

Pont y Frindiau – means Bridge of friends- Welsh university town

Reeder- Seed of the Myriar- telepath

Reuben – inhabits an inter-worldly cavern

Stozcist – Seed of the Myriar. Can manipulate stone.

Tanes- a group of elementals in Dublin

Tenements- the name of the Rugby team populated by Tanes

Teifi- river in Wales.

Tinobar- healing place

Tolbranach – mythical sea creature inhabiting the Caher mountains in Ireland

Chapter One

A staccato of bullets hammered against the wall that had once shone white in the fierce sun of Damascus. Grey rubble wept from the edifice, dusting the man-made passages below: rough constructions of tyres, boards and other heaped remnants of life before the devastation of civil war. Josh ducked his head as he ran, catlike, along the deep seams of the city. Tormaigh, long and thin, whistled through the conflict as he winged ahead. Behind came Echin, waves of dark hair framing his serious face. The armed fighters seemed not to notice the trio, gliding like ghosts, along their guarded passageways. Josh owed his speed to the power of his Mourangil companions, members of a hidden race, indigenous to the planet. To them, the word earth referred merely to the surface of the planet they named Moura. Residing mainly in the luminous core of minerals and stone, Echin and Tormaigh had come to dwell above the surface and bejewel mankind with their presence.

Josh was moving fast and yet every detail seemed etched with clarity. Like a slow moving film, the trapped participants of an endlessly shifting conflict, played out their lives as he passed. A young child, drawing on burnt breath; the livid shock on the face of a woman, wreathed in scarves, who bent over him. Gun-gripped soldiers slotted their young bodies within the barricade. Their eyes were locked in grim concentration, wide with a mixture of fear and power. Some turned their heads in puzzlement as the silken thread of the Mourangils weaved unseen among them.

Leading the way, Tormaigh stopped abruptly in a deserted basin of demolished beauty. It was clear that the courtyard had once been a place of splendour. Rows of broken, upturned tiles littered the huge space. Forlorn stone arches, still intact, edged what must have been a magnificent chamber, now holding nothing above them but air and ruin.

Tormaigh's gaze circled the area, "Again and still again," he said sadly.

They had come to find Danubin, the pernicious leader of the ruthless Virenmor. She had stolen the Chalycion stone, snatched it from Josh's hand as he had tried to defend himself. And now they were here in Damascus to reclaim the jewel that had been held in safe keeping for him down the ages; perhaps the oldest of all the precious stones they had been given.

Turning, Josh saw that Echin was no longer behind him. The Mourangil knelt beside the young boy they had passed. The woman smiled gratefully at him, her tears falling on the boy's chest, where his rapid gasping changed to the even rhythm of peaceful breathing. Echin stood up, his tall body leaning into an accelerated swiftness that brought him by Josh's side in moments. His eyes, the colour of landless ocean, smouldered as they scanned the ruined building.

"The crysonance has gone," he stated simply.
Josh recalled the crysonance as a small mural of crystals that had perched on the wall in Evan's kitchen. It enabled communication between the Mourangils and those, like Evan, who were able to interpret its meaning. The thought of the Welshman, his bluff generosity, brought a sense of warmth to the cold dereliction of Damascus.

Boots grating on broken stone sounded beneath the arches; a group of soldiers had scrambled underneath them for cover. The harsh pop of bullets followed. Echin

7

quickly led them to an exit on the other side of the courtyard, away from the ruin towards a different part of the city. Once more they swept unnoticed, shrouded by the speed of the Mourangils in which Josh was carried, through dozens of battered streets heading out from the centre. Josh, the artist, stood in awe as they came to rest before a large construction. The war-ripped materials of the city, fragmented metal, broken tiles and demolished stone had all been sculpted into defiant beauty. A stunning mosaic of bright colours, an array of diverse substances tamed to harmony, had been erected outside the gates of a school to show the world that Damascus was still Damascus. Echin glanced at Josh, the tight angles of his jaw relaxing slightly.

"There," he pointed towards the centre of the sculpture, at what appeared to be a bicycle wheel. In between the spokes, terracotta tiles had been pasted, forming diagonal arrows around a central amber crystal.

"Place your hand on the crystal Josh," Echin instructed.

Josh's touch ignited a spark within the stone that created orange petals of light between his fingers. Voices within the stone unravelled like a DNA helix. Each one a connection that together created an image, a riot of colour; a vision of a fantastic cavern covered in precious stones.

A pink light fluttered in the distance. Josh followed the glow from this winding thread until it led to the lost Chalycion stone. Hungrily he traced a sliver of light to the pulse of vibrant pink energy in the Chalycion; it was beating against the dark sac in which it was housed. The quickening of his heart was reflected in the rhythm of the stolen stone, visible now to his mind's eye but remaining

locked away in Danubin's unyielding grasp.
Undoubtedly, the stolen gem had remained in Damascus for only a short time. Awareness of the street once again filtered into his consciousness. Josh released his hand from the crystal centre of the wheel. Gunfire sounded in the distance; unfamiliar Arabic syllables were loud nearby as the locals gathered around the sculptured symbol of hope. The wheel had helped him to gauge a strong line to the current location of the Chalycion.

"Istanbul," he whispered brokenly.
Echin nodded thoughtfully.

"Why did Danubin come to Damascus?" Josh asked. He turned as he felt himself being watched. A gathering of men on the far side of the square courtyard fixed curious eyes in their direction.

"I think we may have found the answer to that question," Echin told him.
A giant figure broke away from the group and came towards them. He was almost as tall as Tormaigh and twice as wide as Echin. His face was a smooth dark brown, hair hidden in a red, chequered keffiyeh. The aquiline nose and strong square jaw added to a persona of unrelenting strength, undisguised by his long shapeless tunic. Wide, dark eyes skimmed over Josh, passing to Tormaigh and then hardened as they fell upon Echin. For the first time in his memory Josh was frightened for his lifelong friend. The stranger spoke in English, with the shortened vowel sounds and curved syllables of an Arabic speaker. "Well, Toomaaris," he addressed Echin by his Mourangil name, "do you still think you can find your Myriar?"
The Myriar, the elusive lost gift to mankind, the reason why they were chasing the Chalycion, chasing hope. The

purpose that had forged together a group of gifted human beings known as Seeds; each one planted in the human race with the possibility of bringing mankind to a new phase of evolution. Echin had discovered that Josh was one of the Seeds, the Creta, an artist whose vision extended far beyond the physical appearance of the subject he depicted. And now this man spat the name out with distaste, the word that had come to define their purpose.

"The Myriar is a nonsense. Will you forever watch mankind despoil the land with their squabbles and not intervene?"

"Ulynyx," Echin calmly acknowledged the stranger. On the other side of the courtyard the conversation of the group became more agitated and voluble. Ulynyx turned and spoke in clipped tones. His companions swiftly disappeared within the mauled concrete that was now a maze of dusty barricades.

"We will find each other again soon," this steed of a man said solemnly to Echin.

Tormaigh and Echin were wordless, their faces unreadable as they followed the strong, unhurried figure as he too vanished into the surrounding structures. Josh released a whistling sigh, "Who is he?"

"Clever, clever Danubin," Echin murmured. "She used the Chalycion to draw him out. He is the leader of the Chunii, a powerful secret army that the Virenmor have long wished to control."

Josh swallowed further questions as the sound of gun-shots peppered the nearby streets. "Err…, maybe we should leave?"

Tormaigh gave an unhurried nod and prepared to transport his friend to Istanbul.

Josh heard the familiar and heartachingly beautiful music of the fossilia. He was familiar now with the appearance of these ephemeral, butterflylike creatures. Whenever a human being was required to make a transitional physical state, they gathered around to assist. Gladly he gave himself up to their caress as he became wrapped in the energetic layers of the Mourangil. Lifted above the earth, he travelled invisibly within folds of air. Unaware of time and space he was propelled northwards, suspended in an amniotic haze of trust. The shock of release was profound as Tormaigh's cry thundered the air. Josh's limbs flailed in panic as he separated from the Mourangil, unable to stop the heavy pull of his body as it hurled towards the earth. The dry sand of the desert rushed towards him but then Tormaigh was there once more, like a leaf catching rainwater. Josh felt his feet sink in soft sand, his body assailed by heat in the dry and barren expanse. He turned shakily towards the Mourangil. The bony prominence of Tormaigh's nose and chin was dotted with hard glinting green tourmaline, a sign of extreme stress.

"I'm sorry Josh," the Mourangil stumbled against the stunned young man.

"I'm okay," Josh could feel the fierce heat in his nostrils as he took in a deep breath. "What happened?"

"Silex is gone!" His tone was grim as he moved towards Echin who had followed their fall and was now making his way towards where they stood. Josh recalled the impish Mourangil named Silex, sharp as an arrow tip as she had spoken to each of the group in Wales. Echin said nothing but Josh had never seen him so bleak. A moment later, from the arid ground beneath, emerged the figure of Faer, the third Mourangil; sunlight fell on the feldspar edges of his blonde head and boyish features.

Knowing that the three would have already exchanged news in the wordless way of Mourangils, Josh accessed Mengebara. This human mind place had been constructed by Klim, another Seed of the Myriar. He was a telepath with the ability to amplify non-physical communication. Mengebara had now developed into a mental communication field for all those connected to the Myriar. Klim had left a record of events that had occurred on the Welsh island and like all his communications in Mengebara, it played like a visual record. Josh flinched as he saw Nephragm the Devouril, the enemy that had almost destroyed his friends less than two years previously. Originally Mourangils, the Devourils had followed the dreadful Belluvour in pursuit of mankind's extinction. Nephragm's murder of Silex had led to his own destruction; he had been trapped in the human form which he had taken to deceive the Seeds. Josh cried out as he watched the ugly battle that had occurred on the other side of Europe; the destruction of both Nephragm and the colossal energy of Magluck Bawah. Released from the Secret Vaults where Belluvour was imprisoned, Magluck Bawah had pursued them under the direction of the Virenmor. These two horrific influences were thrown into conflict on the Welsh island resulting in the dissolution of the wondrous habitat that the Devouril had polluted. The other members of his group had barely survived. At the last moment Kier had relinquished safety and plunged herself into the sea to retrieve a pebblelike stone that had transformed her fingers to blades of light. The unfathomable Kier, whom he had come to love in a way that was neither sister, nor lover, nor friend, yet somehow transcended all three.

Josh turned back forlornly to the Mourangils, stooped together like trees forced by the wind in the barren space. They came from a world untouched by human cycles of birth and death. The sacrifice of their involvement with his kind ate at his spirit; the pain of their grief for Silex created an enveloping shadow unrelated to the hot sun. He had no sense of time passing but pass it must have done for he looked up to find that the moon hung pendulous in the sky. Liquid, starlit crystals began to glow beneath Faer's skin. Tormaigh also began to transmute; only Toomaaris remained fully in his human state as Echinod Deem. Faer's voice was barely audible,

"Lioncera calls us Toomaaris. There is little time." Josh recalled Lioncera, the wondrous Mourangil kingdom and the true planetary home of his friends. He waited nervously, aware that the three were involved in a private exchange. These Mourangils had guided and directed the struggles of those, like him, who had found themselves intimately involved in the Myriar; their loss would be unquantifiable. Strobes of light: blue, green and white intermingling, swept the three Mourangils into one body, before separating once again into the shapes of his friends. Faer and Tormaigh came towards him. Tormaigh's outline was emerald green. "Very soon we will know if the heart of man can bring the Myriar to fruition." Faer placed a white crystal hand on Josh's shoulder, his human form now barely detectable.

"We are needed within the Mourangil kingdoms. Kier has retrieved the Stone of Mesa, a fragment of the planet that died and has now been reborn. When this fragment reached the surface, it ignited a chain of events. Soon there will be a realignment of the planets that we call the Sister Spheres and a new age of Moura will begin. She has called us home to strengthen and purify the heart of our planet in preparation. The doorways that allow us to walk the surface as humans are closing," he glanced towards Echin who remained apart, "but you keep with you our most precious jewel."

Josh could not help sighing with relief that Echin had elected to remain with them in human form. But what would it cost his friend? In his heart, he suspected that Echin had already paid a high price for his long effort to bring the Myriar to completion. Josh reached out his hand in farewell. He stepped back as Faer and Tormaigh vanished within a cloud of sand.

Echin and Josh stood side by side, unspeaking. Although he could not fully understand, it was clear to Josh that something momentous had occurred. A line had been drawn, impossible to cross at this point in time. The Mourangil kingdom, with Tormaigh and Faer now within it, lay on the other side. The remaining Mourangil scanned the parched land, then his eyes swept to the sky. He looked sympathetically at his friend.

"Look about you Josh and remember. We go forward into a storm of change that will level all you once knew as real. When the heart of man stands naked before the Sister Spheres only the Myriar can hold mankind to this planet. And still, it may not be enough."

Josh stared at the shadowy outline of miles of desert, hearing the thrumming of a wind that threatened to reshape the landscape at any moment. He felt his fingers tremble and made them into fists. He breathed deeply, the hot air burning his throat.

"Istanbul?" he asked hoarsely.

"Istanbul," confirmed Echinod Deem, "to recover the Chalycion. Even this precious stone is not immune to Danubin's power to turn good into evil. And you will need it very soon."

Chapter Two

In the night and day since the return of their small and exhausted group from the island, the weather had been unpredictable and turbulent. Within the last hour, however, there had arrived an interlude where the wind softened and the swollen river seemed to calm. Kier's breath caught in her throat as Echin's face, intense and troubled, appeared miraculously above the water. Alone by the river, her hand reach towards what she knew could not be present. Her caress moved only the air and yet his eyes reached towards her. They fell to the circles of Mesa embedded in her palm, and to the stone that hung around her neck. The image of Echin shimmered and vanished. She gasped, mesmerised by the black hole that hung suspended beneath the shrouded sky. Light shimmered within the dark space, shaping itself into seven globes: their size, colours and patterns vastly different. Around them alighted pinpricks of stars. She sat gazing at the spheres, losing all sense of time and locality as she became lulled by the faint music that hummed around each one, each a vibrating element in a wondrously complex chord of sound.

"Kier," Klim called. He stood in the front door of Samuel's cottage.
Her head turned, he was clearly unaware of the vision of planets that, as she turned back, flickered and faded into folds of freshwater.

"Evan's asking for you."
Someone spoke behind him and Klim stifled the words he was about to say. He looked quizzically at Kier and then retreated back into the cottage. She stared for a moment at the sky. Clouds already filled the void where her

private visions had played out. She wrenched her body, now stiff with cold, from the embankment and headed inside.

Quickly she climbed the stairs to the small room that had seemed barely big enough to hold the colourful Welshman three days ago. Evan lay on the bed shrunken, older. His grey eyes turned at the sound of her gentle knock on the open door.

"Kier," he smiled, reaching out his hand.

She took it in both of hers as she sat on the bed and kissed his forehead. He was cold, despite the open fire in the old fashioned hearth.

"You're looking better," she told him.

"I feel empty." His eyes wandered to the pendant around her neck. "May I?"

He held out his hand and Kier removed the stone, etched with the planet Mesa and its three moons. She placed it within his trowel like palms.

"So, this lay in the belly of Magluck Bawah?"

Kier nodded, watching Evan close his eyes. She said nothing as her old friend ran his fingers across the pebblelike surface to trace the large circle in the centre, skimming the three smaller ones above. Eventually he placed the pendant back within her hand and enclosed her small fist with both his own.

"It contains none of the taint of the Secret Vaults, nor the violence of the Undercreature. Remarkable."

Kier flinched at the thought of the prison within the bowels of the planet, where Belluvour strained for release. The dreadful destruction caused by Magluck Bawah, the Undercreature, remained too raw to dwell upon. Bending forward, his grey eyes wrinkled.

"I cannot go where this will take you Kier. I am no longer a Stozcist; I feel that I am barely a man."
His ability as a Stozcist, one who can manipulate stone, had been part of Evan's essential identity. The pain in her gut gnawed as she squeezed his hand. Evan was their father figure; benign, sometimes comical, always true.

"You're still with us Evan. That's all that matters. Your strength will return."

"These events will stir the planet. Already I hear the storm beneath the rocks and feel the sharp taste of a hurricane in the air." There was an urgency in his voice that scared her. Evan may have lost his power as a Stozcist, but his attunement to the planet spanned years of his lifetime.

"When you found the Stone of Mesa you set a chain reaction Kier. The planet is destabilised; imperceptible to most, the greatest manifestation will be in its weather patterns. Samuel must stay close to the Teifi, we will have storms such as we have never yet seen. Leave soon."

Kier fumbled as she placed the stone back around her neck; she was shocked that her action in retrieving the stone could have so great a significance for the planet.

"But Evan, I don't know where this stone will take me, or if it will take me anywhere at all!"

An edge of desperation clipped her tone as she stood up and walked to the window. The curtains had not been drawn and she saw her own reflection against the dark sky. An untidy frame of hair hid most of her face but the amber eyes glowed, lit with the vision she had just witnessed and the events of the last few weeks. The loose fitting cotton shirt hung too big and she thought of how little they had eaten over these last days.

"I'll make something to eat," she told Evan, giving him no time to reply as she broached the narrow stairs. Picking dishes from the shelves, Kier reflected on the group of people, unknown to her two years previously, who had now become her family. Perhaps even more than that, as if they had been propelled towards each other forever, bound by a common purpose that perhaps only Echin truly understood. It pained her that they had again become scattered. Josh and her beloved Echin had disappeared to Istanbul with the other Mourangils. Siskin had travelled to Cumbria that morning to be with Clare. The strange combination of musician and soldier made Siskin vibrant company and she missed him already. He spoke little about his relationship with Clare but Kier felt his deep passion for her and his fierce protection of her daughter Juliette.

Sighing, Kier gathered bread and slices of cheese. The absence of Gabbie, chirping like a robin by her side, made the cottage quiet and forlorn. Gabbie, carrying her huge heart in so petite a frame, was bitterly disappointed that neither Klim nor Kier had chosen to accompany her to visit her father in the North. Of the three that were left from their small group, Kier was the least disenfranchised. Her parents, though remote, were still alive, and her best friend and brother Gally, was in America. Klim, who had lost both parents, could not face the memories of Bankside, where he and Gabbie had grown up. Swift, orphaned and stolen by Alex Jackson from the streets of Lima, now considered Evan and his daughter Angharad as family. Of them all, strangely, Swift was most at home by the banks of the River Teifi. Apart from Samuel of course, who they now knew to be a Riverkeeper. The gentle cleric had arrived from the sea to pluck them, barely in time, from the devastation of the doomed island.

She could hear voices from Swift's room as she returned upstairs and wondered how Gabbie would cope with the closeness between Klim and Swift. The small blonde had been awed by the South American's exotic beauty. There was no denying that Swift, a powerful Stozcist, shared a link with Klim that had proved, literally, strong enough to reach into the depths of the planet. The rhythmic purr of sleep could be heard as she returned to Evan's room; she smiled and left the tray quietly by his bedside. Making her way downstairs she noted that her friend had been right, the weather had the low growl of a fierce storm. The door rattled against the wind, light flickered in the hallway. In the living room Samuel sat serenely as ever, reading in one of the cosy armchairs. Kier wandered over to the bookcase, letting her fingers ramble over the leather bound collection of ancient texts. She guessed that it was here, in his private dwelling, invisible in the folds of energy that swam alongside the River Teifi, that his most precious books were kept. She picked one out at random, opening it vaguely as she sat down on the sofa opposite Samuel. The title had something to do with Celtic runes. There was page after page, picturing various types of early inscriptions on stone, some crude and childlike without symmetry. Others were just the opposite, complex lines criss-crossing with precise indentations. On one particular page was an intricate drawing of a wide, damaged stone. Laying the book on its side, Kier adjusted the angle so that the stone now stood upright.

Her fingers roamed the page, carefully following the complex lines radiating out from the centre, hovering over circular indents as if she was touching the stone itself. She felt her palm tingle and placed the glowing outline of Mesa, embedded within her hand, against the surface of the ancient depiction.

"Deep and down," she said aloud, letting her fingers trace the picture. The meaning of the inscription, as so often before, unfolded effortlessly. "The Key of Brunan lies behind a doorway in the city that straddles two continents." She closed the book and looked towards Samuel who had abandoned his reading and now focused intently on her face.

"Kier, what do you know of the Key of Brunan."
She hesitated, placing the book down.

"It's what the text says, in your book."

"Istanbul!" Samuel pondered. "It is divided by the Bosphorus and straddles Europe and Asia."

"But that's where Josh is heading with Echin; where Danubin has taken the Chalycion!"
It had been Josh's last communication in Mengebara, that they were following the stolen gem to Istanbul.

"And so Danubin's theft has brought her enemies just where they need to be." Samuel grimaced at the thought of the leader of the Virenmor, who had all but penetrated his hidden rooms at the university. He came over to sit beside Kier and nodded towards the book, his voice tinged with awe. "In all my time as a Riverkeeper these runes have never spoken to me, and so often have I asked them to give up their secrets. And you, my dear, lay them bare with a single touch, and hardly a glance."
Kier, dazed, lifted her eyes to his, "What does it mean?"

"It means that human time and planetary time have lifted to purpose."

"Samuel that sounds deliberately cryptic. I don't understand."

"I barely understand myself." He picked up the book and placed it on her lap. "Does it show you anything else?"

She hesitated before turning back to the script, concentrating as she pressed her palm against the text. Slowly, the vivid images of places that she had never seen filled her consciousness. "A stone doorway," she muttered, seeing a column of rock. Her mind was then assailed by colour, more than she had vocabulary to name. "A glittering underground kingdom." Kier opened her eyes to find Samuel unaware of her scrutiny and deeply in thought. "What does it mean, the Key of Brunan?"

He seemed startled by her words, struggling to focus. He stood up, the most agitated she had ever seen him.

"You speak of mystical portents." He was pacing the room now, his words tumbling out. "Three keys shrouded in mystery. Toomaaris made them his eternal study, but none of us could be certain that the keys ever existed. He once spoke of an obscure inference that the keys were intimately linked to the fabled Stone of Mesa." He stopped pacing and came back to sit beside her, his eyes alighting on the stone around her neck. His voice shook slightly. "And now this fable has come to life." His eyes swept the bookshelves. "I too have studied the keys over the years, collecting texts that have been preserved in what mankind would call magical libraries."

"And what do you know of them?"

Samuel sighed, "Too little. Even to the bejewelled their names are but a whispered presence. Toomaaris discovered their names: The Key of Brunan, the Key of Talitha, and the Auric Flame."

"But what do they open?"

He shrugged. "I asked Toomaaris that same question once; he told me hearts and minds."

It was Kier's turn to pace distractedly as Samuel continued. "My understanding is that Moura has lodged them where only the power of the Myriar can take mankind."

"But we haven't even managed to form the Myriar. Or found Candillium!"

Candillium, the elusive centrepiece of the gift that Moura had intended for mankind. It was said that all the Seeds would be drawn towards her. Or him, there was no knowing how Candillium had chosen to return to human life; or if the original leader of humankind in Ordovicia had chosen to return at all. Samuel held her eyes a long time before answering and then she had the impression that he had not said what he had first intended to say.

"Those of us who sojourn here for many human lifetimes have long believed that the Key of Brunan is hidden in the Mourangil Hall of Jasmine. You are one of the few human beings to enter Lioncera, the Mourangil kingdom of the west. Within our planet is hidden a number of such places. In each is a consciousness unconstrained by space and matter. Lit with crystal energy, these prismatic entities are part of the essential expression of Moura and they reach out to the galaxy and beyond."

"The Tomer?"

"Yes indeed."

Kier remembered the sense of awe she had experienced in her meeting with the Tomer. She felt that his touch would remain in her heart forever.

"Unethora is another such being," continued Samuel. "It is said that she holds a key to be retrieved by the male aspect of the Myriar."

"The male aspect, you mean Siskin, Klim and Josh?"

"Tradition says that the Key of Brunan will be given only if one of the three final male Seeds of the Myriar can find a way to the city of Jasmine. Even then it may be withheld if Unethora chooses to do so."

The cleric picked up the book Kier had been reading.

"My dear, in these pages may be the secret location of the doorway that your companions must find."

Kier, breathing deeply, once more let her fingers guide her, braille like, through the pages. The shapes again came to life beneath her fingers and brought once more the strong image of a stone doorway. Sat in front of it was a woman, calmly blowing smoke that obscured the writing on the stone door itself.

"She's small, and dark haired," Kier told Samuel.

"There are runes," she opened her eyes in disbelief, "and it's as if her very DNA was made up of the same kind of runes that are in this book." Samuel looked startled. He stood up quickly, the most ruffled she had ever seen him. "I need to send a message," he told her, hurrying from the room.

Kier waited, increasingly anxious. She thought of reporting what they had discovered in Mengebara but decided to wait until she was able to explain it more. The intensity of Samuel's expression when he returned did little to allay her worries.

"Who have you sent the message to?" she asked.

At first, he did not respond, seemingly unaware of Kier's question. Just as she went to prompt him further he turned a serious face towards her. All the easy, languid aspects of the Riverkeeper seemed to have disappeared.

"It has begun," his eyes focused upon her, as if he were seeing her for the first time.

Involuntarily Kier stepped backwards, "Who did you message?" she asked again.

"The Runeshaper," he answered matter-of-factly.

Kier frowned, looking for an explanation.

"She records knowledge that can only be accessed by the Seeds of the Myriar. Some external, in various texts or written in stone. Other knowledge she carries internally. I have just confirmed to her that she holds the location of the doorway."

"Internally?"

"This knowledge cannot be consciously accessed by the Runeshaper herself."

"How then?"

"I don't know," he shrugged his shoulders as if he was not wanting to present her with yet another vital puzzle. Kier turned away and for some minutes neither spoke, seating themselves back among the books in the small living room. Kier glanced at the runes that had seemed alive a few moments before and were now dull images on the page. The force of the rain slapped in bursts against the wooden window pane. It took a moment for Kier to realise that Samuel had begun speaking again.

"It is said that the doorway to the Hall of Jasmine," his expression was distracted as he concentrated, "that the doorway will show itself at a lunar eclipse."

He looked meaningfully at Kier who returned only a blank stare. "There is one occurring over Istanbul in a matter of days," he informed her.

"Okay," she nodded. How was she supposed to know this? Her mind returned to the events that had occurred earlier that evening.

"Just before, over the river," she told him hesitantly, "there were globes in the sky."

Samuel's expression was unreadable. She stumbled to explain, "Well I knew they weren't really there. Like a projection from a film or something." She omitted to mention the Mourangil.

"Globes? More than one?"

"Yes, seven."

"The Alignment!" Samuel's tone was hushed. He paced the floor again, muttering.

"What is it?" She cut off his pacing by standing in front of him.

"The Sister Spheres are planets in the solar system, some visible and some invisible to our technology. As I understand it, when you retrieved the stone from Magluck Bawah, you ignited a kind of flare, a call to these profound bodies. The last time they aligned with our planet, Mesa deposited the possibility of a new kind of life form." Kier raised her eyebrows and Samuel nodded, "Yes, I mean us, mankind."

Kier felt her legs give way and sat back on the couch. Samuel joined her. He sighed and held her hand, turning it over. "When you rescued the Stone of Mesa from the sea you called to it using the same power that was used to bind Belluvour so long ago, the same hand that was used to bind him."

Kier pulled away, her heart rate stumbled over itself as she raced to absorb what the Riverkeeper was saying. She had read and heard how Candillium had used the power of the Myriar to bind Belluvour in the Secret Vaults. She turned back to the book that still lay open and closed it, quickly bundling it back on the shelf. She shook her head, "No," she told him firmly, " you're mistaken." How could she be Candillium and not know? How could she be Candillium and Echin not recognise her?
Samuel looked alarmed, "Kier," he began gently but she had already retreated to the door.

"I need to check on Evan," she said, fumbling with the handle, looking everywhere but at the cleric who went to follow but decided against it, his calm serenity lost for a moment in indecision.

Out in the hallway she glanced at the stairs but could hear Evan's soft snoring from where she stood. The little cottage had become stifling and her limbs were taut, her spine racked with the tension of the last few days. Impulsively she grabbed a coat from the stand in the hall, pulling it tightly against her body. The wind rushed in through the open front door. Hesitating for a moment, she looked towards the sitting room but like a vacuum the agitated air, so reflective of her mood, pulled her into the gathering storm.

*

Josh grinned, he felt he had no choice. The vibrant dancing colours of the Grand Bazaar encircled him in a zest for life that had lately abandoned him. He was surrounded by the bartering chatter of buying and selling. There were bags brim-full of rich golden spices. The smell of roast chestnuts and hot sweetcorn drew in customers from the cold October streets. In the covered arcades, he followed the sound of throaty Turkish vowels as young and old men hopped through their catalogue of languages, guessing the correct greeting for the nearest potential customer. Rows of pillars supported intricately coloured arched ceilings. There was a churchlike glow from gloriously stained glass lamps, hanging like luminescent jellyfish in stall after stall.

Echin steered him towards a narrow tunnel at the end of which was a row of steps that looked as if they had been made in the days of the sultans. Each stone step was twice as steep as the ones that he was used to back home. A rickety handrail spiked the middle of them, shaking beneath his hand as they left behind the busy sounds of trading and ascended into the top of an enclosed courtyard. There was open space, above which light filtered through a cloudy sky and settled onto the bony branches of a central tree. He looked down to see the terracotta roof tiles of small dwellings lining the cobbled yard, enclosing it in this hidden corner of the Grand Bazaar. There was a small walkway lined with ornate railings that bordered the rectangle. It was punctuated by carefully preserved and decorated stone archways, within which were a number of brightly painted doors. He followed Echin towards a small leaf green door; his friend giving one knock before entering.

The dimly lit room was filled with an array of objects: old books, maps, lamps and a number of clay figures beside a stone oven. Weaving around the various items, were tendrils of apple smelling smoke that gave an ethereal impression to the small space.

"In the back," Echin instructed as he led the way through a fabric covered archway.

Josh coughed as he entered the small cave like space where its occupant puffed on what Echin later referred to as a narghile. At the bottom was a blue, bell like structure with a highly decorated stem. The shape of a golden eagle formed the middle of the fascinating object before narrowing to create a tray with coals that heated rich, aromatic tobacco. A small woman blew from an attached long bulbous pipe that emitted steamy, gurgling smoke. She wore a white cotton top, and loose yellow trousers. As she turned to them with a wide smile, Josh noticed that her skin was the colour of an acorn and that her thick dark hair was streaked with grey. In contrast, her eyes were hazel in a face of European contours. She seemed to embody the ancient city that bridged Europe and Asia. Istanbul, the renamed Constantinople, had always fascinated him in history lessons at school. Cartoons of Arabian Nights flashed through his mind as he absorbed the fact that here he was, Josh Allithwaite, standing in the centre of a city where building after building told the story of its ancient past.

With precise and unhurried movements, the woman put aside the pipe and placed two small cups on the table to add to her own. She poured hot tea, without milk, into small shaped glasses and handed one to each of them. As she passed the glass to Echin with one hand, she lifted the other palm upwards. Within it lay a lapis piece that seemed to contain a luminous sheen of stars within its structure. Gently, Echin folded back the small hand into a fist, covering the softly glowing stone. She unfolded her hand. "If not for yourself then for another," she told him, holding his eyes. Echin nodded and this time took the stone.

Josh watched their interchange with no comprehension of what was passing between them, his fingers itched to draw this unusual figure.

"Elanur," Echin introduced the woman, "this is Josh Allithwaite."

Instead of answering, Elanur looked pointedly towards Josh, who politely stretched out his hand. Her eyes became dancing green jewels, excitedly she laughed again. "The Creta," she stated, ignoring his hand.

He paled at the use of the name, a title he had been given by Echin as one of the Seeds of the Myriar. She pulled out a drawer in a nearby wooden table and produced a pencil and paper, placing them in front of Josh. He shook his head in bewilderment.

"It's important," she told him.

Gingerly the young artist looked towards Echin who nodded. It seemed that she was aware of his gift to see the invisible features that revealed the heart of the person he was drawing. Elanur sat back down on the one chair within the small space. Once the pencil was in his hand it ranged back and forth over the paper until, in a matter of minutes, he was finished. Examining the completed drawing he held her gaze, "Do you really want this?" he asked evenly.

In answer, she reached out her hand and he placed within it the sketch, not of a woman or a man, but of a mound of grass covered earth at dawn. A rune covered stone was positioned on its side at the entrance and a stream of sunlight fell onto an opening behind it. She looked at the picture and her eyes lit with wonder as she returned the steadfast interest in Josh's gaze. It made him think of another elusive, mysterious being of their acquaintance.

"I don't understand," he told her. "Are you another Samuel?"

Elanur looked solemn, "If only I were one such as he," she said reverently, "but Samuel has sent through a communication."

"Telepathy?" asked Josh, his face reflecting the awe he felt around the strange figure of Elanur.

"Not exactly," she laughed. She went to the corner of the room and pulled out a cloth covered tray. He gasped with surprise as she lifted the cloth to reveal rows of embedded crystals.

"Is that a crysonance?"

"It's similar," explained Echin, "but designed by the Mourangils specifically for communication between the old ones. Ancient technology if you like. Even quicker than computers and using only the energy that the individual brings with them."

"You have shown me that I must move from this place to another. In return, I have a message for you. Your friend Kier has translated a text that has lingered for almost as long as mankind has lingered." She looked pointedly from one to the other but neither offered a comment. "It appears," Elanur continued, "that Kier was able to decipher the Runes of Unethora. The doorway to the Hall of Jasmine will be accessible during the lunar eclipse in three days. The Key of Brunan is hidden there." She turned to Echin, "Is this why you have brought the Creta to Istanbul?"

Josh glanced at Echin who said nothing. "What is this Key of Brunan?" he asked.

"A legend, until now," Elanur said quietly.

"Three days?" Echin waited until Elanur's nod confirmed the statement. "We have little time. We need to recover the Chalycion as soon as possible."

"The Chalycion is necessary to Unethora's conditions."

"You're sure Elanur?" Echin asked.

"Until now I did not see it, but yes I am sure." Echin nodded in acceptance of her words. A quick glance at Josh stifled the raft of questions he was about to ask.

"Drink," Elanur instructed, placing the tea in his hand. The apple flavoured sweet liquid had a calming effect on Josh. The questions, that a moment before had seemed urgent, became gentle queries that would be answered in their own time.

"There is an exit onto the street," she smiled kindly, removing the empty glass from his hand and holding it within her own. "I will find you later." Josh felt a wash of peace as Elanur held his hand; he found himself reluctant to remove his grasp from her soft brown fingers.

"Thank you Elanur," Echin replied, his voice now solemn and formal. "May your shape define what you see as divine."

"And may the lighted jewel shine in your footsteps," she replied equally formally. Elanur nodded and smiled, once again placing the pipe in her mouth.

A hanging carpet hid a back door, by which hung a number of hooded garments. Echin passed one over to Josh and then pulled opened the door that led down to the streets via a sturdy metal stairway. The sound rushed towards them, chatter in all languages. Josh followed the distinctive notes of Turkish street music and his eyes found a young man playing on a fan shaped xylophone that tinkled down the alleyways. Along the street stood another in Arab dress, playing what Echin called a Saz; a long, three stringed, guitarlike instrument, with a teardrop shaped bowl. The notes were higher than an English guitar, making the music a snake charming dance of exotic sound. Josh's eyes were wide as he took in the fabulously constructed buildings with their domes and minarets.

Echin laughed, "I forget how little you know of each other's culture."

"I've never travelled this far across the world before."

"Same world Josh," Echin told him as he rifled through the contents of one of the stalls. "Culture and language are just different clothes that cover the same human frame."

That was a difficult concept for Josh to accept. His eyes were captured by signs he could not read, foods he could not identify and faces he did not recognise. Except one. "Ulynyx," he whispered quietly, noticing the tall Arab striding towards the bazaar. Echin turned to watch Ulynyx disappear inside. A slight tint of lapis glinting at the edge of his jaw.

"We need to send a message in Mengebara to Klim and Siskin," he instructed. "Tell them they're needed here." Echin waited until Josh confirmed that he had done as he requested. He shrugged on the hooded jacket taken from Elanur's house. Josh followed his example as they dodged the trams and steamy traffic that rolled along the wet road. Echin plunged into a maze of narrow cobbled streets away from the main tourist areas. The October day was damp and cold, and Josh was grateful for the warm jacket, nudging his hands into the pockets. The cold was more pronounced as they lost the cover of the buildings and headed down towards the water.

Echin steered his companion towards a docking area where a boat, packed with passengers, stood ready to leave. He paid quickly and signalled Josh to follow as he jumped across the rubber tyre that acted as a walkway. Minutes later the ferry rumbled out towards the centre of the Bosphorus strait. They eased their way through the interior and out onto the deck. Josh breathed in the fierce breeze and sighed with pleasure at the view of two continents: on one side Europe, on the other Asia. A guide offered a commentary in several different languages to describe the magnificent buildings that dominated the skyline on the European side: Hagia Sophia, the museum that had once been church and mosque, the magnificent Blue Mosque, named for the blue tiles that lined its interior and the preserved opulence of the Topkapi Palace. Further along the straits an Ottoman mansion had been turned into a modern hotel and its luxury stretched languidly along the shoreline. The crew member stopped his commentary to sell refreshments. Echin and Josh found themselves alone when the rest of the passengers moved into the covered interior of the boat.

"Who is Elanur?" Josh clamped both hands onto the rail as the captain angled the boat for the return trip. Echin removed his gaze from the diverse mixture of families, backpackers and sightseers inside the boat. He turned towards Josh, "Elanur is a Runeshaper."

"Surprisingly, that's not a job I know much about," Josh prompted, when Echin seemed not to elaborate further. He leant over the rail, his face damp from the tingling wash of spray. "Are we even talking job, or some supernatural envelope of being? Echin, when I sketched her I drew a mound of earth!"

"You drew a place in Ireland," his companion calmly replied. "You showed her where she must be at the Alignment."

"What?" Josh looked more perplexed than ever. A little girl wandered out on deck. She was about nine years old with long dark hair that was plaited over one shoulder. Josh had noticed her with a group of schoolchildren earlier on. She reached into her satchel and brought out a pencil and paper. Josh was stunned when she determinedly held them out in front of him. He looked to Echin for guidance, but his friend's eyes were fixed on the domes and minarets of the magnificent Hagia Sophia.

"What do you want me to draw?" Josh asked the girl, who shook her head to indicate that she had little English. He drew the skyscape of Istanbul with a quick, accurate artistry. As he handed the paper back to the child she laughed with delight.

"Star," she said proudly, pointing to where Josh's pencil had paused in its arc across the skyline. She gave the drawing back to him to examine. Between two of the most striking buildings the crumbs of the pencil lead he had rubbed together did, in fact, resemble a star. He frowned but the girl was called back inside to re-join her group and left him staring at the picture he had created. Echin looked curious as Josh handed him the drawing.

"How did she know I could draw?" They moved to the opposite side of the deck.

"You've grown Josh, now your gift leaps out for those who are sensitive, for those who are awake."

"Awake?"

"Most sleep, content not to look further than their physical eyes will show. For fear, mainly of what they might find."

"Like a Creta?" Josh returned with a hint of harshness in his tone. The image of his father flitted through his mind, how he had been so difficult to convince of anything beyond his five senses. Josh suspected that part of the reason they had given up the Mountain Inn and moved to Ireland was that he could once more lapse into denial regarding his son's strange gifts. The chatter of the schoolchildren grew louder as they spilled back onto the deck along with many other passengers. The young girl was lost within the group. Josh realised he still had the drawing in his hands and went to place it in one of the bins. He felt Echin's arm on his, "Bring it with you," his friend instructed.

Frowning and shaking his head, Josh rolled up the drawing and placed it in his sleeve as he had been wont to do when sketching impromptu on the fells.

"You were saying, about Elanur?" Josh insisted.

Echin gave a reluctant grin, "A Runeshaper makes and reads maps of a certain kind."

"Ordovician?"

"Not just Ordovician and ancient, there are many intersections within and around the planet."

"Intersections?"

"Points of change, when human time and planetary time interlink for a particular purpose."

Josh looked out across the water at a crowd of skyscrapers almost leaning against each other, on the Asian side of the city. "So, the Mourangils operate on planetary time? That's why you never get old."

"We age, but very slowly in your eyes. Mourangils can inhabit a human form but they never cease to be Mourangil, always linked to the intricate fabric of Moura."

"And Ulynyx?"

"He shares the same organic origin as the Mourangils."

"Like Nephragm you mean, a Devouril?"

"That we have yet to discover."

Echin steered him back towards the throng of passengers, cutting off their conversation. They manoeuvred through the interior of the boat, where tourists sat opposite each other drinking and eating, to find spare seats by the exit, where they sat quietly for the remainder of the trip.

The small cruiser headed back towards the port. Shuffling out of the ill-fitting sliding doors they stood outside the cabin, ready to alight as the boat slowly docked. Josh looked over at the Ottoman skyline, magnificent, even on this cold, damp day.

"You still haven't explained why I drew that mound of earth," he quizzed his friend.

"It's a place not far outside Dublin," Echin said quietly, the wind catching his words so that Josh had to move in closer. "An important site, though most Irish people know little of its existence. From your drawing, we will need to be there by the December solstice. In that time, we must retrieve the three keys."

Josh spluttered, "Hang on, we need to be there? Three keys?"

Echin moved to one side as a crew member came between them and bent to secure a rope to the metal ring on shore. Echin jumped onto the paved docking area. Josh, still floundering, found himself pushed along the outside of the cabin as passengers flooded out through the sliding door. He was forced to wait until the whole boat had emptied before he could shuffle near enough to jump across to dry land. He knew that for the moment at least, he had prised out about as much cryptic conversation as Echin was likely to share.

Chapter Three

At first, she had welcomed the feel of dripping rainwater from tendrils of wet hair that flicked across her face; it pulled her attention away from the deep fear that Samuel's words had engendered. Candillium, the lost centrepiece of the Myriar, returned to the planet – no! She was Kier Morton, the girl that cost her sister's life and wrecked her parents' marriage. Kier Morton who had unwittingly led her beloved friend Adam to his death. The wild careening of branches and leaves, flung in the wind across the grassy path, seemed a fitting echo of flashing screams of memory and fitful confusion. They echoed the bizarre events and terrible energies that had collided around her. The blackness of the track, as it took her away from the river, went unnoticed in the relentless rhythm of her steps. Time and distance were a blur as Kier stopped with sudden awareness; she was completely lost. A profound feeling of dread immobilised her.

The trees closed inwards, the noise of the storm merely a muffled backdrop to the immediate absence of natural sound. The air was thick with a familiar scent that crept beneath her skin. She shivered beneath the raincoat, recognising the stench of rotting vegetation, of stifling, stagnant space. Inevitably now it came: the low, wrenching moan from the jaws of an enemy that had waited timelessly for her arrival. The panther-like Roghuldjn unfurled itself from the dim outline of a withered oak. This dormant enemy, distorted and then spewed across the earth by Belluvour, had been given one purpose, to destroy anyone who could contribute to the formation of the Myriar. Kier cursed her stupidity in leaving the sanctuary of the cottage and the river. Samuel had warned them, had impressed heavily upon them, not to venture out of earshot. She flinched as the dark shape circled her.

"Lioncera will not take you this time," the low, rumbling growl came in snatches as the shadows weaved around her.

"Asin vi Lioncera," she whispered. There was no response. The words that had once brought her escape from this enemy, allowing passage into the jewelled kingdom of Lioncera, were now only echoes within dead space. The storm whirled outside the hideous pocket tailored by this primeval creature, whose long limbs brushed against her legs. Kier kicked out as Siskin had taught her, swift and hard. It was like jumping against a tree, her muscles rebounded with the jolt. Misshapen, grating grunts, that she took for laughter, were quickly loud beside her neck; close enough to fill her nostrils with the putrid stench of the Roghuldjn's breath. Kier recognised the ancient language of Ordovicia. "You are nothing, can become nothing, the ashen leavings of Ordovicia."

She jumped forward then screamed as a long, curled claw, poker hot, ripped through the flesh of her shoulder. The dark outline of the massive Roghuldjn appeared in front of her, eyes glinting an eerie green, the savage mouth open to reveal long, prehistoric incisors. Kier covered her face and turned to run as its strong hind legs bent ready to spring. A heavy thump somewhere to her left found her twisting backwards, to witness shadows within shadow as two huge animal forms collided. A long tail caught her, sent her stumbling. Trembling, she retrieved her balance and ran hard and fast, frantically searching for a way back to the river. The howling thuds and ripping tissue screamed in the sinister hollow behind. Kier lifted her chin, hunting fresh air and escape from the stagnant evil of the Roghuldjn. She ran blindly through the trees, slipping on slick leaves, on and on, round and round. Round and round unknowingly back to where she had started.

Moonlight filtered through the rain as it pounded into the previously arid space. Above her she could see stars where before the trees had bent inwards to cover the infected area. Gasping, pushing wet tangles of hair from her eyes, she tried to process what she was seeing. The body of the Roghuldjn sprawled across the ground, its ancient flesh already rancid and disintegrating. She could not imagine what animal could have destroyed this dreadful enemy. Another Roghuldjn? A low growl sounded behind but before she could turn, Kier felt blood trickling underneath the sleeve of her raincoat to mottle her hand. Her vision blurred, she slumped to the wet ground with the howl of a wolf ringing in her ears.

*

Elanur cleaned her pipe and packed it ready for moving. She began to gather the clay figures she had made, placing them carefully into a box that had individual pockets for each of the delicate ornaments. The tread on the tiled floor was unmistakable and she held tightly to the figure that she was holding, lest it drop from her fingers. She turned as Ulynyx entered, his tall, muscular body obscuring the light. She greeted him traditionally, "May the lighted jewel forever shine in your footsteps."

41

"May your shape define what you see as divine," he returned politely.

"Sit, I will make you coffee," she instructed, placing the clay model she had fashioned to one side.

"No Elanur, it is not required," he answered, squatting with his back against the stone so that he was more on a level with the small woman. He reached for the clay figure that had barely cooled. "Exquisite," he said appreciatively. Elanur's artistic fingers had sculpted a figure of a young woman with long dark hair, gazing upwards, her hand occluding a pendant that lay at her throat. "Who is the model?"

Elanur shrugged, "A young woman in the street," she lied. She turned her back to him, hiding the figure of the Creta she had made earlier, and watching in the mirror as Ulynyx replaced the one he had examined.

"You have seen Toomaaris?" he asked, as she turned towards him once more. The tone had changed, his smile lingering uneasily.

"Yes indeed," she answered, waiting.

"Alone?"

"Not alone Ulynyx. The Creta was with him."

He stopped smiling. "You verify that the boy was indeed the Creta?"

"Yes."

He raised himself above her, "It will do no good," he said softly. "As we both know."

Elanur fixed her expression.

"The lunar eclipse occurs in three days," he went on, "and I see a difference in you. The presence of the Creta has perhaps activated what has been hidden within?"

His eyes glinted coldly as he came nearer. "He has lost the Chalycion, there can be no possibility of him entering the Hall of Jasmine. Did you give him the location?" Elanur, fidgeting, wished that she had not packed away her pipe, but this she could answer truthfully. "I did not. You know it is locked within me, passed down in the DNA of generations of my family. Coded, it is said, in a way that can be discovered only by the Seeds of the Myriar. But it was not asked of me."

"You know that Belluvour reached from the very depths of the Secret Vaults to destroy the centrepiece of the Myriar. Without Candillium the Seeds cannot have developed in power as Toomaaris had planned," Ulynyx reminded her, questioningly.

Elanur remembered the despair she had felt, when the news of the girl's death in England had come to her, a decade ago. His hand rested on the worktop and Elanur quietly removed the figure she had made from its surface. Carefully she placed it with the others in the box at her feet.

"Has he lost the Chalycion?" Ulynyx flicked his hand arrogantly. "The game-witch of the Virenmor was in Damascus. My men saw her with the stone and followed her to Istanbul. Clearly the Myriar's power has passed to the Virenmor and she will seek the Key of Brunan."

"Unethora would never let it pass to one such as she." Impatiently, Ulynyx took her hand, his voice impassioned. "You are Elanur, Runeshaper. Belluvour stands on the edge of return. Only my army, the Chunii, can defend the continued existence of mankind. Let me try to find the location inside you, Elanur. I am a Mourangil, it will not hurt you."

She stood quietly for a moment and then cried out, holding her head, slumping down on the chair.

"There is no need," she told him, her face filled with awe. "Your presence, my powerful Mourangil, has brought the doorway to the front of my consciousness." She smiled beatifically as she described the location in Hagia Sophia, one of the most iconic buildings in the city.

*

Danubin heard the final call to prayer of the day from her sumptuous apartment not far from the Topkapi palace. She was exhausted and still racked with pain from her accidental contact with the parts of a crysonance that had somehow found their way into the construction of the sculpture in the centre of Damascus. It disturbed her deeply to think that the sculpture had been made without a Mourangil hand; that the artists who had put it together, had salvaged the most powerful of elements from the ruins of the old city. Already its influence could be felt in the air of hope surrounding the sculpture. The Chalycion had, of course, led her towards it. It had taken all of her long experience and strength of will to carry the Chalycion so far. The stone, even with the baryte next to it, proved to be the most difficult that she had yet encountered. Only a momentary contact with the hidden crysonance had been made. She peeled the glove off her left hand to reveal the blackened fingers. The baryte, she carried as protection, had not been able to prevent the violent response, but the unexpected contact had served her purpose, as it had acted like an alarm bell; Ulynyx had been drawn from the hidden city.

Ulynyx was a dark arrow whose poison was both pleasure and pain. For so many years she had looked to find the leader of the Chunii, the impenetrable army. In Damascus, she had witnessed in recent years, how he had interfered; binding together people to oppose the chaos which she had created. He had become powerful and ruthless and, as she had planned, had followed her to Istanbul. She had not, however, expected him to stride into the middle of her most covert cell and deliver the shocking news. Danubin stroked the desk, within which was hidden the stolen Chalycion, as she recalled the meeting. Ulynyx seemed neither Mourangil, nor Devouril, nor man. The devastating tale of Nephragm's destruction and the defeat of Magluck Bawah had left her stunned. Even so, her body and appetite responded to the strong male presence and she thrilled with the idea of capturing this long sought-after enemy; of commanding the hidden soldiers of the Chunii. He had relayed, without comment, the story of events on the Welsh island. She had no idea where he had learnt this information but did not doubt its truth. He had come for the Chalycion, of course, but its trace was hidden by the obdurate stone in which it was enclosed. Before she had marshalled her resources, still bedazzled by his presence, Ulynyx had left. However, with her long experience of such things, she had read the unspoken signs, knew the weapons to use against an arrogance that, to her, was as prosaic as it was human. It would cost her the Chalycion she decided, pulling tight the glove on her left hand but it was a price she was willing to pay.

Danubin reminded herself of the reward, so very close now; Belluvour would be with them soon to reclaim his dominion. She fluffed the red and gold cape that she

wore around her shoulders, preened her designer hair and
flashed white teeth at herself in the mirror. She had
become the final leader of all the Virenmor, and now that
the bonds were almost broken in the Secret Vaults, she
must be the one to prepare his way on the surface.
Danubin reached for the drawer hidden within the ebony
desk. It was a replica of the one destroyed at her mansion
house in Wales; even she needed some constancy. There
was, after all, little left. She thought back to the events of
the previous few weeks and the bitter taste of Abigail's
betrayal. She had been shocked by the revelation that
Abigail was in fact a Tane. That she, Danubin, leader of
the Virenmor, had failed to recognise Mactire and his
gang as elemental creatures; changelings that appeared in
human state, but could become mythical creatures at will.
She now understood that Abigail was, in fact, Mactire's
sister Loretta. That the Tanes, whom she had dismissed
as relics of history, were still in existence. Changing into
the form of a white unicorn, the girl had played a
significant part in her failure to destroy two of the Seeds.
The betrayal was filed and counted; she would take
particular pleasure in executing retribution.

She forced her mind to focus on the small pouch
that she had placed on the desk. Carefully she fastened
the baryte pendant around her neck and only then brought
out the black pocket of material that housed the
Chalycion. Even so the gloved fingers of her good hand
smarted. She controlled her urge to fling the Chalycion
onto the table, allowing it to roll gently from the pouch.
The body of the pink, striated stone, had dulled to a
cloudy grey. Sweat broke on her forehead; she chewed at
her lip, her mind wrestling with the power of the
fearsome object. It took all of her long experience and

skill to glimpse an energy affiliated to the stone and to recognise that it was that of Arwres, the jewel she had located in Capel Cudd y Bryn. The Chalycion smouldered an angry red stripe and Danubin laughed in triumph and then in surprise.

"Of all the places!"

Sweating and pale, she packed away the Chalycion with the baryte, allowing the drawer to slide closed, invisible within the heavy table.

Chapter Four

Gabbie sat in the kitchen that had become a second home in her primary school years. Shrewdly and sadly, she saw that her new life made her old friend uncomfortable. Danielle talked rapidly about her plans to move away from Bankside as soon as she had enough money.

"Must have been great to do all that travelling," Danielle's face lit with wistful enthusiasm.

Gabbie smiled and nodded. Her thoughts flitted back to the crazy summer that had now passed into a cold, damp autumn. It had been a time of jostling fear, amazement and desperate hope. Remarkably it had only been a few days since she watched the island in Wales disappear into the sea and Kier lift the Stone of Mesa from beneath the waves. More remarkable still was the fact that she had been away from her friends a mere two days, but it felt like a year. Already she found herself longing to return to those with whom she had shared events that she could not even begin to explain to her dad, or anyone else in Bankside. She wondered if she should have come back to her childhood home at all but smiled as she recalled that her father had been delighted to see her, and she him. It had been a wonderful relief to see him happily settled in the new home Kier had helped to find, just outside the small town.

"No one seems to know exactly where Luke's gone," Danielle said, looking up, her dark hair cut sleek against her face. Gabbie remembered that she had passed her hairdressing exams last year. "His mum comes into the shop, says he messages them now and again from Tunisia mostly, but he never seems to stay in one place." There was confusion and hurt in Danielle's eyes. "We split not long after you and Klim went away. He got really messed up." She sighed and stopped straightening the contents of the ponderous case of makeup and hair products on the table. "How 'bout you and Klim?"

Gabbie noticed the eagerness in her friend's voice; all the girls once had a thing for Klim. She shook her head to dispel any thoughts of Klim and Swift together in Samuel's cottage and made her mouth form a cheerful smile, "Friends. How's the hairdressing going?"

The glass in the door rattled against the wind as Ben, Danielle's brother, arrived. Gabbie jumped up to help as he wrestled with an overly large sports bag and the gale outside. Once his bag was safely on the floor he hugged Gabbie, looking her over with appreciation.

"Looks like you've been working out a bit little 'un." It was the way he had referred to her since she was five. She had never quite managed to conquer her hero worship of Ben. Memories of him were full of sporting triumphs and images of him running on the crag. Now he was happily married with his own kids, and she had been pleased to hear that he had finally achieved the dream of building his own gym.

"I used to run with my boss. Well, she's like my big sister really. In Australia, we ran every day along the cliff top path from Bondi to Coogee in Sydney."

Ben whistled, "I hear it's great there, never know, might go some day."

"You should," Gabbie agreed. "It was awesome." She tried to make her smile reflect her admiration for the city where the beaches were immaculate, the centre vibrant, the atmosphere electric. And yet she had ached for home almost the whole time.

49

"I used to swim a lot in the outdoor pool at Bronte beach. It was freezing." She put her arms around her shoulders and gave a shiver. "I even had a gym membership!"

"Sounds great, but it's a long way to go for a gym session." Ben reached up to a shelf above the sink. He slid a key across the table. "Go and check out mine if you want, I'm not in tomorrow. It's still being fitted out but there's enough to keep you busy."

"Great, thanks I will." She looked enquiringly at Dannielle as she picked up the key.

"No way!" was her friend's reaction. "I don't do exercise."

"Just drop the key through the letterbox when you come out," Ben shouted as he left the kitchen. "It's a spare." Gabbie gathered her things, ready to leave but tangled her scarf in the chain about her neck. She pulled it free, bringing the pendant she wore into view.

"Ooh," Danielle exclaimed, reaching towards the glowing stone. "Can I see?"
Gabbie found herself reluctant as she allowed Arwres, the precious Myriar stone, to be handled by the other girl.

"Wow, where did you get that?"
Gabbie did not answer. Her eyes were focused on the stone for it had turned a deep red. Within the cloudy interior, she saw a face she had not seen since for over a decade.

*

His clothes were heavy with mud, and slicks of sodden soil crept underneath his fingernails, as Klim foraged for signs of Kier's presence. It was three in the morning and together with Samuel and Swift, he had been searching since midnight. Almost ready to give up, he caught the stench of an evil he had hoped never to find again. Since regaining the Iridice, his father's stone, his gift for telepathy had become multifaceted. It led him now to an eerie hollow where he was plunged into images of the attack on Kier by the Roghuldjn. Minutes later he discovered the torn, bloodstained strip of Kier's coat. He described to the others the foul creature he had met once before on the crag at Bankside.

"There was another battle, between two creatures. I think Kier somehow escaped in the middle of it but, for some reason, returned to the site. It's hard to figure out what happened then." He examined the sensation of a sudden absence of feeling. "She either blacked out," he hesitated, "or…"

"She blacked out," Swift insisted, her face pinched with exhaustion and dread. Samuel's gloom added to the sense of hopelessness.

 Klim was aware of a strong and uncharacteristic anger with Kier, whom he had come to love deeply as family. He was at a complete loss to explain what had made her run away in the middle of a storm. Taking a deep breath, he gazed with increasing fear around the putrid hollow where she had almost, if not in fact, met her death. He pushed away the thought as Swift reached for his shoulder; she could barely stand. He took her hand and forlornly they followed Samuel back towards the cottage. Klim had been helping Swift to recover from her long ordeal of the previous weeks. Pursued by the Devouril Nephragm, she had used her gift as a Stozcist to navigate dangerous pockets of matter beneath the surface. It had taken all of her strength to find a way back and then to survive the struggle with Nephragm. Klim had experimented with transferring positive energy from himself to her with considerable success. Right now, he struggled to shake off his own negative emotions. Swift spoke little, returning to her room as soon as they reached the cottage. Throwing off the grimy raincoat Klim followed Samuel into the kitchen, where the cleric had placed glasses on the table.

"Swift's gone to check on Evan and then to bed," he said.

"How is she?" asked Samuel.

"Healing, I think."

"Brave, miraculous Swift. If Nephragm had found her on the island with the others ..." Samuel ended his speculation with a shake of his head.
Klim nodded, "She knew how vulnerable she was to him, that he had come to find her."

"I still fear for her." Samuel poured out a liberal quantity of Evan's brandy into both glasses.
Klim picked up the glass and let the smooth liquid heat his throat. The kitchen door flew open, its glass rattling in its small panes. Samuel closed it absently with a flick of his finger. Klim shook his head, a wry smile around his lips as he looked towards the firmly closed door, "So cool."
The gloom was broken for a moment as Samuel returned his smile and then it quickly descended back into place.

"Be sure you know what you are doing Klim." The cleric was sombre as he stood up to leave the room. Klim finished the brandy. Perhaps it was as well he was leaving for Istanbul in the morning as Echin had requested. He acknowledged his deepening link with Swift, his confusion of emotion. The storm pressed noisily against the door but it stayed firmly shut. What if Kier was still out there, lying somewhere, dying of cold? He pushed away the glass and let his head fold over his arms, too exhausted to climb the stairs.

*

Dawn nudged the sky over Stonehenge. The king stone slid downwards, slotting into the surface, key tight. The chilling sound of its falling was echoed throughout the planet, as one by one the great Waybearer stones sank into the ground, closing the interface between the surface of the earth and the Mourangil kingdoms that lay within. These great standing monuments had stored the memory of humanity on the planet; they had assisted the Mourangils to explore human form upon the surface. A voice, her own, ringing with fear, forced away the dream and brought the sound of hurried footsteps nearby.

"Killian!" Kier was astonished to see the Irishman. Breathing heavily, the Tane came across to the bed, on which she lay propped up on soft pillows. Gently he slid his hand behind her head, raising it forwards, offering a glass of water. She was desperately thirsty and confused, her body was stiff and weak. Gratefully, sipping the clear, cool liquid she peered disbelievingly at Killian's face. There was no denying his misshapen nose, so many times broken; his crooked grin and the glint of emerald eyes that reflected his elemental origin. Her head, too heavy to hold without his support, flopped back onto the pillow as he removed his hand.

"You're awake then!" The voice came from the corner of the room, wolfish eyes scrutinised her face.

"Mactire!" The words fell out in a hoarse whisper. Her mind swiftly returned to the fearsome encounter with the Roghuldjn, remembering that the creature had been destroyed by another. Finally, she recalled hearing the howl of a wolf, before she slid from consciousness in that dark place. Kier stared neutrally at the handsome and charismatic figure that stood in the doorway. One she had seen previously turn into an adlet, an upright Icelandic wolf. Mythical, elemental Mactire.

"You saved me," she was torn between gratitude for her survival and distrust of the Tanes. They held no love for humanity in general. Mactire bowed his head in acknowledgement but said nothing.

"Where is this place?" The room was cosy, homely even. Clean curtains, fresh flowers, wooden dressing table.

"We're outside a little village on the east coast of Ireland," he explained. "An old domain where the Tanes once lived out of earshot and slingshot from the rest of the world."

"Why am I not back with Samuel?" she demanded, confusion summoning a strength in her voice that tore at unused vocal cords.

"Mostly," Killian told her mildly, "because we couldn't find him. We'd already been looking for days when Mactire came across you about to be devoured by the Roghuldjn."

Mactire came towards her. Kier noticed bandages peeping out under the blue shirt he wore; the previously sharp, jade coloured eyes had dimmed to a soft green. She remembered that Samuel had told them that his cottage could be accessed by invitation only. She also remembered Echin's words that the adlet form of Mactire was slowly dying.

"How long have I been here?"

"Since last night," Killian informed her, as he signalled to Mactire to help him raise her to a sitting position. Kier's brow furrowed in concentration as she tried to compute that she had been unconscious for a whole day. Pain ripped through her right shoulder, her left hand reached across to feel the area padded with dressings. Mactire signalled to Killian, who passed across a medicine bottle from a small table on the other side of the bed. With gritted teeth, she allowed the two men to lift her gently into a more comfortable position.

"It'll help the pain," Mactire told her, pressing a small plastic measuring cup to her lips; the sticky liquid tasted of peppermint.

"Thank you," she said, trying for a smile. "You make good nurses."

As the Tane stepped back she moved to speak again but was assailed with a need to close eyes that had become leaden, the words she intended to say had already drifted beyond her.

*

There was a biting winter chill in the air as Gabbie walked up the hill, her hands pressed into the pockets of her a tracksuit top. She dodged parts of a broken slate, one of the many that had become dislodged from rooftops in the previous night's gale. The wind had dropped now; Klim would have been able to tell her if it would start building again later. He had a way of knowing the weather. She sighed and her breath was a soft mist in front of her. She missed him. Bankside seemed smaller, emptier. She wished she could have talked about it to Danielle but things were different, she was different. Lifting her chin, she raised her eyes to the grey morning sky, getting darker by the day. All the times she had walked up this hill but never really looked at the buildings! They were terraced, deceptively big inside with three spacious floors. One side was residential and the other filled by shops and businesses. She had never noticed before the round turret on top of the otherwise ordinary looking building that Ben had turned into a gym. Vaguely, she remembered her dad referring to the 'old Co-op place, where those with funny handshakes used to meet.' She knew nothing about the Masons, apart from the fact that they had lots of secrets. Looking at the place now she noticed that the windows on the top floor had been covered with boards.

Gabbie shivered as she pulled out the key from her small bag. Her fingers were stiff with cold as she let herself in and climbed the stairs. In the main room, on the second floor, she weaved between boxes of still packaged equipment but the treadmill, bike and cross trainer were in use. She took off her jacket, adjusted her trainers and leggings before stepping onto the treadmill. She was fast now, and once in her rhythm her mind flitted about like a pinball trapped in a machine. Klim's image was never far away. She remembered how he hadn't wanted to come back with her to Bankside. How he had looked at Swift so protectively. She ran harder, everything, apart from the weather, which was a lot worse than usual, seemed so normal back home. But she knew she had left home behind a long time ago, maybe Klim knew that too. She pulled hard at the water bottle, adjusting the strap of her vest top. Hitching her bag over one shoulder, she noted with satisfaction that she had run ten kilometres.

Gabbie whistled as she wandered through a door into another gym. This was the room she had noticed coming up the hill. The windows were blacked out and old wooden panels lined the walls. A false pine ceiling added to a sense of secrecy. Her eyes followed the metal trellising that faced the entrance to the room and lined one side. She smiled as she walked towards a professional looking boxing ring to her right. Ben had boxed professionally at one time; she pictured him sparring in his own place. It was no surprise that this part of the gym was already in use. A pair of blue boxing gloves lay in the centre of the roped square. Nearby was a box filled with equipment. The tail end of a hand wrap reached the edge of the new trainer on her left foot; she bent down and wound the two inch tape back to its source in the box.

Abruptly she turned, certain she had felt someone enter this strange room that shut out the morning and was built for privacy. The dim bulb gave an aura of interrogation; she felt the fine hairs on her arms prickle upright. Gabbie noticed that the door was closed tight, but she had no recollection of closing it behind her. The wood lined room suddenly held a coffin like claustrophobia. As he turned back towards the boxing ring she saw, with horror, that the tape she had replaced now lay as she had first found it, stretched untidily across the floor. The rasping breathlessness of panic escaped from her lungs as other tapes spilled out of the box. They unrolled at speed, weaving up and down throughout the metal trellis, gathering towards her.

Gabbie reached the door and pulled at the handle but it would not open. The white tapes rose to reach around her waist but she fought them with a fevered energy, stamping on the fibrous material to loosen its hold. In seconds, there were other reels snaking towards her. They wrapped around her body tightly, so that she felt her lungs struggling to expand against her enveloped ribs.

"Where is the stone?" asked a voice from behind the panels. "Give me Arwres."

"Danubin!" gasped Gabbie. It had to be. Gabbie had never seen her in person but she felt certain that this was the work of the leader of the Virenmor. One of the white ribbons of tape released itself from her throat. There was an empty space where Arwres usually hung; Gabbie had removed the stone before coming to the gym.

"Where?" insisted the harsh, disembodied voice. Gabbie tore at her bonds, screaming now with fury she managed to free her hands and pull at the wraps that crushed her chest.

"I know who you are, Danubin!" she yelled defiantly. "You can't have Arwres. You can't have me!" Immediately the ghostly strands of tape wrapped around her more tightly than ever, suffocating, choking. Gabbie felt her knees sag and she dropped to the floor, kicking over the bag she had brought with her. The few contents scattered: Ben's key, her own house key, a hairbrush, water bottle and the small ornamental mirror her mother had once given to her. Her vision grew blurred, the mirror rolled towards her face and opened. Danubin's voice whispered from a face she had never forgotten.

"Really Gabrielle?" The cruel sneer ravaged her mother's face. "We will see."

The room dimmed to black as one of the wooden panels exploded from the wall, splintering the room with oak shards. The wraps fell limply to the floor around her. She grabbed at the door which opened at her touch and ran, fleeing the building out onto the street. The screech of brakes on a four-by-four awakened her to the fact that she was in the middle of the road. She crossed to the other side and leaned heavily against the building opposite.

She looked up towards the boarded windows, searching for Mengebara, hastening to let the others know of Danubin's attack. Nothing. Panic-stricken, she searched again for the mind place that Klim had constructed for them. Still nothing; she was unable to access anything from the others. None of them used a mobile phone because Mengebara had given them a means of communication that needed nothing but their waking consciousness. Bereft, she stumbled back down the hill alone, more alone than she had ever felt in her young life.

Chapter Five

Klim had crawled up to bed in the early hours. After a fitful sleep, he was now even more determined in his view that Kier was still alive. He could feel her. It wasn't the same as his links with the others, harder to describe. As if it was on a level so deep he couldn't figure it out. He had awoken convinced that if she had died, an essential part of him would know. His eyes picked out the irregular pattern on the ceiling. There had been some movement over the river when he had disturbed Kier the evening before. He ruminated that this might be a clue to her disappearance. He was reluctant to give up the search but he felt certain that she would not be found anywhere near the cottage.

The rhythm inside his head, a firm basal heartbeat of strength and agility, was one that he had come to know well. When Siskin was near, he could join his friend's understanding, at least on a simple level, of the particular melodies of each individual. It was the Lute's gift, to hear their essential and unique musical signature. It extended further to a manipulation of sound waves, to the point where Siskin had created a sound driven vehicle. He had named it Suara. Klim was proud of his own role in amplifying Siskin's power by using his own gifts of manipulation in the field of thought. Always ready for flight since working with Siskin in Nicaragua, he quickly dressed and ran to greet his friend.

It was Evan's first time at breakfast since he had been injured. Siskin grinned, greeting the Welshman with a handshake and a curved arm around his back. "Good to see you back on your feet."

Evan's presence lifted the younger ones who would have spared him the news of Kier's disappearance, had they been able.

"I love this land, this stone, this river," Evan told them in his mournful bardic way, "but without Kier, it is a garden whose rare flower has been stolen."

"Surely our time would be better served here, trying to find Kier?" Siskin looked worried. His blonde hair was tied back in a ponytail, his strong features and graceful movement, an unconscious part of his presence. "It's just so unlike her to run out in the middle of a storm. Could she have been tricked again?" They all remembered the Devouril, Nephragm, inhabiting the body of Kier's beloved friend Adam, to lure her from the safety of the book shop in Pulton.

Samuel sighed. "It was my fault," he told them, rubbing his face with his hands.

The small group turned towards him with incredulous expressions. He sighed and gave an account of the interchange between himself and Kier the previous evening. "I told her that the Stone of Mesa had been lifted by the same hand that had bound Belluvour in the Secret Vaults. Candillium!" Swift, still pale, nodded in agreement.

Samuel told them of her discovery of the runes and the interpretation of their meaning. Eyes widened as he spoke about the ignition of the Stone of Mesa, the coming alignment of the Sister Spheres and the Key of Brunan. His companions seemed both enthralled and shocked. "I should not have pushed her, though the times are upon us."

"Then all the more reason for us to stay and look for her," Siskin commented.

Klim put his hand on the cleric's arm. "Are you certain that Kier is in fact Candillium?"

"She is Kier and only Kier unless she finds the voice of Candillium within her. But I am certain that Candillium, if only for that moment, was the power that ignited the Stone of Mesa."

Klim saw the deep relief in Swift's face. He himself, had never doubted that Kier held the centrepiece of the Myriar somewhere inside her.

"I always knew it," Siskin nodded with satisfaction, standing up, all soldier now. "And I think Kier knows too Samuel, she maybe just can't face it right now. Don't blame yourself. I won't leave until I find her."

Samuel's tone became urgent. "I spoke to the river and the earth," he said matter-of-factly, as if it were a conversation they could all share. "I guarantee that Kier is not present any more in this part of the world."

"She is alive!" Klim interjected. "I'm certain."

Samuel looked carefully at each of them. "She is not within our reach at this time. Of that I am sure," he said sombrely. "I believe the way to help her is to continue our attempt to recreate the Myriar. Kier's finding and translating the runes, at this time, was no accident. We have been given tasks that must be fulfilled. You and Siskin should get to Istanbul urgently and assist Josh in finding the Key of Brunan."

"Swift," he cut off her protest as she moved to stand, "I will need your help to stop these catastrophic floods. The Teifi is swollen with the impulse to escape its borders." Swift dropped her head, nodding her assent.

"Echin will come back to find Kier," Evan insisted, "if she really is Candillium, and I too believe that she is, then that is our first priority."

"Can't we message him? He should know," Klim suggested.

Samuel looked out towards the simmering storm then turned back to the Welshman. "If you will trust me, I advise you that it will do no good to bring him back here just now. Place nothing in Mengebara. The doorway must be opened by the male aspect of the Myriar, that is the priority."

"But Echin will know that," Evan reasoned.

"He is outside the Mourangil kingdoms, aligned to human destiny, and he grieves." Samuel's voice was heavy with fatigue.

"Outside?" Evan queried.

"The Waybearers have closed their doors to the surface with the approach of the alignment. Moura draws her jewels within. Faer and Tormaigh are unreachable."

"What!" exclaimed Siskin. Klim sighed heavily, his hand closing around the Iridice, his dad's stone, the stone of the Reeder. Swift sat silently, pale underneath the soft brown of her skin. Evan put his arm around her. Siskin stood, slowly putting on the woollen hat that covered the soft blonde of his hair. He nodded towards Klim as he stood. "We'd best be on our way."

Klim nodded numbly. The loss of Kier, Tormaigh, and Faer touched that dark hole of despair that had threatened to engulf him since his mother's death. And he was already struggling with another separation. The loss of his closeness to Gabbie had been the hardest part of his time away with Siskin in South America the previous year. There had been little chance for either of them to understand each other again, especially with his deepening attachment to Swift. His movements were uncharacteristically heavy as he made his way upstairs to pick up his rucksack. Swift stood waiting on the bottom step as he came back down. The dark, almond shaped eyes held his. "Give this to Josh," she told him, placing a pendant in his hand, the chain dropping between his fingers as she covered the stone. The wind rattled the small cottage as they stood there facing each other, neither one releasing the other's touch. Siskin came out of the living room.

"Ready?" he asked Klim.
Klim nodded as Swift removed her hand from his. "What is it?" he asked her, opening his palm and looking up in surprise to find a pulsating, striated, pink quartz like material. "The Chalycion?"

"A.....what do you call it," her Spanish accent rounded the word, "fax!"

"Fax....oh a facsimile," he corrected.

"Si," she replied. "I think it will be of use. Its name is Licia and it will tell you when Danubin is near."

"But how?"

"She held other Myriar stones of power for some time. Your Iridice, and Siskin's Amron Cloch were manipulated to her purpose. I used both stones to find a trace of her, like a signature that embedded in your jewels. I inserted the same trace into Licia. It will respond to her presence."

Klim placed the stone carefully in his pocket and kissed Swift on the cheek in farewell. Both men made their goodbyes. "Will it be any warmer in Istanbul?" he asked Siskin.

"Maybe a bit, but probably just as wet," answered his friend, pulling a heavy coat around him. "Right then," Klim replied, "that's something to look forward to."

*

A deluge of rain enhanced the confusion of the crowd as they alighted the boat. People scattered across a large pavement area, edging through queues around various ticket booths. Josh scanned the area to find Echin. A silver haired man in a suit stood to one side but Josh was unable to see his friend. As he moved towards the stranger Echin's easy smile met his, he stood exactly where the man had been standing. The young artist shook his head. "There was someone else standing here, older, grey hair," he stated with conviction.

"Illusion only," Echin told him. "I don't wish to advertise my presence here."

"It was you?" Echin nodded, his guarded expression silencing further conversation.

Echin steered him away from the docks and up into the city. The haunting call to prayer echoed from a nearby mosque. They entered a café and ordered a strong Turkish coffee that the Mourangil seemed to have a taste for. There were a number of low armchairs and tables populated mainly by tourists. It was only when they had settled in a secluded corner that Josh felt able to share his thoughts. "This illusion thing, could you teach me sometime?" The young artist fiddled with the small cup of syrupy liquid.

Echin put down his coffee cup. "The Tanes have touched on this art and believe they are masters. However, apart from hiding their elemental self, they have not been able to create personal illusion of this order. The Virenmor practice a corrupt version in their projections and manipulation and are in fact nearer to mastering the skill. The Virenmor cannot reach the heart of man however, the mystery of selflessness is beyond them. For this reason, their constructs are merely that, distorted versions of material form. As the Creta, and a Seed of the Myriar, you have already travelled far beyond this and recorded the illusory folds of reality that make form. To learn the skill of creating the illusion that you are someone else, you merely need to take a step backwards to the beginning of that process. Instead of weaving between the layers of your images to explore a new plane of existence, you need to create only the image of new shape and let it overlay the existing one. Who would you seem to be? It's easier to hold if it is not a copy of another but an illusion you have created from your own imagination."

Josh took out a pencil from his pack and hesitated, "I've only ever worked from life."

"Then perhaps it's time to expand your style," Echin suggested.

Josh put down the pencil thoughtfully, "I'll have to give it a bit of time." His eyes were a mixture of curiosity and self-doubt. Josh's natural place had always been in front of a sketchpad and for the first time he felt seriously challenged. His fingers itched to draw the characters of those who sat around him, to pierce their identities with a razor sharp pencil. The paper remained blank when Echin signalled for them to leave.

It was dark when they emerged from the café, though the streets remained alight with shops and hotels. Josh looked wistfully at the luxurious interior of a huge Ottoman style hotel, but Echin led him down the cobbled streets into an altogether different aspect of the city.

*

"Give it back Aiden," the light Irish brogue was a woman's voice.

"She's not going to miss it now Loretta, you said yourself she's hardly alive."

Footsteps sounded angry beside the bed. "Show some respect man," it was Mactire's voice, strained.

Vaguely she was aware that it was Mactire's hand under her head; she had become accustomed to his touch. The chain that she had so quickly become used to wearing was replaced around her neck; the weight of the Stone of Mesa was comforting as it nestled at her throat. Kier felt the uncomfortable pinch of a cannula in her right arm. Her mouth, though dry, felt comfortable and clean. At least one of the Tanes, she thought, had professional training. The weakness of her body was overwhelming. The effort to open her eyes or form words was beyond her. It seemed that only her ears still served her.

"Sean, I've never heard of anyone recovering from a Roghuldjn attack where the skin was broken. And it was deep. How did you think to use the stone?" Loretta asked her brother.

"Desperation to tell you the truth of it, IV antibiotics weren't touching the infection." Placing the stone on the wound seems to have encouraged her power to heal herself. I just wish I'd come to it earlier. You really think it's too late?" Kier was surprised at the emotion in his voice.

Loretta sighed. "You have as much training as I do, so you can see for yourself." There was a hesitation then her voice became filled with sympathy, "Ah, I didn't know how you felt about her. I'm sorry Sean, quite honestly her chances of survival are negligible."

Chapter Six

"Early October still sees a good many tourist in the old city," Echin explained as they made their way through Sultanahmet. Iconic buildings, spires and minarets gleamed in the morning light. Early visitors were taking advantage of the less populous streets. Stall holders had not yet refreshed their bartering voices. "By the end of the month most of the street vendors will be gone." Echin purchased hot chestnuts for both of them, passing the paper bag to Josh who was grateful for the warmth. A damp drizzle trickled beneath the hood of his jacket as he watched a hardened stall holder set up against the rain. Another wore what looked like a miniature lampshade but was in fact a small umbrella worn in a band around his head.

"Where are we going again?" Josh checked. Echin pulled the young artist back just as a yellow taxi whizzed past. "Other side," he warned, as Josh remembered that the Turks drove on the right-hand side of the road. He was steered through a sloping alleyway that brought them into what looked like an old church. This impression was confirmed as Echin continued to lead them through an unused Christian chapel and out into a maze of small dwellings.

In the middle of the conclave was a stone staircase that led down to a further level of intimately close white buildings, one of which had an arched blue doorway. Echin pushed gently and it opened to his touch, revealing a narrow corridor from which Josh could smell an already familiar aroma. Elanur sat smoking through the long pipe on a bench in a modern kitchen, her clothes now much more elaborate and her hair dressed in jewels. She came laughingly to greet them.

"Come in, come in," she said merrily. "Take a pipe and some coffee."

To Josh's great delight Klim and Siskin were seated on the bench opposite the small woman. Both, he thought, had a dazed look that he took to be the result of their exclusive exposure to Elanur.

"Good to see you," he said, shaking Siskin's hand and then Klim's. Elanur stood by quietly, observing as they made their greetings. She poured coffee for the new arrivals and then returned to smoking the bubble pipe, lifting it to one side in order to speak. "Danubin has been found."

"What?" Josh abandoned the thick syrupy coffee and pulled his chair closer to Elanur. "Where? Has she got the Chalycion?"

"Is she on her own?" Siskin asked.

Elanur clucked, waved a finger to scold them and smiled.

"Quietly, give me time to tell you."

She waited until Echin and Josh had brought stools and placed them opposite the others. She pulled her own stool against the wall beside the Mourangil. "She was not on her own I think,"

Echin looked over at Elanur who nodded sadly.

"Ulynyx?" he queried.

"Ulynyx," she confirmed.

"In the old city," Echin guessed and Elanur nodded in affirmation. "There are so many ancient jewels in the old city that the Chalycion is less likely to be traced," he explained. "There's an enclave that Red Light has been watching for some years. That's partly why I asked you to come," he looked towards Siskin and Klim.

"Red Light?" asked Elanur.

"I've worked for the organisation over many years," Siskin explained, "and more recently so has Klim." He nodded to his companion who, even as Echin mentioned the name, had straightened his back, ready for conflict. "It was only last year," he continued, "that I found out that Red Light had been set up originally at Echin's instigation. It's a multinational charity, collecting funds and promoting political action. Within its operating facility, I was part of a team that chased down and brought to justice some of those responsible for human trafficking."

The hard edge of his voice made Josh feel grateful that Siskin had never had cause to hunt him.

Echin sounded unusually tired, "The enclave in Istanbul stirs hatred and fear between East and West, East and East, West and West. It plays an important role in the ever revolving conflict, maintaining enmity where crucial cooperation is needed. It's no surprise that the Virenmor have a hand in its existence, but Ulynyx?"

Elanur's expression was veiled, "We still do not know what part he plays," she said softly.

Echin's expression softened a little but remained distant as he fetched a set of maps from a drawer in the kitchen dresser. He placed them on the table, but before he could continue Elanur, her eyes encircling the group, spoke softly. "You are already much intertwined," she commented, "and masterfully secretive. But you should have told us before that the heart of your group has been lost."

Klim looked shocked; both he and Siskin looked towards Echin.

"Kier?" The Mourangil's tone was tense. Josh felt the blood leave his face. He braced himself against the whitewashed wall. Siskin looked suspiciously at Elanur.

"Elanur will have stolen most of your secrets already," Echin commented with uncharacteristic irritability. "If there was any doubt of her, you wouldn't be here." Klim sensed a trace of discomfort in Elanur at Echin's words, but he joined with Siskin in recounting the events of the previous evening, informing them of Samuel's insistence that Echin should not be troubled with Kier's disappearance. Echin said nothing but quizzed Klim carefully about the events of the night Kier had left the safety of the house. Despite Echin's assurance regarding Elanur, neither he nor Siskin felt happy to discuss the fact that Samuel believed he had driven Kier from the cottage; how he had communicated to her that he believed Kier to be Candillium. Instead Klim concentrated on explaining what he had found during the search.

Elanur gave a gasp of revulsion as Klim told of his recognition of the presence of the Roghuldjn. Echin became more intense, his expression locked down into the inscrutable contours that were impenetrable, even to Klim. "Recovery of the Chalycion is paramount right now," the Mourangil told them. "You must lure Danubin back to the café at the centre of the cell. Somewhere in the city will be a hidden lair, you'll need to follow her closely to find it."

Josh raised his eyebrows and considered that the other two looked far too keen to face Danubin again. He pressed himself further against the wall, as if it would shut out the fear that had threatened to engulf him since the news of Kier's disappearance. Drawing in his breath he pushed away his personal anxiety and concentrated on

Elanur's words. Over the following hour she explained in detail the pattern of comings and goings, the personnel involved in a café in the old city. Echin disappeared outside. Once the briefing had finished the friends found him in a small garden, enclosed by tall trees at the back of the building. He was deep in thought as they approached.

"This is your place?" Klim guessed.

Echin turned, his thoughts only slightly turning with him. Slowly he looked around the enclosed garden. "I suppose so," he told them. They knew he was reluctant to consider the concept of ownership. To him the planet Moura offered its materials as they were needed, the places and buildings he had collected were freely given according to the needs of the time.

"The dwelling is given up to Elanur's use right now," he went on. "The bedroom window looks out over the Bosphorus and the stars embed their reflection in the water at night."

"Hmm," Josh countered, a look of exasperation on his face. "I'm guessing there's more than one bedroom. So, is there a reason we stayed in that wonderfully comfortable hostel last night?"

It brought what was becoming an increasingly rare smile to the Mourangil's lips, "Yes Josh, there was."

*

Josh, whose sense of direction was even more accurate than that of Siskin, had directed the two members of Red Light straight back to the run down hostel where he had spent the previous night. It was a barren attic room with no other amenities than a battered and barely clean bed. Echin had explained that it also happened to overlook the café in which Danubin and Ulynyx had been seen. Siskin and Klim worked together wordlessly, scanning the area from the large window. Josh nodded with appreciation once again at the domes and minarets of a city that evoked an age of magical empires, the stuff of fairy tales. His eyes followed Siskin as he scrutinised a number of youths huddling over a charcoal fire. The hostel was only a short walk from the main tourist area, yet this part of town showed little evidence of fairy stories. It seemed that this small enclosed area was a centre for the disenfranchised, a magnet for social unrest at a time when violent war was a mere border away.

The afternoon wore on; Siskin and Klim lay on the bed, trying to catch a few hours' sleep. Josh wore around his neck the copy of the Chalycion made by Swift. The difference between the two stones was subtle, she had managed to imbue the replica with much of the original. What even Swift could not replicate however, was the long years of usage, the imprint of Candillium and so many others who had guarded it from harm down the years, including his mother Marianne. Josh's expression was bleak as he allowed himself once again to recognise the guilt and frustration that the precious jewel had been stolen whilst in his care. The artist slipped from his sleeve the picture that the young girl had asked him to draw on the boat. Picking up a pencil and turning to the blank side of the page he began to do something he had not done since school before his gift as a Creta had matured. He drew, not from life, but from his imagination, creating faces that emerged from a different energy of mind. Quietly he practised, as the other two dozed, the new skill that he had seen Echin perform. When he was as satisfied as he could allow himself to be, Josh stood in darkness by the window, watching the café through the night vision goggles that Siskin had supplied.

The evening stars had begun to decorate the sky when the news came through from Swift. Siskin had messaged earlier in Mengebara, in reply Swift confirmed that Kier remained missing. Immediately the depressing little room became even more so. It was nine o'clock that evening when Josh awoke his two companions whose habit of instant alertness always made him jump.

"Play time," he told them.

Chapter Seven

Sitting in a hidden nook at the top of a cobbled street was the café that Red Light had identified as the heart of a terrorist cell. It was considered particularly dangerous as there seemed to be no consistent national affinity; no other purpose apart from ensuring continued and poisonous conflict. It was surrounded by several dwellings in poor repair with crumbling windows and brickwork but the café itself appeared reasonably well maintained. A woman sat cross-legged in the doorway, a young child wrapped in blankets upon her lap. She looked at them with the lugubrious stare of hard poverty and desperation. Klim had given her most of his money before Siskin nudged him away. Klim noticed with satisfaction that the small room on the top floor of the hostel, where they had been positioned, had been well chosen. Most of the building was hidden by one of the many rooftop sheds, this one painted in bright yellow, and the window from the top room of the hostel was barely visible. Situated several streets away, it allowed a good view of the street they were in but was unlikely to be noticed by those below.

The café was full of locals and Klim was surprised to hear Siskin order drinks in Turkish. "It's just about all I know," the musician told them in response to his friends' querulous look, as he ordered three glasses of the traditional raki drink. Klim felt the tight pressure of time as he downed the raki. They ordered a round of bottled beer. Searching for Danubin in a city of fourteen million, Siskin had explained, was a non-starter. They had to bring her to them. Elanur had confirmed that the café was the heart of Danubin's political rustling in Istanbul, though she had rarely been spotted within it. The place was a mixture of sparseness and warmth. The building itself had a faded elegance in its solid structure. The whitewashed walls covered old stone and the small arched windows gave the place an atmosphere of another age, lingering stubbornly in the architecture. The colourful and dimmed Turkish lamps offered a sheen of welcome but the tables and chairs were barely upright. Josh twice adjusted the leg of the table to stop their drinks spilling.

As the evening wore on, Klim sensed that their continued presence had turned mild animosity into scrutiny by the few locals talking quietly on the other side of the room. All attention however became redirected to the noisy entrance of a group of men carrying heavy luggage. "Weapons," Siskin noted, picking up his drink. "Four newcomers, guessing automatics."
Klim had adjusted to seeing Turkish officers wearing guns but glancing over at the new arrivals, all with heads covered in a chequered keffiyeh, he saw nothing obvious about the large brown holdalls they had deposited on the floor nearby. He trusted Siskin's instinct however and reached out his mind towards the hard looking face of the nearest man. Fear and passion warred in a mind that was besotted with a belief system that fuelled his right to take what he wanted. A train ride of destruction was Klim's assessment of the youth, who was probably around his own age. The older two, fierce and determined, were awash in blood and violence. Klim felt a sense of relief that the girls were not being exposed to these hardened soldiers, misogynists that denied women rights of the most basic kind. All but one woman, to whom they were clearly answerable.

Klim saw the mental signature of Danubin etched irrevocably on the minds of each. Danubin, with her own savage cruelty, fed their power and solicited young men and women from all over the world to create a culture that condoned acts of heinous barbarism. Like a snake in a chaotic jungle she wound between the pillars of their self-erected importance, stoking the lust for power, even as she also laced each mind with fear. Klim turned away seeing that the fourth member of the group was returning to the others from the men's room. Although he was the tallest of the four he was also clearly the youngest. Gabbie would have called him hot, Swift beautiful. Klim recognised a brand of film star good looks, made even more charismatic by the haunted expression of his dark young eyes. He probed to find a fragile film of toughness, memories that clung to his mother and sisters, self-loathing and fear. An invincible connection to the other youth made Klim sure that they were brothers. He turned away from the boy's agony of existence.

In Mengebara the Reeder relayed what he had learnt from the minds of the four newcomers and confirmed Siskin's assessment of the automatic rifles that lay hidden within the bags on the floor. The atmosphere in the café had become charged, a tinder box of potential violence. Only Josh, who had least experience of violence and combat of the three, seemed to be calm. Klim let his mind connect again with the group, this time searching for specific intention towards themselves and another couple of tourists in the café.

"What!" he said quietly lifting his drink. "Is this your doing?" His incredulous look was mirrored by Siskin who watched in Mengebara the picture that Josh had depicted to camouflage their presence in the café. He had created the illusion of naïve looking tourists, a family of three. Siskin and Klim were overlaid by middle-aged parents, and Josh appeared as an academic looking young man, presumably the son.

"How long can you hold it?" Siskin allowed himself to look uncomfortable and become ready for moving.

"Once I have it in place," Josh explained, "it's kind of like settling into a balance. I can hold it for another hour or so maybe but not if we split up."

"Wish that you had warned me of this before I drank the beer," Klim looked towards the gents. "And why do I get to be the mother?"
Josh gave a half smile and the side of Siskin's mouth lifted, even as his eyes continued to scan the room.

"That one is a hair-trigger," Klim's glance flicked towards the older of the two brothers. "I think we should leave."

"Are we likely to be followed?" Josh asked.
Siskin shook his head, "We're small fry," he told them. "There's no need to use the replica to draw her out, my guess is she's already on her way."
Klim nodded, "She's at the forefront of their minds and I'd say any time now."
Siskin walked slightly behind the others as they made their way to the door, but he made sure that he was near enough for Josh to maintain the illusion. The thinner of the youths watched them descend the street from the café door. With relief, they rounded the corner; Josh slumped against a doorway, finally dropping the illusion that he had crafted.

"I need water and sleep," he told them. "I didn't know I'd be so exhausted."

Siskin automatically scanned the street before emerging into their natural forms, linking Josh in a good imitation of a drunken stagger.

"I underestimated the danger in scouting out the café. Well done with the illusion Josh."

"I was only practising," Josh told him. "I didn't expect those four to show up and Danubin to be on her way!" Entering the hostel, they glanced at the disinterested old man on what vaguely passed for a reception desk. Once in the room Siskin checked for any evidence of entry or tampering.

"All clear," he reported.

"So then," Josh said, claiming the bed and stretching out his legs, his hands folded behind his head, "we just need to wait." He was asleep in seconds.

*

The storm had gripped Wales and South West England. There were stories of trees crushing vehicles, widespread flooding and rivers rising at alarming rates to swallow bridges in poor repair. The Teifi brimmed like a simmering stew but held to its banks. Samuel and Swift had battled all day, him keeping the river in check and her holding and remaking old stone so that the ancient bridges, now at the level of the water, still held. Evan, moving stiffly, added the last seasoning to the meal he had prepared. The wind, rising yet again, rattled the windows in the small kitchen. Samuel, though he had little rest, moved towards the door he had so recently entered. Swift went to follow but he spoke to her gently, "The bridges will hold, stay," he reassured her.

Alone with Evan, Swift removed her boots and made her way into the living room. A few moments later, alerted by the sound of books toppling, the Welshman came running after her. "Swift!" He bent awkwardly over the slight figure that had fallen to the floor, clutching her shoulder. He ignored the pain of his injured abdomen as the young women rolled in agony, murmuring in fast Spanish. His eyes darted over her body but could see no sign of sudden injury. "English please Swift," he pleaded. The dark eyes opened and she shifted her position to sit upright, leaning heavily into the settee. Seeing Evan's hands around his stomach she coaxed him to sit in the armchair. Vaguely he was aware of the storm outside dimming, and the front door opening. However, his focus was on the young woman who sat with her hands clutched around her knees, only the top of her dark head now visible as she hunched over. "Swift," he said gently and was rewarded with a lift of her head. Samuel came into the room and behind him was Echin. The Welshman's normal effusive greeting was quickly put aside when he saw the grim expression on the Mourangil's face. Swift reached her hand towards Echin who took it and sat down beside her. "Cariad," Evan began, taking the armchair opposite once again. "I'm fine Evan, nada, it's nothing," she told him. "It certainly isn't nothing," his concern rang loudly in the small sitting room, "I thought you had been attacked, wounded." Swift's chin came up, her eyes were raw with unshod tears. "It's nothing for me," she choked, "I'm not the one who has been injured. It's Kier, I think she's dying." The dark eyes were tortured as they fell on the Mourangil. "Tell me," he said tonelessly.

"I can feel her, there's a wound, a horrible wound in her shoulder. It's poisoning her body."

"Where is she?" Samuel asked.

"Across the sea, hidden," she answered, a look of confusion crossing her face. "I can't see where she is." Echin questioned her gently and skilfully but it was clear that Swift's connection with Kier was visceral, picking up mainly her physical suffering.

"She's isolated, even the energy of Mengebara is lost in that place."

"She's alone?" Samuel queried.

"No, not alone. I think she's being cared for, but it's not enough. They don't have the skill, she's dying."

"Swift," Echin turned towards her. "Let me try something while the connection is still near."
She nodded. Evan held back expressing his fear for the courageous young South American who she loved as a daughter. Echin placed himself in front of her in a kneeling position; she adjusted her own limbs to mirror his. He reached for her hands and both were soon enclosed within a blue sheen of light that travelled from the body of the Mourangil to the young woman. She, without hesitation, searched for the sense of Kier, for the painful suffering of her friend, sister, mother; for she had become all of these to the younger woman.

The energy of the Mourangil added to her own to create a powerful wave that pierced the wall surrounding Kier. Both saw her, lying unconscious on a bed, dressed in a white garment. The room appeared a simple bedroom with none of the standard equipment of a hospital ward. Life was ebbing slowly from her injured body. The wound in her shoulder had healed but all that held Kier to this world were the strands of power emitting from the pendant around her neck. Swift slumped against the Mourangil who gently lifted the slight form and laid her on the settee. He turned with solemn eyes towards Samuel. "She's been gone over 48 hours."

"There was no purpose in bringing you from Istanbul. No one, in all our history, has ever recovered once blood has been let by the Roghuldjn. It is beyond the skill, even of Madeleine." Samuel, exhausted, still in his wet outdoor clothes, slumped into an armchair. "Your burdens are already too great."

Evan was highly disturbed by the conversation and the tension between his two friends. "Where is she? Where is Kier?"

Echin ignored his question, his eyes held those of the Riverkeeper.

Swift roused. "We have to go there!" She looked puzzled, her eyes darting from Samuel to Echin. "We can help her."

Echin's voice was as old as the river outside. "We would not find her in time. As Samuel has told us, Kier stands on the brink of death."

"I can hardly believe that she is still alive," Samuel spoke quietly, regret in the dark eyes as he raised them to the Mourangil. "Roghuldjn poison usually kills inside twelve hours."

Evan cried out in tragic Welsh.

"Look after Swift," the Mourangil said to Evan. Then he turned and folded his being into the air around him.

"Toomaaris wait!" Samuel cried out, but he had already gone. Frustrated, Samuel turned to the Stozcist.

"But where is Kier? Who takes care of her?" Samuel asked the Stozcist.

"I could not see," answered Swift, her eyes shining with tears.

The young woman sank her head wearily against the broad chest of the Welshman, who reached out a protective arm to hold her close. A few moments later she straightened and reached for a glass of water on the table. As she held it up she saw the distorted reflection of Samuel gliding quietly behind her and out through the door.

Chapter Eight

"I don't like this," Klim sat cross-legged on the floor, his eyes apparently absorbed in the grubby off white wall of the attic room.

"What don't you like?" Siskin, stood at the window, keeping his gaze fixed on the people entering and leaving the café.

"That I can't feel Kier or Gabbie."
Josh lay on the bed, coming around from sleep. He sat up in response to Klim's words. "You said Kier's still alive and Gabbie's in Bankside."
The Reeder said nothing, his thoughts consumed in the attempt to find some trace of the two women.

"It may be just distance," Siskin suggested, but Klim shook his head.

"Danubin!" exclaimed Siskin, recognising the smart European entering the café. Klim joined his two friends at the window and Josh put his hand on the stone that Swift had given them. The striations within the rose coloured stone began to pulsate.

"It's tuned into her like Swift said it would," he told them, feeling the soft tug of the stone towards the café.

"She's wearing a red top and black skirt," Siskin noted automatically.

"I thought she'd have a couple of bodyguards," Klim commented, remembering the two ex-mercenaries that accompanied his uncle most of the time.

Siskin shook his head. "Not her. She's a different breed of Virenmor, invisible to Red Light until now, though she's obviously been working this cell for years."

Siskin pulled on his black woollen hat. The angles of his jaw jutted in detestation.

"Secrecy, it's like a cloak she wears. Her brand of evil is subtle, it depends on deceit and manipulation."

"I can't believe she's on foot," Klim remarked.

"She may have got a taxi nearby," Siskin replied.

"Remember how powerful this woman is, she fears no man. She's just as likely to be five minutes away, somewhere no one has penetrated. You sure you're ready for this Josh?"

Josh didn't answer, the look he gave his two friends said clearly that ready or not he would carry out the task he had been set. The two young men wore hooded, dark sweatshirts. Siskin lowered his voice as they opened the door, "Klim'll take up the rear, you stay with me." Josh nodded and all three men exited the squalid room. A few minutes later they were hidden in the shadows of the street below. It had gone midnight and the area was quiet as they made their way stealthily towards the café.

Klim had divined that the four armed men were now upstairs in the café. Although he could establish a mental link with those he knew well, he had only developed a cursory connection with the volatile strangers he had met earlier. He felt a sense of profound loss for the youngest of the men. He appeared imprisoned with poisoned obligation; surrounded by intractable, disturbing violence. Klim's awareness reached out to the small smoke-filled room above the café. Danubin's sinister presence made him wary, making sure that he did not probe too much. Klim signalled to the others when he felt her influence lift from the destructive mentalities she manipulated. He indicated to the others that she had left the room.

The three friends had hidden out of sight in an alley at the bottom of the hill. It gave Josh a clear view of the café doorway when he inched forwards. In only a few minutes Danubin had descended the steps and stood examining the street. He stepped backwards into the shadows, making a fist with his hand to stop the tremble that had occurred momentarily at the sight of his enemy.

"She's not alone," he whispered.

Danubin walked slowly down the hill on the opposite side from the alleyway, where the three men now crouched behind an old crate. Josh caught the glazed eyes of the youngest of the four strangers as Danubin weaved a possessive arm through his. Klim nodded. "Drugged," he whispered. Quietly the trio emerged from their hiding place and began, what seemed to Josh, a strange and surreal journey through the ancient centre of Istanbul. As Siskin had guessed, it seemed that Danubin was based somewhere nearby in the richer part of the old city. They had to find where she was keeping the Chalycion stone, without placing themselves in the hands of Danubin.

"Let Licia lead us." Siskin, all soldier now, halted in the streets behind the famous Topkapi Palace. Josh nodded his understanding. Placing his hand around the pendant he felt a tug that he knew would lead him towards Danubin. Slowly and carefully they continued to follow the dangerous footsteps of the leader of the Virenmor.

Like so many other cities, the rich and the poor of Istanbul stood physically side by side but miles apart in their realities. Amid the glittering Eurasian buildings were lonely derelict sites. It was to one of these that they were drawn, just in time to see Danubin steer her companion inside a wooden door. Siskin had been certain that Danubin would have elected for sumptuous luxury. He scrutinised the unlit house, its overgrown, fenced off garden.

"It's a construct," Josh said, examining the old door that was solid and impassable.

"Like the games that she creates to deceive players into violence?" Siskin queried.

"More solid, polished," Josh replied, taking in the irony of his words as he saw the run-down illusion that alluded scrutiny by its sad portrayal of dereliction. The Creta's eyes were open, perhaps assisted by the Licia stone he wore around his neck.

"What do you see, Josh?" Klim asked him and Josh transferred his thoughts to Mengebara, where they could share the massive pillared structure.

"It makes the Topkapi Palace positively mundane." Siskin whistled at the contrast between the ruined building and the marble turrets and minarets that Josh had shown them.

"It has to be me, alone," Josh told them with an authority that brooked no argument.

Klim began to object but Siskin scrutinised the young artist and saw the determination, and something else, an undefinable need in his expression. It was true, that of all of them, Josh seemed the least susceptible to Danubin's manipulation. He recognised the glow of power that now surrounded Josh, as it had once done in the small out-building in Pont Ffrindiau the day he entered a picture and brought to them all their first vision of the Myriar. Nodding to Klim, Siskin stood aside for the Creta. "We're just here," he whispered.

Josh prepared to enter what looked like a wall but was in fact a door at the side of the building.

"Can you sense anyone else in there Klim?"

Klim tried to scan the house. "I'm not picking up any other imprints inside, but Danubin is well capable of shutting me out. Go carefully," he added, nervous now for his friend.

Once inside, Josh noticed that there was a familiarity about the place. It became obvious that the building was a hidden copy of the one in Wales, where Danubin had robbed him of the Chalycion. The long corridor contained store rooms and empty cells. Josh checked in one of them, a cave like prison with blood stains on the wall. He tried to subdue his revulsion, wondering what kind of atrocity Danubin had enacted within this place. An image presented itself as he concentrated on the Licia stone that Swift had linked to Danubin. He saw the young man she had taken to her private rooms in a parallel corridor. He felt sickened by the vision of the young face, unmanned, spent, his mind raped of emotion by the fixating drug of her power. A wave of nausea swept over him but he continued along the narrow passage until he reached a central, domed area.

Several corridors exited from the centre space. He felt his throat constrict with gnawing fear that he would become trapped once more within the illusory constructs of one of the sinister games with which Danubin trespassed on the physical world. His knee banged against a heavy table. Marble. Steadying his breath, he remembered Samuel discussing a large, marble table with a hidden button that opened Danubin's study. Licia now tugged towards the personal quarters in another limb of the building. It seemed incredible that Danubin would replicate the furniture from the building in Wales. Josh reckoned it was worth a try; his fingers traced underneath the table to depress a single button. He gasped at the almost silent swish of a door opening on the other side of the circular space. Quickly he took himself inside the windowless room. There was a small ebony desk, nothing on its surface. Frustrated he checked that Licia was still tugging towards the far corridor, aware that the open door would be visible to anyone entering the central space. It came to him with a voice he had shut out of his memory; Loretta describing the desk where Danubin had hidden the stones of the Myriar. Another replica but this desk seemed identical. However, it was clear to Josh that the mechanism on this was different. Loretta had explained there was a shell like depression at the back of the table which required the whole palm of a hand to unlock it. Carefully and slowly he slid his hands behind the table allowing his palms to connect and disconnect as he explored the smooth surface. Licia tugged, Danubin was moving. He shot up to try and close the doors but he was unable to shift them. Back at the desk, he carried on searching and found the depression, made for a woman's hand. He let his palm slide into the space, pressing upwards as Loretta had described. A drawer to his right slid open. Josh could hear steps now, she was coming closer. Hastily he opened the small pouch, Echin's words echoing in his mind. Jackson had protected himself against the Perfidium, and the Iridice, by the use of baryte that Nephragm had manufactured. Quickly he removed the clear, glass like substance and placed it on the floor pressing his heel firmly down upon it. Without effect! The footsteps were closer. Quickly he picked up and pocketed the baryte stone and placed the Chalycion, still on its chain, around his neck. It was with amazement that he watched Licia, the copy that Swift had made, flow into the Chalycion. The small lines of pink that criss-crossed its surface pulsated in rhythm with his own heartbeat. Even in Danubin's infected quarters he knew a sense of overwhelming peace. Calmly he exited the study, knowing that his movements had grown in speed without effort. In seconds of real time he had found the switch in the marble table, the silent door was closed and he was back in the corridor from which he had entered. Behind him he heard heels clicking on the white floor. Josh hid at the edge of the corridor and watched as Danubin, gowned in a flowing red dress, led the half clothed youth on a leash and metal collar.

"Who are you?" the boy said in agonised English, struggling within a haze of drugs.

"Anyone you need me to be Tarek," she said in a voice that rang of lust and rust.

Barefoot, behind her, the boy searched the large, central area for escape. Suddenly Josh ran from the connecting corridor, as Danubin strode towards her study, stamping on the long leash so that it was jolted out of her hand. She turned with a cry, fury leaping to her face. She twisted her mouth, speaking hurried words that he could not understand. In moments, the central space became as it had been when she had captured him in the Welsh mansion. Medieval torches sprang high above him and a portcullis slammed to the ground behind. Closed doors now sealed each of the corridors leading from the chamber. Josh froze with panic, reliving the moment when he had been caught in her trap; bound tightly in a spider's web.

She was across the room in seconds, a screeching harpy, reaching, as before, for the Chalycion. The long leash tugged beneath Josh's foot as he released the boy, who fell backwards onto the floor. Danubin stumbled as the boy thrashed around in an attempt to stand. Josh did not need his pencil to see the distortion of human personality behind the perfectly shaped face. Her eyes narrowed in confusion, the torches flickered, behind him the portcullis grated.

Later, Josh would equate that moment to how he felt inside the picture he had once created and entered. As if time was a concentrated bubble into which he had stepped. His determined focus was all that kept the bubble intact and inside that space his power as a Creta grew. As he faced Danubin he felt a surging glow of energy, that began with himself but was amplified by the Chalycion. Josh had no way of knowing that Danubin was blinded by her vision of the Creta, a Seed of the Myriar, wearing a stone of power. That, without the baryte, she was unprotected from the pulsating, burning light of the stone. He was only aware that she had turned her face away from him. He took his advantage and landed his fist on her cheek bone, feeling it break as she fell to the floor, unconscious.

The construct she had created collapsed and the medieval chamber became as it had been previously. Danubin lay unmoving on the cold tiled floor; Josh could see the rise and fall of her chest beneath the lurid red gown. The boy she had called Tarek looked towards Josh, his eyes wide above the metal collar that Danubin had locked around his neck. Josh picked up the leash and pulled him by the arm down the corridor through which he had stolen entry into Danubin's lair. Together they stumbled out into the starry night of Istanbul.

*

The anticipated lunar eclipse headlined the papers; astronomers worldwide were appearing on TV to give their expert opinions. Europe had been pummelled by storms. Story after story of freak weather events emerged. Overnight Siskin and Klim had found a way to send Tarek to a safe house in the Ukraine where he would be able, perhaps for the first time, to make his own choices.

Siskin stood up, peering through one of the small, arched windows. Elanur served apple tea in dainty sherry glasses, urging the musician to sit. Klim felt awkward picking his up, not quite knowing how to handle the stem. The hot liquid was tasty and refreshing and, along with his companions, he quickly finished the drink. The narghile bubbled and Elanur, having offered the pipe to each of them, was now contentedly smoking in between sips of Turkish coffee.

"You have done well," she congratulated them. "To have snatched the Chalycion from within the house of Danubin, a house that none have previously discovered, is a most laudable achievement." She shaped her mouth in what Klim thought was meant to be a reassuring smile, but he found it quite disturbing as if she was trying to hide something. Like Samuel she had no mind print and this seemed strange to him, far more than the cleric. Like a maze, he figured, her centre was invisible and the attempts to find it would take him down many confusing paths.

Restless, Siskin stood again. "Where's is Echin?"

"Where he is most needed," Elanur replied calmly. "As always."

Siskin rubbed the back of his neck. "This doorway Elanur, if he doesn't come, can you help us to open it?" Klim was also aware of a gnawing fear triggered by Echin's absence. He had not dared to reach out to Kier again or even acknowledge to himself and the others that she may no longer be with them. Added to this he had messaged Gabbie several times overnight in Mengebara without reply.

"You sailed the Straits of the Bosphorus two days ago, I think." Elanur looked directly at Josh. It took him a moment to understand that her formal language was describing the brief boat trip he had shared with Echin.

"Do you remember the schoolgirl? The young girl for whom you drew the skyline," she asked. Josh nodded, surmising that Echin had told her about the incident.

"You still have it?" she queried from a wreath of smoke.

"Back in the room," he nodded, puzzled.

"Is it relevant Elanur?" Siskin asked her gently.

"Of course," her lips pressed together firmly.

"I'll go get it then," Josh decided, standing. Siskin moved to follow Josh, "Klim?" he prompted.
Klim caught an expression on Elanur's face that made him shake his head in response to Josh's invitation. "I'll wait here," he replied.
Siskin narrowed his eyes in surprise but carried on towards the door. They had been gone only moments before Elanur closed the pipe and the coffee was put aside. Standing, she spoke firmly to Klim, "It is time."

"Pardon?" Klim stuttered, confused and a little daunted by the intensity of the Runeshaper.
Elanur took a seat opposite and Klim felt the power of her mind press against his. "If you and your friends cannot find the doorway to the Hall of Jasmine then you must give up the Chalycion to another."

"And just who would that be? What 'another' do you mean?" Klim felt a rising anger, his voice becoming harsh.

Elanur, her proud chin uplifted, looked at the angular stern features, the dark eyes that held hers. She focused on the Iridice that hung around his neck. "You risk everything by delay."

"What do I risk Elanur? Explain!"

"It is for Toomaaris to explain!" she was angry now. "He should be here. We have hours only left to open the doorway. The Reeder, the true Reeder, would not need to be told!"

The small women stood up defiantly as if to leave. Klim slid in front of the door, preventing her exit. She had challenged an identity that he had mostly sought to hide or deny. That he was a Reeder of the Myriar, able to see into the minds of others, to communicate to others on the plane of thought. He was able to build a safe haven of telepathic communication for those connected to the formation of this evolutionary gift. Elanur had pulled from his consciousness a frenetic, wing beating defensiveness. In that moment, he felt a shift inside. He looked again at the Runeshaper. It was as if he had pulled down the face of a clock to uncloak the mechanism that lay behind. In the space of moments, the edifice of her mind had become visible to him.

"You goaded me," he stated.

She returned to her seat, her features now relaxed into a weary smile. "I had no choice. There are only hours until the eclipse. It is your gift to claim the knowledge that I carry within; the location of the entrance to the Hall of Jasmine."

"I see it," he told her. "I also see Ulynyx." Until now the name had referred to a daunting figure of a man described by Josh. Now his intimacy revealed Elanur's fears; they were written on her mind like graffiti on a beautiful painting.

"What do you know of Ulynyx?" she asked anxiously.

"I know what you know of him." His simple statement made Elanur turn away. "I know," Klim continued, "he has created a secret army to challenge the madness and the violence. I know that Toomaaris fears that the Chunii have manifested another madness of its own, that has become like the monster it professed to destroy. I see your long devotion to both of them and that you are torn between their different directions. I see that if we do not reach into the Hall of Jasmine then our future on the planet will certainly be lost."

"Go Klim," she advised. "And keep your distance from the leader of the Chunii. I think even Toomaaris underestimates his ambition."

Elanur bowed her head and felt Klim's gentle touch on her shoulders as he left the building. "At last," she whispered.

Klim ran, he ran with all the focus and agility that he had used to stay alive when hunted by those with so called power. Those like his uncle Alex Jackson. They had money, a sadistic self-interest and physical brutality. The power that he now felt inside was none of these things, it was the power of simple recognition, of understanding. He was the Reeder, a Seed of the Myriar. The rain had slicked the pavements on the dockside as Klim slid across towards the old city of Sultanahmet. His mind searched for the imprints of the others and he used Mengebara to instruct them to wait for him. Ironically, they were practically positioned in the location of the doorway.

Chapter Nine

The Waybearer monoliths had populated the surface of the planet since his first emergence from the womb of Moura. And now they were closed and would open only after the Alignment, if at all. He stretched his awareness over the plains and across the cities, into the high reaches and hidden valleys. He traced the steps of mankind where they had fallen, in all but the most remote of places.

The possibility of extinction hung invisibly over the race of men. Ulynyx stood tall and let his eyes roam across the city of two continents, proudly crafted by human inspiration and labour. Their fate was in his hands. Toomaaris was blind, the Myriar a foolish quest that had failed in its infancy. In a matter of hours, the doorway would show itself and he would present the elite of the Chunii to Unethora and accept the fabled Key of Brunan. Ulynyx shifted position as he tried to bury the uncomfortable edge of doubt. The Creta was in Damascus and he knew that on the other side of Europe, Nephragm the Devouril had been defeated.

Shrugging away these thoughts, he turned towards the vast hidden caverns where, even now, the ranks of his army trained tirelessly. Toomaaris, for all his long sojourn among mankind, had not come to know this race as he, leader of the Chunii, had come to know them. He would provide all that was needed; had he not already shaped his followers to strength and agility? Soon he would create a human society worthy of Moura. Again, doubt pricked his mind; Danubin had yet to bring him the Chalycion as he was sure she would do. He had sensed its residue about her but knew he could not force the game-witch of the Virenmor. And if, he reasoned, the stone was in her possession, then it could not be held by the Creta. Ulynyx was certain that without it, the boy who had accompanied Toomaaris in Damascus, could never be accepted within the Hall of Jasmine.

Restless, he paced the walls of his hidden city. The Stone of Mesa had lain dormant since the last Alignment, unknown even to his kind. He dug his blade into the sand as he recalled Elanur's belief that only the hand of Candillium could have recovered the stone and ignited its power. The men and women around him noticed nothing, their consciousness pulled hither and thither by petty arguments and rivalry. An immense power had been released that would call the Sister Spheres to Moura. Together these planets would decide what, of this world, would be discarded. In the work of a moment, a shift here, a turn there, it was possible to begin the process of the extinction of a whole species.

In Mourangil legend the Myriar was to have shown man how to bring together the three keys of Moura long before the Sister Spheres would once more align together. In truth, none knew the real purpose of the keys, but Ulynyx had no doubt that it would help determine if mankind would continue to live on the planet. Toomaaris had made it his long study but had spent so much time on the surface that few could share the workings of his mind. And fewer still had looked to understand what he had made available. It was said that the three male Seeds of the Myriar, each carrying the stones of power, would need to be present at the entrance to the Hall of Jasmine during the lunar eclipse. The hour was almost upon them. Toomaaris had not formed the Myriar and Danubin had at least one of the stones in her possession. Only he could provide a solution. As a

Mourangil and leader of an elite race, Ulynyx had no doubt that Unethora would entrust the Key of Brunan to his care. Elanur, the Runeshaper, had shown him the hidden doorway to the Kingdom of Jasmine. She alone bore the secret location by which means the fabled city could be accessed. The Myriar, he reasoned, would never be needed, for there would be no further necessity to bring mankind beyond their present stage of evolutionary development. They would dwell in the world he would create for them on the surface of Moura.

Ulynyx called to him one of the Elite soldiers that were never far from his side. He sighed and covered his face with a black keffiyeh as he handed the note to Amed, First in Faith of the secret army. He had even created a new language for the thousands who now followed his words without question.

"Be quick and clean, she must feel no pain."
He watched as his words, the death sentence he had pronounced, began to manifest in Amed's mind. Amed studied the note bearing his instructions. He nodded his acceptance; he would personally perform the execution. Ulynyx placed his hands behind his back and walked away from the Elite. As his falcon eyes scanned the city, he would have been surprised to notice that the onyx jewel that glinted at his elbows and chin, had much the same characteristics as the obdurate rock through which a Mourangil cannot pass.

*

"Slow down Klim," Siskin steered him into a nearby café. "We need to talk this through. You said hours not minutes, okay?"

Klim released the sense of urgency that had gripped him since he had plumbed the vast mind of Elanur. He had reached not just into Elanur's thoughts but to the encoded material that formed the bedrock of her being. Her challenge had made him seize his identity as the Reeder of the Myriar in a way that meant he could never again shrug it aside.

Siskin had chosen one of the large, well populated eating houses in Sultanahmet. He led them upstairs into a quiet area, where a number of people were drinking coffee. The musician nodded to the leather couches that had just been vacated. Klim gathered his thoughts as they ordered coffee and he placed himself opposite his two friends. He leaned forwards, elbows on his knees.

"Show me the drawing you made," Klim instructed Josh. "I was able to find the doorway to the Hall of Jasmine hidden in Elanur's mind, it was totally different to anything I've done before. As soon as I asserted my identity as a Reeder I could see it, the material was encoded in her DNA. It was unbelievable! She herself can carry the knowledge but it can only be passed on by using the gifts of the Myriar. When you drew her Josh, you were able to unravel the most important factor. You discovered that by the December solstice the Myriar must be fully formed and present at the location you drew for her."

"Echin said it was a place in Ireland."
Klim nodded, "It's where all of us need to be when the Alignment takes place."

"What is this Alignment?" Siskin eased back into the chair as the coffee was served. He turned expectantly towards Klim, once the waiter was out of earshot.

"A group of planets that last came together when the planet Mesa ceased to be."
Josh whistled.

"We're running out of time. In a matter of hours, we have to be at the hidden door to enter the Hall of Jasmine during the lunar eclipse."

His friends looked blank, waiting for him to elaborate, but instead Klim reached for the pencil drawing that Josh had retrieved. "The child was part of a chain of events that Kier activated when she read the runes in Wales," Klim explained. "It activated receptors on Elanur's DNA that were able to recognise that you are the Creta. In turn, without the physical awareness of either, a connection was made with the young girl."

"Multi-dimensional communication." The other two turned and looked at Siskin, puzzled. "Just like me hearing melodies, you expressing knowledge through your art, Klim reading thoughts. Our communication is multi-dimensional." Siskin shrugged his shoulders as his two companions exchanged glances of amusement. Klim brought their focus back to the picture.

"Anyway Josh, you marked the spot at which the doorway can be found."
They peered over the drawing, focusing on where Josh had over weighted his pencil to form a grey spot. It was very near to the building outside of which he had stood with Echin. The artist recalled what he had read on the information board next to the huge, domed structure surrounded by tourists in Sultanahmet.

"Hagia Sophia, Byzantium's Basilica, built in the time of the emperor Justinian. Once a Christian church, then a mosque and now a museum. I didn't notice I'd marked it until the girl told me I'd drawn a star on the building."

"The locals refer to it as Aya Sofya but look more carefully." Klim pointed to the picture. "Look just where it is marked."

Klim stopped talking in response to the look of concern on Siskin's face. The musician lowered his cup of coffee and Klim knew he was hearing what no one else could hear. He drifted to the window with Siskin to locate the source of the sound. A young European with a shaved head and a dark backpack was moving through the crowd towards the café. Immediately Siskin started towards the stairs, signalling to the other two to hurry. At the bottom of the steps Siskin waited while his two friends exited and then went looking for the man he had seen enter below.

The distinctive shaved head and black rucksack bobbed in the centre of the crowded café. Even as Siskin located the fanatic, the man pulled at a tag on the corner of one shoulder. Siskin yelled but the sound was lost in the blast. At the entrance to the café the musician was blown into the street. Splinters of glass and debris littered the tram tracks and passers-by screamed in horror as body parts rocketed through the shattering windows. Fierce fires erupted. Quickly, the squeal of ambulances and police tearing towards the ravaged building, added to the general cacophony. Klim and Josh dragged their friend behind a low wall in the gardens and scanned the crowd. He signalled to Josh to duck as the distinctive face of Danubin came into view, her eyes fixed on the writhing bodies of the injured. It was obvious she had not found what she was seeking, as she weaved in between the rescuers to peer into the devastated building.

"Now," Klim whispered.

Together, they helped the still dazed Siskin to stand and passed behind the crowd, unobtrusively winding their way back to the grubby hostel.

*

Elanur had packed away her pipe and her coffee urn. Her clothes were folded in an old-fashioned trunk to send on; she had never been interested in air travel. On the trunk, she placed a name and address, neither of which could be traced back to the individual who now stood, hands on hips, checking to see if she had left anything identifiable in the small space. She rose, hearing the shuffle of feet outside her door. Thinking to find Klim and the others returned, she was surprised to see Amed alone. It took her only moments to comprehend his intention. Shock and profound sorrow racked her body, so that she sat involuntarily and let him make small talk to hide his task.

She hoped it would come quickly and cleanly. A great sadness filled her, she would leave her final work undone. In her heart, she spoke to Toomaaris, asking forgiveness that she would not be there to shape the runes in Ireland at the Alignment. Amed had lapsed into the new language of the Chunii; asking that Elanur be cleansed of the crime that had caused his master to order this execution. Elanur's clear eyed stare led him to believe that she knew the secret language. He spoke intently, still in the language Ulynyx had made their own.

"Only the Chunii can speak these words and are evolved enough to understand them."

Elanur replied sadly in the language that she was not evolved enough to speak, "So already you have fenced in your minds to any that do not meet your approval?"

"You dare imply that our Lord is wrong, that his words are not only to be used by the cleansed?"

"And yet, as you see, unclean as I am, they are revealed to me."

"Then that is why I have been sent to cleanse you," the soldier told her, conflict bubbling sourly within him. He was acutely aware that Ulynyx intended Elanur to be killed without knowing her fate. Her calm acceptance and her knowledge of the Chunii language unnerved him. Elanur closed her eyes, awaiting the fatal strike from the blade she knew was hidden in the leather strap between his shoulder blades.

Chapter Ten

The suicide bombing and its tragic result took prime place on the news. They had uncovered the old-fashioned, dusty tv set on what passed for a dressing table. In fact, the shabby piece of furniture was an old wooden filing cabinet covered in scratches.

"You sure we have to find the entrance tonight?" Siskin checked with Klim.

The Reeder nodded and Siskin, his arms covered in cuts from the blast, looked pale and weary.

"Security's so tight in Sultanahmet," he said, "we'll be lucky to get anywhere near."

They picked at sandwiches but none of them had any appetite. A knock on the door caught them by surprise, there had been no preliminary footsteps. Klim went to answer the door as Siskin positioned himself at the side of the wall. Taking a sharp knife from his boot, he raised it in readiness before signalling to Klim for it to be opened.

"Echin!" Josh exclaimed with relief.

Siskin's look admonished Josh, who lowered his voice and closed the door.

"How's Kier?" Josh asked the question, tense.

The Mourangil's enigmatic face told them nothing, his words were terse. "Alive. Just. She's hidden by the Tanes in a forest on the east coast of Ireland. Their elemental fields are virtually impassable."

Siskin swallowed, "Elanur was so right when she described her as the heart of our group. We can't lose her."

"The only way you can help her is by finding the Key of Brunan. We need to be very careful, Ulynyx also hunts the doorway to the Hall of Jasmine."

"Swift, is she okay?" Klim asked.

Echin nodded his reassurance, "I couldn't have found Kier without the link between them. I couldn't do much, just bought us a little time. Very little time."

"The Tanes?" Josh's tone was harsh.

"If it wasn't for Mactire she'd be already dead." Echin's statement silenced the artist. He turned towards Klim and scrutinised him carefully, "You found the location from Elanur?"

Klim nodded, he was still profoundly affected by the intimate contact with the Runeshaper. An edge of wonder tinged his voice as he explained what he had discovered in the body-mind of Elanur.

"And Elanur…could you tell if the location came to her conscious awareness?"

Without hesitation Klim answered a firm "Yes, Elanur knows."

Echin suddenly exited through the badly painted door, his movements urgent. When Klim opened it seconds later, the long corridor was empty.

*

The blade clanged on the stone floor of Elanur's kitchen.

"You would kill the Runeshaper?" Echin's angry voice rang out. Elanur opened her eyes to see the cold stare of the Mourangil who stood tall and unmoving behind Amed.

"I have heard of you," Amed spat, his skin turning a sallow yellow. "Toomaaris the weak, who could have been strong. Toomaaris the dreamer whose hope hangs on to a lost promise! The Chunii will save the race that you failed to protect!" He sprang forward, deftly lifting a small knife from his waist band. Echin seemed to move without haste and yet too quickly for the Elite soldier, placing himself against the wall at the back of the room and away from Elanur. Amed followed, lunging viciously towards Echin's chest, who stepped to one side before the other had registered his opponent's action. The Chunii soldier hit the wall with the full force of his fury and fell unconscious to the floor. Echin picked up the small knife and the larger curved blade that was to be used for Elanur's execution. He threw them on the table with a look of disgust. He looked towards the Runeshaper with a reassuring smile. "He'll think even less of me for leaving him alive! Are you all right Elanur?"

She nodded, sad and weary, sinking into a chair. Echin stepped towards her and placed his hand on her bowed head.

"That Ulynyx could do this!" She wept at his betrayal, as Echin stood quietly beside her until she had spent her tears.

"We should leave." She stood up, catching her breath. Echin took the blades and placed them in the small clay oven. He closed the door and with a flick of his finger flames arose to swallow the metal. Gently he led Elanur from the house and out into the garden. It took him only minutes to return to the house to remove her few belongings and to check on Amed.

"It'll be some time before he wakens," Echin told her, guiding her into the street.

The Runeshaper took a last look at her home in Istanbul.

"I liked my little place," she mourned. "At least I had packed everything ready to go." Her mouth twisted as if she had eaten something bitter. "I was to be killed so that I could not give the location of the doorway to the Seeds. So that Unethora would know there was no possibility of the Myriar being in place by the Alignment. For all his confidence, he fears that you will succeed."
Echin squeezed her hand. "Your bags are already with Baris. He'll look after you and take you to the train. You need to hurry."

"Drive safely, at least for once," he told the young Turk once Elanur was safely deposited in the passenger seat. She seemed to have aged ten years in a day as she placed her small fingers over his on the open sill of the car window. He leant in to kiss the top of her forehead. Baris started the engine and the car began to crawl slowly forwards. "The lunar eclipse," she whispered breathlessly. "Ulynyx will be in Aya Sofya."
Before Echin could reply Baris had driven off and the van was lost in the manic traffic of the roads that edged the old city.

*

The silence of Aya Sofya was broken by the scurrying feet of the Chunii. They had entered quietly, passing though the arched columns of the ancient building now turned museum. Ulynyx cast aside the thought that Amed had failed to return. It was not without regret that he had ordered the despatch of the only one who could direct the Seeds of the Myriar to the doorway of the Hall of Jasmine. He had chosen six of the Elite to accompany him to the location that Elanur had given him, an archway, at the back of which lay a stone wall. Many visitors had stood in this plain, rustic space, out of keeping with the shining gold mosaics that adorned many of the walls. Its stark undecorated stone hid in the shadows and made a striking contrast against the low hanging chandeliers and richly painted iconic figures that populated the interior.

"Is there a key Lord?" asked one of the Chunii.

"No key," he told them. "Only the mystical Key of Brunan that Unethora will present to me in the Hall of Jasmine. Do not fear when I embed with the jewels of our planet for a short while, I will return to you." Excitement shook his voice as it had been decades of human time since he had returned to the Mourangil kingdoms.
The Chunii bowed their heads as Ulynyx spoke, never before had they heard of such things. They stepped back in awe as, with a dramatic sweep of his dark cloak, Ulynyx disappeared and an onyx jewel appeared in the wall before them. The men gasped in wonder; one pulled his black keffiyeh across his face. His astonished eyes looked reverently towards the unadorned wall from which the jewel had now disappeared. As they seated themselves in the small space, preparing for an overnight vigil, they were disturbed by a loud, cracking sound. In horror, they watched as a jagged tear reached diagonally from one corner of the rectangular wall to the other. The soldiers fell backwards as Ulynyx appeared at their centre. His face was breathless and pale with fury.

"Nothing!" His eyes swept the small alcove. "This is not the doorway!" He reached out his hand and blasted a hole in the thick stone.

"She lied," he hissed, his voice contorted with anger and shock.

The hardened soldiers of the Chunii stepped out of sight amongst the shadows of Aya Sofya as they heard the sound of guards, from the square outside, rushing towards the site of the damaged wall.

"Back!" Ulynyx ordered. "Go quickly."
The skilled soldiers made their shadowy exit unnoticed. Outside Ulynyx looked towards the sky where the lunar eclipse was set to commence.

"Back to Ulyn," he ordered. "I will meet with you there."

Chapter Eleven

Echin led his friends along a cobbled hill to an old green door, on which two tiny stone hands provided an unusual knocker. It opened easily but behind this were a pair of imposing metal gates. Josh, tense as he felt, could not help giving a wry smile when he realised that the Mourangil intended to tackle these with something as mundane as a key. Carefully closing the heavy door, Echin reached for a switch just beyond the gates. Soft lamps revealed the rectangle of an extremely old building. What had clearly once been the site of sumptuous luxury, was now uninhabited and in a state of disrepair. The Mourangil walked towards a courtyard at its centre.

Trees, long established, housed birds that chirped notes of alarm at the disturbance but quickly settled to quiet. The trees framed an exquisitely sculptured statue of an angel. It was clear, that at one time, a fountain of water had arisen from the back of the noble face to form a spray. It would have given a wing like nimbus to the beautifully carved figure. Echin reached up and found a tiny handle on the halo; it emitted a scraping sound as he slowly moved it clockwise. The angel grated to one side to reveal the entrance to an underground stairway. Echin pointed towards the sky as he descended the steps; a shadow had begun its progress across the moon.

"We have very little time."

The Basilica Cistern, the ancient water reservoir used in Byzantine times, lies beneath the city of Istanbul. Echin had found them a way in that by-passed the carefully guarded entrance. The haunting underground cavern was supported by rows of stone columns salvaged from all over Byzantium. Seeing their awed faces Echin smiled, "You had to have been there," he told them softly.

One by one they reached the bottom of a circular stairway that brought them to the far end of the cistern. They followed Echin as he stepped over a metal chain that cordoned off the stairway, as it was thought to lead to a dead end. The dim light revealed they were standing on a raised wooden platform that extended into walkways around a hall of stone columns. Echin stood aside for Klim to lead. Slowly the Reeder gazed at the old stones whose rippling reflection extended across the water below. He began walking carefully on the damp boards as carp swam ghost like in the water beneath. Eventually he led them off to one side, where one of the columns was supported by a block depicting the head of Medusa; the dead eyes and snaking tendrils of her hair even more menacing as the head lay askew at the bottom of the pillar. This was clearly a spot for tourist interest as around it was a wide area of viewing platform. Klim had unravelled a clear vision from Elanur's mind and his eyes scanned the shadows. They alighted on a stone with no markings, almost invisible in the darkness. He led them along the walkway to reach the column at the far corner of the cistern.

"Is this it?" Echin asked him.

"But don't you know, Echin?" asked Josh, puzzled. The Mourangil shook his head. He squatted with his back against the damp wall that supported this corner of the cistern. His hushed voice echoed in the cathedral like space. "You've found the fabled Waybearer stone that works in reverse to those we use to create our bodies above the surface. It was lost to us. When the cistern was built in Byzantine years, it must have been brought here, like so many others, from places across the empire. A perfect model of early recycling." He indicated the variety of different stone columns that had been gathered to help provide fresh water to a growing city.

"This Waybearer stone was created by Candillium, using the gift of the Myriar. To those who are also touched by Moura's gift, it will allow access into the Mourangil kingdom. In its current location, it should enable entrance to the Hall of Jasmine."

"This Key of Brunan …how do we obtain it? What happens if we can't?" Josh bit his lip anxiously. His watch told him that the time of the eclipse was merely minutes away. Klim's dark eyes glimmered in the soft light, echoing Josh's uncertainty. Siskin was on alert, ramrod straight despite the trauma of the blast.
The Mourangil looked calmly at the young artist, "You will find it."
Josh swallowed and squared his shoulders. The dim lights inside the Basilica Cistern flickered. "It's time," Josh told them. "The lunar eclipse has begun, but how do we get into this Hall of Jasmine?" Klim shrugged his shoulders and raised his palms. He turned to Echin who was concentrating on the stone column and did not respond. The column remained motionless, as it had done for almost a thousand years when it had first been placed underground. The Mourangil gave a half smile.

"I recognise it," he murmured. "It was one of the four supporting pillars of the house of Aleth." He turned to the others, entranced. "The centre of music in Ordovicia. To have survived all this time and come all this way!"
Siskin reached out his hand to touch the worn pillar.

"There's a melody inside the column." He concentrated, his hands pressing into the stone. "A song," he hummed softly. "I've heard it somewhere before."

Siskin, the Lute of the Myriar, became absorbed in the music that only he could hear. Finally, he detached himself from the column. "It's stopped." The silence was broken by the occasional drip of water as the blind, white carp meandered below. Josh raised his eyes to the ceiling imagining the progress of the eclipse and the closing of their small window of opportunity to access the ancient kingdom. Siskin began to hum again, as if he was completing a phrase of music that was incomplete. Such an old melody, calling them from a distant place they faintly remembered. A song that had, in fact, never been heard since Candillium inhabited Ordovicia.

The column began to change, tendrils of the outer stone stretched across to them, forming human hands. The hands reached out to Josh, who found his heart beating frantically as he placed his own hand within the ghostly fingers. He gazed around him, waiting for the same thing to happen to the others. It seemed the ghostly arms had all they wanted as they wrapped themselves around him, pulling him within the column. He heard Klim cry out in alarm and saw Echin move to restrain him. At that point Josh ceased to notice the others. The melody that Siskin had hummed now echoed from beneath the stone. The glorious fossilia crowded around him as he passed from the Basilica Cistern into a world far, far beneath.

Chapter Twelve

Josh opened his eyes, aware of the sensation of loss as the fossilia disappeared. He breathed in an air of a different quality, as if he could taste the purity of its elements. The vast underground space was punctuated by waterfalls that had no definable summit as they plunged into pools of cerulean blue. Red streaks blinked amongst living stones, thousands of embedded jewelled stars that he sensed were in a state of great agitation. Faer and Tormaigh stood either side of him but here was not a place of human greeting and custom. For friendship's sake, they had become their human selves, acknowledging him with brief smiles. Josh felt an overwhelming relief at their presence. A multitude of glittering flower shaped crystals, in colours, for some of which he could find no name, formed a sky above that flashed shades within shades of violet blush. Five figures were engraved on a stone podium, a few feet away from where he found himself.

The definition in the sculptures felt remote as the statues stood back to back, facing outwards, on each a suggestion of human countenance. Josh gasped as the grey stone fell away from the figure immediately opposite to where he stood, revealing burnished gold. There was a face, heart shaped, female. A glow framed her head as light filtered through bands of golden threads that wove a glittering pattern above a long, elegant neck. The figure moved forwards in a rippling gown of flickering light. Countless precious stones were threaded in and out of the gown to create a tumbling cascade.

The eyes opened as the figure stepped forward creating strobes of luminescence. She slowly came to stand directly in front of Josh. He was immediately transfixed, plunged into prisms of light that erased both fear and courage, for he could feel neither as he became lost in their embrace. A female voice whispered but he did not hear with his physical ear, her words pressed into his mind.

"I am Unethora, and you are the Creta, one of the Myriar. You may enter the City of Jasmine." Instinctively he understood that his physical being within the cavernous city was akin to standing in the driveway of a mansion. Tormaigh and Faer, either side of him, placed their hands upon his shoulders. Josh allowed his inner self to be propelled between layers upon layers of intricate crystal presence and willingly gave himself up to the wondrous light of awareness. This then, was the vast world of the multifaceted Mourangils. They had inhabited the earth from its inception, and he felt the history of the planet embedded in their bejewelled presence.

What he had seen previously as ponderous solidity was now teeming with life and motion. A starlit universe that weaved through deep and mysterious channels hinting at worlds beyond. The scrutiny was intense. Josh felt naked within it and yet he did not flinch. Unethora was not gentle in her perusal. She swept through his mind, picking out certain episodes to examine more thoroughly. Among these were his devotion to Echin, and the pain of his father's denial of his son's true purpose. She swept past swathes of memories that he had no recollection of still holding; he felt her light pass through his mind fixing on his early days and the pervasive presence of his mother, Marianne. He felt divorced from the emotional claims of the events that had collected to portray his life. Josh watched impassively as Danubin stole the Chalycion from his hand and allowed the majestic Mourangil to rifle through his grief at this event.

The lights dimmed and Unethora halted her communion with him, but Josh sensed that he had not completed his task. He felt overwhelmed by the unfathomable grandeur of this being. However, Josh was now aware of the presence of the fossilia, gathering to guide him from the hidden kingdom. He knew he had failed, that Unethora had not found within him whatever it was she had been seeking. There was a tourmaline flash on one side of him, a crystal of feldspar on the other. Josh knew that, for the first time, he was seeing Tormaigh and Faer in their Mourangil forms.

"Nothing can be hidden here Josh, you must trust," Faer whispered.
Josh, becoming aware once more of his physical self, placed his hand on the Chalycion. It was with surprise, that in his mind's eye, he was hiding the entrance to a narrow cave. Lights flickered around him as he saw himself step to the side of the entrance, one he had concealed without conscious effort. Unethora's presence shone into the hidden place and there she found memories of his meeting and interaction with the other Seeds. The sense of family that had been engendered as he had come into contact with Siskin, Klim, Swift and Gabbie. Here were hidden the inner struggles as he faced their enemies, his entry into the picture he had painted, finding the image of the Myriar. The secret of the Vortex was revealed, as was his barely acknowledged passion for Loretta. Weaving through it all was his deep devotion to Kier. Breathing in a wave of charged air, he opened his eyes and was again within the magnificent Hall of Jasmine. Alarmed, he discovered that Tormaigh and Faer

116

were no longer by his side and the Creta stood transfixed as the statuesque figure turned back to the dais. Beneath the starlit cavern, the golden chandelier gown shimmered back to grey stone. Josh was quickly surrounded by fossilia, folded in their dazzling embrace as he made the transition away from the Hall of Jasmine.

The Basilica Cistern was cold and damp, in contrast to the glittering kingdom. Josh wondered how Echin could bear to be parted from the world of the Mourangils. Even as his eyes were trying to refocus, panic turned him back towards the stone column. He banged on its surface.

"I didn't ask for the key!" Bedazzled, he had found the Hall of Jasmine and left empty handed! Klim and Siskin were beside him, within the shallow water that surrounded the column of stone.

"I didn't ask," Josh cried again in dismay.

"You didn't have to," Klim told him, his gaze fixed over Josh's shoulder.

Josh turned to see that around the base of the column was a circle of gold. It shimmered in the water and illuminated previously invisible engravings that were marked on the stone. Siskin placed the memory in Mengebara, carefully reading the engraving. He hoped that it would make sense to Kier. Josh bent down to watch as the gold coil unravelled itself from the base of the column and wrapped itself snake like over his forearm.

"It's light," he told them. "Silken." The Chalycion glowed bright pink in greeting.

"Well done my friend, you have obtained the Key of Brunan," Echin put his arm around Josh's shoulder. He looked towards the steps they had used to enter the Basilica Cistern. "Let's hope we're not too late for Kier."

They ran across the sodden, wooden walkway and climbed out into the courtyard where Echin stopped, stricken. In the sky beyond the trees hung the pale yellow disc of the newly displayed moon. Startled cries could be heard from observers in the streets as another shadow, unexpected and ominous, moved irregularly over its surface. The small group pressed against the sculpted angel as the earth shook beneath their feet and dust hissed from the dilapidated building. Echin held out his hand towards Josh and the golden coil released itself from the Creta and wrapped around the outstretched arm of the Mourangil. He whispered to the Key of Brunan, stroked the coil and released it to the sky. It transformed into a huge, golden bird that launched itself beyond the ancient buildings and headed out to sea.

*

The White Chapel beckoned Kier; the place high in the Northumbrian woods where she had first found the bound devil depicted in stone. She had been just a young girl when Martha, her sister, had leapt to her aid, a triangle of fallen glass piercing Martha's heart. The door was open, rust spotted locks lay tangled on the path. The empty building had been swept clean, the roof whole. The door closed tomb like behind, its sombre echo bouncing from stark white pillars, each one like a memory unjudged. She feared to look again at the chained devil that had once opened its stone eyes to chill her bones.

The ancient stone remained standing in place. Kier released her breath as she forced her gaze to its surface. Nothing. On either side, nothing. The image of the four circles that were now engraved into her flesh, no longer framed one side of the old, upright tablet. Where the bound devil had been locked within the opposite surface there was only smooth and barren stone. Flinging open the heavy door she ran from the building into the starlit evening. Her breath rasped and rattled, trying to escape forever the prison of her body. And there among the gravestones was an empty, grassy grave beneath the stars. So restful, so easy, just a few steps and she could lay her head on the sweet smelling ground.

It came again from the sky, a sudden presence in the air above the White Chapel, heading towards her. Kier's hands rose protectively above her head and then fell as she heard its call, the ancient song of the House of Aleth. As it flew towards her, the golden bird glimmered. The night sky turned to sunlight, suffusing her with warmth. Under her feet, the grave returned to solid ground as she stepped across its surface.

Kier opened her eyes. Mactire sat an arm's length away in a chair, sleeping. His head was cupped in one long hand, leaning awkwardly against the armchair. She saw, not for the first time, that his feral, handsome face, held the suggestion of his Adlet form. Under her gaze his eyes snapped open, his expression focused and challenging. They softened a little; there was even a rare smile as his eyes fixed on her pale face, moving to the combed and plaited dark hair that was arranged over one shoulder. "So, you decided to stay with us after all." There was wonder in his tone. Tenderly he placed one hand in hers and then his fingers probed at her wrist finding a strong and even pulse. He seemed to understand that speech and movement were beyond her. Gently, he replaced the passive arm. The pain had gone. The rage and enmity that had entered her body in the viral attack of the Roghuldjn, had been extinguished and cleansed. Her eyes roamed over Mactire's chest, the black T-shirt seemed unruffled by dressings or bandages. He placed his hand over the right side of his thorax, following her thoughts.

"Tanes are not as vulnerable to Roghuldjn poison. Plus, my wounds were contusions rather than open cuts. My elemental form is one of the few predators feared by the cursed creatures. Down the years we've cleared their infective presence from as many forests as we could. But obviously," his face was grim, "not all."

A wintry looking sky peeped through the window above Mactire. A surge of strength sent her sitting bolt upright.

"Belluvour is unbound." Her voice, hoarse with disuse, choked out the statement. Mactire stood, rearranging her pillows to support her. "The potency of his binding has ended," she told him, her forehead wet with effort.

"Kier, you have to rest," Mactire told her evenly, waiting until she relaxed back against the pillows. "We know," he continued. "It happened during the lunar eclipse three days ago, we're already searching."

Kier acknowledged the absence of other sounds in what she sensed was a busy house. The others then, had been despatched to find news. He had elected to stay with her. Relief, written clearly on the handsome face, did not erase the pallor and exhaustion that sent him slumping wearily back into the armchair.

A few minutes passed and Kier summoned all of her strength. Slowly she forced herself upright, flung back the covers and raised herself to standing. She ignored the tremble of her legs beneath the long white shroud in which she had been dressed. The Adlet form bristled around the muscular outline of his human body as Mactire moved towards her. Kier, focusing her will, held out her hand to stop him.

"How do you know?" His voice strained, had regained the hard, mysterious edge of the Tanes. "How could you know that Belluvour has escaped from the Secret Vaults? You've been here, beside me, all the time."

"How could I not know?" she returned gently. Mactire held her eyes, her voice had quickly grown firm. He watched her warily, this woman who had returned from the edge of death like a reforged sword.

"He's in human form on the surface," she told him

"But how?" Mactire responded. "The Waybearers are no longer in use so how can he make a human form?" He looked troubled. "Or like Nephragm, has he stolen the form of another?"

"He would never demean himself to wear a true human form," she spoke with utter confidence. "It isn't the first time he formed himself to mock the race he considers repugnant."

She clearly saw the image of a dark face, vicious hatred in hollow eyes, a human parody. Then alongside came the vivid stench of torn flesh, the agony of flame, the hurling fields of energy in the mountain of Obason. "I remember," she whispered.

Mactire said nothing. She stood, so pale that she seemed almost transparent, her amber eyes looking solemnly from the thinned face. Around her neck was the glowing Stone of Mesa, the planet with three moons. One of the moons was now filled with gold and within it was the engraving of a majestic bird. Kier reached for the small pile of clothes beside her bed.

"Thanks for your help Mactire," she said, looking towards the door, "I need to leave now.

Chapter Thirteen

"Gabbie love, there's some breakfast downstairs for you."
Her father sounded strained and tired.
Twisting among the sheets guilt stabbed at her, forcing her eyes open. Days had passed and she had barely left her room. The small, neat house was a new build on the edge of town, she even had her own en suite. In Gabbie's eyes however, it had none of the feel of home that she had felt in the little railway cottage, destroyed in the earthquake. The view from her window, overlooking farmland and out to sea, was her favourite part of the new house. She had watched the sea and the sky alter their pose with the sun and the moon as she recycled the same thoughts; letting them swirl in and out of her mind, dragging her ever downwards into a pit of fear and doubt.

Kier had taught her about judgement, how not to react to the world in the way others tell you to. Her favourite phrase was 'do what your heart tells you to do'. She was the antithesis to what a successful business woman should be, the least materialistic person she knew. And yet she attracted people and success in a way that was effortless. It was hard to believe that Kier had singled her out as a personal assistant, to be her closest associate. Now of course, all that was history.

It was a mistake that they had perceived her to be part of the Myriar. She had always known it, but now, well now it was out of the question. The stone of Arwres lay in the small, silver jewellery box her father had brought from Prague; she allowed herself to check that the stone still nestled in the soft velvet. Of course, she would give it back, eventually. She took up her position, knees to chest on the bed, eyes gazing across the Irish Sea, waiting for her mother to arrive.

*

"You'll never make it Kier," Mactire insisted. "He's looking for you. You're not strong enough yet."
She was certainly strong enough to appreciate the animal magnetism of the man who sat opposite her, pouring the creamy milk that he had just extracted from the goat in the garden outside. It was a place of evergreen beauty, protected by the magic of the Tanes, filled with summer flowers, though she knew that it must be almost November. The coffee was milky and warm, the bread freshly baked and spread with fresh butter.

"Is this your home?" she ventured.

"As much as anywhere," he replied.

"I love it," she said simply. His sharp intake of breath made her regret her enthusiasm.

"Kier, you should be dead already."
She laughed at his bluntness, loving the honesty of it, fearing the truth of it. "But I'm not. And I have things to do. Belluvour or not, I need to find my friends. How is it that I can't reach our mind place here?"

"Mengebara?" His voice was tinged with awe. "The community of interconnected minds! Don't tell me... Klim? He recreated it!"
She nodded.
He laughed, "Wait till Loretta hears!" His tone softened, "He's suffered greatly has that lad." She was touched by his empathy and impulsively reached for his hand.

"Kier," his eyes lingered on hers, hungry.

"Mactire," she said softly, meeting his intense gaze.
"Sean." It was a good sound on her lips, his real name,
"You confuse me."
She drew her hand back. The force of his emotion was
inviting. The handsome face charmed and thrilled, but
she was long bonded to another. He seemed attuned to
her thoughts for he stood up and started clearing the
table. "Ah well at least I do something!" The brogue
deepened as he made fun of himself. "What else can a
poor Dubliner do to raise attention from the most
beautiful woman on the planet!"

"You didn't answer my question," Kier insisted. "Why
can't I reach Mengebara when I'm here?"
He deposited the dishes on a counter behind him. "The
world of Faerie really exists Kier, we tap into it in our
elemental form. We built this place within it, a separate
dimension, so no one can reach you here."
But Swift had reached her, Kier thought, her eyes fixing
on the colourful garden through the open back door. In
the death throes of her pain filled body, she had found the
connection to the Stozcist. She had then sensed the
presence of Echin, blotting out even her pain, giving her
strength to stay alive. Mactire, bringing her to this hidden
elemental dimension had almost entirely cut her off from
friend and enemy alike. Kier knew with certainty
however that the Mourangil had sent the Key of Brunan
to find her, though it had almost been too late. She hoped
that the boundaries of the Tane dwelling place would
stand against the Devourils. Her heart told her that they
would soon know one way or another.

"I have to go," she repeated, and knew that it must be
soon. Mactire would not hold her against her will but she
could not be sure of the other Tanes.

"You would be safer here." It was his last attempt to sway her but it was half hearted. He knew she would have to leave.

"I'll take you," he said, resigned.

Kier was dressed in Loretta's leggings and a bright green shirt, a measure of how thin she had become. Mactire threw her a jacket, his own she thought, then his green eyes glinted wolfishly as he took her hand. The path from the kitchen door took them through a walled garden, replete with vegetables and fruit. At the end of the path was a beech hedge that stood at least twenty feet tall and carried on for as far as she could see in either direction. A wooden door marked the border of the home of the elementals. Mactire placed his hand on the handle of the wooden door and the nearness of him made her tremble. He kissed her gently on the lips and walked a few steps back to the bridge, his green eyes luminous.

"Sean," she warned, "this place is not inviolate. You must be careful."

Mactire scrutinised her face. "Be safe Kier Morton," his Irish brogue sang lightly, ignoring her warning.

"You've got to be kidding!" she cried as she looked towards the path that stretched out in front of her. "A yellow brick road!"

"Killian's little joke," he said smiling. He stood waiting as she stepped out onto the gleaming pathway.

"Do I just click my heels?"

He gave a mocking, lopsided grin in reply. His eyes filled and he turned away abruptly. Kier took a second step and the doorway closed quickly behind her. The beech hedge disappeared and the yellow brick road was lost in a thick pine forest. Descending into the late October chill, she pulled on the jacket Mactire had given her. After only a few minutes walking, fatigue pulled at the muscles in her legs. Kier sat down on a tree stump and breathed in the scent of pine; with relief, she was now able to connect with Mengebara. She frowned in disappointment that there was no communication from Gabbie. Her heart lifted however to see the recovery of the Chalycion and the finding of the Key of Brunan. The same golden coil that had now formed itself into a golden bird on the Stone of Mesa, that had brought her back from certain death. On contact, the key imparted all knowledge of its journey; its long wait in the Hall of Jasmine for the Creta to arrive and of course its inviolate connection to the Stone of Mesa.

In Mengebara Siskin had placed an image of the old stone angel that formed an entrance to the Basilica Cistern. It seemed to spark memory. Kier did not follow that thread of thought however, focusing instead on the column that had provided the way to the Hall of Jasmine. The House of Aleth flashed before her eyes, the heart of music in Ordovicia. Finally Kier placed in the mind place her own memory of events since the night she had left Samuel's cottage. It seemed so very long ago.

Abandoning Mengebara Kier began walking through the empty forest. Mentally she reached towards Gabbie, using the closeness they had built. A sense of despair constricted her throat, the ebullient young woman seemed lost in a grey sea of surrender. Kier quickened her step, cracking the dry twigs as she continued downhill. Only then did it occur to her that she had no way of getting back to England. A cold wind brushed her neck and she pulled the wool lined jacket more closely around her. She placed her hands into the oversized pockets to keep them warm and found a roll of notes. She counted more than enough to carry her back across the sea. Mactire, it seemed, had compensated for her lack of practical foresight.

"Thank you, Sean," she whispered, smiling.
The thrush, on a nearby rock, looked up from teasing a snail out of its shell.

"You're so very welcome," it chirped in Mactire's brogue. The world of Faerie, it seemed, still lingered.

Chapter Fourteen

The conversation they had avoided all these years finally found them in the modern kitchen as Gabbie pushed away a cereal bowl, still half full. "Dad." Her father looked up from his breakfast, his eyes full of concern, and what she had now learnt to recognise as fear. Kier had once told her that someone very learned and wise had written that fear was just the absence of love. Yet here was her father who loved her, she had no doubt of that. She had no doubt either that he was afraid of what was surely written on her face, the question she was about to ask. "Why did she leave, Dad?"
Andrew Owen twisted his head to one side, avoiding eye contact. His daughter waited, hating the pain she was causing. Even in those first years after she had gone, the young girl she had once been never spoke about her mother. It was their unwritten rule of survival.

"You should eat more, you're too thin." He pointed to the bowl but she placed her hand over it and held his blue-grey eyes with her own. Andrew placed his elbows either side of the empty plate on the shiny breakfast table. He looked out of the patio doors, his eyes tracing the line of the neat lawn at the back of the house.

"In many ways, she was never really here Gabbie."

"What do you mean?"
He turned towards her. "I wanted to tell you a hundred times but just couldn't," his voice broke and Gabbie wished she hadn't started the conversation. But it was too late now.

"Get your coat," he said in a way that made her feel like a little girl again. "I want to show you something."

He left the table, heading towards the hallway for his car keys. Gabbie looked perplexed but her father was already heading for the door.

"Just a minute," she turned back and ran to her room, picking up the silver box and sliding it into the pocket of her coat. She had a small rucksack permanently packed, following Klim's example. Her father was waiting in the driver's seat of his van. She grabbed the bag, locked the front door, and jumped into the passenger seat next to him. Andrew worked for himself these days, employed by the council to do odd jobs for the elderly. She'd never seen him as happy. Then she'd come back and brought with her nothing but misery. Silently she resolved to leave soon but not until she had the answers to questions that she should have asked years before.

*

Swift almost fell into the kitchen, drenched and exhausted. "It won't hold much longer, Samuel says we have to pack up and leave."
Evan dropped the knife and the potato he was peeling and ran to help her close the door against the tearing wind.

"How is it that the Riverkeeper cannot tame the Teifi and the Stozcist cannot hold the bridge?" he asked.

"I can stop the bridge from breaking apart but the river has already burst its banks," shock edged her voice. "It's not safe Evan, not for any of us. This is a power beyond even the Undercreature or any of the horrors we've faced before."

"The Unbound?" He looked at the young woman whose courage had been so instrumental in destroying Nephragm and Magluck Bawah. She paled as he spoke. Suddenly the door flew open and Samuel marched through, his clothing dry, though he had been out all day trying to quell the effects of the storm.

"The Teifi trembles, it quivers with doubt, ready to wash away what the Unbound considers unnecessary. In remote places of the world volcanic forces agitate towards eruption, preparing to wipe clean the face of the earth."

"Samuel," Evan cut through the cleric's words. "Why do you say this?"

A cold bitterness was stamped on the face of the normally serene Samuel.

"The Teifi recognises its old master Belluvour and bends towards his will. These are the whispers embedded within its currents."

Evan looked alarmed and opened his mouth to ask about his daughter. Samuel pre-empted his question. "I've already given Angharad the order to evacuate, she's safe. We have merely a few hours before this cottage will be swept away. The river has given its warning. Pack!" He headed towards the sitting room. Swift and Evan ducked as many precious books hovered in the corridor, before sliding neatly into the trunks that Samuel had opened and positioned with a flick of his wrist.

Later, on the path above the river valley, the three friends watched as the Teifi reached up greedily to sweep the small cottage into its belly. Before them Samuel kinetically manoeuvred trunks of books and other items saved from the cottage. Swift and Evan now carried on their backs what little they had brought with them. In the copse, where Siskin had parked only days before, a small van provided transport for the trio and enough luggage space for Samuel's trunks. Swift stretched out tired limbs across the seat in the back as Samuel drove inland. She dozed for a few minutes but roused to the building darkness as the fierce storm shook the van. However, a few miles further inland the wind abated and the late October day became relatively calm.

"It's very localised," Evan commented. Samuel gave a terse nod.

"Evan!" Swift cried out in alarm, holding the Stone of Silence in her hand. Samuel had pulled off the main road taking a short cut through a small village. "Turn around Samuel!" she begged. "It's a trap!"

Without hesitation Samuel swung the van around to find that the road was blocked by a farm vehicle, brandishing a huge serrated bucket, that was descending towards them. It was easily big enough to crush the small van and Evan's string of Welsh curses did nothing to offset its descent. Swift added her rapid Spanish that bubbled out in panic. Samuel said nothing but flicked his hand causing the vehicle to circle towards a ditch to their left. The van quickly skirted around it as they heard other vehicles approaching from the rear. The Riverkeeper again waved his hand to pull the vehicle, with its dazed occupant, back into the middle of the road. As the van raised its speed Evan regaled the village behind with bardic warnings, his face was triumphant as he patted Samuel's back.

"How did you know, Swift?" Samuel asked calmly.

"The Stone of Silence," she replied. "It turned black."

He nodded with satisfaction. "Though if I'd seen the roadside sign," she said, looking back as they drove away from the side road, "I think maybe I would have guessed!"

The sign for Capel Cudd y Brynn, was barely visible under the graffiti. Swift felt her stomach lurch as she remembered her last trip to this place when she and the other Seeds of the Myriar had been entrapped by Danubin.

"Maybe not the college Samuel," she ventured, with a shaky voice.

"My thought exactly," Samuel replied as he turned the van to head north.

Later that evening the three sat in Evan's neat and functional hotel room in Shrewsbury. Swift gazed outside and was grateful for the absence of rain and wind. It was clear to them all that they had been particularly targeted.

"Danubin," concluded Samuel. "She knows of my affinity to you and to the Teifi. She is Belluvour's instrument."

"He is really unbound?" Evan stared unseeing at his own reflection in the dark windows.

"He is here. On the surface. The power that obliterated Ordovicia," confirmed Samuel.

"We have to find Echin," Evan searched in his pack for the Crysonance. "And where is little Gabbie?"
Swift looked restless. "What is it?" he asked.

"Danubin couldn't use the Chalycion in the same way as she used the other stones, to connect to the Seeds and each other. However, I noticed when we first found the stones that Arwres and the Chalycion had been cut from the same rock."
Evan paled. "Then Danubin would be capable of manipulating the stone to find Arwres. To find Gabbie."

"Do you think that's why she hasn't contacted us in Mengebara?" queried Swift.

"What!" Evan exclaimed. He rarely used the mind place.

"Not for ages." Then Swift's face broke into the first smile they had seen on her face since Klim left.

"Have you found her?" asked Evan.

"Kier," Swift reached out her hands to them both. "She's back!"

Swift acknowledged Kier's greetings and apprised her of the events at the cottage and her fears that Danubin may have targeted Gabbie.

"She suggests we stay safe here," Swift relayed.

*

"Kier! She's messaged and she's on her way back to England!" Klim was jubilant. The others nodded as they too picked up her messages and the Mourangil, who did not intrude into the mind place, smiled his relief.

"I wish she had waited until we could travel with her," he said quietly.

"You think he might be here?" Siskin looked around the busy tube station. Echin, scanning the crowd, shook his head. "No, he will not show himself yet. His way has always been to use others to complete his purpose until the last."

Siskin chilled at the bitterness in his companion's tone. They were grouped to one side of the main crowd, in the tiled walkway, out of earshot. Klim was becoming increasingly anxious. "I can't find Gabbie, she hasn't responded to anybody." There was a note of alarm in his voice as he continued his mental exploration of the mind place. Now that he was back in England and could still find no means of communicating, his worst fear was confirmed.

"She's no longer connected with us in Mengebara."

133

"How can that happen?" Josh looked deeply troubled.

"Either she broke the link subconsciously or deliberately, by her own choice." His voice had taken on a tinny quality. "We should move," he continued, noticing that they were beginning to attract attention from some of the other passengers.

The three Seeds stopped as one when the message from Swift came through. Siskin had a murderous look in his eyes as he relayed the events in Wales; his eyes glanced at Klim whose stricken face showed that he had acknowledged the threat to Gabbie.

"We need to split up," Echin told them. You three find Suara and make the drive north. I'll go ahead."

"But," Josh objected, recalling the reason why they had chosen to return across Europe by train, "that'll make you more visible to..." he hesitated.

"To the Unbound," Echin finished for him. "Not if I'm alone. The Visperaals will help."

Siskin gestured his incomprehension with open hands.

"They are straals that inhabit the air. I can pick up areas that have been polluted by Devourils or the Virenmor and steer my way clear. Be careful Siskin, there's a good chance the Virenmor will have tracked the vehicle."

"I left it cloaked using a sonic signature inside a rented garage. It should be safe," Siskin reassured him.

Echin nodded his appreciation and passed a scribbled note to Siskin giving Gabbie's new address in Bankside.

"Right then, let's go."

*

They had driven without speaking, listening to the local radio for the last hour. It was the first time Gabbie had seen the lakeside town where her dad had grown up. He had rarely talked of Shimmerfell and as a young, inquisitive girl she quickly lost interest in the place that seemed to have little significance for her father. She had been so wrong about that. He had been in a state of heightened emotion since they left Bankside and were it not for his years of driving experience she would have doubted his ability to handle the vehicle. It was, she decided, one of the most beautiful spots she had ever seen. It was immediately obvious that the town had been named for the shimmering water of the lake, spreading long beneath an undulating semicircle of hills. Along the lakeside a walkway stretched between an avenue of trees, where fallen autumn leaves lifted and fell in the October breeze.

They had left the van in the café car park by the lake. Her father set off at a strong pace, skirting behind the boathouses and on to one of the smaller fells. Gabbie increased her pace, almost running to keep up, her eyes drinking in everything around her. They reached the first rise and he set off down a track she would otherwise have missed, ignoring the notice that trespassers would be prosecuted on this private land.

"It wasn't always like this," anger edged his voice. "The council should be ashamed of themselves, selling this land to those lot."

Gabbie saw that he had brought them behind what looked like a huge hotel.

"Our house was here," he told her, pointing at a patch of land that had been made into a pitch and put golf course. "Compulsory purchase for the good of the town. No thought that my family had lived here for generations."

135

He strode through the small golf course with its colourful numbers and manicured, miniature lawns. On the far side was a small wooden fence that he stepped over without difficulty and Gabbie followed, hitching her small legs over with an effort. It was as if she didn't exist for all the awareness he showed of her presence.

When she caught up with him it took her a little time to see that they were in the grounds of a ruined church, standing in a small local graveyard. Her father knelt at a graveside, his eyes tear filled and his attention nowhere she had ever been or could ever go. She placed her hand on his shoulder and read the inscription written in bold black letters on white marble. He turned to catch her as she sank to her knees, his face a plea for understanding and forgiveness. "Here lies Maria Owen, beloved wife to Andrew and mother to Gabrielle."

"Dad," she cried. "What does it mean? Why didn't you tell me?"

A thousand more questions screamed for expression but her father's slumped shoulders, the tears running down his face, made her bury her head in his chest as they knelt side by side over the cold stone.

Chapter Fifteen

Kier drove a hired Jeep to the edge of the cul-de-sac. It was here she had helped fund the new buildings to house those affected by the earthquake, a little over twelve months previously. Gabbie and her father now owned one of the three properties at the head of the cul-de-sac. The wind blew leaves across the driveway leading up to the front door that was indented an inch, it was open. There was no vehicle outside and dead, shrivelled flowers bowed sadly in the living room window. It was the middle of the day and none of the three properties in the small close showed any signs of life. Still the hairs on the back of her neck prickled with a sense of being observed.

Without warning a fist banged on the window next to her head. Outside was a stocky, balding man, in his fifties. Kier decided to take a chance and she opened the door.

"Is there something I can help you with?" he asked, his tone belligerent but softening when Kier smiled.

"I'm looking for my friend and her father, Gabbie Owen."

He took a minute to ponder her words and then stepped away from the door so that she could get out of the car. Once she had done so he reached out his hand.

"Reg Dickson. I live in the house next door. Gabbie and her father left about three hours ago, but I think something's happened in the house since then."

"Why do you think that?"

"About an hour ago I thought there was going to be a storm. The whole close darkened, I had to put the lights on. A storm cloud settled over the house, but only over this house," he said pointedly. "And then I thought I could see shapes in the windows."

Kier suppressed the fear that had begun to take hold.

"The door is open," she remarked. "Have you been inside?"

Reg looked surprised and uncertain. "It was locked when they left, I checked. I run Neighbourhood Watch," he added in explanation. She walked towards the front door of the house but Reg hesitated. He held Kier's arm to stop her from entering.

"Ten minutes before you came, the cloud cleared. It just lifted."

Kier nodded. Gently removing Reg's restraining arm, she moved forward through the front door. There was a hiss of burnt ash as flakes rose and fell, covering the whole of the ground floor. A toxic smell of burning. The open plan living space had been singed; drawers and cupboards were upturned and brown burn marks edged the wood. The soft furnishings, papers and books were mostly ash. It was as if a firebrand had passed through the house and its touch was everywhere.

Kier 's eyes stung and a shock of memory flattened her against the lounge wall. Nephragm the Devouril in his natural state above ground; a coal black body and oversized animal limbs. And way back beyond this was another memory lodged in her mind, created in a hollow in Obason. Belluvour, the stench of his volcanic hatred, the fire of fierce prejudice, the destructive force of his presence.

"Are you all right, love?" Reg asked as her face registered the shock that immobilised her. He looked aghast at the state of the house. "It's like there was a fire with no flames!"

Kier, finding movement possible again, hurried to the front door and bent with her hands on her knees taking in great gulps of air. The old man patted her back as she quelled the urge to vomit onto the pristine lawn.

Reg yelled a warning as a shimmering glow at the kerb quickly materialised into a black BMW four-by-four. The windows were shaded. He had heard nothing of its approach. Shocked, Reg pulled at Kier's arm. "Quick, get back." Kier, still bent double, lifted her face. Reg looked to see if her laughter was hysteria; relieved, he saw joy spring to her face as she moved nearer to the vehicle. Kier had immediately recognised the sound-driven car that Siskin had constructed, one that could be cloaked in chords of invisibility. There was a vague hum as three men emerged from the vehicle and Kier held out her arms towards them. It was clear to Reg that he was witnessing a family reunion. One by one they enveloped her in an embrace and she held them tightly, utterly grateful for their presence.

"Where's Gabbie? What's happened?" Klim's questions tumbled out.

"The house has been blasted, scourged," Kier replied meaningfully, her gaze fixed on Siskin. Turning quickly to Klim she added, "Thankfully Gabbie and her father left before it happened." She looked at Reg for corroboration.

"Three hours ago," he repeated.

"Reg! What are you doing here?" It was only at that point that Klim noticed the old man who had stood silently aside at their arrival. He was shocked to see the face of Reg, who owned the hotel at Bankside where he had found a place of safety and work. Klim was hard-pressed to recognise the jutting chin and steel-hard eyes of the man who looked so suspiciously at them, to place it alongside his memory of the amiable and somewhat limited hotelier. Reg peered closely at Klim; his face broke into a massive grin, bringing back the kindly man who had given him shelter from his uncle.

"Unbelievable!" Reg appraised the young man, finally placing a hand on his muscled shoulder. "Just look how you've grown lad," he said, his eyes filling. "I wouldn't be ordering you about these days."

Klim smiled as he spoke with sincerity. "Thank you for everything you did for me. I never got the chance to say it before."

Reg patted him on the shoulder, "I was glad to do it lad." He stepped back, a slight blush colouring his face, wiping his eyes on his sleeve. Together they moved towards the house.

"The door was left open?" Siskin checked.

Kier nodded and looked towards Reg who gave to the others the same account of events he had given to her. One by one they entered.

"Dam!" Josh picked up the residue of a singed cushion and moved to open a window to release the chemical smell.

"Like a blow torch," Siskin examined the remains of a second burnt cushion.

Klim emerged from Gabbie's room at the back of the house. In his hand were the broken remains of the small ornamental mirror she used to carry at all times.

"You're sure Gabbie got out, Reg?" His face set in concentration, the edge of alarm in his voice.

"Certain," Reg stated firmly. "She was here three hours ago and then she left with her father."

Josh picked up the ash from the floor and allowed it to pass between his fingers. A cold, bleak wind howled through the front door and snaked through the grey detritus.

"Devourils," Siskin locked the angle of his jaw, his chin jutted upwards.

Kier nodded, "It's unbearable to think what would have happened if Gabbie and her father had still been here." Josh, his fair skin a shade paler, turned an empathetic glance at Klim, "But where is she?"

*

In late October, the small café by the lake was still busy indoors. Gabbie remembered her days in the bookshop when she looked from Pulton out across the bay to the mountains. And here she was on the other side of that bay, learning that her first steps had happened in the heart of those mountains, in the Lakeland town of Shimmerfell. She had wept, they had both wept, but her anger and confusion had not dissipated. When her father came back with tea and cake she felt the ghost of a memory, a little girl having cream removed from her face by a woman, laughing. The buried memory of a buried mother.

"I never ever wanted Patrice to supplant your mother," he told his daughter. "She came to Shimmerfell when you were three."

"And mum collapsed and died later that year?" He nodded but she could not tell him. She could not say that she was almost certain that somehow the woman he called Patrice, would have engineered the death of her mother, if it had meant she could manipulate events to suit her plans. The more her dad spoke about the 'smart' and 'stunning' visitor who had helped him to put his life back together, who had treated Gabbie as a daughter, the more certain she became. Danubin. In her life, in her home! Why? She had seen it in Ben's gym, felt the shock of mutual recognition. The terrible thought that their great enemy and leader of the Virenmor, was her mother. But now, here in Shimmerfell, she had discovered that her real mother had died when Gabbie was an infant. Her dad had been a handsome man, but from what she knew of Danubin, it was likely that their little family got in the way of bigger plans. She listened as her father explained that Patrice had persuaded him to sell to the new hotel and use the money to make a fresh start in Bankside.

"You took to calling her mummy." Andrew Owen was wracked with emotional exhaustion as he explained how everyone in Bankside assumed they were a family and Patrice seemed happy with that.

"She stayed for about a year, just after you started primary school." He hesitated, "But I got to a point where I didn't trust her with you anymore. There was something," his mouth shaped into a self-mocking grin. "Maybe it was your mother nudging me, I often wondered about that."

Gabbie said nothing, waiting. His emotions, tightly coiled for so long, were now pulling him relentlessly in all directions. Her dad seemed like someone else, someone she hardly knew.

"She took you to Manchester, to the Trafford Centre." Yes, she remembered that day, felt the excitement of the woman called Patrice, how carefully she had dressed 'her Gabrielle,' as she always called her. How her hair had been coiled and ribboned. Patrice had let her carry the small pretty mirror so that she could practice her smile. Her father continued, "I never learned what her intention was that day but I didn't go to work like I'd said." His face reddened with anger, "Instead of going to school she took you to Manchester."

He moved the tray forward and placed both elbows on the table, his voice hard. "I drove behind in Reg's car, out of sight, all the way. She'd packed everything she owned and a few of your things. I reckoned she was never coming back. When I found her in the Trafford Centre, she was waiting for someone, I think. You turned and ran towards me and she was furious. All the faces she had worn came down then and I saw her, really saw her." His voice had risen causing Gabbie to place her hand over his folded arms. He jolted himself back from the memory and reached for a sip of his coffee. "I'll never know," he continued evenly, "if she was really trying to take you away. Once I had hold of you she simply picked up her bag and turned her back on me. I never saw her again."

Grief assailed Gabbie, her middle felt like a hard, empty shell, hollow with all the lost years without her real mother, with every hushed remark at the houses of her friends and every playground slight. And fear. What would have become of her in Danubin's hands?

"I want to go home Dad," she said simply.

Andrew Owen looked at his daughter, his eyes a plea for forgiveness. "Every day you grow more like Maria," he told her.

Gabbie felt crushed, overwhelmed. "Take me home Dad, please."

Her father slowly nodded and stood up, lifting his jacket from the chair, turning to locate the men's room.

"Upstairs," she pointed, collecting her coat.

"Won't be a minute," he replied, heading for the dainty, metal staircase.

Gabbie's coat rattled. She put her hand into a pocket, locating the source of the noise as the small, silver box she used for the precious Myriar stone. She had stopped wearing Arwres, feeling that she had no right. Now, her connection with the stone felt stronger than ever. She left her coat on the chair and took it from the box, placing the jasper in the centre of her palm. Its usual rust colour had turned blood red. Gabbie was certain that the stone was screaming a warning that she was in mortal danger. When she placed the pendant around her neck, it seemed that she was no longer in charge of her own body. Immediately the stone tugged towards the door and Gabbie's limbs were primed with urgency. She ran out of the café, picking up speed as she continued downhill and plunged headlong into the lake.

The water was freezing, her jeans heavy around limbs that knew they must keep moving. She swam like she had never swum before; all the fitness training, the muscle she had gained over the last months, gave her a speed and power that took her to the central, small island. It took her father the same amount of time to descend the steps and mumble that Gabbie had walked out without her coat.

Darkness started to descend over the small town. Over the lake a deep shadow coalesced into a coal black mass so that Gabbie could only feel, no longer see. Her hands found a hook in the smooth mossy rocks of the island. The blackness totally enveloped the island and she chose to sink deep underwater rather than be exposed to the sulphurous black cloud. She swam around the circumference of the small land mass, surfacing underneath a wooden, boarding stage. Gabbie snatched the preserved air as she felt the weight of the darkness above. Fear, unreasoning panic and desperation gripped at her throat, burning the tender mucous lining of her windpipe. She could not breathe, she could not see, she could not hear. The island was now a seething mass of internal combustion. An avalanche of small writhing bodies, fluttering wings, hard shells fled into the water around her. Wild, atavistic screams encircled from above. Despair opened like a tunnel beneath the water and she felt her legs being pulled down beneath the surface. Terror robbed her of will, of fight, of thought, as she descended deeper, plunging downwards like a weighted arrow.

*

"I have found her," Klim's momentary relief was swamped by fear. "She's in water," his eyes snapped open in horror. "The Devourils are there!"
Siskin put a hand on his arm and Klim slowed his breathing, focusing his mind on the thread of connection, following it back to Gabbie, grasping for a sense of location. "She's in a lake surrounded by mountains and there's an island in the middle." He opened his eyes in panic, "North, that's all I can see."
They had left Reg shaking his head as the BMW vanished into its invisible state. Siskin had uncloaked the vehicle once he was on the main road and now pulled into a lay-by near to the motorway roundabout.

"What kind of island?" Siskin quizzed.

"Small, not far from the shore."

"It could be Shimmerfell," suggested Kier, who knew the area well.

"We'll go with that," Siskin decided.

Josh felt the Chalycion tug and saw that the pink striations had started to pulse. "She's wearing Arwres," Josh told them. "The stones will pull us towards her."

"I don't need a stone," Klim told him, his face grimly determined as Siskin restarted the vehicle.

Chapter Sixteen

Beneath the lake, in the silted turmoil, Gabbie's barely open eyes were drawn to an amber light. It shone with a physical force that dispersed the debris around her. She was hopelessly tangled but slowly the foliage began to lose its hold on her struggling limbs. Arwres, the source of this light, floated beside her in the water, but it was too late. She turned her head, feeling her eyes bulge with the pressure of starving lungs. Finally, the hunt for air became unbearable and her mouth opened. Into it passed Arwres, still on the chain, settling onto her tongue. A sensation of fresh, breathable air was emitted from the Myriar stone as oxygen propelled into each lobe of her lungs. The image of a newly formed crystal, adsorbing air and sunlight, storing it within for this critical moment, passed vividly through her mind so that her body, transiently, felt a part of the wondrous jewel. She thought of Swift, understanding for the first time, how what she did was possible. Inevitably, Klim's dark eyes looked soulfully from her rich store of shared memories as she felt exhaustion overcome her.

*

Kier was grateful that she had not taken the offered front seat as Siskin wove in and out of the cars on the motorway, that could neither hear nor see him. Josh, next to her, turned away, choosing not to look. Klim, at the front, having complete confidence in his friend's dexterity, concentrated on the location ahead. It would normally have taken an hour to drive from Bankside to

Shimmerfell but they turned into the outskirts of the town forty minutes later.

"The lake," Klim instructed and Josh confirmed; the pull of the Chalycion towards Arwres became more pronounced as they veered downhill. The road ahead was blocked with police cars, an ambulance and TV vans, that could not see Suara quietly manoeuvring into the café car park. The vehicle was completely in view again when they parked in a slot, occluded from the main road by a tall laurel hedge.

Klim jumped from the passenger seat to run towards the lake, where a crowd of onlookers had gathered but Siskin whistled him back up the hill. He opened a private gate leading around the back of the café, where it joined with the lakeside path. They kept above this path and moved amongst the trees, out of sight from the crowd below.

"Oh no!" Siskin had stopped at his first sight of the lake. Kier felt she was watching some post-apocalyptic movie as she followed his gaze. The island's vegetation had all but disappeared, singed to ash. Scattered burnt twigs abounded in the water where fish floated belly up. Birds that had been caught in the onslaught were sad, feathered skeletons. The wooden tourist boats, chained at the edge of the lake, were untouched. A reporter stood by the boathouse and was being filmed against the wretched backdrop. He adjusted the microphone and ran a hand over well-groomed hair. "Not an hour ago the beautiful Lakeland town of Shimmerfell was the site of a previously unheard of natural phenomenon. It seems that from nowhere a cloud, of what witnesses have referred to as 'burning tar', descended onto the island in the centre of the lake and reduced it to what you now see. The only

consolation is that this occurred out of season or the lake would otherwise have been filled with tourists."
Siskin turned back to the others. "Keep going, we might get a better view of the island from higher up."

"Someone's on the path," Klim commented, as small stones scattered towards them. The tall figure of Echin rounded the corner, he was moving at speed and almost ran into Siskin. Their feelings of relief were cut short by his worried expression.

"Where is she?" Klim choked.

"Alive," he answered as Klim turned away, wiping his eyes. "Can you take Josh and meet us with Suara on the other side of the lake?" Echin asked Siskin, who nodded and immediately turned around. Josh was already in front of him. "She's badly shocked but in one piece," Echin told Klim, gently. His eyes found Kier and for a moment she felt the same jolt of recognition as the first time she had seen him on the sands at Pulton.

"What else?" Klim probed.

"I think you're better placed to decide that." Echin started back the way he had come.
Kier was soon running to keep up as they scrambled alongside the lower reaches of one of the fells. After some three miles of running, they began to descend to the far side of the lake. The water was screened from the lower fells by a number of well-established trees. With no place for easy disembarkation and without a clear path, this area was usually untouched by tourists. Echin led them down between the trees to where a small hide for bird watching had been erected, with a narrow dirt track leading to the main road.

"I'll send Siskin here," Echin was already heading down the track, indicating that Klim and Kier should enter the hut. "Tell Gabbie I found her father, he knows she's safe."

Klim entered the small, wooden cabin owned by a local ornithological group. The heavy glass windows were firmly closed and the long bench that ran underneath them was not in use. Gabbie was huddled in a pile of blankets on the floor, in the far corner of the hide. Her wet clothes were nearby, her damp, blonde hair pasted across her face as she slept. Klim drew nearer as her breath gave a laboured rattle. Gently, he removed the strands of hair to one side. "Gabes," he whispered, using his old schoolyard name for her. She became awake slowly, reluctantly. Kier could barely make out the shape of her small body inside the tumble of blankets.

"Klim," Gabbie whispered mournfully, her eyes holding him lest he move away. He folded a protective arm underneath her. "Kier!" she cried, eyes lighting as she saw her friend who came over to hold her hand. "I should be dead," she told them simply. "Arwres saved me."

"Your dad knows you're safe," Kier told her. Gabbie nodded sadly.

"They were Devourils," she told them, pulling the thick blanket closely around her. "We need to warn people."

"We'll talk to Echin," Kier promised as Gabbie's eyes closed.

Siskin opened the door to the hide, Suara had pulled up soundlessly outside the hut. Gently Klim lifted Gabbie, ignoring offers of help, a fierce determination on his face as he carried her outside, laying her in the back seat. Kier joined him as they slid either side of the slight form, allowing his knee to frame a pillow for the damp, blonde head as he stroked her hair.

"I have to go back to Andrew," Echin told them, closing the door. He moved towards the driver's window.

"I don't think we're that far from Stromondale." Siskin nodded in agreement as Kier looked at the sleeping body of Gabbie, who they had so nearly lost.

"Where will it end?" she muttered.

"Wherever it ends," Klim stated firmly, "we'll be together." She looked across towards him and squeezed his free hand.

"I'll second that," said Josh, turning around in his seat.

"And me," Siskin affirmed. Kier closed her eyes. Somehow. Somehow. Somehow. Let it happen somehow, she entreated the hidden source deep within, that I fully find you in time.

Chapter Seventeen

Siskin sat in the original part of the building, securely divided from the main hotel. Clare had curled in a chair beside the stone hearth, where they had stoked a blazing fire that partially distracted from the storm outside. On his knee lay the sleeping form of Juliette who stirred only slightly as he tenderly lifted the little girl, bathed and dressed for bed, and placed her in the room connected to her mother's. Returning to the hearth he looked to see how Clare had taken his explanation of the group of friends who were now housed in the main building. In fact, there had been very little explanation at all, she accepted without fuss that they were in danger and needed a place to stay.

"I don't pretend to understand," she said in response to his searching look, "but you know I would never refuse you any help that it's within my power to give. Besides, before Min left she told me that she had created a protection for the Barley Field. She said that was why she had come here, to make sure we were safe. Maybe the strangest thing is that I didn't think it strange at all." Siskin smiled at the memory of the old woman who sat constantly knitting in the little shop, examining everyone that entered and left the hotel. Echin had told him that she was, in fact, a Mourangil. Siskin knew that, if not for her presence, Danubin would have stolen Juliette for the second time in her young life. Instead she had used a dummy to lure him from the canal boat in Dublin when he had so nearly led them all to their end. Alarmed, Clare saw the sadness descend around him and placed her hand upon his knee.

"There's only an elderly couple who will leave tomorrow morning, otherwise the hotel's empty."
Siskin smiled and took her hand in his. "Can you mark it as full for this week?" he asked. "I'll reimburse you for any loss."

"There's no loss," she smiled. "I wouldn't have expected as much custom as you've brought in this weather."

"The last two arrived about an hour ago when you were bathing Juliette," Siskin added. He smiled, "An avuncular Welshman and a young Peruvian girl."
Clare squeezed his hand, watching his eyes. "The woman who came in with you is very beautiful."
Siskin laughed, "Kier? Yes, she is. And yes, I do love her, like a sister."

"Hmm," Clare muttered in mock disbelief.
He decided not to go on to describe how important Kier was to all of them. Instead he pulled her towards him and led her towards the bedroom, erasing for a brief time the shadow of Devourils and Virenmor.

*

The November day soon became a chilly evening; the old stone of the Barley Field Hotel grew dark in the unrelenting rain. Siskin lit the fire in the main suite that comprised of a living room, with large comfortable seating, and a large open hearth. It had been assigned to Gabbie and Kier who had never left her side. She had persuaded Klim to leave as they settled in but he had returned again less than an hour later. Echin had left to find Evan, Swift and Samuel but had returned without the cleric who, he told them mysteriously, was needed elsewhere.

Once they had all gathered the musician produced bottles of wine, beer and snacks, conjuring an almost party atmosphere. Everyone had the chance to shower and change. Clare had found clothing for Gabbie in her stock of unclaimed items that residents had left over the years. The fact that they were all together lifted their spirits and even Gabbie smiled a little. Siskin took charge. "I suppose this is our time for debriefing." He sat behind the counter of the kitchenette looking relaxed with a pint of ale and the remains of a cheese sandwich by his elbow.

"Still a soldier Siskin?" asked Kier smiling.

"In part maybe," he agreed, "but a poor soldier I've been when I was not there to protect you. I still don't understand how it happened. How you came to be alone in a place where the Roghuldjn could attack."
Kier bowed her head, lifting it again on a deep inbreath.

"I was careless and stupidly preoccupied," she admitted to them. In as much detail as she could remember, she told them about the attack by the Roghuldjn and her stay with the Tanes. She did not mention Samuel's words that had first sent her out into the storm, unaware that Samuel had already detailed the events of what had almost been her last evening.

No one made a sound as haltingly, she explained the near fatal effects of the wound inflicted by the vicious and ancient enemy. The Stone of Mesa, now with its glowing, golden moon, lay in her uplifted palm. "It held me to life until Swift and Echin found me. Until the Key of Brunan unlocked the way back." Kier's hand caught that of the young South American who sat on cushions by her feet.

Josh shook his head. "I had no idea how important it was. I almost failed to obtain it in the Hall of Jasmine."

Kier's eyes fixed firmly on the man she knew as Echin in this life. She wondered why she had never truly read what was now so clearly written in the depths of his eyes as they held hers; like a bell waiting to be struck so that it could reveal the composition of its being. She trembled with the knowledge that he had never not known her, he had always recognised Candillium within, just as some part of her had always known the Mourangil of Ordovicia.

Echin wrenched away his gaze and turned to Josh, "I never had any doubt in your ability to be exactly what you are, the Creta of the Myriar."

Evan's rich Welsh tone broke the silence for Josh felt unable to speak. "I still don't understand why Danubin took the Chalycion to Damascus and then to Istanbul."

Echin's eyes had returned to Kier's face. He did not bother to remove them as he answered. "She took it to Damascus to bring Ulynyx into the open."

Josh then described his encounter with the leader of the Chunii. "I haven't tried to draw him yet, though he's one of the most hypnotic figures I've ever seen."

"So, he's a Mourangil?" Swift asked.

Echin shook his head. "Sadly, I think his actions will have splintered him from his original being. Elanur deliberately misled him about the location of the doorway to the Hall of Jasmine but I don't believe he would ever have gained access."

"So, once Danubin had drawn him out," Siskin
theorised, "he was led to Istanbul where she has
obviously been working for some time."
Josh's face twisted in distaste. "Her lair is a replica of the
place in Wales," he informed Kier, who had shared his
captivity in Danubin's mansion, "and just as deadly."

"Not only that," continued the Mourangil. "Istanbul has
many very old stones, long precious. Even the Chalycion
would seem one amongst many and we would not have
found it again without Josh."
Josh told his story of the recovery of the Chalycion,
patiently answering the women's questions about their
time in the old city. Gabbie cried out in horror as he told
of the bombing, engineered by Danubin in revenge, that
cost so many lives. Swift's dark eyes were afire as he
went on to describe Unethora and the Hall of Jasmine.

All the time Kier and Echin continued their silent
communion. She now had no difficulty in seeing the pain
of separation from the jewelled kingdom in the eyes of
the Mourangil, who had chosen to remain with them.
Josh halted as he spoke of their fear for Gabbie when
they discovered her separation from Mengebara. Siskin's
voice was gentle as he addressed the young woman.

"Are you able?"
Dressed in a blue sweater that she wore as a dress,
Gabbie's colour had returned. She pulled herself forward
to the edge of the sofa looking around her, hands laid in
her lap, spine straight. She began with the attack in the
gym, a story none of them had yet heard.

"Of course, I knew it was Danubin, imposing a..."

"Construct," Josh supplied the word she searched for.
She gave him a grateful nod. "Imposing a construct on
Ben's gym. She wanted Arwres and thought to kill me. I

felt her presence even though it was projected from far away."

"She used the Chalycion to find Arwres," Echin explained, shaking his head. "It's the only one of the other stones she could reach. I should have foreseen it but I underestimated her power. What we could not have known is that she had a previous link with the building and Gabbie; that was how she was able to carry out the manipulation from so far away."

Gabbie's blue eyes were fierce as she continued her story.

"Before the woman I thought of as my mother left me, she gave me a small mirror. It fell out of my bag as Danubin searched for Arwres. I'd taken the Myriar stone off for the gym. I sensed her, understanding that she kind of improvised once she realised where I was. Looking back, I suppose I could feel the point where she saw that she could use what was in the room in front of her."

Struggling to find her words again she looked towards Josh who suggested, "Game plays?"

"Yeah," she nodded, "I suppose it was like that." Gabbie shuddered, "She made what was already in the room come alive." She moved her hand in an undulating movement across her face that scrunched as she hissed snakelike. Despite her seriousness there were flickers of amusement from the others. They fell away however, as her voice dropped to a whisper. "She couldn't find Arwres and upturned my things. But I saw her face in the mirror, the one she had given me. And then she saw the mirror and recognised my face in return. It was Danubin, the woman I called mother."

Shock stilled the room. "So that's why you removed yourself from Mengebara," Klim said gently.

Gabbie swallowed as she remembered the desolation of loneliness that had assaulted her in that moment.

"I just couldn't find the mind place in my head, I wasn't able to contact any of you."

"You didn't want us to know," Klim suggested. "The shock and horror of your discovery cut the links."

"Danubin is your mother?" Evan interjected.

"No!" her voice was stronger, firmer. "She was never my mother after all. That's why we were in Shimmerfell." Gabbie then went on to complete her story, with what she had learnt from her father. "You spoke to him?" Gabbie turned to Echin, although she already knew the answer from Klim.

"He's safe and returning to Bankside tomorrow. We've arranged other accommodation. The house, having been so intensely focused on by the Devourils will start to disintegrate, it probably has already. We've found an old railway cottage on the other side of the line."
Gabbie nodded approval. "But what if they come back?" Her voice trembled.

"Danubin no longer has any way of reviving the connection, unless you seek her out," Echin reassured her.

"I won't do that," Gabbie said coldly. "Not just yet." The threat, coming from the small blonde, reminded Klim of the times when her storms of temper would not be subdued until they had played themselves out in the force of emotion.

"Your dad believes there has been an electrical fire at your house and that it isn't safe for him to return," added Echin.

Gabbie rubbed her forehead. "I tried a few times to tell him about everything, with us I mean," her hands raised in an open gesture that encompassed the room, "but I don't think he could handle it. It was the same with my mum and Danubin, she called herself Patrice then, he never told me the truth, couldn't cope with it himself. I think she murdered my mother." Her eyes welled and Klim reached for her hand, Gabbie leant into his shoulder.

Swift turned away from Klim and Gabbie, "We need to talk about what happened in Wales. The cottage is gone, swept into the river."

"Why would Samuel let that happen?" Siskin was appalled.

"Belluvour," Kier stated coldly, looking to Echin for agreement.

The Mourangil hesitated, connecting to memories that none around him could share. "He was truly magnificent once and we all bowed beneath the force of his passion that shaped the surface, dispersed the waters from new lands and stroked the mountains to edged majesty. He may no longer have the power to make volcanic change as once he did but he still holds the charismatic energy that, even as the bound one, allowed him to have such influence."

"You think he specifically targeted Samuel?" asked Kier.

"Danubin will have guided him to the Teifi and Samuel as a way of attacking the Myriar."

"But surely that does not mean that Samuel cannot stay with us?" Swift looked as if she would leave to fetch the cleric there and then.

"He really is needed elsewhere," Echin told them in a way that halted any further discussion.

"So already the Unbound strikes at our centre." Kier said without emotion.

"How?" Gabbie's face had become even paler. "How did this monster get out?"

"Monster?" Echin repeated. "I have never called him so, and yet what he did was indeed monstrous. But many of my kind believe his rejection of the human race to be based on his love of Moura. They have forgotten that his actions wounded Moura even more deeply than the ravages of mankind."

"The bonds have barely held him this last decade," Kier said, looking towards Gabbie. "Had it not been for the recoil of murder he would have been unleashed on the human race several years ago."

Gabbie frowned, "What murder?"

"My sister," Kier managed to keep her voice level but shifted restlessly in the armchair. "I've only just come to understand it myself. He found me. In the furthest reaches of the Secret Vaults, he drew me towards the Waybearer stone created by Nephragm. It was intended to allow access from the Secret Vaults to the surface and it succeeded, in part."

"So, this was the secret hidden within the White Chapel in Mengebara?" Kier nodded, acknowledging the truth of Josh's statement. "It was also," he continued, "the scene that I drew when I looked into your heart in Samuel's lodgings at the university; when he demanded that I drew all in the room to ensure that Nephragm was not amongst us." On his face was registered the shock he had felt as he depicted the moment of her sister's death.

"Such an attack," Kier explained, "signalled that the bonds were almost broken. Even so it cost him greatly and until very recently he did not know that he had killed my sister and not me."

Josh had been sketching silently. He passed the drawing to the graceful woman in the chair opposite. He had drawn Kier just as she was, sitting, listening, speaking within their group. Pinned to her shoulder by a bright stone was a long cloak. Within the swathe of rich material Josh's clever pencil had managed to suggest an infinite universe of stars. It intermingled with the outer reaches of the page as the eye followed the mystery of every space.

"You are Candillium, are you not?" Josh's voice was gentle.

A spasm of grief passed over Kier's face. "Yes, I was once Candillium," she told them evenly. "Leader of Ordovicia and the new race. I know that buried deep inside of me there is her power and her memories. Sometimes it has come to the surface and when I lay dying I knew, without doubt, that it was I who held the centrepiece; that I had not fulfilled my promise of bringing the Myriar to fruition. I felt the irony that my body is primed so that I would survive all but the touch of the Devourils and the Roghuldjn."

Echin stood across the room as if held in a vice. "The Roghuldjn are Belluvour's deformed manifestation, sent to hunt you even in Ordovicia in the last period of that time. We patrolled the borders to keep them away."

"I remember tiny snatches," Kier replied, "but most of the time it's like a dream I can't hold onto. I haven't connected the two things up but I hope that you will help me." She looked at Echin, the hunger in his eyes was like a physical pain to her. No wonder his presence on the sands at Pulton had left her so shaken!

161

"But I do know that it is not as Candillium that I will find the centrepiece within me but as Kier Morton." Siskin came across and held her hands, kissing her cheek. He returned to the counter and there was a long silence, broken only by the clink of glasses as he poured champagne, passing a flute to each of them.

"To Kier Morton," he toasted.

"To returning," whispered Echin, as they raised their glasses towards the woman who sat quietly amongst them, searching for a being that was all the more elusive for being contained within.

Chapter Eighteen

Clare sat on the bench in the garden watching Juliette playing with the girl Siskin had introduced as Swift. The exotic beauty slid out of sight as Juliette closed her eyes.

"You are getting warmer, said the grass," a soft Spanish voice came from the lawn. Juliette ran onto the grassy garden. After she had circled around a small boulder a deep throaty voice came from behind a tree trunk, "Warmer said the tree."
Juliette ran over to the nearest tree, where she jumped on Swift's crouched form and the young woman groaned loudly. "Oh, how did you find me?"

"The grass and the tree told me," Juliette giggled, delighted.

"That's a good trick," Clare laughed.
Swift looked up and taking the little girl's hand came over to sit beside Clare. "Throwing my voice? I've always been able to do it, my grandmother encouraged me and after she died," she shifted uneasily with the memory, "it saved me a few times in Peru."

"Life must have been very hard."

"No more than for you I think," Swift turned shrewdly towards the older women.
Juliette pulled at her new friend's hand but her mother coaxed the little girl back inside the hotel for breakfast. Swift remained on the bench, wrapped in a thick jumper. It was no wonder Juliette wanted to get out into the garden for it was the first dry day in over a week. They had all been cooped up for too long. It had been two days since they had all sat down together but no one had any heart for moving on. The Mourangil had made himself absent yet again and Kier still seemed largely lost to

herself. Evan sat in the lounge working his way through the bookshelves and sipping brandy in his coffee. Kier and Josh had braved the weather and explored Stromondale. Klim and Gabbie had hardly left each other's side and the gnawing pain in Swift's insides stabbed at her incessantly. Klim hardly made eye contact with her and Gabbie virtually spoke to no one except him. Kier, hands in the pocket of a long coat, now too big for her thin form, came out of the main building. Swift made room for her on the bench.

"So good to be in the fresh air." Kier pushed her hands deeper into the pockets against the cold. Laughing, she pulled leaves from her friend's hair that had become lodged during her game with Juliette. Impulsively Swift covered her hand with her own, resting her head against it. "Remember on El Silencia?"

Kier nodded, "When you thought I was going to pay for your bracelets in English two pence pieces?"

The young woman laughed, "You knew?"

Kier smiled and placed her arm around the thin shoulders.

"We both knew that there was a connection, but we didn't understand then."

Their thoughts turned back silently to the events in Peru that had triggered all that had since happened.

"Can they find us here?" Swift asked, hesitantly.

Kier was forcibly aware of the changes that had occurred in Swift since she had first known her, little over a year before. There was no fear in her voice, more speculation. Kier shook her head. "Stromondale has been closely protected since the kidnapping last year. Siskin is reluctant to risk more than another couple of days though and it's really all we have anyway."

"What will happen then?"

164

"Then," Kier breathed in deeply, "we begin the last leg of the race." She looked up at the skies, "The clouds are gathering again," she warned. "I came to get you. Echin's back, everyone's gathered inside."

They walked back together to find that Siskin had pulled a large, square coffee table between the two sofas in the living space. On the table were a number of things. Kier immediately recognised the old book from which she had read in Samuel's cottage and Gabbie was pouring through it.

"You went to find Samuel?" Kier looked carefully at the Mourangil who nodded. "Is he safe?" She had not seen the gentle cleric since the dreadful night of the attack and she missed him.

Echin smiled, "He misses you. I wish there had been time for him to meet with us here."

Kier smiled her thanks and relief. It seemed he did not wish to discuss where he had sent the cleric or why. Echin's absence had given them no opportunity to be alone. She wondered if Kier Morton could ever match the image of Candillium that he had held in his heart down through the ages.

"I can see it Kier!" Gabbie was following the text, that Echin had supplied, with her index finger. "I understand what it means!"

"You're an Inscriptor, Gabbie," she told her friend. "You can read and write in languages that are no longer in use. That's why you find learning languages so easy."

"But I thought that was you."

"Kier shows some aspects of all the Seeds," Echin explained, "and has a particular affinity for ancient text. However, you Gabbie are the last Inscriptor of the Myriar."

The tiny blonde put a possessive hand on the pendant around her neck; in her heart, she had never accepted that it could be meant for anyone else.

"So, we're really it then?" Josh had started drawing automatically, using the pencils and paper that were on the table.

"What I don't understand," said Siskin, " is that we're hardly representative of the world right now. We're mostly westerners, the largest continents are not amongst us and yet we few are to form the Myriar?"

"You think in terms of one life, your world fragmented as it is now," Echin explained. "The Seeds have been all races of men, on all continents, down through generations. To work together now you are following the pattern that was chosen for Candillium in this life. Humanity is the country, the culture, the community of the Myriar." Echin looked towards Gabbie who bent over the old book and began to translate the text. Kier, when she read, had remained Kier but the mobile face of the young woman transformed its features as she spoke in a voice that seemed no longer to be her own. It transported all those in the room into a pocket of time that even then was out of step with the point at which it had been written. As if the words had leapt forward to belong here and now in this moment and this place. Kier felt her body tingle with memory as Gabbie translated from the book she had first found so very long ago. In the way of the Mourangils, Kier found her inner self was able to step into the memory and observe the events of this other age, this other self.

She beheld a curtain of water at the entrance to a mountain cave, where each droplet lit to crystal in the sunlight. Stone steps burrowed into the mountain, a silver stream winding its way across the floor of the cave. Kier sat cross-legged at the edge of the stream, cupping her hands, drinking the water. Her skin tingled with delight as she drank the cool, light filled liquid that seemed to fill every hollow space inside her. Standing, she turned to pass through an arch that led to a walled enclosure. It was lit with crystals: luminous greens, pure whites, soft blues and shimmering yellows. On the wall to her left her fingers traced the surface of a lapis jewel that glimmered with a universe of threaded possibility. On the ground, stone seats shaped around a central dais. There, laid open and bare, was a book. The paper was made from alu, the base material used for so much in Ordovicia, shining white in the soft glow of crystal. The small space became filled with sound, the murmuring of the stream and the crystal. At the same time as Kier registered each note, a rune appeared on the surface of the book, a melody captured in images that spoke of Moura's intention. Candillium felt the jewelled heart of the planet. "Yes," she whispered, "I will be the centrepiece of the Myriar."

The lapis stone caught her attention as it glimmered to her right. It seemed to enclose a whole ocean. Even as she reached out to touch the stone, the lapis jewel shimmered. It was the first time that Toomaaris the Mourangil had walked in human form. His skin had the sheen of crystal and shone faintly blue. It was clear that he had carefully studied her kind. Like her he wore woven alu cloth and his dark hair was tied in the knotted stallion tail worn by the men of Ordovicia. She felt the warm pulse of human life as she reached out and took his hand in hers. In those days, his face was a simple reflection of his emotion and its force was equalled by the overwhelming strength of her response. She recognised the power of the Myriar as it shone from every pore of his body and, with his touch, the gift of Moura flowed effortlessly through a conduit of love into hers. It became embedded within her essential being for all days.

Kier detached herself from the memory when Gabbie stopped speaking. Siskin, Josh and Swift sat opposite on one sofa with Gabbie, Kier and Klim together on the other. Echin and Evan sat to one side on stools in the kitchenette. Kier lifted her tear filled eyes to find that those of Echin had never left her face. She was certain that he had walked silently beside her as she had found the memory at the heart of all her longing. The room was completely silent. Gabbie had described the first meeting of Toomaaris and Candillium; the moment when the centrepiece of the gift of Moura had been passed to humanity. Kier ached with the memory. Neither she nor Echin spoke, in fact he had turned away. No matter that she had once been Candillium, she was Kier Morton now. After all the long years of living above the surface, of watching for her return and guiding the Seeds of the Myriar, Toomaaris was also Echinod Deem, remote and apart.

Evan broke the silence, "Is there more Gabbie?"

Gabbie glanced at Kier, who smiled encouragement.

"Each rune is a collection of pictures," explained Gabbie. "This is just so difficult!"

"Perhaps Kier?" Swift suggested but Gabbie shook her head and continued. "Moura has imposed conditions on her gift," the Inscriptor told them. Everyone straightened with attention as Gabbie closed her eyes and passed her hands over the runes. "What was given to mankind freely, in the first flush of their presence on the earth, can no longer be awarded so simply." Gabbie's voice rivalled

Evan's bardic tones as she pressed on. "In the Hall of Jasmine, the Key of Brunan is hidden. It can only be retrieved by the male aspect of the Myriar, from the city that straddles two continents."

Kier nodded and then explained. "The runes are dynamic, altering themselves as mankind has altered. This is the part of the text I relayed to Samuel and he in turn passed to Elanur. I could see no further than that. Go on Gabbie."

"In the Realm of Resonance, will be found the Key of Talitha, which must be recovered by the female aspect of the Myriar." Gabbie placed the book back on the table. "Well I read it." She shrugged her shoulders. "Doesn't mean it makes any sense! What's a Realm of Resonance?"

"Think of the ruffs worn by the men in this country in Shakespeare's time," Echin suggested.

The teenagers looked at him blankly. He picked up a pencil and drew an elaborate, circular collar comprised of narrow, stiff folds. "Looked at as a whole," he explained, "the central space forms a circle and only the lines of the ruff are visible, even though each contains a deep fold as it spans around the centre." Encouraged by nods he went on but seemed visibly troubled. "Reuben's cave is one fold and there are many more hidden and connected to Moura, anchored as invisible attachments around the planet. The Realm of Resonance is another such fold." He hesitated, directly addressing the three women. "It is also the most difficult of all to reach and to return from. Linear time has no meaning there."

"It said the female aspect." Swift's voice was a whisper, concentrating. "Does that mean we have to go alone?"

"I'm afraid it will only allow access to you, Gabbie and Kier. Or like the Hall of Jasmine, may permit entry to only one of you."

"Can't we go as back up?" Klim's fear had heightened with the serious expression on the face of the Mourangil. "What will happen to them?"

"I've no idea," Echin told him bluntly. "It's a place that exists only because mankind exists. A world of reflected shadow and light."

"Hmm," Gabbie sounded unimpressed. "So how do we get there? It says nothing in the book to help us find this place." She flicked through the enigmatic runes.

"The writing on the doorway in the Basilica Cistern!" Siskin pointed to the words that he had copied from the ancient stone column when Josh exited the mysterious Hall of Jasmine.

Gabbie leant over to carefully examine the words that Siskin had managed to copy onto the large sheet of paper.

"*In the shared mind place of the Myriar Seeds, the female aspect may cross to the Realm of Resonance. In their footsteps will be left a fertile field, in which to start the new beginning or strip barren forever the harvest of possibili*ty."

"Great! Well that's clear then!" Gabbie concluded with a smile to the others.

"Mengebara!" Klim examined the words carefully. He sighed, "If I'm supposed to have a clue what to do, then I've got to tell you I don't!"

Evan, leaning over the sofa behind Klim, patted his shoulder. "It'll come. If you need to do something, it will come." Klim raised his eyebrows, wishing that he could share even a little of the Welshman's optimism.

Chapter Nineteen

A screech in the wind turned her panic stricken face towards the Aegean Sea. At the top of the hidden temple Danubin stroked her injured face and hid from the adamantine glance of the one she had served over many lifetimes. He had whispered to her from the Secret vaults as she slept, he had led her through a maze of dark power, made her a weapon, a swirling force, a curse. So long had she planned, so meticulously had she crafted the obdurate dwelling, leaving only a cup of marble at the tip where she now overlooked the ruined city. Across the centuries she had used her skills to prevent access to the mysterious island, preparing in secret the sumptuous abode. The building was surrounded by a collection of ancient pillars, the remains of long treasured architecture, sacred tributes to old gods. Fittingly, she felt, she had created the ultimate temple to the ultimate Lord. Her eyes fell on the ruins below; much of what she had preserved was now scattered over the ancient site of worship. Each day the majestic buildings crumbled a little more.

Every boat that had attempted to land since Belluvour had come here, had been swallowed in the angry current of a sea that warred with itself. The small airstrip was lost in a tainted grey fog. The walls of the palatial temple were dotted with embedded Devourils. Sour, glass like crystals produced a gaseous miasma choking the air. Bereft of form they moved as burning tendrils, communicating around her like the torn strands of a whip. Belluvour had finally escaped his bonds. The whole island trembled with the presence of this alien creature dressed in human form.

*

"It doesn't make sense Klim, why would the doorway to this place be in Mengebara?" Gabbie frowned and shook her head. They sat side-by-side on the sofa. Since the discussion that morning, the small group had milled around the hotel, drifting in and out of the cosy living space in Kier and Gabbie's room.

"Y' know," Klim offered, "when I began to put together the mind place, I felt I was using a different kind of energy."

"What do you mean?" Swift asked from her seat directly opposite him.

Klim hesitated, searching for the words, as Kier entered the room, dark circles under her eyes. She had used Clare's internet to Skype her brother Gally and Klim felt the anguish emanating from her. It had been months since she had seen her brother, who now lived in Los Angeles. Gally had been captured and tortured by Nephragm in Pulton over a year ago and he knew that Kier had deliberately kept him in the dark about the events that had happened since then. Kier sat down quietly in one of the armchairs by the fireplace without speaking. Klim forced himself to concentrate as Gabbie shook his knee to say he hadn't answered the question.

"It kinda hovers around us," he continued his explanation, "but we don't know how to use it. I could feel other places out there, well in there I suppose. I think that one of those other places could be this Realm of Resonance."

He looked to Echin who had remained in the kitchenette but it was Kier who answered. "In Ordovicia, the mind place held our history, our collective consciousness." She

172

was unclear how much of what she knew was from her reading and how much was from the elusive mind of Candillium. "People could dip in and out of their memories, hear the voices of those that had passed. There were some specific groups that connected for certain purposes but each person in Ordovicia was born with a connection to Mengebara. And you are right," yes, she did remember, "on the outer rim was the edge of connection with other dimensions."

"Klim, I don't want to go without you." Gabbie had turned to him, utterly open in her affection and need for him. It was an irresistible combination; he kissed her hand, whispering reassurance. Swift chose that moment to move to the kitchenette to fetch a glass of water.

"If the doorway is in Mengebara then I need to help them find it," he looked directly at Echin.

"Not this time Klim." Before he could object, Echin continued. "This is for the female aspect. Remember what Gabbie read about the conditions that Moura has imposed. You will have things to do elsewhere." Although he spoke gently, the Mourangil was firm and his statement went unchallenged. Swift returned to her seat as Evan turned from the armchair opposite Kier.

"I think," his shrewd eyes moved between the three women, "that everything now depends on your allegiance to the Myriar and to each other."

Swift and Gabbie avoided eye contact, neither had yet been prepared to acknowledge the gaping hole that had arisen between them because of their love for the same man.

"But..." Klim began.

"How do we do this?" Gabbie interrupted, reaching for Swift's hand that was offered stiffly in return.

Kier came over to stand beside them. "I've done something like it once before with Josh, Faer and Tormaigh," said Kier. "Maybe we could use the garden room?" Siskin quickly nodded his approval.

"Right now?" Gabbie's voice had lifted a pitch. "Do we have to go now? Don't we just need to practise first?" Echin's gaze seemed fixed on Gabbie.

"No," Kier clipped.

Gabbie looked around. "Well, what do we need to bring?"

"I don't think we will need anything but ourselves," Swift answered.

The young Inscriptor looked towards Kier who nodded her agreement. Siskin drew the discussion to a conclusion and stepped in, "We'd best say our goodbyes here."

It seemed to Kier such a short time since she had found them again and now they would have to split the group once more. She wondered why Moura should require them to be apart. Evan, Klim, Siskin and Josh briefly hugged the girls in turn; Gabbie turned away as Swift clung to Klim. Once they had left the room and entered the corridor Echin gave them little time to dwell on their loss. "It's very difficult and dangerous to place your physical self within the mind place," he lowered his voice so that only Kier caught his words, as they moved towards the garden room. "Even more so to venture from there into the Realm of Resonance."

He was so near that Kier could feel the hairs on her skin prickle in response to his magnetic presence. She could brush her hand against his but something held her back, as if he had erected a forcefield around himself just for that purpose.

"Focus your minds on the Key of Talitha," he told them, "and on the fact that you're all needed back here. Leave as soon as you have the key."

"Sounds like a good plan," Kier sighed and his wry smile acknowledged the ridiculous simplicity of his words. He stood to one side and Swift and Gabbie, both tense and absorbed, passed into the garden room. Kier followed the others but turned as Echin spoke, his voice choked. "Come back Kier," he said softly, turning away, leaving before she could reply.

"Have I not always?" she whispered to the empty space.

The large windows looked out upon a walled garden where herbs had been planted in pots. Clare often used this space to play with Juliette in bad weather. The room was virtually empty apart from a few scattered cushions on the carpeted floor. At Kier's instigation, the three women arranged themselves on the cushions to form a triangle. Sitting cross legged, they joined hands. Swift and Gabbie followed Kier's example and closed their eyes. The last time that Kier had placed herself within the mind place, her physical body had remained within Samuel's lodgings. The Mourangils had assisted herself and Josh to view the collective structure of thoughts and the individual way that each member of the Myriar had stored them. She trembled as her awareness touched the barrier, surprisingly fragile, between mind and body. The shooting pains of guilt, the underlying fear, the shadow of grief; all such regular inhabitants of her everyday mind, she now forced away. None of these could be allowed to gain purchase if she was to manage the difficult task of bringing all three of them safely into Mengebara.

Kier felt the complete trust of the two young women on either side of her and relaxed, seeing the entrance to the mind place as a walled garden with a wooden door. Projecting this image to Gabbie and Swift, she felt a jolt as their consciousness came together with hers. Normally there was no formal entrance to the mind place, it came to them at will. But now all three shared the vision of the firmly closed wooden door. There were three grooves where the lock would normally be found and Kier placed the Stone of Mesa in the first groove, Swift followed with the Stone of Silence and Gabbie accessed the last with Arwres. When all three Stones of the Myriar were in place the door slowly swung open. Outside the garden room Toomaaris watched through the glass door as Kier vanished inside a golden light. A flash of diamond enfolded the graceful figure of Swift and Gabbie was covered by an amber glow. He sighed with relief as they disappeared one by one, leaving nothing behind but the weight of their absence.

Mengebara had grown, there were many more empty spaces. Kier recognised the area of their most recent memories and headed towards blocks of washed stone, in the centre of which, was housed a deep well. Followed by the others, she stopped to raise a cup to her lips and felt the clear, cold liquid trickle its way into the hollow of her stomach. Her vision altered, shapes moved around her, the deliberate memories shared by the others. Swift and Gabbie had followed her example and each now examined the recent happenings as they had been recorded in the mind place. The ruined island in Shimmerfell hovered large in a grey cloud above the sheltered abode of Stromondale. Gabbie shivered when she saw the interior of her father's house, corrosively attacked by the Devourils.

Kier led them beyond the well to the individual rows, where each member of the group stored involuntary memories. These became visible only when, like now, they were able to step inside the mechanism of Mengebara. Kier compared them to the last time that she had visited the mind place in this way. The stone rows of Swift now included a silvery cloud of soft rock that filled the back of her area. Gabbie's herb garden, originally so full of colour, was now in its autumn, with dead leaves and bare stalks littering the ground. The White Chapel in Kier's garden was still standing in the centre but had been covered by trees, one of which had now prised open the door. Cracks had begun to form in the marble structure. Josh's ornate garden was interspersed with door size painted canvases depicting different parts of the world. At the centre was the figure of a white unicorn. The bonsai trees representing Siskin's memories had grown larger and more convoluted, though still carefully trimmed. The hum of internal melody rang through Mengebara. Klim's reed bed was, of course, even more densely populated than before.

"We haven't time," Kier told her two companions as they both made to enter the area of the reed bed. The two young women switched direction and followed her beyond these constructions, along a pebbled path and to the border of the area that had been enclosed by a high stone wall.

"Don't think we can go that way," Gabbie examined the view on either side. "The doorway's not here."
Swift nodded her agreement, "The stone is strong and protective; it does not mean to be breached."

177

Kier put her finger to her lips. The faint sound she had heard became more defined. A whimpering cry of a woman stifled with fear. She pressed her ear against the wall and heard the shuffling of feet, orders shouted, the slap of blows delivered.

"Soldiers," Swift had come alongside, eyes closed as she also listened. Gabbie looked up but could not see the top of the wall. One woman's voice became many, a mournful weeping.

"We have to get to them." Gabbie frantically hunted for a gate or a gap in the wall.
A voice, speaking an unfamiliar language with a Spanish accent pierced the background noise of war. Swift trembled with recognition. "Mateo," she told them nervously.
Kier looked blank but Gabbie remembered the story that Swift had told her on the crag at Bankside.

"He sold you to Jackson, he was your friend. You're sure?" Swift nodded, biting her pale lips.

"We have to help," Kier told her gently. "You are far stronger now. He will not subdue us."
Gabbie had no knowledge of what language Mateo spoke but she translated the meaning without difficulty.

"The young one on the left is mine," she paused and shook her head. "Foul!", she spat out the word. "They're going to rape the women. I think the men of the village have been gathered together and he's telling them to prepare for death and that this punishment has come to them because they show no righteousness. Or something like that." Her eyes darted either side of the wall. She scampered along the path, trying to find some mode of entry. Kier waited and eventually Swift nodded that she was ready. She placed her hand against the stone and it slowly became suspended liquid beneath her touch. It seemed to Kier that she could distinguish every individual layer, every particle of the stone's composition. Swift extended her hand above her head and then to either side as she scratched her fingertips in two lines to the ground. She had created a gateway. Gabbie turned at Kier's call and hurried back, breathless and startled by the shimmering block of stone.

"Do we even know if we can get back?" she asked the other two.
Kier shrugged her shoulders. "I just know we have to help whoever is suffering on the other side of this divide." In turn, the two young women nodded their assent. Following Kier's example they took a deep breath and followed her quickly into the entrance that Swift had created.

Chapter Twenty

"We didn't get much time to say goodbye properly," Klim followed Josh and Siskin to the door of the Garden Room where Echin stood looking at the empty space. The Mourangil walked to the centre of the circle that the women had formed. "The Myriar is changing her. Even as Candillium she never undertook to bring her physical body into the mind place. Now she has safely guided all three of them across the threshold."

"If that is meant to be reassuring," Klim told him, "it isn't. What would have happened if she had failed?"

"You created Mengebara as it now stands Klim, so you may be best placed to answer that question," Echin replied.

"But it was done by intuition not science."

"Yet science and research often follow intuition. Somehow in creating Mengebara you have allowed the fractional possibility for the absorption of the physical into the abstract." Klim looked at him blankly. "Kier," Echin continued, "has managed to weave the physical strands of their three bodies into fine entities that can enter into the world of collective thought."

Klim looked around the empty room. "At least we should be able to find them in Mengebara."

The three men accessed the mind place as they had now done dozens of times but Klim opened his eyes with alarm. "There's no connection with any of them!"

Echin dropped into his own private reverie. "They have found a way through but my heart tells me that they have not reached the Realm of Resonance."

"Well, where could they have gone?" Klim's voice was loud, his forehead knotted with tension.

"The power of the Myriar belongs to all mankind. It is now manifest even if not fully whole. At the borders of Mengebara it is possible that an urgent need calls them, a task that the women must complete before they can find the Realm of Resonance."

"Will it be dangerous?"

"Almost certainly." It was the first time that Klim would have welcomed the Mourangil's absence. Evan noisily entered the room with a tray of drinks and the men gladly took the beers that he offered. He picked up his own glass of brandy. "The Crysonance," he told them, "tells of the jagged discordance of war, the march of pain across the surface, the impending doom that sits ready to swallow mankind." Evan's deep, musical voice made his ominous words more poignant. Siskin raised his glass towards the Welshman. "Then we will be ready to meet it." He drained his glass; the others followed, draining their own.

"I'm ready," Klim said, his rucksack was already packed. Josh indicated that he too was prepared to leave. Evan went to speak but Echin stopped him with a shake of his head. "Angharad has need of you," he told him. "You're going to be a grandfather again." A rush of joyous Welsh rang throughout the small room and Evan's eyes lit bright for the first time since he had been injured. Siskin turned towards the door, where on the other side, Clare was chiding Juliette as the child's feet tapped along the corridor amid shouts of 'Siskin'! One hand on the door handle, he turned back to the others, "Give me ten minutes," he said, "then I'll be ready."

*

The heat slammed against Kier's body as the wall disappeared and they entered the horrific midst of war. Immediately she was aware of a village setting. A simple living space with a cool, sand dusted floor, crowded with women and children. The hand painted, abundantly coloured walls had been dimmed by scattered dust and splashes of blood. Kier guessed that they were in Africa but it could have been anywhere, for this scene has been played out the whole world over, on every continent habited by man. Whenever men have abandoned their hearts and filled the space with lust and greed, the same result has followed. All the spurious rationale for their savagery, be it fanaticism, so called nationalism, rebellion turned dictatorship, or whatever lies they told themselves, this was the outcome. Those who were not beaten, brutalised or raped, joined thousands of the displaced and dispossessed. They have wandered the oceans in crowded, unseaworthy vessels; herded and packed, they were squeezed through tight borders. Shunted in walking lines, miles long, they have trailed along waterless paths in search of sanctuary. All this because their beloved homes had become infested by the same fatal sickness that had gnarled its rabid course through history and was now present in the village they had entered.

The village women stood back, afraid and confused but Gabbie began to chatter in the language she had so briefly heard. Some of the children came to touch the strangers and then ran back to the safety of the women. The keening of a grandmother, rocking back and forth, stilled to something like hope. The villagers desperately held their hands towards the outside where men and boys, fathers, brothers and sons had been gathered in the open area to be shot. The women crowded against the sides of the dwelling as Kier watched from the doorway. The men were herded pitifully against a backdrop of magnificent mountains, that had no doubt witnessed the tragedy of human conflict for uncountable years. The sky, high above the swirling dust and noise, was a serene blue, beneath which, crowded together were the grim, despairing faces of men and boys, on many of which hard labour had traced premature lines. Ragged clothes, hands coarse with effort, were witness to long years of exploitation. Now they were penned together with less care than had been given to the cattle that had been snatched to serve the voracious needs of the army.

The soldiers were dressed in khaki, luridly accessorised with gleaming strips of machine gun bullets. Their faces were hidden by striped scarves with slits for eyes, in the same way that other men had created covered, faceless woman to serve their own fears in the name of tradition. They raised their guns at the order of their commander, as Kier stepped out into the sunlight with Swift and Gabbie by her side. In his peripheral vision Mateo, the commander, noticed their exit and expecting resistance, he swung his gun around to point at them. And then saw Swift.

"Sylvana," he whispered her christened name, his confused eyes greedily drinking in the tall beauty. Kier stepped forward, ignoring the guns that were now turned as one in her direction. The power of the Myriar thrummed in her veins when she signalled to Gabbie who, without hesitation, came to stand beside her. Kier spoke directly to the soldiers and each line was echoed by

183

Gabbie's voice, translating clearly into their given language.

"This is not war, it is hate. This is not for love of God but love of power. That power is only an illusion so that you are left with nothing but hate. And its poison will choke you." Kier paused and pointed to the imprisoned men. "Whatever you try to inflict upon these people will rebound upon you." She turned to the village women, huddled together outside the entrance to the dwelling. "Any of you who try to force a woman, will lose your manhood."

The hardened men glowered at her. Mateo, who had lowered his gun in shock, now pointed it firmly at Kier. Swift ran in front of her friend and Mateo screamed at her to move. She held her ground. "Fire," he instructed the squad of soldiers, ready to execute the villagers.

Swift suddenly ran towards Mateo. Kier, seeing the deadly impulse in the South American, cried out for her to come back. Mateo, throwing his gun to one side, turned towards Swift. "And you are mine!"

Machine gun fire rattled across the standing bodies; fathers trying to shield their sons, young men holding their brother's hands, flinching with the onslaught of deafening gunfire. Miraculously no bullets were felt, no death inflicted. Astonished, the soldiers frantically placed their hands where spurts of blood had erupted on their own bodies. Groaning and cursing, they slumped against each other as they fell down. Mateo halted, fear crossing his face and for a brief moment Swift's rage was quelled, as she was reminded of the boy who had once been her best friend. The thought quickly vanished as he lifted his fist to strike her. Swift's rage was fearless, she stood her ground waiting defiantly to be struck. Gabbie, flung herself at Swift, pushing her away from his attempted assault but Swift was on her feet in moments as Kier blocked her advance. "Look! There's no need, wait." Mateo fell to the ground in agony. Every part of him felt on fire, his hands covering his genitals that burnt even more than anywhere else. He screamed as his eyes turned to Kier, knowing that he was unmanned and would never again take a woman.

Swift, enraged, pulled away Kier's arm and moved to where Mateo spat out curses in Spanish as he squirmed on the ground. Standing over the spluttering young man, she knelt down and reached towards his chest. Swift pressed her hands heavily on to his body and the earth below slowly began to envelope him. Gabbie shouted but Swift did not hear. She pressed further until all but his face remained. Mateo, eyes suddenly clear inside a grey mask whispered, "I am sorry." He was twice her weight but Swift lifted his limbs from the embrace of the earth, bringing him fully and abruptly back to the surface where he lost consciousness. Her rage died in her tears for their lost childhood, for the boy who had betrayed her and that she had once called friend.

Chapter Twenty-one

The wind brushed against the black onyx stone dwelling that Ulynyx had created in his first wanderings on the surface of the planet. It sat a little apart from the rest of the subterranean city in the desert, where he had housed thousands of rescued men, women and children. The boys had now grown to become soldiers, the backbone of his army. The stone dwellings beneath the sand dunes, seated deep in the earth, were invisible, even to the technology now available to mankind. The human race, he reflected, had been stubbornly blind to the real technology, the grace of Moura. He had teased underground streams and rivers to weave around the city he called Ulyn. At his request, walkways opened to reveal cool caverns lit with crystal, now turned dim. Once they had been brighter than sunlight and had cradled the ravaged and the desperate. Even Toomaaris had chosen to embed there in the early days of the city.

Ulynyx had shaved away the side of an overhanging mountain and planted grass and trees. Twice each day sprays of water erupted from mountain streams, as they followed the pattern he had set. A hidden oasis flourished within the hollowed mountain and he manipulated the layers of space to fold within themselves. As such they were invisible to the rare onlooker from above or those travelling the known routes, by what barely passed for roads. He turned his eyes towards the gathering cloud of sand in the distance and shrugged away any thoughts of the old communion of Mourangils above the surface. Ulynyx would have evicted from his storehouse of memory, if it had been possible, the day that Toomaaris refused to share essence with him, Ulynyx, leader of the Chunii and his Mourangil brother.

Toomaaris had arrived only hours before a group of his soldiers shuffled into the largest of the caverns. Ulynyx had originally named it the 'Hall of new beginnings' but lately, in the new Chunii language, it had become the 'Hall of No Regret'. Had he lived the span of a human the wretched vision would, by now, have vanished with death, however he saw it once again in the cloud of sand that swarmed in the distance.

She had been the most beautiful of the girls he had rescued and Ulynyx had seen that her intelligence outstripped her peers. They had pulled her lifeless body onto woven leaves and laid it before him. Blood from the gash at her throat spilled over the white linen dress as the First of the Chunii told of her treachery. At first Ulynyx had felt a human sorrow, tracing with his fingers the lifeless face. It had not been merely for her beauty that he had favoured Mwabi. When she spoke, it was with the wary care of one who knew that words could take her, more surely than an arrow, along paths she feared to walk. Yet she had walked them after all. In the space of time it had taken him to stand, rage had replaced sorrow. Ungrateful for all his guardianship and provision, she had intended to leave Ulyn and make known to the world the secrets of the hidden army. He had instructed that his soldiers slit the throat of any individual that left the borders of the city without his express permission. When Mwabi refused to return, they had carried out the sentence as he had demanded.

Mwabi had been the first he had chosen to take to his bed in the way of men. He had decided to give the gift of his Mourangil being to mingle with her own and to create a new beginning. The infertility of his many attempts had soured his thoughts towards her. He had ordered her body to be burnt but the image of her perfect form, stained with blood, returned to him often. He had not seen Toomaaris since that day, until he stood before him in Damascus.

Ulynyx wandered around the hidden city receiving worship as was his due. He watched the young women vanish inside their homes, still awe stricken by his presence. The wind stirred behind him but the gathering sandstorm was dismissed with a flick of his finger, redirected around the city. A gasp came from nearby and he marvelled, once again, that his birth right should appear such a miraculous power in the world upon the surface. In the upper reaches of the city he had taught his men how to move silently and he saw them now, moving with care, awaiting his guidance. Amed was hunched in discussion with the other Elite as he strode towards them. Ulynyx flinched as he saw the dressings on his back, a result of the flogging he had imposed after the failure to kill Elanur. He had found his current First in Faith squirming in the sand when they had returned from Aya Sofya and would have struck him down, had not his mercy answered the cries of the other soldiers. The Elite stood frozen as Ulynyx removed his sabre and threw it, so that its point landed within an inch of Amed's foot. He strode across to retrieve it as each man held their position. He had taught them well.

"Be ready," he told them in the language of the Chunii. "It has begun."

*

Klim felt a chill at the base of his neck, that trickled down the length of his spine; it made him stop and cover the Iridice with his hand. The forest crowded about them until nothing seemed familiar. Not the swaggering tall trunks that bent like giraffe necks towards them, nor the leafless branches snapping like firecrackers in the undergrowth. Here was a living, alien world that his telepathy could not soften nor understand. Nor could he reach the minds of the others, not even Mengebara, as if someone had simply turned off the power supply to their mental electrics. Siskin, a sharp blade of concentration, let his eyes cross Klim's in a sweep of the strange terrain. In that one glance was written reassurance, readiness, warning and alarm. Josh had retreated into his own thoughts and seemed little bothered by the sense of threat that now surrounded them. Echin looked back with interest and reached, for the second time, into the space between two trees. Once again, and even more forcibly, the trees groaned as they bent down towards him. Something slithered beneath Klim's feet and he was quickly pulled to the ground. Siskin, always as graceful as a dancer, rebounded from a collision with a solid, gnarled trunk. Echin laughed and Josh, pulled out of his reverie, looked up.

"I'm asking permission, Mactire," the Mourangil said loudly. "We need to speak."

A ghostly griffin glided past and flew between the trees above their heads but then vanished. Klim remembered the battle with the Tolbranach in Dublin when the Tanes had come to their aid. It had been Oisen who had taken the form of the mythical winged creature with its eagle head and lion body. Suddenly a door, much like a garden gate, appeared where the magical griffin had vanished. One by one they followed.

Oisen, now tall and muscular in his human form, reminded Klim a little of Siskin. As fearsome and strong as he appeared, the elemental's short, sandy hair and grave blue eyes hinted at an artistic gentleness. With just a nod of greeting he waited until all three were inside the gate, then led them to the house where Kier had once found herself recovering from the near fatal attack of the Roghuldjn. The building was larger than Samuel's cottage but possessed the same sense of timelessness. Where Samuel's place had been filled with books, this however, was like a leprechaun's hidden treasure chest. Klim had a quick eye for antiques, it had been one of his mother's interests. As Oisen led them through winding passages Klim saw that priceless, small statues and paintings were tucked away in various nooks and crannies. Eventually they reached a bright dining room, with an ornate, wooden table that could have easily belonged to a Gaelic king. Probably had, Klim reflected. At the head of it sat Mactire, facing the entrance. The cheerful, curly headed Danny, youngest of the Tanes, sat next to him and Killian stood behind them both. Klim recalled when Killian had come to their aid that summer, in the shape of a mythical chimera and without Kier, it would have cost him his life. Loretta and Lorcan, Klim surmised, were no doubt manning the Vortex, the marvellous hidden experiment that plumbed the depths of the planet.

"I told you she would give us away," Oisen said matter-of-factly as he took a seat at the table.
Klim thought Mactire looked different somehow, now older and sadder.

"What do you want?" The wolf stared out of the man.

"I've come to ask the same of you, Mactire." Without invitation, Echin pulled up a chair at the other end of the table and faced the wary eyes opposite. His companions remained standing behind him. "What is it that *you* want?" The Mourangil rebounded Mactire's question back at him. "In a matter of weeks the cycle will be ended. The Sister Spheres will align as they did when Mesa dropped the first stardust of human seed, including those of your own race."

"We are not of their kind," insisted Danny.

"And yet," Echin responded, "the double seeds of your race were intermingled with theirs. You breathe the same air and are sustained by the same planetary ecosystems. Should Belluvour succeed in rendering the planet uninhabitable to humanity, how do you think it will hold you?"

Oisen was as white as the ghostly griffin of his elemental self. "We've shut down the Vortex. His presence is like a tainted fog, we can see nothing since he escaped the Secret Vaults."

"Weeks, you say?" Mactire asked tersely.

"The December solstice," Echin confirmed.

"So you found the Runeshaper?" There was a touch of awe in his voice. "Then it's true, Kier is Candillium. And the Myriar? Is it really possible?"

"Neither the Chunii nor Belluvour believe so," Echin told him. "And yet they are both afraid enough to hunt us down."

"The Chunii! They exist?" Killian's eyes widened.

"It's too late," Mactire turned away. "All too late."

Echin spoke without emotion. "Your elemental form is dying Mactire because it is linked to your hope."

Mactire's fist came down with a bang upon the table but the Mourangil did not stir. His chair flew back as, with a growl, the Tane transformed. The handsome face and athletic body distorted, twisting into animal limbs. Grey fur covered his form until a giant Adlet wolf stood before them, teeth bared. The three men closed around the Mourangil and in turn the Tanes were soon beside the Adlet. Killian put his hand on the shoulder of the wolf, "Easy Sean," he said gently.

The breath of the great creature came in spasms, as the green eyes looked upwards and the mouth emitted a howl that Klim thought would crack the moon itself. Slowly, the fabled creature of the North vanished and in its place, once more, was Mactire. Klim felt a great sorrow to see that he appeared defeated and exhausted.

Echin slowly stood up, "You are needed, all of you."

"You have Candillium," Mactire replied dismissively. "What do you need with us?"

"Think Mactire," the Mourangil replied. "What do you hope for? When did despair creep inside this being, who can tangle with matter, explore the universe in an old Dublin terrace and be there to save the centrepiece of the Myriar when no one else saw the danger?" Mactire sat rigid in his chair as Echin continued. "I remember the Mountain King who once stood before me in this place. He spoke of a future where the Tanes and the Seeds of the Myriar would lead the new age of Moura. An age where the old borders were lost and the Sister Spheres would lend their influence to reshape the surface. Where all could hear the music of the stars and the voice of Moura. Where the magical kingdoms of imaginative belief planted sparks of rich possibility into the fertile mind to bring forth a new way, a new beginning, a new hope."

"Myth and legend," Mactire murmured unconvincingly. Echin signalled to the others to head back the way they had entered. Before following them out of the room, he turned back to the elemental beings. "Myth and legend," he repeated, "and what have the Tanes been all these years but myth and legend?"

Echin strode from the building and caught up with his three companions.

"That went well!" Siskin looked at Josh and shrugged his shoulders.

Josh gave a twisted smile, "Well we got out again at least!"

Chapter Twenty-two

The men and women of the village were overjoyed, hugging and holding each other in amazement. Kier and her two companions quietly turned back towards the hut. For some time Swift examined the space where she had created the doorway, although it was now solid. The villagers had taken guns from the soldiers and a few of the men were herding those who were still alive, those who had chosen not to shoot, over to one side. Kier came over to examine them, peering closely at three terrified youngsters. Gabbie spoke to them, confirming what Kier had already guessed. They had been groomed for service by a well-oiled propaganda machine and this was their first encounter with the reality for which they had left their homes. All three were weeping, one had soiled his newly issued trousers. Kier looked at the oldest of the village men who seemed to have taken charge, he appraised the three boys and nodded towards Kier. She turned away, secure that the fate of the misguided youths would be fairly considered.

Kier gazed at the small collection of simple dwellings, beads of sweat tingling on her forehead as the strong sun stroked her cheek. She felt a vibration at her throat, where the Key of Brunan nestled in the engraved moon on the Stone of Mesa. She watched with wonder as it shaped itself into a small bird, no larger than a wren, and flew from the engraving. The tiny wings fluttered, shimmering in the heat, disappearing beyond the village. Gabbie and Swift were mesmerised by the beautiful creature and with Kier they followed its path from the village. High above them the small bird dazzled in the sun. It flew towards the mountains whilst the three women followed, climbing on worn rock that formed the mountain track. A tree with bare white wood, leafless, akin to the ones she had seen in Reuben's cave, seemed to gain direct nourishment from the sun. It shone iridescently in the shimmering heat. The golden bird rested on one of the many branches of the white tree.

The track ended where the mountainside indented to form a cliff face and the narrow path opened out into a huge bowl before it. Gingerly they made their way around the edge and, tired from the climb, nestled their backs against the mountain. Kier acknowledged that thirst would soon drive them back to the village. Suddenly Swift gasped and jumped up, holding her hands over her ears as a crack appeared in the bottom of the sheer rock face behind them. Kier and Gabbie sprang alongside the Stozcist and all three stood watching as a seam appeared at the bottom of the mountain. Kier remembered once before standing here, a cascade of water had curtained around her and splashed a fine spray over her hot face. As the image filled her mind, water wondrously fell from a thunderous sky and began to form a lake in the hollow, empty crater below. Turning back to the mountain she saw that a gap had now appeared at the bottom of the rock face. It looked a tight, not to say impossible fit. Kier looked towards Swift, whose face was a solemn mask as she shook her head. "It has to be you first. The mountain has opened because you are here."

Kier nodded to show her acceptance. She smiled with pleasure as the golden bird flew down to her wrist, where it perched for a short while before rising to her throat to become embedded once more in the engraved circle of the Stone of Mesa. She knelt and eased herself into the small space; Gabbie and Swift, ready to follow behind.

The tunnel appeared to carve itself in front of her hands, as Kier, hot and thirsty, staving off the rising panic of confinement, scrambled along the floor of the mountain. The Key of Brunan glowed in the darkness. Stopping, she lifted her head and shoulders without thinking. Instead of the painful scrape of rock, the tunnel expanded upwards. Kier realised with a sense of amazement, that the tunnel was shaping itself in response to her movement. Taking a deep breath, she straightened her back. Kier squatted and still the walls of the tunnel extended around her. Gradually she straightened to her full height, aware of a sharp intake of breath from Gabbie behind. The ceiling that had wrapped itself around her now became a vaulted roof, barely visible. She felt tears sting her cheeks as winking lights of crystal and amethyst revealed a forest of stalagmites and stalactites. In the distance, she saw that a silver waterfall shimmered. Without doubt, this was the place where she had first met Toomaaris the Mourangil.

The three women held hands as whispers reverberated around the empty cavern that Kier had last entered in another lifetime. As before, a silver stream ran down the centre, bubbling in echoing ripples of running water. Three silver goblets stood empty beside the stream. Kneeling, Kier lifted one, dipped it into the water and signalled to Swift and Gabbie to do the same. It was as if she had thirsted all of her life for this water; like a tree nourished to its roots, able to reach the leafy limbs of its being. Turning to the younger women she saw that their eyes glowed and their bodies were tinged with a faint, silver light. No one spoke but each turned their head in an awareness of an arch that had appeared nearby. They raised themselves from the stream, entering beneath the arch to an enclosed space that sparkled with Mourangil jewels. The stones of power that they carried with them coloured in response and the Key of Brunan emitted flashes that came and went in an excited dance of light. Arwres shone amber upon a shining piece of feldspar that edged from the wall of rock. The Stone of Silence pinioned a piece of tourmaline in its diamond glow. Kier laughed, placing her hand underneath the feldspar that fell into her hands. Swift repeated the process with the tourmaline and together they laid the stones gently on the rock floor. In seconds Faer and Tormaigh emerged.

The two Mourangils were dressed in what she now recognised as the alu cloth of Ordovicia.

"The wing of an eagle, a snow tipped mountain," Kier said softly, holding out her hand to Faer who took and kissed it, his eyes luminous. She turned towards Tormaigh, extending her other hand. "A blade of grass and the night sky," she told him gently as tears ran down the faces of all three. For a long time, they held each other's hands in the miraculous cavern. Kier's whole body heaved in a massive sigh for what had been, for who had been, for all the suffering that had occurred down through the ages because she had not been.

"Kier are we still in Mengebara, what's real here?" Gabbie tugged at her friend.

"Gabbie, Swift!" cried Faer. The Mourangils embraced the two young women joyfully. Faer stepped back to Kier and placed his two hands on her shoulders. "Does Toomaaris know that you have recognised Candillium within you?" She nodded in reply. "And have you spoken?"

Kier sighed, shaking her head, "No, not really." She looked at Faer who seemed to have no problem in relating to her both as Candillium and as Kier Morton. "It's like we're the closest of strangers."

Faer seemed to understand, again put his hand on her shoulder, which she covered with her own.

"Every day," Kier told them, "I learn something more from the buried memories of Ordovicia, but there are so many things still deeply hidden. I can't find them until they make themselves known."

"But there isn't much time left," Gabbie pointed out. "That's what everyone is saying."

"The Waybearer doors are closed, so how is it that you are here?" Swift spoke as she continued to examine the glimmering crystals that winked within the protected space.

"When Candillium first walked into this cavern the source, the heart of Moura, came to meet her. It offered her a link, the finest and purest of threads that could weave between the physical, blur the boundaries of the mind and nourish the spirit deep within." Faer glanced towards the silver stream. "Even now it flows to relieve your thirst and because of that the boundaries are broken in this place; the Tomer has allowed us to come to you. This stream flows only in the presence of Candillium and will allow only those of the Myriar to quench their thirst."

They were all a little awestruck as Kier smiled, gold flashing from the stone around her neck.

"The Key of Brunan!" Faer reached to examine the coiled gold within the Stone of Mesa.

198

"Josh was very brave," Tormaigh commented. "Unethora was not gentle when she verified the Creta."

"You know that the Sister Spheres are returning very soon?" Faer asked.

"The December solstice," Kier repeated what Echin had told them.

The glance of excitement and apprehension between the two Mourangils was now obvious to Kier. She had no doubt that previously she would have seen them as impassive. It came back to her in a surge of hope how much she had loved these two beings in the past and still loved them in the present.

"We have to find the Realm of Resonance," Gabbie explained, "to bring back the Key of Talitha."

"What is the Key of Talitha," Swift questioned, "and why do we have to bring it back?"

"And why doesn't Echin," Gabbie demanded, hands on her hips, "ever tell us this stuff?"

"Because my little friend," Tormaigh wore his awkward, thinking expression as he towered above her, his long fingers moving along a bony chin, "he lacks our erudition in these matters."

Kier laughed, "I seriously doubt that."

Swift began to tremble, she was never comfortable inside a cave. Tormaigh pointed to where a stone seat circled a raised dais. "Even a Stozcist can remain here without fear," he reassured her. As they moved nearer to the dais a book made of alu paper opened. The pristine, blank pages folding apart at the centre. "There are three keys," Tormaigh began, his green eyes glowing emerald amidst the winking lights set into the walls of the small enclosure. "The Key of Brunan, to be recovered by the male aspect of the Myriar. To the female aspect is allotted the search for the Key of Talitha. The third key is the Auric Flame."

"The Auric Flame," repeated Swift.

"The most elusive and powerful of the three. We believe that Brunan is of the present."

"That's why it was able to keep me here, help me hold on to life, and to show us the way to this place," Kier postulated.

"Yes, indeed," Faer agreed.

"And Talitha?" asked Swift.

"Resolution of the past creates possibility for the future," Tormaigh said, looking closely at Gabbie and Swift. "Talitha lies within that dimension where the past resonates against the backdrop of human existence."

"So, the Auric Flame represents the future?" said Kier.

"Toomaaris believes that it encompasses all three."

"And why do we need these keys?" Gabbie queried, looking confused.

Swift's tone was abrupt, "It seems obvious that without the Key of Brunan Kier would not have survived." Tormaigh, his glance darting to Kier, explained further, his tone gentle. "As the race of man develops, the Myriar continues to be a vehicle for evolution. Like the Mourangils and all other living beings on the planet, mankind possesses the potential for a direct link to Moura and through this planet to others. The Myriar is the embodiment of that link and also of the primordial connection to your original home on Mesa. Over all this long age Mesa has reforged its composition. The touch of Candillium upon the fragment of the original planet began a chain reaction. Universal law brings the Sister Spheres to align once more in the exact formation that they did so during your inception here. During the

Alignment, it will be determined which species of the planet will continue to survive on the surface and those that will begin the process of extinction."

"Extinction?" Gabbie repeated, alarmed.

"A new epoch," Faer replied. "Toomaaris discovered that the three keys existed and he believes they are integral to the new epoch, in a way that has not yet been revealed. In your language, they are fabled planetary heirlooms."

"And Belluvour, now that he is unbound?"

"Ah," said Tormaigh, "we feel the powerful sway of his influence in the fabric of the planet. Danubin is at last united with the one she has chosen to serve."

"Ugh!" was Gabbie's comment. Tormaigh's expression was grim. "Already mankind has created vast swathes of the planet that eat away at that which sustains you. The dark energies will exploit these places very quickly and they will work to add to man's own ability to cause destruction. The Devourils and the race of man compete for life upon the surface. The obdurates already begin to populate the Barins."

"The Barins?" Gabbie asked.

Faer sighed, "The Barins are what we have come to call those areas where the current ecosystems have been altered or destroyed to the detriment of all life. Much was entrusted to mankind and now Belluvour bends his power to show that you have betrayed that trust."

Kier swallowed, "And Ulynyx?"

"Ulynyx, like so many of our kind, had little faith in the return of Candillium and the evolution of the Seeds of the Myriar. On the other hand, he abhorred, as did all Mourangils, the destruction of Ordovicia and wished mankind well. In these later years, he strived to help your race and achieved many laudable changes, effectively preventing the Virenmor from stirring hatred and mistrust in some of the world's most vulnerable places. He lent his energy to some of the most revered of your kind and helped to enable miracles of human endeavour."

"And now?"

"Sadly," Faer glanced towards a large onyx jewel that seemed dull and lifeless in comparison to the glittering stones around it, "he has succumbed to the same ambitions that he despised. He is no longer a Mourangil. Perhaps when he sees this fully he will turn to Belluvour for his continued existence or it may be that in his blindness he will continue to oppose the unbound one."

"And what did you and Tormaigh believe?" asked Kier. Faer reached for her hand. "That your love would reach to us from whatever realm you inhabited, that Moura was implanted in your being. That you were ever the jewel at the heart of Toomaaris and he was ever embedded in yours."

Kier's eyes filled, "And can't you ever give us your company again?"

Tormaigh shook his head sadly. "At times of Alignment the Mourangils serve only Moura. We support with our embedded presence during this time of encompassing change. Later, when the Sister Spheres have departed, we will look once more to the surface."

 Kier asked softly, "What about Toomaaris?" Swift looked stricken at the question. Of the three women, she seemed to align more with Echin's Mourangil form than the human being that had become so vital a part of their lives. Kier was answered by an expression of grief and pain that she wished she was still unable to read.

"He has given up the jewelled kingdoms," explained Tormaigh.

"For us?" Gabbie's eyes filled.

"For the Myriar," Kier corrected.

Gabbie was undeterred as she turned to her friend, "For you," she stated with certainty.

Kier could not speak. Deep within she felt the truth of Gabbie's words and it was too much.

"The book!" Gabbie moved quickly towards the dais to see that shapes had appeared across the white page. Kier went forward to read them but Gabbie had already begun to translate what she was seeing. "They're making sounds," she said in wonder and concentration. "Notes of music and each one brings an image." As she spoke a deep, booming, bell like sound resonated from the dais.

"We have to find the White Chapel," the Inscriptor stated.

Kier looked utterly confused as Gabbie continued. "The White Chapel is the doorway to the Realm of Resonance."

Chapter Twenty-three

In the Great Grecian Hall, the pillars were scorched black, as the Devourils left a permanent tattoo of their presence. Those who had left the kingdoms of the Mourangils inhabited the stone she had so painstakingly prepared. The dark energies of her vicious presence in the world had wound the ancient marble to obdurate. It had taken her lifetimes of infected evil but she had succeeded. The one who had supplied her dark power, elevated her into the elite corners of malignant force, now stalked the marble floor of the great open air temple. He inhabited the body he had created so long ago to goad Toomaaris with its mockery of human life. He strode like a dark Apollo, sleek black obsidian skin covering a perfectly formed body, yet absent of genitalia. This facet of mankind's ability to generate was wiped from the concept he had first created within the Waybearer when he had stolen Candillium and roared his volcanic malice across the land of Ordovicia. The eyes were lidless and had no iris, dark orbs of fathomless hatred.

Danubin trembled as his rasping voice rebounded within the great hall. She knew his language of old, for it was the language of destruction and despair, one she had come to use so often. "Already there are vast areas that man has made uninhabitable, destroying the hand that feeds him. In these Barins we can create our cities, build new kingdoms above the surface that are void of the infection to which Moura was subjected so long ago. Danubin you will bring to us the bodies that you have prepared for our service."

She could hardly speak or stand, her back crawled with the sensation of fear that had been her weapon of choice to inflict upon others. She knew little of its disabling effects upon herself. By sheer will she forced her legs to hold her upright and with a deep breath propelled her voice.

"I will call them to this place Lord," she answered, "and I will prepare for them cups of death, as once we administered to your enemies long ago in Mesopotamia." He dismissed her with a perfectly sculptured hand that nevertheless appeared deformed in its parody of human gesture. She had little thought for the lives that she was about to sacrifice, those that she had manipulated and blackmailed into service. And she knew that Belluvour, should it be needed, would snatch her own body in an instant. Further, that the energy of her demise would not be captured by the Secret Vaults and transmuted into another powerful figure to serve his purpose in human history. Released from his bonds Belluvour clearly intended to grind all humanity into a dust that could never reshape itself again into human life. The Virenmor were to be used and discarded, including herself. The bitter truth scorched her being more than any of the painful burns that had recently been inflicted in the course of her service.

Still trembling, she nodded her assent to issue the call her people had waited generations to hear. The call to paradise on this remote Mediterranean island, the call to directly serve the Lord that had at last, and largely by the hand of the Virenmor, loosened his bonds and escaped the Secret Vaults. She looked around at the swarm of dark presence in the once beautiful chamber and felt the rising bile in her throat. Walking, mustering all the

control of long practice, she turned towards the exit.
Once outside in the polluted sunshine she vomited
uncontrollably.

*

After they had left the Tanes's hidden domain Echin
directed them to the boat they had used when staying in
Dublin. In the aftermath of the battle with the Tolbranach
Siskin had given little thought to the long, canal barge.
Echin had arranged for it to be waiting for them on a
canal in County Wexford, in the east, near to the village
where the Tanes had created their elemental space. Echin
had already made changes, covering the boat in runes
written by what seemed to be a light emitted from the
largest diamond Siskin had ever set eyes upon. The runes
appeared like a fine liquid stream upon the wood. Once
they were in place Josh had been enlisted to paint the
outside of the boat. The natural beauty of his art had the
Mourangil laughing as the Creta began to produce
stunning colour, the precursor to a magnificent landscape.
   "We need less attention Josh, not more," Echin told
him. "Simply another name and a coat of paint."
Josh shrugged his shoulders and began covering up his
flourish of colour in favour of a dark blue. He created
stylish white letters however, for the new name,
'Marianne'. Echin nodded with approval at the name of
Josh's mother which completely covered the runes he had
created.
   "They're not far away." Josh reminded the Mourangil
that his parents were based in a nearby county of Ireland.
   "I promised you and myself that I would not
deliberately bring her to danger again."

The young man nodded, resigned to the situation. "I know, it just seems a long time since I was there."

Echin had left them to continue the changes and later Siskin, walking on the deck to breathe in the verdant, Irish countryside, heard the poignant tone of homesickness lace through the artist's naturally buoyant melody. "If you've finished that you might give me a hand," he suggested.

Siskin had completely refurbished the interior using the same techniques that had been used to create his unique, sound driven car. He had also injected some of the new melody he had formulated into the current systems. Klim amplified the sonics, planes of sound unused by mankind but accessible to Siskin, using the same subtle manipulation of energy that he applied to thought. The Reeder was fitting the solidified power source, in the shape of something resembling ceiling lights, into the wooden interior. There was a row of two seated sofas on either side of the narrow aisle, where Siskin pointed to the windows, "We need to see without being seen Josh." The artist noted the number of small cabin windows and went to fetch his kit from outside. He was applying a paste to the last of the windows when Echin returned with food. The Mourangil whistled with approval.

"If it had wings we could fly it!" Klim laughed.

"We don't need wings," Echin told them. "Switch it on Siskin."

The musician obliged by singing a low chord and the receptors within the boat's interior came to life. Echin laid the sandwiches he had brought, on the table and stepped back, concentrating. The interior was suffused with a misty glow, emitted from the receptors that Siskin had fitted into the ceiling. Only the outline of each person was visible in the soft cloud within the boat.

"Awesome." Josh and Klim were hanging over the rim of the barge. In a matter of seconds, they had been transported three hundred metres down the canal.

"Hope it's cloaked," Klim added.

"It is now." Siskin fiddled with the flickering transmitters, his lips were shaped to whistle but this appeared soundless, as it was not a frequency to which his companions could respond.

"There are a few modifications we can make so that you can transport without me," Echin commented. He called Klim over to explain to him the mental connections that the Reeder would need to make in order to be able to teleport the barge. Over the next twenty minutes the mist came and went within the interior and the barge moved back and forth along the canal.

Echin continued to examine the boat whilst the others ate. Afterwards he dragged Siskin outside to make some adjustments. Josh was pouring coffee into good sized mugs when they returned.

"Klim, how's Mengebara looking?" asked Echin. In answer Klim sat apart and began to gather his concentration, this time slowing down his breathing and subduing the disturbing fear that had gnawed at his insides since the women had left. The others cleared away the remains of the supper and waited patiently until at last Klim opened his eyes. In them was a look of discovery. "I'm beginning to understand, finally," he seemed hesitant.

"What?" nudged Josh.

"The words that Kier read, 'Into Mengebara will pour the army of the Iridice'. "I think it's about changing minds."

Echin nodded his approval. "Belluvour," he told them, "has long discovered that the best way to kill mankind is to get the human race to aid in the process. He can better destroy man with man's cooperation. There are areas, named the Barins, where even the Mourangils have been unable to balance the damage that your race has inflicted upon the surface. The wide stretches of deforestation, the islands that have been abandoned due to rising sea level, the deltas that have choked because of redirected rivers. By the December solstice," he continued, "Belluvour will seek to accelerate the destructive processes that man has put in place. A human race that has wiped out its own source of survival has already begun the process of extinction. He will also target all those who have attempted to redress the deterioration. Unless we can prevent it, many good people already attempting to align themselves to Moura, will soon perish."

"Isn't it a little late for changing minds?" Siskin suggested.

"I don't think so," Klim told him. "I can sense it, the desire to make things right. It just somehow has to be channelled."

"We will also have to face an army of Devourils who, thanks to Danubin, have now usurped human bodies."

"What! She's placed on the planet more Nephragms?" Josh choked on his horror. Klim's mouth twisted in remembrance of the powerful Devouril to whom his uncle had given allegiance. "How?"

"Danubin joined the camp of Ulynyx after handing up an army of the Virenmor to Belluvour."

Siskin felt his breath leave him in a long whistle. "You have someone in the Chunii?"

Echin did not answer his question but continued. "Their stolen bodies will last until around the December solstice. They can inhabit and extend these polluted places, they need no sustenance but their own Devouril state. However, they are not like Nephragm, who stalked the surface of Moura for so long. He knew the human race well and used his knowledge to cause greater harm. Many of these beings were Mourangils not so long ago. They have been persuaded that the continued existence of the human race is no longer in the interests of Moura." A cloud passed over his face. "They will vastly accelerate the damage already caused and they will do so in human bodies, as a way of emphasising that mankind has brought about its own destruction."

Siskin felt his determination become a palpable force.

"What of this Ulynyx? Are we fighting a battle on two fronts?"

"Sadly yes," replied Echin. "Ulynyx and the Chunii wish our destruction as much as Belluvour. He's crazed with his own idea of power and control over the human race. The Myriar is like one of your fairy stories to him, he has never accepted that Candillium could return or that man could nurture the Seeds down through the generations."

"So, which do we tackle first?" Siskin looked like a soldier ready for the challenge.

"Neither."

"Because they're coming after us!" Josh guessed. Echin nodded.

"Great!" Josh replied, his face grim.

As if a signal had just been given the door at the back of the narrowboat suddenly burst open.

Chapter Twenty-four

"The White Chapel? You're sure?" Kier stepped nearer to the dais. The silver stream tinkled in the main part of the cavern. The walls in the arched alcove were starlit with Mourangils in their natural state. The Key of Brunan blinked its light upon the runes and the result was a mist of silvery sunshine that shone over the convoluted shapes. The sound became clear, a throbbing and mournful bell that had summoned her to the place where she had first seen the Bound One depicted in stone. The place where her sister had been murdered instead of her, where the Key of Brunan had found her on the brink of death.

"But how do we find the doorway again?" Gabbie looked at Swift who nodded with resignation.

"I will try," she told them.

Faer looked thoughtful, "Kier, think. How did the White Chapel come to be in Mengebara?"

Gabbie caught her breath, "It's inside you," she said confidently.

"But it's a real place!" Kier shook her head.

"Didn't Faer say the Realm of Resonance is about the past?" Gabbie persisted.

Tormaigh nodded encouragement. "I think Gabbie's right. You three have already linked your consciousness on this journey. If you can find the source of the memory within you, I think you will all be able to pass into the Realm of Resonance."

"Swift?" Kier turned to the Stozcist. "Do you think so too?"

"I will go where you lead me, inside or out."
Kier squeezed her hand. She led them back to the silver stream. Slowly she emptied her mind until all she could hear was the stream trickling through the cavern. She sat cross legged, cupping her hands and then reached into the silvery water. Swift and Gabbie mimicked her movements, knelt on either side. As Kier scooped the water to her lips her whole body trembled with its liquid touch. She focused on the White Chapel in the Northumbrian hills. She recalled the forest around it, how rich the air felt, but the vision dimmed. Kier could not, even in memory, travel back there. She opened her eyes, defeated. Her friends looked at her with concern. Tormaigh and Faer knelt opposite on the other side of the stream.

"Try again Kier, we will be with you," Tormaigh reached out his hands to hold hers. Kier let herself sink into the memory that she had relived so many times. The White Chapel appeared just as it had done on the fateful day of her sister's death.

The cavern shimmered and fell away. Standing up, Kier found that she was on a path, high up, the sun near to setting. The leaves were green with summer and she called to her friends; the two young women were just visible at the point where the track curved upwards towards a forest. They came forward and she laughed at their childlike apprehension. What beautiful jewels they wore, glittering diamond and amber in the ebbing light.

Two other shapes outlined the path. It seemed as if a single, strong blade of grass had risen from the ground, more like a standing palm leaf of beguiling emerald. It

212

dispersed the mottled shadows of the forest and Kier was fascinated by the prisms of light caught within it. She took a step forward to move down the path but was halted by the sound of wings, swooping into place. A magnificent white headed eagle draped its huge, dark wings downwards over old grey stone. The feather tips were edged with white crystal feldspar.

The two young women caught up with Kier, who turned back along the path into the thick of the forest. In the middle of a clearing was a very old church. Kier felt her breath catch at the sight; a searing pain struck her chest. The sounds of the forest were now blotted out by the rapid pulse of her own rushing blood. She turned away but the tallest of the two young women, grave and stately in her beauty, reached out her hand. The small blonde with her heart shaped face, that was not made for sadness, nevertheless seemed equally serious. Holding hands with both Kier turned back towards the church and saw that the solid, hardwood door was open.

Inside, the white altar beckoned her. She heard a plane overhead, a droning sound that pierced the sky. All three trembled and turned towards the back of the chapel where a girl, around fifteen, stood clearly horror stricken; her eyes fixed on a standing stone, the size of an old way marker often seen on country roads. The droning became louder and a second girl, a little older, came running in just as glass shattered above where the first was standing. In a moment, she had thrown aside the younger girl but a shard of glass, falling like an arrow from the shattered, stained glass window, pierced her heart.

The younger version of herself vanished as Kier ran to her dying sister. "Martha!" she keened, unable to save the one who had saved her. Kier could not move, could not think, only roll into a ball of disabling grief. She had no idea how long she had spent huddled within the maelstrom of emotion on the floor of the chapel. It was the touch of sun at the back of her neck that made her raise her head. On either side lay Swift and Gabbie, she knew them now. Both were fast asleep, they had curled against her as she descended into a well of regret and despair. Vaguely she remembered shaking away their attempts to comfort her. Every nuance of emotion that she had fielded from her everyday existence, that had balled itself into a fist within the dark spaces of her mind, every drop of poisonous guilt over he sister's death, had all been spilled.

Kier walked peacefully to the back of the chapel and examined the old stone that had been the source of her grief. All markings were now erased. The Key of Brunan appeared as a golden bracelet around her wrist as she laid her hand upon the tablet. It shattered, disintegrating into a heap of dust. There were no tears left. Gabbie and Swift jumped awake at the sound of the stone breaking.

"Kier?" Gabbie said gently, as if to a child, looking so young herself as she rubbed her hands across her eyes. Kier nodded in response. "It's okay," she said softly. The young blonde ran down the aisle to wrap her small arms around her friend's waist, holding her tightly. Swift examined the marble altar. "It has the feel of a Waybearer." Kier placed her hand against the cold surface that became warm to her touch. Swift had both hands pressed towards the centre and her eyes were closed in concentration. "More voices," she said, with an edge of fear.

"Mateo?" Gabbie asked anxiously.

Swift had taken her hands away and stepped down from the raised altar, shaking her head.

"This is the way in," she said confidently. "We have found the Realm of Resonance."

The Key of Brunan uncoiled itself from around Kier's wrist and touched the centre of the altar, where Swift's fingers had created a circular depression. The golden key floated like molten liquid into the hollow and filled the space. The chapel, as it was standing, fell away. Brunan formed a golden archway and Kier could see that it led into a long passageway lined with bare sandstone. She reached for her friend's hands on either side. "Together," she whispered as they stepped forward.

*

Siskin and Klim had pulled the others down to the floor, even as the Irish brogue yelled at them to stand up.

"Sorry boys, no time to knock. There's Devouril activity showing up in the Vortex and it's heading this way!"

The narrowboat filled with Tanes. Mactire's grin was wide as he took Josh's outstretched hand. Killian grimaced as he squashed in last.

"How did they find us?" Klim turned to Echin and then back to Mactire. "And I thought the Vortex was closed down and only looked underground."

"We looked underground the better to see what's about us. Loretta's reopened the channels and found a way to observe the dark shadow above the surface."

"How did you find us?" asked Siskin.

"Once you have crossed over to our elemental world it leaves its mark on mortal men. Interestingly we couldn't follow Echin or Kier but you three were a breeze."

"It isn't us that the Devourils are following" stated Echin calmly. "Danubin's thirst for revenge lies with the Tanes."

Mactire looked towards Siskin who was already in the process of cloaking the boat, ensuring invisibility. "Then we need to move faster than a canal barge," Mactire's tone was urgent; he and the others were already turning back towards the towpath.

"Wait," Echin called to them. Mactire shook his head. "Don't be daft man, we can't stay here. This narrowboat's no place to meet them."

"Hold on!" Echin shouted. The interior of the boat became lost in white mist, echoes of a music whose sound could only be dimly heard added to a sense of vibration. The Tanes were visibly unnerved as the mist disappeared seconds later and Killian hurried to the door.

"We've moved and we're no longer in Wexford!" There were cries of amazement from the others who ran to confirm Killian's observation. Klim eased himself between them and steered the boat over a remote stretch of the canal, where large reeds edged the towpath on either side. Echin ushered them all inside, signalling silence. "Keep it cloaked," he instructed Siskin.

Siskin felt the onslaught first, the thick oppressive drone, like thousands of cockroaches clicking together, thickening the air directly above them. Even inside the safety of the barge they felt choked by the dark shadow that now blotted out natural light. Siskin looked suspiciously at Mactire who stepped back angrily. "No Lute, we didn't bring them to your door on purpose!"

Echin stepped between them. "They're heading north." Mactire's anger subsided into pallor as he took in the import of the Mourangil's words. "Loretta! Where are they now?"

"A few miles outside Dublin."

"Hang on, we'll move nearer."

Echin signalled to Siskin and Klim. "You know how to move this without me?" They each nodded in answer, seeming equally disturbed.

Impatiently Killian interrupted, "I'll meet you there!" He began running down the aisle.

"No! You won't last five minutes in elemental form." Killian tried to free his arm from the Mourangil's hold.

"It's what they're looking for!" Echin insisted. Suddenly they all fell backwards as the boat tilted.

"Sorry!" Siskin adjusted the controls and brought the craft level once more. Klim concentrated on amplifying the sonics. In seconds, the interior of the barge once again dissolved into a shapeless, white cloud as the two men transported the narrowboat, unseen, to the outskirts of Dublin.

"Get some seat belts in this feckin' thing, will ya!" Oisen slumped into one of the seats.

"At least you can fly," returned Mactire, hanging on.

"Do you think they know about the Vortex?" asked Danny.

Echin helped Siskin settle the boat into its resting place, as he replied. "I think Danubin will have put significant resources into finding the woman who betrayed her. You said Loretta has been working on the Vortex again. They may not know what's in the house but, if she knows it, Danubin will have given up Loretta's location to Belluvour. He would prize the capture of an elemental."

217

"The Liffey!" Killian shouted as he recognised his surroundings through the portholes. "Make sure we can be seen for God's sake man, or someone'll hit us. It's busy on this stretch!"

"I've brought it as near as I can," Siskin said calmly.

"Danubin never knew about the Vortex," Mactire reasoned.

"It must be shut down," Echin insisted. "Permanently."

"We already made that decision. It is too risky to continue. We figured that if we can track Belluvour that way the Devourils would eventually become aware of our observation." He swore under his breath, "I hope she managed it in time." The Tanes emptied from the barge in seconds and Josh followed. Echin called to Siskin and Klim as they too made to leave.

"Cloak the boat Siskin. Nothing will come near."

"But…" started Klim.

"Stay here both of you," he added. "We will need to move as soon as they get back. With or without me…. remember don't wait, I'll find you."

He left through the bow of the boat before either got a chance to say anything more.

Chapter Twenty-five

There was no sound from their endless trudging within the tunnel, no echo of feet upon tiles, no whisper from any other but themselves. Gabbie was lagging behind her long legged friends. "How long do you think it will take?" she called to them.

It was getting darker. "I've no idea," Kier whispered. "We need light."

A few seconds later the walls on either side became filled with runes, as light flashed on both sides, bouncing from the jewels worn by the three companions. Gabbie swallowed as she read the runes; like the others they evoked sets of images. She looked towards Kier who continued forward, even as the story of each of them played out along the walls.

"What does it say?" Swift was the only one of the three who was unable to translate the shapes.

"It's the three of us," answered Kier. "I can see you both as girls and myself too, it's showing some of the events in our lives. Do you want me to describe it Swift?"

"No," she replied firmly.

Gabbie's eyes filled with tears as she saw herself as a toddler, holding the hand of a woman she knew to be her mother. She went to touch the wall but as fast as the images appeared they vanished in favour of others, each further along than the last, so that they had to keep moving in order to see them. They saw Swift on El Silencio in Peru, running from Mateo, discovering for the first time her talent as a Stozcist. Gabbie watched as the young girl ran past them and plunged the beach into darkness during her battle with the Devouril, Galinir.

219

Further on, the sky was bright once more and she had in her hands the Stone of Silence.

On the other side of the wall Kier watched the events on Whistmorden, their battles with Magluck Bawah and finding the Stone of Mesa. It ran like a movie screen with no chronology to note, as some scenes were repeated several times in each of their lives. Kier heard Gabbie's gasp of horror when she saw Danubin approach her mother; it was clear that the cup she offered contained a lethal dose of poison. Her mother's last thoughts, and these were open to them, were of the little girl she would leave behind. Gabbie, choked with emotion, stopped walking but Kier noticed that Gabbie continued to move as if she were on some airport escalator. Kier saw her look away and she guessed that Gabbie would gladly have given up her gift, at that moment, if it meant that she, like Swift, could not see these images.

Kier could see that there were glimpses of herself working as a chambermaid, finding Adam in a homeless hostel, playing with Martha and Gally. Swift, hungry, eyes dancing with fear, trying to sell woven bracelets to tourists. Gabbie sitting under a large oak tree with Klim, the Iridice shining its cats-eye in the moonlight. How little we really see of other people's lives, and perhaps even our own, she silently reflected.

Without warning a thundering sound came from behind, like rushing water. Kier put out her arms and flattened the three of them to one side, while the shadowy shapes of men and women ran past them, almost flying, disappearing into the tunnel ahead. Gabbie shivered, the tunnel had become darker and the lights on the walls had stopped. They walked on, hand in hand, trudging silently. Equally as suddenly the noise had ended.

Gabbie was slightly behind the other two and inched forwards between them as they came to an abrupt halt. Ahead everything was black, a complete void. A voice commanded, with words Kier could not understand. It seemed alien, there was no sense of humanity. Behind, the tunnel stretched out dark, long and straight. The voice rang out again.

"Do you understand it Gabbie?" asked Kier.

"Yes," she replied and Kier saw that she held back the automatic 'can't you?' Echin had said that Kier had some of all their particular talents but the trait was the strongest in each respective Seed.

"It's telling us to go back," Gabbie's voice trembled. "It says we don't belong here."

"We have to cross," Kier concluded simply. She was certain.

"But we can't see," objected Gabbie.

"Our eyes are often the blindest part of all," Swift stated, her voice remote. "In the deepest parts of Moura, I have no eyes to see but matter weaves around me and I sense its presence. I will go first if you wish."
Kier reached for their hands. "We go together."

"I feel as if you're telling me to go sky diving without a parachute," Gabbie had begun to shake. Kier squeezed Gabbie's hand tight against her own and waited until the trembling stopped.

"Ready?" She asked.

"Ready," lied Gabbie.

*

Josh ran like a deer but he could barely keep up with the Tanes, who skirted in and out of the alleyways towards

221

the three storey building that looked so ordinary. Yet it housed such a powerful secret in the middle of this quiet Dublin street. Entering through the back door the Tanes had vanished inside. Josh had halted in the cobbled alleyway to catch his breath when a hand on his shoulder pulled him back. "Wait," Echin whispered, going past Josh and indicating that he should follow him to the right of the building. Josh squatted beneath the window, where they were hidden from the back door by the stone steps that led up to it. The Mourangil signalled to Josh to stay put and disappeared through the stone into the building. The moon was ready to take possession of the sky, it hung milky and full, waiting for darkness. The Mourangil resurfaced in a matter of minutes and Josh felt his heart chill at his friend's words. "Get out of here," he said chillingly. "The room is full of Devourils. Mactire's van is round the front." He passed Josh a set of keys. "Give it ten minutes then go. If I can get the others out I will but don't wait for me, I'll catch up when I can."

Josh took the keys but shook his head. "No."

"We can't risk you Josh, you're one of the Seeds."

"I'm not going anywhere except in there."

Echin looked at his young friend. "They have the Tanes but can't recognise their true nature. It seems impossible to me that they won't recognise you as a being of great power." He glanced to where the Chalycion lay at Josh's throat, glowing in the moonlit night. "I can no longer see if the stone illuminates you or you illumine the stone. The Devourils have stolen the bodies of the Virenmor, they may try to do the same to you."

Josh nodded, his light blue eyes glinting determination, as he started to head for the steps. Echin pulled him back, resigned.

"It's just possible that they're too blind to notice your true nature. Hide the Chalycion. I'll take you through," he indicated towards the wall. "They're all over the building. It can't be on your body."

Josh folded the Chalycion in a large, brown leaf that he picked up from the yard and buried it in the soil that edged the nearest bush. He remembered what he had learned of illusion and that he was the Creta. Concentrating on the area he created an illusory appearance of concrete. Bending over the precious and now hidden stone, he took in a deep breath and sighed outwardly. He asked himself the question, 'Am I ready to die today?' After a moment of probing self-examination, he had the answer - *'yes.'*

*

The darkness was complete. Kier remembered that she had stood in this place once before, not long after Martha had died and when Gally had returned to university. Increasingly she found that she spent hours alone, her parents' bickering now replaced by their inability to communicate with one another at all. Mostly they tried to hurt each other by absence or perhaps they couldn't stand to be in the house without Martha or with their other daughter who, Kier believed, they blamed for her death. She often sat in her sister's bedroom and chatted to Martha, feeling comforted by a sense of her presence. Many hours she sat lost in thought, lost in the sound of her own breath. On one such occasion Kier had found herself in a dream like state, still waking, just where she was now standing. Alone and fearful, she had known that she had the choice to enter this space. Perhaps she lacked the courage or the confidence to cross, for she had retreated back to the barren, Cheshire home.

"Ready," Gabbie said, her warm, small fingers tightly gripping Kier's hand. On the other side, she felt the cool clasp of Swift whose shoulder rubbed against her own. Kier stepped into the void.

There were no physical sensations, none. No sense of air moving around her nostrils, of light upon her face, no touch, no vibration that whispered against the drum of her ear. And yet there was movement, there was light and there was sound. Fine threads of energy constricted and released like breath. Waves of blackness unravelled their composition to reveal plunging purples and diamond stars. Phrases of music instrumented all with a sweeping tide of haunting melody. It spoke to her of letting go as she travelled in a river of her own debris, clinging to jagged branches of doubt and fear, fighting through tangled weeds of rejection and regret. Exhausted, she gave in to the flow, beginning to let the river wipe away the life she had failed to embrace.

"You do not belong here," the music was inside her, coming from her throat as Kier remembered her body, raising her hand to grasp the Stone of Mesa. The Key of Brunan stretched like silk to encircle her wrist and she saw its golden light shine towards an embankment across to her right. Kier hauled herself onto ground that was anything but solid. Kneeling, she watched the dark water pass by, a morass of charged energy. A diamond flashed and Swift pulled herself onto the left hand shore. Down the centre of the torrent the tiny figure of Gabbie thrashed blindly as Arwres winked an urgent amber. The Key of Brunan stretched from Kier's wrist to wrap itself around the small body, holding her against the fast flowing water. Kier tried to pull her back to the bank but other hands were reaching for the golden cord. Swift calmly stepped out into the water and the flow around her became a still pool, waist deep. She pulled Gabbie's still thrashing body into the stillness of the pool and together they alighted onto the opposite bank. The Key of Brunan dropped into the water, where it vanished into golden droplets to return once again, moments later, onto Kier's wrist. Swift looked towards Kier, as she continued to calm Gabbie and Kier nodded quietly in return. They each turned towards the path that again lay ahead of them.

Chapter Twenty-six

Once again Josh asked himself 'Am I ready to die today?' It was the most liberating question he knew and he had asked the same question most days over the last year. Since the first time it sank in that he was a part of someone else's hope. Since the first time he had placed the Chalycion jewel around his neck, treasured from the early stirrings of civilisation. All of what he had been only mattered in that it made him more of what he was now. Even his love for Loretta was pinned below the surface; he had to be able to move into the only thing of importance, a different love, one shared by five others and the rest of mankind.

So yes, he was ready to die today because then he could project himself to a point at the utmost outer corner of his consciousness, that left everything behind apart from his intrinsic being. And that is how he travelled through the stone with a Mourangil for the first time, fully conscious, allowing himself to sink into the fathomless depth of an individual who nurtured and nourished and who shone with the light of Moura. Even with the danger surrounding him his fingers itched to paint the tremulous image of the dense energy that, at the touch of the Mourangil, moved aside to accommodate their presence. His glimpse of existence as one of the jewelled beings begged the question, once again, how Echin could give to them so much of his time and threaten his continuation as a Mourangil.

The shuffling of feet sounded in the outer corridor. As quietly as possible they entered through the fridge door, where Mactire had previously showed them how he used light illusion to hide the entrance to the Vortex. Josh was immediately aware of a chill that raked up the hairs on his forearms and on the back of his neck. The impulse to run was almost overpowering and his limbs began to freeze. Somehow, they worked themselves to follow Echin as he stepped into the central chamber that housed the Vortex. The back of the house was basically artwork. A sham to hide the laboratory that contained the Vortex over three floors. The steel doors were open but the huge column of diamond laced glass, that filled the centre of the lab, had been replaced by a central, solid pillar. So Loretta had succeeded in shutting down the Vortex. Echin went quietly ahead towards the hall that led to Mactire's study on the left but Josh crept towards the lab, his body concealed behind the steel doors, his head angled to search for Loretta.

At the computers around the pillar sat a number of ordinary looking people concentrating on screens. Ordinary, that was, until one turned his head and fixed his gaze on Josh. The eyes were hard, black obsidian and looked at him with a detached curiosity. In the flash of that obsidian eye, before Josh could move, the stolen human body of the Devouril was next to his. His heart contracted but with such speed, there was nowhere to run. There would be no need to draw this figure, so clearly alien to all things human. He wore the jacket and trousers of a professional executive but his movement was awkward and stiff. Josh dared not look round for Echin but instead said nothing, did nothing. The pretend man, as Josh phrased it to himself, reached out an arm to grasp him, black shards glinted at the knuckles. He did not resist. The hold was not painful but firm, leading him through the large, hidden room and out into the front of the house where Mactire had his study. As they walked across without speech Josh reflected that this was not the clouded emotion of Magluck Bawah, nor the broiling hatred of Belluvour. There was no humanity here but nor was there the gratuitous human violence of the Virenmor and Danubin.

The body had been kept in good shape but he doubted that the Devouril had any awareness of this fact. Josh thought back to what Faer and Tormaigh had told him about those who had chosen recently to follow Belluvour. It was his guess that these detached, distorted beings could well be the ones to which he referred. The small study was full of the Tanes who looked deceptively mild and somewhat confused. Mactire raised his eyebrows as Josh was added to their captive group and the door was locked again from the outside. Josh lifted his hands and shoulders in a gesture of puzzlement.

"Not what I expected either," Mactire told him tightly, his eyes flicking to the corners of the room. Josh took it as a warning that hidden cameras or microphones had been installed and that these were accessible to the intruders. He scanned the room and immediately became aware that Loretta was not with them. The warning in Mactire's eyes and the hint of a shake of his head told him not to ask about her. And where was Echin? Automatically Josh put his hand towards the Chalycion but then remembered he had removed the stone. He let his hand rest on his throat and closed his eyes, mentally banishing its residue from his body in order to conceal any trace of the stone from these creatures. His eyes opened to scan the room.

The shelves, previously stacked with books and papers, were now empty. He wondered if this had been done by Loretta and Lorcan. The latter's face gave nothing away and Josh was certain that he should not provoke anything that would reveal the true nature of the Tanes or himself. Half an hour later the door opened and Josh turned towards the man, for it was a man this time, who had just entered the now crowded room. The tall, long nosed figure fixed his hard, malicious gaze upon him. It was clear that he had been observing the room, hoping for more information. And he had just handed himself to them! He should have listened to Echin.

Josh hoped that his revulsion showed in his face. The last time the gruesome figure had presented itself he had been inside the gaming set created by Danubin, within her home in Wales. Standing next to the leader of the Virenmor this man had worn the instantly recognizable robes of an Inquisitor. So, the Devourils had not chosen to destroy all of the Virenmor after all. This one undoubtedly recognised him. Behind the man, whom Josh could only think of as the Inquisitor, came the automaton like Devouril, flicking his strange dark gaze from the Virenmor to Josh. The Inquisitor reached for Josh, who pulled against the vicious grip, only to feel a wickedly sharp blade scrape his side.

"This one, Geoden, will make a fine prize for our Lord," he rasped.

Geoden inspected Josh with increased attention. Josh remembered the look of bleak despair that had appeared on Echin's face when Faer had told him that many of his kind had left Lioncera and joined Belluvour. He remembered the distress of his friend when he heard that Geoden, was one of these. Unlike Echin, Josh could find nothing but a sense of the alien in these strange creatures, hearts as empty it appeared, as the obsidian of their eyes.

229

"This one is..." The Inquisitor did not finish his sentence, for he fell to the floor unconscious. In his place stood Echin, who passed the blade he had taken quietly to Mactire.

"Toomaaris." Geoden's voice shook a little.

"Geoden, of all, I did not expect this of you." Echin stared coldly at the Devouril. There was a long stretch of silence and Josh wondered if they should attack Geoden but a glance from Echin told him otherwise. The Mourangil placed himself at the front of the group and the Devouril's eyes fixed upon the still figure of the Inquisitor.

"I haven't killed him." Echin's bitter words were flung towards Geoden. "He'll still be able to help you do Belluvour's work."

Geoden spoke in his fractured voice, "Stand aside Toomaaris. In these bodies we can destroy each other and that is not my desire, even if Belluvour would have it otherwise."

"Let them go," Echin told him. Geoden turned and raised his hand to carry out the gruesome task he had planned. Attached to his wrist was a hidden device resembling a gun. Echin instantly recognised the substance that had been prepared for ejection.

"The Odiam! In the name of Moura, Geoden, Belluvour goes too far!" Echin's explosive anger had no impact on the Devouril.

"Only a drop of Odiam was needed for the solution," Geoden explained dispassionately. "It is the most efficient tool to cull these creatures who infect our planet. Belluvour has diluted its composition so that it is merely an irritant to us but kills the humans instantly and painlessly. The black flame of internal combustion is invisible to them and its reaction with their body is faster than their human synapses can compute. The flame swallows the dust of their bodies and so leaves no trace. I will take to Belluvour the unicorn girl who we have already secured. The female Virenmor tracked the elemental to this place but we did not expect to find a Seed of the Myriar." His eyes fell upon Josh. "The others die. Step aside Toomaaris."

Lorcan, who was nearest, lunged for the Devouril. His expression was the vacant stare that the Tanes wore before transforming into their elemental form. In an instant Geoden had vanished, even as he released the toxic solution that travelled to its target as an invisible bullet. Lorcan was rendered to a hiss of air, his body dissipating to nothing. The Tanes reeled in shock. In seconds, a Devouril had appeared at each corner of the room. Echin spoke quietly and clearly, "I will go with you in exchange for their lives."
Geoden hesitated, Mactire bared cruel teeth. "Where's Loretta?" he demanded. Geoden ignored him but turning back to Josh, glanced at the unconscious figure by his feet. Echin showed the same absence of emotion, his voice detached as he spoke. "Think Geoden…what can they do without me? How would the Myriar form without a Mourangil to guide them? You have never believed in the possibility that mankind can use Moura's gift, there's no need to soil the light of your being any further by killing these hapless creatures." Geoden listened but turned his attention back to the group and to Josh in particular as Echin continued. "In capturing me as the bigger intention it would seem as nothing to ignore the presence of these humans."

Geoden dropped his hand to his waist. The dark, empty eyes turned away from the group and Mactire made to strike but Josh, seeing the expression on Echin's face, put out his arm to stop the Tane from transforming. Geoden moved his mouth in a sickly smile, as if he could see all that was happening behind him. He followed closely behind as Echin led the way. Once they had stepped over the unconscious body of the man known as the Inquisitor, Echin stood to one side. "They leave now," he said, carefully watching the Devourils, as the Tanes and Josh reluctantly made their way towards the front door. The last that Josh saw of Echin was the drop of his shoulders as he turned back towards the steel encased room.

"Wait!" Josh told Mactire, as he raced around the back of the building to retrieve the Chalycion. Mactire followed, now fully changed into his Adlet form. As Josh replaced the Chalycion around his neck he felt a sweep of air above him, followed by the appearance of a dark cloud heading south. The Adlet howled his grief to the rising moon.

Chapter Twenty-seven

Gabbie awoke alone. The thrashing river, Swift's insistent calling, still swirled in her head. When she finally opened her eyes she lay on her own, on summer grass that spiked her face. She remembered struggling for breath, holding on to a golden rope, until the tall figure of Swift strode towards her and helped her to the river bank. She had no recollection of being parted from the other women, who had set off down a path side by side. Vaguely, one part of her remembered that she was here for a purpose. Wherever here was.

The sun was high in the sky, there was no shade; yet there was no sense of burning or redness to her exposed skin. Standing up, she looked around at the vast field that seemed to stretch for miles in every direction. In the distance, the plain rose to a horizon and she felt certain that the place she was looking for must be in that direction. As Gabbie walked she became aware of her feet pressing on the grass, a skylark busily singing above the clouds. Out of breath she reached the top of a hill and sat looking eagerly at the vista below. She knew it now of course, she had been there many times. The terrain stretched beyond where her eyes could take her. She waited, as she had done on previous occasions, pulling her arms around her knees. Gabbie shouted with joy as she saw her mother walk out from under the eaves of the city. She waved excitedly, her heart beating wildly, and then she was running into the arms that had enfolded her from her first breath.

Later, they were sat in a house that overlooked a vast field, on the edge of the city, talking endlessly of everything and nothing. Gabbie recognised that this was an ongoing conversation and that she had partaken in it many times. In particular her mother asked Gabbie not to think harshly of her father and Gabbie was surprised at the hard ball of anger that had begun to eat away at her insides. When she looked down she saw that she was now holding a heavy ball of lead shot, like an old cannon ball. She handed this to her mother who smiled and whose touch disintegrated the heavy weight. "We meet here often when you sleep," her mother told her, "but I see you are now awake, how are you here?"

A peculiar sadness draped over Gabbie's shoulders as she tried to recall something she had forgotten. Seeing her distress her mother gently placed a hand on hers. "It doesn't matter," she said, "let's go and find Pembicaro." Her head glanced towards an opening in the stone wall. Pembicaro was there on the hillside, restlessly shaking his head, one hoof stamping impatiently.

Gabbie ran out and with a leap, was on his back in one swift motion. Riding across the vast plains of grassland on the black stallion was a joy that lit her blue eyes and lifted her heart. Her head hung beside his as the hooves pounded out great strides. Softly she kissed the long damp neck. "I missed you," she whispered and Pembicaro lifted his head and called out breathlessly in a magnificent throaty yell that celebrated that they were together again.

*

"Get back to the boat," Mactire led the way, running ahead, now returned to his human form.

"We have to go after them," insisted Josh but Oisen pulled him along. "Where to man? Go," he instructed.

Josh ran, still trying to process that Echin and Loretta had been taken. Breathless, he jumped aboard the narrowboat after the Tanes. Klim had been waiting up top and closed the door behind them as they entered. "Where's Echin?" The question was met with grave looks from everyone. Siskin was standing towards the rear of the barge as they bundled in.

"Leave," Mactire instructed hoarsely. He threw down a blade onto the table. "Echin gave this to me." Engraved on the steel were the words, "Waste no time. Go to Bankside."

"Do as he says," Josh instructed.
Siskin glanced towards Klim, who nodded his readiness to attempt the transition. "Buckle up!" Siskin shouted as they dashed into seats and clung on, as the musician fiddled with the dials to produce the strange thrumming vibration that signalled his communication with the internal melody of the narrowboat. Klim concentrated on a quiet stretch of canal in Bankside, merging with Siskin's sonic communication. A mist covered the interior of the barge and all sight was lost. Minutes later Klim's strong outline, deep in concentration, became visible. The absorbed face of Siskin, his whole body humming with power came next. Gradually the boat appeared as it had been in Dublin, transported in those short minutes across the sea. Mactire pointed to the white, circular ceiling fixtures.

"They use us," Siskin explained. "I think that's the best way to put it. Echin said they were from the newest, old power source on the planet!"

"And how did they get here?" asked Mactire.
"He called, they came."

"Who gives a flying feck!" shouted Oisen, his voice strained. "It'll matter little or nothing to Lorcan. And where will we find Loretta now that those anathema have taken her?"

Beside him Danny began to sob, then all the Tanes started to keen. They bowed their heads back and forth and their voices, in unison emitted an animal whine. The door to the cabin, at the back of the boat, opened. Unbelievably, and to Josh's great relief, Loretta stepped forward. Her eyes were wide with concern as she looked at each of the Tanes in turn. Then she gave an agonised scream, "Lorcan!" Mactire stood and put his arm around her, lowering her into the seat beside him. Loretta began the mourning song of the Tanes, in a language only Gabbie would have understood. The others joined in the sombre melody and Josh sketched idly as the song evoked images of elemental animal kingdoms, hidden realms of Faerie and the fierce and passionate loyalty of the Tanes.

*

Swift could not remember being parted from Gabbie. It was clear that the Realm of Resonance drew different paths for each of them. The river had disappeared and she was now in a desert. In the distance, she could see mountains and beneath their shadow were a number of caves. The sun was low in the west, the air was cool but her bare feet felt the warmth of the day's heat as her toes filtered the sand. The yawning howl of a wolf ripped into the silent landscape, where the pack gathered on a ridge above the caves. Below this were her parents in the mouth of a dark cavern. They were cooking on a stove, apparently unaware of the wolves. She ran towards them, wanting to warn them of danger, but as she approached her father pulled across a fence, high and solid, that would keep out the wolves and also their daughter.

Tears ran down Swift's face, tears she had cried a thousand times. Some place deep inside her, she knew that the fence had been built by her, that she had promised never to seek them out, even here in the Realm of Resonance. They had sold her to the woman she had called grandmother, the woman who had stepped in to prevent her being given away for money to those who would have abused and sold her on again. It had cost the old woman a life's savings and it had been her who had renamed the little girl, Swift. Her grandmother had been, from that moment, a constant and loving presence. Even when she died Swift felt that some part of her was always with her. The old woman had told her that even the thick veil of death could not hide her love.

The sun was an orange globe in a pale pink sky. Swift moved away from her parents to the other side of the mountain and another cave. She had long known that she could lend her will to pass through the dense, molecular structure of stone and other materials below the surface. However, where she did not lend her will to this process and tried to exist within a cave for a prolonged period, the stone pulled at the Stozcist's energy and drained her human life. Despite her residual fear of being caught underground, she was drawn inexorably to the dark, arched opening in the mountain. At the mouth of the cave her grandmother appeared, two wolves nuzzling the small figure, one on each side. Swift's breath caught in her throat and was released in a gasp of amazement and joy. The old woman opened her arms and Swift ran laughing towards her. After a long embrace, and as her grandmother stroked her head, Swift saw that in the setting sun the landscape flowered with life. Several trees could be seen where a river had produced a flourishing oasis. Her grandmother lived peacefully in the wolves' cave and Swift, feeling secure, petted the animals who then ran out into the night. She settled in, watching her grandmother light the candles, noting that the cave was open and would not make her sick. Her grandmother prepared two pallets for them, piled with soft blankets. Swift inhaled the fragrance of rich spices from the bean stew, cooking above a small fire at the mouth of the cave. She filled two clay bowls, whilst her grandmother brought bread and spoons from a box nearby. They sat on the blankets together, eating the stew.

"What has brought you here?" asked the old lady, who had dedicated the remaining years of her life to a small girl; a girl who had become the beautiful young woman beside her.

"It doesn't matter now," Swift answered, removing the Stone of Silence from around her neck and placing it beneath the pallet. "We have everything we need."

*

Siskin exited quietly through the narrowboat door so as not to disturb the grieving Tanes. A few minutes later he was joined at the stern of the boat by Josh and Klim. It was about three in the morning and a crescent moon hung low in a starless night. Coots and moorhens piped from the reeds on the opposite bank.

"It seems daft," Klim voiced what they all felt as they leant over the rail at the edge of the boat, "to find anything that still feels like normal. What happened Josh?"

Josh, his face a mere outline in the darkness, explained what had occurred in the Dublin terrace. Klim shivered with revulsion as his friend described the Devourils.

"Danubin was determined to get her revenge on Loretta." As Abigail, Danubin's assistant, the elemental had deceived the leader of the Virenmor. She had been instrumental in preventing Josh and Kier from being killed by Magluck Bawah. Josh glanced towards the interior. "She must have been so stressed to change her form. Bastards!"

For some time, they stood silently. It was Klim who finally voiced what weighed so heavily on all of their minds. "Will they kill him? Echin?"

Josh groaned, turning from the rail. "No."

"We can't know what they'll do," Siskin reasoned, tonelessly.

A tired female voice came from behind them. Loretta emerged from inside, adjusting a blanket around her shoulders. Josh held out his hand and brought her to sit alongside him on a wooden bench. She rearranged the blanket so that they could both huddle together in its warmth. "They were watching you all the time from a room upstairs. I couldn't believe it when you all arrived." She shook her head and continued. "They'd come for me. Not just one, a whole swarm of the things. I think that's how they are, working in numbers. Echin got me out. He waited for his moment when they went downstairs leaving me tied and gagged. The Virenmor creature," her voice changed, "he was despicable!"

Loretta dropped the blanket and pulled the jumper she wore from her shoulder. On it was the mark of a hot poker, still painfully red. "He said I needed branding like the animal I was."

Josh was hoarse with anger. "You should have said before. We'll find him, he'll pay for this!"

Loretta soothed him, "Echin released me. He helped me escape out of the front door before heading to the study. He told me where to find the boat. Those things, they're Devourils?" she asked.

Josh nodded, "Looks like they're primed to kill us indiscriminately. I don't understand why he wouldn't let us fight." Josh shook his head in agreement. "They were quick, sure, but between us we could have made a fight of it."

It was Loretta who answered, "I dismantled access to the Vortex but the connections will take some time to dissipate. That kind of battle energy would be the one thing that could have called Belluvour straight to us. We're not ready for that yet."

Siskin rubbed his forehead. "Sounds like the Devourils believe that we can't form the Myriar without a Mourangil. I think Toomaaris is hoping that we'll be left alone once they have him."

Klim frowned. "So, you think he doesn't intend us to follow and attempt a rescue?"

"Quite the opposite," Loretta explained. "He expressly forbids it. He said that on no account should any of us enter into the territory of the Devourils. Something about the stones not working there."

"And Bankside? Did he say what we are supposed to be doing here?" Siskin queried.

"He just said to lie low on the least populated part of the canal, outside of the town."

"Then we need to head further north from Bankside itself," Klim suggested and Siskin agreed. "There's an even quieter and more lonely stretch up there."

"As soon as it's light," Siskin said wearily. "I need sleep," he added, leaving the deck. Klim followed. Snuggled beside Josh, Loretta's breathing quickly drifted to the quiet and regular rhythm of sleep. Josh, so grateful to have her beside him, held her close. He tried to close his eyes but it was impossible, continually his thoughts returned to Echin. And Belluvour, he fretted, what unthinkable horrors would he inflict on the Mourangil?

Chapter Twenty-eight

The path had taken Kier downriver, beside the raging torrent in which they had been transported. She concentrated on trying to find a way across to Swift and Gabbie but found it hard to think of anything but her feet crunching on the uneven surface. "The Realm of Resonance," she repeated to herself. A place of entanglement. Focus on Talitha, Echin had told her, leave as soon as you have the key. Time seemed to have no relevance. It felt like only minutes since she had left the river and yet her jumper and jeans were bone dry. With a cry of relief she broke into a run, seeing a bridge that would take her across to the other side. Distractedly she acknowledged a dusky feel to the sky as she slowed to a walk. Just as she came to the bridge she noticed a yellow flower peeping out from the undergrowth. An evening primrose. She and her sister had sat at their bedroom window so many times, waiting for the flower to open, vying with each other to be the first to see it.

Kier moved away from the river to examine the flower more closely. It was only then that she noticed a narrow path heading downwards. On one side ran a drystone wall, over which she could see pastures stretching into the distance. On the other side were overgrown brambles that, as she came further down the path, reached out their long ropes of thorns, between patches of stinging nettles. The wall to her left gave way to reveal a mass of similar bushes. Kier ducked underneath a thorny archway and flecks of blood appeared, as she felt the irritating sting of contact with the overgrown tangle. Her hand came up above her eye, The Key of Brunan was still wrapped around her wrist.

Since leaving the river it had grown dull in appearance and hardly visible, but now it glowed golden in the half-light.

Kier reached an old stone bridge, no more than three paces in length and less than a full stride in width. Covering the first third of the bridge was a silver birch tree that arose from an embankment in the river below. The long, drooping leaves stirred as she neared; the bark was a mixture of dark veins and strong, white ligaments that added to the sense of movement. She stepped onto the bridge and felt the tingling of the air as it collected above the water. A number of small streams were drawn into the main river from different directions. She counted them, seven in total, all of them meeting underneath the old bridge, perhaps to join the great surge of water that had brought her to this path. "Seven Rivers," she let the phrase roll on her tongue. She seemed to know it so well but the reason for its familiarity eluded her. Hidden away as it was, she wondered how often the ancient bridge was used. On the other side of the bridge was a high, granite wall. Engraved upon it, covering much of its visible surface, were strange looking symbols. As she looked they seemed to come alive, golden lights winked at her momentarily.

A door appeared within the wall and reminded her of the magic she once thought was real; the entrances and exits she had noticed with a child's eyes but knew they were secret and outside her parents' world. Spellbound she watched, mesmerised by the shimmering wall. Confidently she approached to examine it but as she reached the middle of the bridge the overhanging birch bowed its long leaves. She found herself surrounded by the ghostly touch of elongated, finger like branches and leaves that brushed against her body. She heard a murmuring that grew to a voice, "Candillium," it whispered. Then, from within the birch, she heard another voice, one she knew well. "What kept you so long?" Martha asked as she dropped from the tree to land lightly beside her sister on the old, stone bridge. Kier, speechless, held out her hands and felt the face of the sister who had given up her life for hers. The long brown hair that fell to her shoulders. The finely drawn, intelligent face. The sincere blue of her eyes. And in that moment, in that place, she saw clearly the many other lives that Martha had lived on the planet.

"Erion," Kier said softly, seeing that the first of these lives had been beside her in Ordovicia. Erion, who had played the Pipes of Aleth. The first Lute, killed by an Irresythe.

"Candillium," replied Martha, reaching out in her turn. Together they sank among the leaves on the ground and rested against the white bole of the tree. The sisters watched the moon through the dappling pattern of the birch and slept, entwined, as they had done as children. When the sun rose, they ran along the bank of the river, throwing and catching fallen branches. However, dusk came quickly. Kier splashed herself with water from the stream, as the wall over the bridge became alive with lights. And meaning. *Though I am Mourangil and you are not, yet we are the same and you will always know me.*

Kier knew those words, she had said something like them once. She frowned, unable to solve the puzzle and called for Martha who came to sit beside her. But the wall was merely granite once again. Kier peered across the stream but already the words she had read were drifting from her memory. In sudden shock, she saw blood dripping down into the stream below. A shard of glass cut into her heart. There was no pain, just blood, as if her body were not her own. Martha reached out and gently pulled. Kier groaned, bent double. The shard of glass splintered into the water. Martha's hand pressed on the wound until it ceased to exist. "There," she whispered softly, wiping away Kier's tears, "it can't hurt you anymore."

Kier noticed that the golden bracelet that she wore now shone in the moonlight but she felt a sudden sense of urgency. "Toomaaris," she whispered. She looked towards the granite wall and recognised the exit from the Realm of Resonance. Quickly she sprang up, looking for her sister. Martha was not there. Gabbie and Swift! The memory of her friends flooded back. She needed to find the path to the river.

"Wait!" Martha ran back down the embankment. "Take this." She handed her a single rowan berry. Kier looked puzzled. "Do you remember when we sneaked out into the garden and hid underneath the large rowan tree?" Martha asked. Kier nodded. "The berries hung like small bunches of grapes but we remembered that red meant dead and we weren't allowed to eat them. But we decided........."

"You decided," corrected Martha.

"That we'd build a game around it. Each berry contained a fairy with red wings. We had to find the bunch where most fairies were hidden and then we threw them one at a time into the air so that they would fly." Martha leant over and kissed her sister. "The path's that way." She pointed behind Kier who turned to see the overgrown track leading down to where she had first stood. When she turned back, Martha had gone. Kier paused by the bridge, holding the rowan berry. She threw it high into the air and was thrilled as it darted from one side to another to hover by her eyeline. A strange pixie face squinted at her. It fluttered its red wings and landed in the second moon of the Stone of Mesa around her neck. The Key of Brunan quickly left her wrist and embedded itself back inside the first moon.

"The Key of Talitha." Kier placed her hand around the pendant that now contained the two keys. All she needed now was to find Gabbie and Swift. "Like walking in quicksand," she murmured.

*

"So this is England," Mactire stated as he followed the others from the boat. Loretta, still pale from her confrontation with the Devourils, gratefully took Josh's offered hand.

"You've never been?" Siskin was surprised.

"Scotland and Wales only," replied Mactire. "The Celtic leanings. Anyway what brings a New Yorker over here?"

"My mother was born in the Lake District, not too far away. After deciding that the military didn't bring out my best side I started working for Red Light." Siskin looked down the long stretch of canal surrounded by fields. "I reckoned this was as good a place as any to settle." They walked along the deserted towpath in ones and twos, an assorted convoy. Between them they looked like part of a touring sports team. All were athletic and the Tanes had that scrummed-down appearance that came from the fray of intense sport. They were indeed part of a hurling team named the Tenements, a fast paced and wild hockey like sport popular in Ireland. They were soon overlooking gardens that had shed their rich autumn coat ready for the icy touch of winter. As the canal brought them closer to the town and as they became parallel to a main road, Siskin nodded towards the Christmas lights in the shops. He remembered that the winter solstice was approaching fast, a matter of weeks only.

"It's hard to think they know nothing of Devourils and Mourangils," Mactire stated, "or Tanes."

"I'm not sure about that, I have theories," Loretta commented. "It's my next project, looking at the different types of knowledge we absorb and how we absorb it."

"Sounds interesting," Oisen added. "Let's hope we stay alive long enough to do it."

They all fell silent. That morning the Tanes had left the boat and found a remote spot where they could share their grief in private. Deploring the fact that there was no body or remains, they created another way to honour Lorcan. The funeral pyre rose high and could be seen from the boat. Each of the Tanes placed within it something that reminded them of the clever, gentle, bear like being. Josh had given Loretta a sketch he had drawn, showing Lorcan in his strong elemental state. Instead of placing it on the pyre, she kept it close.

"Why are we here in Bankside?" Josh finally broke the silence.

"No idea," answered Siskin.

Mactire stopped walking. "How do we find out?"

"Still no idea," Siskin replied ruefully.

"What about Kier?" Mactire asked, more hesitantly. "Where is she?"

247

Siskin turned towards Klim. Even in the prosaic light of a Bankside day his dark eyes and the angular features of his face made him appear like some fate stalked hero in a story. Klim looked carefully at Mactire, at Siskin's prompt, trying to decide if he could be trusted with knowledge of the women. Mactire's sharp mind clouded with anger. "Do you think we would hurt her? Didn't we just save her life?"
Undaunted Klim searched the Tane, there was still no mind print.

"We have never had any love of the Mourangils," Loretta said evenly, her hand resting gently on her brother's arm. "Before recently we blamed them for their neglect of the Tanes. It's only in these last weeks that we have come to understand that, but for Toomaaris, we would not even be the few we are."
Mactire was met with curious faces. "Ah well, if you're really interested?" he looked around the empty towpath, walking at the front, Siskin and Klim behind.

"I'd like to know for one," Josh affirmed, moving forward to listen. Klim and Siskin signalled their agreement. Mactire sat down on a nearby bench and they gathered around. "The story of the Tanes begins with a revered being, said to have dropped from the stars, who placed the gift of magic amongst our people. We called that revered being Myriar. It's only recently that we discovered what the Myriar really represents and that this same being now walks amongst us as Toomaaris the Mourangil."

"Echin!" Josh exclaimed. "We had no idea he was so involved with the Tanes."

"Nor we," Mactire admitted. "Nor what price we may have to pay," he added wryly.

"He saved all our lives," Josh reminded him, bristling. Mactire stretched out a hand in a pacifying gesture. "Easy Josh. I only meant that we have come to see that we have a part in all of this. Samuel," he continued, "told me that we are splinters of the Myriar. And when I met Kier," his green eyes were fierce with passion, "I knew that our fates were bound to hers."

Klim nodded faintly to Siskin, he could trace no deception behind Mactire's words.

"She's in the Realm of Resonance," Siskin told them.

"Jasus!" Danny shook his head. "I thought that was just a myth the leprechauns told."

"How did she even get there?" Mactire demanded, agitated.

"Be calm," Siskin told him, lowering his voice, although the canal was surrounded by fields on either side. "She's not alone. It's part of what the women have to do. The Key of Talitha is there."

"These are grave matters indeed." Loretta squeezed Josh's hand.

By tacit agreement they started walking again, each lost in his or her own thoughts. They came to a stretch of the canal where the path intersected a public field. It allowed them room to gather again. "I've been thinking," Klim told them. "That once the girls have crossed into this Realm of Resonance they're going to find it difficult to come out again, even if they want to."

"Of course, they'll want to," insisted Danny.

"Echin said it had a similar pull to the other realms we've been in," Josh added in a worried tone.

The talk of other realms piqued the interest of Mactire and Loretta and they leant closer as Josh continued.

"They catch you," he told them. "It's hard to explain. When you're there it's only the finest thread that connects you to this place. And the longer they stay, that thread will become more and more invisible to them."

"Echin," Klim added to the explanation, "told me that the exit points will be determined by those who are trying to leave that realm. That only the force of their attachment to each other and us would pull them out. Echin figured Bankside would be a place that would draw all three of the women."

"But," Siskin argued, "they could just as easily find Samuel's place or Evan's house in Wales."

"Apparently all three have experienced strong emotional events in their lives that would propel them towards this place. I'm saying it as he said it. The Realm of Resonance itself would seek out a point where the intersection could happen, leaving a sign for us to read if we look carefully."

The group shuffled into pairs as they started walking again, each one mulling over what Klim had told them. They stopped to allow a young family to pass them by, a little boy looked forlornly at his empty seed bag and the ducks who were following his footsteps, hoping for more. Klim pointed up ahead where there was a major widening of the canal and a variety of different boats moored on both sides. Just by the widest point was a large pub, there were even some hardy customers outside, sitting on tables that catered for summer custom.

"I think I know where we might find that exit," Klim said, his eyes still on the pub that fronted onto the canal. Siskin glanced at Klim and laughed when he saw that new owners had recently taken over the place and renamed it, 'The Glimpse of Hope'.

*

Danubin emerged from the palace like building in the city of Ulyn. She was exultant. She had known it the moment she first saw him, as his fiery glance answered her aching need with a lust of his own. She was the ultimate gamer, she had played him perfectly; a Mourangil's power lay at her feet. But, she told herself, the game was still in play, go carefully she whispered, go very carefully. The strident figure came out to join her and she smiled as he rested a possessive hand on her shoulder. At her careful prompting Belluvour had sent her to Ulyn so that he could bring Ulynyx to heel. She had introduced the leader of the Chunii to the mutual pleasure of intimate embrace; taught, teased, and brought the once noble steed to submit to the reigns in which she had entangled him. Those reigns would, of course, remain invisible to Ulynyx who had made the human state of arrogance so blindingly his own.

Belluvour had been besotted with the poisonous army she had given him and had not taken seriously the threat of the Chunii. It was only when she revealed the failed attempt of Ulynyx to gain the Key of Brunan that he had turned his dark gaze in his direction.

"How do you know this?" Every question that Belluvour asked was an interrogation.

"You taught me, Lord," she had replied, "to look towards the folds of our human existence, to bring your touch to the realms that are threaded around us. Over the many lifetimes I have served you, I have implanted watchers who have alerted me to the powerful shift that has just occurred."

251

"You said the attempt failed?"

"Ulynyx failed." She herself had witnessed the attempt, for she had long ago targeted that area of Aya Sofya for remote observation. "My divinations have disclosed that the Myriar Seeds have found the Key of Brunan."

Danubin shivered with the memory of his ashen presence close beside her, the unstable wrath that threatened to erupt into volcanic destruction. Beneath the island came the rumbling of tortured bedrock. When he spoke it charged the air. Without effort and when he desired, his voice could be heard throughout the island. It was all the more nerve racking therefore when his voice remained a mechanical monotone. And, on this occasion, he had kept his words for her ears only. "Stolen," the lidless eyes looked out to the turbulent sea. "Unethora would never give Brunan to the infection of humanity. Toomaaris has found a way to steal the key in his foolish attempt to reshape Moura's doomed gift."

Danubin, with long practiced skill, had emptied her mind of thought so that its pattern would not be revealed to the Unbound. She concealed her spiteful hatred of the Seeds of the Myriar that was now laced with fear. Despite everything, they had survived her carefully constructed attempts to destroy them. In particular Josh Allithwaite's intrusion into her own secret space was a bitter memory. She had quelled the image of the Creta revealing his full power, the boy had grown beyond her manipulation.

"Ulynyx has made the keys his long study, he will certainly seek Talitha. If my Lord wishes I will find his lair in the secret city of Ulyn."

Danubin had waited, focusing her mind on the few untouched columns of Doric beauty that were left on the island. She had designed the open platform, at the centre of the magnificent temple, to enable a view of the whole island. Her eyes brushed over the infestation of Devourils that now populated the island in the stolen bodies of the Virenmor. She had no idea if Ulynyx had in fact studied the whereabouts of the keys but it had been her own secret pursuit. The shock that these mythical instruments of power had now arisen had been profound. It was impossible to read the Unbound, to gage his emotion, even for someone such as she. Of one thing however, she had come to be certain, he feared these keys. Her time on the island had revealed that their possession was vital and that they could be manipulated by beings of power such as herself.

"Go," he had commanded. Belluvour, with little effort, had arranged natural tunnels beneath the ocean to provide a way of transporting his army. Entrance to these tunnels was through a number of staircases located in some of the pillars. The underground transport system consisted of dense obdurate passageways containing channelled waters, where boats moved like railway trains. Belluvour had forbidden all but a few of the Devourils to move in the Mourangil way through air and water, for he had discovered that this shortened the time that they could inhabit the bodies of those they had murdered.

It took her a day to travel to the nearest barin, a delta stripped of foliage to promote the harvesting of oil. Not once had Danubin let her thoughts stray to her real purpose for fear that the Unbound would discover her intended betrayal. The Chunii was a deadly army, not to be underestimated and long before Belluvour would discover her treachery, Ulynyx would utilise her information to end the threat of the Devourils. Danubin was determined that she would use every skill she had so dearly bought in her many lifetimes to find the Seeds of the Myriar. Ulynyx was convinced that the Myriar could never be formed. She was not so sure.

Although her own long experience of human kind was enmeshed in corruption and malice, Danubin had been too often thwarted by Toomaaris and the Seeds to be blind to their power.

"You are sure that Belluvour fears the discovery of the keys?" Ulynyx asked her, as they stood together, overlooking the city of Ulyn. She placed her hand on his and upturned her face towards him. "I am sure my Lord," her expression remained carefully thoughtful. "Does it trouble you?" she said artlessly.

He dropped his hand and paced behind her, she waited patiently. "I was deceived in the location of the Hall of Jasmine, Unethora could not know I sought the Key of Brunan." She nodded understandingly and Ulynyx continued. "Elanur once told me that the second key, Talitha, resided in the Realm of Resonance. I know not of this place, but she seemed certain that none could reach it there. That it was lost to us."

Danubin was sure that somehow the woman who had once been Candillium would find a way into that realm. She herself had dabbled there on some occasions, using distorted spirits that were still tangled in the river of their previous lives.

"Then there is no need for any of us to fear it's recovery my Lord," she let her hand brush his thigh as she spoke.

As they walked back to the magnificent hidden building that comprised Ulynyx's personal quarters, the leader of the Virenmor congratulated herself once again. She had burrowed away to find knowledge that no one was aware she now possessed. The more she tapped into her dark sources the more she wanted the three mysterious keys. Like the stones of power, she thought, she would bring them under her dominion. Perhaps already Talitha had been retrieved. So much the better, she decided. Danubin had no doubt that the key could be taken easily from the lifeless body of Candillium.

Chapter Twenty-nine

The Key of Talitha flew just ahead, leading Kier back towards the bridge. The tiny ruby figure was encircled by Brunan and twirled delightedly within the dancing, golden ring that flickered into different shapes as they moved. The keys captured her attention as she crossed the bridge so that she hardly noticed the broiling river below. Only after a few strides, stepping from the wide walkway, the two elements slid abruptly into the Stone of Mesa and became buried in the grey engravings of the two moons. Only then did she notice the water bubbling loudly behind her. Her throat tightened as Kier saw the swirling patch of blood. It grew in circumference as it came nearer to the riverbank and began to colour the grass beside her. Ahead, she watched in horror as bloody footprints strode purposefully into a wide field, where she heard, but could not see, the pounding of a horse's hooves.

*

"The Glimpse of Hope," Klim read from the newly painted sign, looking towards the pub on the side of the canal.

"And that it is," Mactire strode ahead of his companions.

"But does it serve Guinness?" Oisen too had picked up the pace but Danny was quicker and pushed ahead of Mactire. "We'll soon find out," he promised.

"I hope someone has money," commented Klim.

"We always have money," whispered Mactire with a mischievous grin. "Leprechaun gold, don't y' know."

"Take no notice," Loretta said as her brother shifted to join the others. She sneaked her arm within the cradle of Josh's as he walked with his hands stuffed in the pockets of his jeans. "Though Sean always carries plenty, it'll be in Euros".

Siskin laughed, "No good in Bankside then," he said, removing a card from his pocket. "I'd best go pay."

The pub surprised Siskin, or rather his reaction to it did. A sense of homecoming that he hadn't felt outside of New York. The day was clear and dry and richly autumnal. There was also that hiatus in the seasons where the land stood on the brink of change and the days seemed to get all mixed up with a bit of everything. The sun shone clear and bold but the air was crisp. Fallen leaves floated on the water but the light coming through the bare trees gave a wintry feel. The smell of wood smoke drifted up from the narrowboats and two swans took centre stage in the middle of the water. The view opposite stretched out towards the distant Yorkshire hills. Siskin sighed with a sense of well-being, in the midst of all the turmoil, here was a sense of peace.

It seemed that all of them had wordlessly agreed to put aside their grief and fears, for a while at least. Inside, oaths were being sworn in a rich Irish brogue and he guessed that Mactire had discovered that his money would not be accepted in Bankside. Siskin turned inside to put it right, laughing at how parochial the mythical Tanes could be. Strangely, he couldn't recall the old name of the pub and suspected it had been renamed by a local, who had been part of the tragic earthquake that had shaken the small town a year ago. Siskin entered as Mactire was trying, with all his charm, to persuade the young women behind the counter to take his Euros in exchange for the beer. The girl, though young, was exceptionally pretty and had heard enough blarney to make her impervious to the Irishman. She looked hopefully at Siskin as he entered and smiled with relief when he handed over his bankcard.

"Seriously, you lot need to come into the twenty-first century," he told Mactire, who was little concerned who paid as long as it meant he would not be parted from the rich black, white topped pint of liquid that stood on the bar in front of him. He squirmed with the first taste.

"Argh….. English Guinness, what will they ruin next?"

"I'll have it," Klim told him, reaching out his hand.

"Off laddo," Mactire lifted his pint out of the way. "Go get your own."

A log fire crackled in the hearth that was positioned on a raised area at the right hand corner of the pub. The group made their way towards it and relaxed in cosy, leather armchairs. "We should eat while we have the chance," Siskin decided, standing to go and find menus. "I've got it covered," he said in response to Mactire's raised eyebrows and unasked question about how they would pay.

"He seriously has it covered," Klim told him. "Siskin is Eamon Keogh."

The Tanes laughed with surprise at hearing the name of the famous song writer. Mactire smacked his forehead with the palm of his hand. "The Lute! Of course! Well now we'll have to have a little music after our meal." Siskin said nothing, hoping that the moment would pass. They ate, realising just how hungry they all were. The sun set early, the customers outside had left or come into the pub, where there was now only standing room. The waitresses, dressed in neat uniforms, weaved deftly in and out of the crowd.

"What about that song now?" Mactire shouted to Siskin, over the heads of the crowded bar as he collected another round of drinks. It seemed that just as he spoke the place had become suddenly quiet and his words rang out, only to be seconded enthusiastically by the crowd.

Siskin heard the call, for call it was. Within this moment was another. It was as if the voice of every Lute throughout the history of mankind now summoned him to sing. He stood up, his blonde hair drifting loosely around his shoulders. His eyes were the colour of a leaf fallen from the tree, caught in the autumn light and now neither tree nor leaf but its own dappled shades. As the pub filled up, the heat became intense sitting at the table nearest to the fire. He stood up and removed his jumper, to the cheering of a group of women at the bar. The grey T-shirt underneath revealed the muscular physique of a man to whom physical discipline was an everyday part of life. Around his neck the purple amethyst caught the firelight and flecked golden. In the dimmed atmosphere of the pub it seemed that he was positioned in the centre of a natural spotlight. The room was silent with expectation, even the clink of glass ceased as the bar staff turned their eyes to the performer.

Siskin began his song to a unique thrum created by Amron Cloch. Clear as a spring wind, full as an autumn harvest, enticing as summer and deep as the mysteries of winter, Siskin sang of Moura. The vibration of his voice reached every heart as he lifted the melody. He told the story of five seeds planted in a garden, nourished through the seasons, as old as mankind is old. The song was simple, the melody held the bitter-sweet tang of nostalgia and the stimulating excitement of finding a rare and beautiful jewel, where it may easily have been overlooked. After the third time, the audience joined in easily with the chorus:

> *We call to our hearts your promise.*
> *We bring to our knowledge your gift.*
> *We remember the time of our coming,*
> *The way that the spheres did shift.*
> *We see in our hearts that your promise*
> *Has grown weary of all we became*
> *But the time of our coming is leaving*
> *And the spheres have now shifted again*

.

The pub was full of locals at this time of year, and as with all gatherings of people who have brushed long and carelessly against each other, there was a melee of real and imagined slights. All the toxic festering of unrequited love, the unresolved bitterness of envy and the unreasonable expectation of inadequacy. To each and every one present, regardless of how solidly these views had taken residence at the forefront of their thought, they now seemed like childish squabbles that had been outgrown.

As Amron Cloch flashed its strobes of colour they bathed in the clean sensation of a newly found love. It was a love that had fuelled their every moment of self-recognition, every act of kindness, every selfless thought. The same love, the same heightened sense of untangled emotion that reminded them of a time without hatred and war, a time that in some starlit corner of their consciousness, connected them with a power that breathed behind their breath and stoked the fire of renewal. At the end there was silence, the call for an encore was suppressed by a sense that what had occurred on their very doorstep was somehow momentous and complete. Like a dam breaking, came a flood of cheers and clapping. The stranger with the heart rending voice walked from the pub and out into the clear night, aware that he had fully embraced, for the first time, that he was a Lute of the Myriar.

*

Although the vicious, second master of the Virenmor had been known to his colleagues, at his insistence, as the Inquisitor, his current origins were quite prosaic. He had been born in London as George Smith. He knew that he had been kept alive only as long as it served the purpose of the alien Devourils, that swarmed over the paradise island like a plague of locusts. Not locusts, he corrected himself, for locusts ate. Even he was revolted at seeing these organic machines inhabit the bodies of his fellow Virenmor. There had been little loyalty within the Virenmor number, except their blind devotion to their bound Lord. However, seeing the inhuman Devourils walk mechanically and mercilessly in their forms ate away at his sense of personal power.

He distrusted Danubin's absence, suspecting she intended to abscond when she realised, as he did, that there would be no elite human race, no human race at all in fact. Daily, there was a continual show of images across the sky, for Belluvour needed no screens to project the human documentaries for his followers. Cities ravaged by conflict, species neglected, the planet wounded by greed and ignorance. The Virenmor had been deluded into thinking that he prized their elite qualities and admired their ruthless command of the ordinary man. The Inquisitor had conceived endless lives of power ahead, with Belluvour providing the thrust of their progress as he had done in the Secret Vaults. But instead this creature was consumed by a vast rage that targeted all humankind.

The Inquisitor had soon discerned that Belluvour's infected, hidden emotion was a secondary symptom of another primary hatred that centred on their old enemies, Candillium and Toomaaris. And here was that very Toomaaris giving up his freedom for a few no-matter lives. He had saved the Creta, a fact that the Inquisitor found most significant. The Inquisitor had not risked his master's fury in revealing this fact to him, nor, to his knowledge, had Geoden. Toomaaris's calm acceptance and continued refusal to speak was clearly and successfully engineered to enrage Belluvour further. Belluvour's sickly parody of human voice carried eerily over the island. "Give him water, feed the human body of my brother Toomaaris. He has chosen to inhabit this form so long that his fate is now entwined with the race that has befouled our world for long enough. But we will keep him alive to witness the extinction and suffering of those more precious to him than the brothers embedded alongside you in the birthstones of Lioncera."
The Inquisitor stood on the shore, watching the terrifying currents that circled the island and sent waves crashing like cymbals against each other.

"It is time to begin the cull," Belluvour's voice announced, "and to excise this living virus from our world, so that we can shape Moura into health once more and make our new kingdoms upon her surface."

A shadow blotted out his own. The Inquisitor trembled, making himself turn and bow. Geoden came to meet him and he tried not to vomit, knowing that he would have to mingle his being with this terrible creature and endure the prolonged pain of another journey in the stagnant despair and determined purpose of the Devouril.

Chapter Thirty

"It's everywhere," Josh announced, looking up from the iPad Loretta had purchased. "It's all over Facebook and YouTube's flooded with hits. Eamon Keogh," he quoted from one article, "the new Beatle. Long known as an outstanding songwriter his impromptu performance of a new song in a local pub has placed him at the forefront of interest in the music world. He has yet to respond to several offers."

"Never mind the song, Josh," Siskin interrupted. "We have to find Echin."

"But the girls will come here. I'm sure of it," Klim reminded them.

Siskin had cloaked the canal boat and moved it further along the remote stretch of canal.

"They're all full of stories about the Alignment," Mactire said, entering the narrowboat and waving a sheaf of newspapers. "We're talking only two weeks."

"What about the third key?" Loretta asked. "Shouldn't we be finding that?"

"Echin's the priority," insisted Siskin.

Mactire sighed, "If any of you three turned up looking for Echin I think he'd kill you himself. You can't get that close to Belluvour. It's clearly a job for the boys!"

He looked around at the other Tanes who all nodded their agreement.

"And what about me?" Loretta demanded.

"Have a close look at this stuff," Siskin interjected. He reached up to remove one of the circular power sources that Echin had installed. Loretta took hold of the white matter with interest and the spark in her eyes said it would take little for her to become fully engrossed.

"I reckon Swift might be able to help you out when she gets back." Klim chewed his lip, the women had been gone over two weeks now. Mactire patted Klim's shoulder. He stood up, followed by the other Tanes.

"Come on lads," he said as he gave Loretta a peck on the cheek. They made their goodbyes sound like they were off for a pint and only Loretta's teary eyes said otherwise. She watched them exit one by one and then turned towards the kitchen. Josh followed her.
Siskin turned to Klim. "We'll head back to Stromondale and pick up Suara." Klim shook his head. "You go," he said, "I'll wait here for the girls." Siskin gave no argument. He grabbed his jacket and placed a black, woollen hat on his head. "I've ordered two hire cars, one to get me there and the other one I'll leave in The Glimpse of Hope car park if you get desperate. Though I think you'd be best sticking to the boat. I should be back tomorrow, around midnight at the latest," he added.

"Then I'll come looking," Klim said as Siskin reached the door.

*

Danubin shied from the column of bright light to her left as she strode from the water. Memories were always more difficult to dispel in the Realm of Resonance. The leader of the Virenmor shrugged them away as she concentrated on the lock of hair she held, the hidden trophy of her earlier possession. It enabled her now, through long practice of the occult, to follow the girl into this most dangerous of places. The hair was very blonde and curled around her long fingers. It had been a long time since she had stolen it from the sleeping child, for it

265

was her way of retaining some connection to all those over which she intended to exercise her power. Overnight she had used it in her dark divinations to discover that Gabrielle, had indeed, passed into the Realm of Resonance. All her workings however, showed that she was still alive, and so Danubin could only conclude that the girl had been selected herself to find Talitha or that Candillium had accompanied her to this place.

Impatiently, she quelled the tremble of uncertainty, a fear that came with the realisation of the way the fates had wrapped themselves around the Seeds and the Virenmor. How could it possibly be that little Gabrielle should be an Inscriptor of the Myriar, wearing the very stone, Arwres, that she had worked so hard to uncover? Danubin had since learnt that it had been her own activity that had alerted Silex to summon Gabrielle to where the stone lay waiting. The shock she had felt following Arwres to Bankside to find its residue in the child! She had the girl in her care for over two years, a Seed of the Myriar! A child she had intended for the Virenmor, recognising even as an infant that she was filled with latent power. Remembering the day that she had planned to abduct Gabrielle, she now told herself that had her father come upon them anywhere else, other than the busy Manchester shopping centre, she would not have given her up so easily. Years later she acknowledged that there had been an unanticipated complication; after all those lifetimes, she had experienced the discomfort of genuine care.

Beneath her feet the red coals crackled but they did not disturb her. As living flesh, she was not subject to the pain of the reflective universe that her current life had created. She strode through the leafless landscape, barren of all vegetation, illumined only by the blood red moon. After all, her favourite colour was red, she told herself, amused; confident she had long ago mastered this realm. In the distance, she heard the beating of hooves and the exultant neighing of a horse. Like a sniper scanning through night goggles, the hazy brightness of a woman and a stallion began to take flickering shape. Danubin saw the way the two beings intermingled to become one graceful, galloping movement and an emotion, akin to regret, touched her. In the Realm of Resonance, it pierced her like a blade and quickly she shunned it away. The rider was clearly alone and Danubin could only assume that the resonance had claimed her, that she had failed in her purpose to discover Talitha. The child, after all, had none of the experience that she herself possessed. One way or another she was confident that she would find the key.

Using her undamaged hand, from the folds of her cloak, she removed the ritual knife. It was not the fabled Perfidium that was once again lost to them, but one of her own making. Rubbing the lock of hair between her fingers she called to Gabrielle. Gradually the pace of the gallop slowed to a trot, she could hear the animal's heavy breath as it moved towards her; the voice of the girl as she came almost alongside. She had grown, just as Danubin had foreseen, her power still not fully claimed but even so one of great stature that must now be levelled to the ground.

*

Swift knelt by the water and filled the stone pitchers. The oasis bloomed around her; tiny birds hummed and she was surrounded by the vibrant colour of exotic plants. Everywhere she had explored brought another surge of excitement and she was sure that she would never grow tired of knowing this place. In the reflection of the pool she saw her grandmother walking towards her. Frail, yet deceptively strong fingers came to rest on her shoulder. Swift covered them with her own, turning her face towards the woman whose love graced her whole being.

"It calls," she said, placing in Swift's fingers the Stone of Silence. Swift felt the stone pulse as the diamond moulded to her touch. She placed the stone in the pool and stood up, looking away towards the setting sun.

"We cannot linger here much longer," her grandmother told her. "You know this, my little one."
Tears streamed down Swift's face as she held the old woman, who barely reached her shoulder in height.

"I won't leave," she told her.
Gently the old woman held her hands, "But I must," she said quietly. "This is a place of tangled webs, neither you nor I will visit here again."

"But, when will I see you?" cried Swift.

"Our love binds us." She placed her hand over Swift's heart. "You will find me here, truly. Implanted within there is a thread that will never break and you can follow it to me whenever you wish."
Swift placed her hand over her grandmother's and nodded. The old woman shimmered and disappeared. Swift sobbed and sank to the ground, closing her eyes and placing her hands on her heart, where the warmth of

her grandmother's touch still lingered. Swift's breathing stilled as she sensed within a flicker of joy, the deep love they shared, the energy of peace. She opened her eyes and the oasis had disappeared but there on the sand was the Stone of Silence on its chain. Without thinking she bent down and placed it around her neck.

The fence was almost in place for the evening but Swift let her hand slide within to halt its progress. She pulled it back and looked on the faces of her mother and father, shame and regret. Swift stood facing the two strangers and felt the cold ball of pain that any thought of them always engendered. In the Realm of Resonance, it manifested itself as freezing ice; she held in her hand a hard snowball that was too cold for her fingers to hold. Swift threw it down and as she did so, the fence fell away. "The wolves have left now," she told them simply. "You won't need it anymore." She turned and walked away, feeling the diamond gently tug against her throat. Looking down it seemed that the sunset was reflecting in the Stone of Silence, for it had turned a deep and bloody red.

The Auric Flame

Chapter Thirty-one

Ulynyx hid in a fold of air close to the Arc de Triomphe. He admired the beauty of another city built by men. His eyes tracked the long stream of traffic as it emerged from the tree lined avenue. Tourists and Parisians on foot filled the immediate area and he remembered that the Christian season of Christmas would soon take place. Danubin had told him where and when the attack would be and he had come to see for himself. He watched as the Devourils appeared silently, mingling with the crowd in the stolen bodies of the Virenmor. Danubin had told him little of her own part in this, only that Belluvour had murdered her fellow Virenmor and stolen their bodies to house his Devourils. Panicked cries of alarm rang out as people discovered loved ones, neighbours, and strangers inexplicably vanish from their sides. People ran screaming in all directions as the indiscriminate attack took children and adults alike.

Ulynyx moved further away as he caught the stench of the Odiam, thickening the atmosphere. Invisible to the crowd he watched as the Devourils weaved across the ground at incredible speed, eliminating the armed security guards. The leader of the Chunii was hard pressed not to cry out from where he hid above the crowds. Shocked, he watched as people gradually disappeared to nothing when the poisonous Odiam was injected with sniper precision. The structures around them were blackened, singed by the presence of the unknown enemy. Ulynyx, transfixed, was unaware of Geoden's approach.

"You are weary, Ulynyx," he spoke in the language of men. "Come and embed with your fellows in the Obdurates of Greece."

Stunned, Ulynyx realised that he was perceived as another Devouril, forever forbidden from the bejewelled cities within Moura. He could barely recognise Geoden in the stolen form but he knew that he had spoken without guile. A great cry sounded and Ulynyx raised his head in confusion, realising that the sound had come from his own lips. In Geoden's dead eyes was a glimmer of the jewelled beings they had both once been as he dropped the stolen arm and vanished. The culling, as Danubin had named it, had been the work of only a few minutes but had been simultaneously repeated in Tokyo, Beijing and Moscow. With a torturous sigh Ulynyx too vanished before the first sirens rang in the Champs-Elysees.

*

Echin sat cross-legged on the floor of the metal cage. He was unable to change to his Mourangil form or become lost in the air because of the proximity of the Odiam. Unlike the diluted substance that Belluvour had manufactured to use for wholesale slaughter, this was the same matter that he had seen in Obason so long ago. The toxicity of its nearness robbed him of strength and was an oppressive weight upon his spirit. In order to prevent him changing form, the cage had been rigged so that the moment the mass changed significantly within, the release of the Odiam above would be triggered. At night, he was lowered to a chamber lined by obdurates so that he could not embed. Here he was fed with food that had not been nourished by sunlight and gave only the bare

271

minimum of manufactured nutrition. The only exit from the chamber was the metal cage in which he now stood and the only chance of escape was during the day when he was exhibited in the cage. Echin was well aware that his imprisonment was intended to entice Belluvour's oldest enemy, Candillium, to the island.

Belluvour strode across to the cage. "See Toomaaris. They drown even their children rather than share a plot of land." He pointed to the sky nearby. With a flick of his fingers, news programmes were redirected to fill the space. Thousands of refugees were fleeing to Europe as the wars in the Middle East became more and more intolerable. Desperate families risked death on a daily basis trying to find some haven that was not stricken with the same diseased conflict.

"I was right to deny them the keys," Belluvour said quietly. Triumphantly his dark orbs shifted towards the Mourangil. Echin stood. His tall human presence strode to the bars until he was eye to eye with the Devouril who was but a step from the cage. "The keys were Moura's first gift." Finally, Echin understood. "You were entrusted to implant them within their evolution, to bring the newly evolved Ordovician race into conjunction with Moura."

Belluvour's sneering mouth confirmed what the Mourangil had guessed. "They were not worthy of Brunan and Talitha," he hissed.

"You hid the keys," Echin accused him. "You were lord of the surface world and would not share it with any being who challenged your power. And what of the Auric Flame?"

Enraged, Belluvour turned his back on the cage. His fist pounded an ornamental pillar and he watched it crumble

272

to dust. Echin, his eyes calmly watching Belluvour, lowered himself once again to the floor of the cage and sat in contemplation, searching his memories.

"What did you offer Durane to betray Erion, her daughter?"

The cruel mouth formed a grin at the memory.

"What I gave her," came the response as the Devouril vanished from the ruined temple.

Chapter Thirty-two

Loretta, standing at the back of the narrowboat, puzzled over the white substance that Siskin had left her to study. Josh sketched, his pencil moving across the page like fingers on a grand piano. Klim came out of his cabin, wearily running his hand over dark, uncombed hair.

"There's nothing in Mengebara," he told them. "Siskin said he'd be back tonight." He looked through the small, round window, the short winter day was almost over. "It's only a week until the solstice."

"What's wrong with you lot, why don't you use devices to help you to communicate?" Loretta raised her arms, palms upwards. "I feel as if my hands are cut off having to leave mine all behind!"

"But it means the likes of you can't track us and hack us!" Josh challenged, his tone light. Before she could reply he added conversationally, "And don't pretend you never tried."

Green eyes glinted hard in her delicate features but a touch of a smile reached her lips.

"If he's not back tonight I'm going looking," Klim decided. "I wish we had news of Echin and the girls."

"If he's not back, I'll go with you," Josh agreed. He retrieved the sketches he had been working on. "These might help." He placed the papers on the table near Klim and Loretta. "This is the first time I've been able to draw the girls since they left." He had depicted three figures, each one invisible to the other, placed behind the points of a walled triangle. The three women looked like ghostly wisps of fog, barely recognisable as Kier, Swift and Gabbie.

"It's like their together but apart," Josh swept his hand over his head, puzzled. Unable to come up with any clearer definition he picked up the next sketch. Echin looked out from a metal cage between marble pillars. A sob escaped Loretta's lips. She quickly recovered.

"At least they're all still alive." Klim grated. Loretta pointed towards the cage that held Echin.

"There's something on the mechanism above, it's rigged." Josh and Klim peered over her shoulder.

"Belluvour would have to hold him in human form," Josh surmised. "I'm guessing it might be something to do with that."

"Sean will spend a good while getting the lie of the land when they do find him." She stood up, wringing her hands, "If Echin can't change form then there's no way the boys will be able to free him from that cage without killing either themselves or him."
Josh tried to reassure her, "Sean's too smart to try something he can't pull off."

"But he's stubborn, as are the rest of them," she countered, pulling on her coat. "I need some air."
Josh grabbed a waterproof, "I'll come with you."

They bundled out into the harsh December day. Josh raised a hand to ward off leafless branches flying across their path. The canal was dotted with blown debris and the rain stung cold on his hand. They pulled their coats tight around them as they trudged along the towpath, their faces buried and oblivious to the hidden figure who moved out of a small copse of trees once they had passed.

Alone on the barge after Josh and Loretta had left, Klim was surprised to hear footsteps on the towpath outside. On this secluded stretch of the canal and in this weather, he decided, it must be a particularly determined walker. They had left the boat open to view, as the canal was too narrow to safely keep it hidden. He concentrated on the sketches Josh had drawn, hoping to pick up some kind of link. There was still nothing from the women. As he turned to the image of Echin, the Iridice turned hot against his skin. With building excitement, he took the chain from his neck and held the stone in his hand, letting its energy help focus his thoughts. He began to see in his mind's eye, the metal cage in which Echin was imprisoned. It became more firmly delineated the more engrossed in his task he became. Klim noticed that his image started to contain other objects, pillars, a stone floor, an open air platform. It felt so vivid that Klim was able to push his thought outwards so that the picture in his mind hovered like a futuristic television screen over the table. He focused on the floor of the cage and felt a whisper of warm air across his cheekbone. He could smell the sea and then saw Echin, eyes closed, sitting cross-legged, resting in the centre of the cage. To Klim's delight, the eyes flickered open and looked straight towards him. 'Klim! Well done!' Echin projected his thoughts telepathically.

"Yes! Are you okay?" Klim answered aloud. Echin nodded slightly, "Did Kier and the girl's get back to Bankside?"

"So, we were right, will they come through to us here?"

"You're in Bankside still? Then they're not back." Klim swallowed. "No they haven't made it back yet. Could they come out somewhere else?"

"It will be Bankside if they're still all together. I placed an attunement crystal, some time ago, in the back wall of the storehouse in The Glimpse of Hope."

"Eh?"

"It will create a pull towards the Myriar stones. Like an anchor." Klim explained what Josh's sketch had told them. "They were all in the picture."

"Did they appear any different?"

Klim toyed with the idea of trying to hold up the sketch but abandoned it. He didn't want to risk losing the connection with Echin by concentrating on another task.

"It wasn't detailed enough to tell. It was like he was sketching just outlines but you could see each one clearly. Where are you?"

"I'm on an island in the middle of the Mediterranean."

"Can you show it on a map in Mengebara?"

"No, we can't use Mengebara now, it has to be kept for a greater purpose."

"Eh, what?" Klim felt nervous.

"It's time Klim, you have to find the army of the Iridice, remember? Where are the Tanes?" he asked before Klim could comment. "Mactire's on the way to rescue you." Echin gave a slight shake of his head. "There's no way he'll be able to get to me. Only another Devouril could come here unseen. Bring him back if you can."

"We'll try. These keys," asked Klim, " what do they open?"

A wistful smile passed over the Mourangil's face.

"Hearts," he said. Then his expression turned cold. Klim saw a shadow pass in front of the image. It reminded him of the fearful picture that Josh had drawn depicting the natural state of Nephragm, except that this was squashed into a smooth and hairless human frame. Klim jumped backwards dropping the Iridice, stunned by the dark eye shaped holes that bit from a sculptured, obsidian face. Shocked, he was still frozen, staring into space when Loretta and Josh returned.

277

Josh bent to pick up the Iridice but Klim did not react. Loretta spoke gently to him and eventually her words stirred him enough to speak. "Belluvour," he said. "I saw him, and he saw me." Klim haltingly explained what he had discovered and the visual connection he had made with Echin. "I don't think I can risk creating the link again," he told them sadly. "Could he see where you were?" asked Josh. "I don't know what he saw," Klim answered, wanly. Loretta brought a glass of water and she carefully examined Klim's face as he sipped the cool liquid.

"Did he speak?" Josh asked, afraid of the answer.

"No, I broke the connection. Well, I think Echin kind of pushed me away."

"I do not think he stained you," Loretta concluded.

"What do you mean?" Josh asked.

"Shocked and dismayed I think, but his shadow is not written in your life force."

"You think he could do that from one glance?"

"Without a doubt," she said almost conversationally, "but you are whole Klim."

With her words Klim rallied and his voice became urgent. "Echin said we have to stop Mactire trying to find him."

"But we can't reach him, we don't know where he is," Josh looked over at Loretta who had walked across to the other side of the barge.

"We don't have Mengebara, but as Tanes we have some telepathy. It's of a different order than yours Klim but I can signal my brother to return."

Klim gasped as she shimmered to become the breathtakingly beautiful white unicorn. As the graceful creature made dance like movements with its head Klim

278

whispered to Josh. "What happens to her clothes? Should I fetch a blanket?"

Josh smiled. "Something to do with the illusion of matter and its manipulation on the elemental plane."

Loretta had transformed back to her fully clothed self by the time Josh had finished speaking. "They'll be back tonight," she announced.

Klim thought he had a glimpse of her mind print as she came back to sit wearily down beside them. He had sensed a residual regret, as if given the chance, she would remain in the form of a unicorn and journey to find the enchanted woods of Faerie.

"Look, let's head up to the pub for an hour or two," Josh suggested. "At least we can get some general news." His companions took little persuading. In minutes Loretta was linking arms with both of them as they headed towards the pub along the towpath. There was a lull in the wind and rain; Loretta stopped to reach into her pockets for gloves as the cold smarted her fingers. "I bet it's not as bitter as this in Dublin," she said. "I think winter's come all over the world," Klim replied and the melancholy in his voice made Loretta pull his arm closer. "You have the right of it sure enough," she said softly.

Inside the Glimpse of Hope was a scattering of regulars, scant custom for a Saturday night leading up to Christmas, Josh thought. There were two large TV screens and they made their way towards the one more discreetly placed by the raised platform, where they had sat previously with Siskin and the Tanes. That night of music already seemed a far memory, though it had happened less than a week before.

They had deliberately timed their visit to catch the main evening news, where images switched through major cities around the world. The reporter called the phenomenon the 'necrotic plague', where men, women and children disappeared, leaving only the faint smell of burning. There was no visible fire but scientists were investigating the possibility of a kind of spontaneous combustion. Not even the bodies were left and the numbers affected were increasing every day.

"Do you think this is some illusion, like Nephragm created when he took Gally?" Klim watched in horror as stricken relatives wandered in shock and panic, searching blindly for loved ones who had been beside them moments before. Josh peered closely at the screen. He stepped down to the bar to fetch the remote and paused the programme. Carefully he examined the images, flicking back and forth to each crowd. "Devourils," he whispered. "Look, the same people turn up in the crowd before each episode." He pointed out the ordinary looking people, magically resurrected around the world and present at each of the attacks. When he switched back to live TV, the same faces were depicted as being wanted in connection with the devastating events around the world.

"Looks like someone else has noticed," Loretta told him. "Are these people who vanished really dead?" Josh paled, "Yes. Everyone. It's how they took Lorcan, Loretta." He reached for her hand as her face fell. "Using a thing called the Odiam. It leaves no trace. They move at incredible speed, so even the camera didn't catch them." The report ended with an exhortation to avoid forming large crowds in the cities. Josh brought the remote back down to the bar and found that he was the focus of suspicious and frightened faces. Lines of Christmas decorations, glass baubles, tinsel and the expensively arranged artificial trees, seemed a mocking backdrop to the events just played out.

The brief visit to the pub had left each of them silently reflective as they made their way back on the towpath in the black, starless night. Loretta and Josh set to making supper but Klim had no appetite. Alone in his cabin, Klim sat on his bed staring at the wall. He thought of Echin and knew that there was something that only he could do, and he needed to do it soon. Slowly he let all of his worry for the others, even for Gabbie, drift away. He switched off all that Siskin had taught him about planning and calculations of risk. Klim let his breath come and go, deeper and deeper, sinking into the rhythm of his mind.

Calmly he entered Mengebara and saw that the mind place had now altered beyond all recognition. The small gardens of each individual had become one huge field of soil, ready to receive whatever grain was to be planted within it. Intuitively he understood that Kier, Gabbie and Swift had literally ploughed the way. Klim became aware of an ominous sound in the distance; as he listened, he began to distinguish its source. The sheer number overwhelmed his senses, human minds, chaos and panic, a sea of collective fear. There was so little order, so much confusion; with hope being buried in levelling despair as they clamoured together. He closed the outer borders of Mengebara and the disturbing frequencies skirted around the edges of the mind place. Detaching himself from the agonised pressure he jerked upwards, heading towards the kitchen.

"I don't know what to do, there's too many, no control, no order," he announced desperately. "What Klim? What are you trying to do?" Alarmed, Josh persuaded him to sit down and Loretta passed him a glass of water. "Kier called it the army of the Iridice."

"Into Mengebara will pour the army of the Iridice," Josh quoted, thoughtful. "Toomaaris said we can't use our mind place any more. It was for bigger things." Josh tried to access the mind place. He whistled, "It's vast. Goes on for miles." "In what way?" asked Loretta.

"It's like a huge ploughed field. It's walled in but there are shouts and screams from the other side."

"Devourils? Virenmor? Are they attacking us from the inside?" Loretta shifted her seat nervously. "No." Klim was sure. "I put it in place so that we could communicate but it's changed, moved on." Josh sat opposite his friend. "In what way Klim?"

"Well," he tried to find the right words, "it's the Myriar in us. It doesn't just belong to our group. The more we find the power of Moura's gift, the less it belongs just to us."

"I think I know what you mean," Josh agreed. He sketched the ploughed field that Klim had described but he had drawn the image in more detail, showing the brown earth winking with lights that covered the page. "I think," he said evenly, "they're seeking refuge Klim. All over the world people are shaken, the Devourils are an enemy they can 't see or fight."

"Perhaps," added Loretta, "many have found inside themselves a sense of the Myriar and they seek its presence. At some level, the human race knows that its very survival is threatened."

"It doesn't have to be tonight Klim," he told his friend.

"But there's hardly any time!" he objected. "There's enough," Loretta insisted. Klim, his eyes stinging with exhaustion, desperately hoped that she was right.

Chapter Thirty-three

Siskin gently lifted Clare's head from where it was tucked beneath his shoulder. Exhausted, and reluctant to leave, he had slept past midnight. He had hoped that he would be back at the boat by the time his companions awoke. A light from the window caught his attention. Clare rarely pulled the blinds; she loved the view across the mountains. He wondered anxiously if it was even later than he thought if dawn had already begun to light the dark winter morning.

It was not dawn that had arisen in the mountains but a different kind of light. Flashes of yellow and purple splashed across the dark sky. With them came an alien melody. Strangely, it had elements of an early science fiction movie he'd seen; twangs of sound that were meant to represent the mystery of the universe. It made him smile that some cord of memory must have pulled the unknown composer towards the sound he was now hearing. It reverberated like a sonic earthquake, releasing the brightly coloured energies that painted the mountains. He had no doubt that what he was experiencing was Moura's own preparation for the Alignment.

Awestruck, he sat down on the bed and his hand reached for the thin fingers that, even in sleep, automatically entwined with his own. Amron Cloch, the Song Stone, thrummed in harmony with the planet. He sat listening, soaking up the sound, until dawn broke in earnest. He dressed and said his silent goodbyes to Clare and Juliette with gentle kisses on their foreheads, noiselessly leaving the hotel. Siskin climbed into Suara, the vehicle reverberated to his touch as he pulled out from the sleepy village, wondering if he would ever return.

*

Klim felt that he'd slept a whole night but in fact it had only been a few hours, when he was awoken by the boat rocking with the weight of the number of bodies scrambling into the small space at the entrance to the barge. He heard Josh unlock the saloon door and then Mactire's voice. As he went to step out of his cabin, Loretta flew past to greet her brother and the other Tanes. They spread out amongst the two-seated sofas and tables.

"It took you long enough," she scolded.

Mactire sank into the seat nearest to Loretta. "We found Echin but we can't get to him, there's no safe way through the sea."

"Even the air currents have been manipulated," Oisen added." They're like propeller blades."

"But he's alive?" Loretta asked. "You saw him?"

Oisen nodded, in his griffin form, his distance sight was eagle-sharp. "Looks like he's on show in some kind of metal cage."

"Did you see Belluvour?" Klim asked.

"To tell you the truth," said Killian, his open, game-battered face defeated, "I've never been so scared in my life. I only had a glimpse of his back but he made my flesh crawl. It's hard to explain."

"Well I saw him, and he saw me," Danny told them. "Even from a distance it was like he knew every dark thought I ever had. He made you feel you should be punished and he could do you the favour of supplying that punishment."

The others turned towards him in surprise. Danny's face remained deeply thoughtful as he spoke. "I was on the mainland opposite the island, yesterday morning. We could only see the place in our Tane forms," he explained. "He was just there, befouling the sandy beach. He saw me but he only saw an oversized fox. One glance, that's all it took and I'll never forget it."

Loretta went to him and held his face. "You were lucky you had your elemental form on you Danny, but you're not the only one to see him in these last hours."

She turned to Klim who gave an account of his brief conversation with Echin; he squirmed as he recounted his contact with Belluvour.

"Kier's coming here?" Mactire straightened.

"Echin seemed to think the three women should have already returned by now if they were together." The mood turned sombre.

Danny rallied. "There's little to gain from speculation. At least we know definitely that Echin is still alive."

Oisen shook his head. "But why are they holding him like that?"

Mactire opened one of the cans of Guinness that Josh had left for him on the table. "It occurred to me that the only way to find out what's happening on that island is to get caught. Especially if you are the one being that Belluvour is not likely to kill until Candillium herself is there to witness it. I think Echin allowed it to happen." The others followed Mactire's lead, reaching for the cans of beer on the table.

Aiden shook his head in doubt. "He deliberately gave himself up. That's a hell of a risk!"

Loretta looked towards Josh and Klim, "I think Sean's right but I don't think it was planned until he was at the

285

house. If Echin hadn't offered himself then Geoden would have wiped us out in the blink of his unnerving eye. Or taken us to the island," she shivered with the memory of her capture.

"Maybe," Josh said, "he overestimated his ability to get out of there."

"I don't think we can help him right now," Klim looked grave.

"Where's Siskin?" Mactire's sharp eyes searched around the boat.

"I'm not sure," Klim told him anxiously. "He was supposed to be back by now."

"So why aren't we out looking?" Oisen shrugged his shoulders and lifted his arms, showing both disbelief and concern.

Klim said nothing but reached for the jewel that had belonged to his father and that he now knew was a fabled stone of the Myriar. He glanced upwards to find expressions that varied from Mactire's raised eyebrow of clinical interest to Josh's fervent encouragement. Holding the Iridice he concentrated on finding Amron Cloch. The milky stone flickered; purple flecks appeared and Klim could hear a soft thrum of sound.

"Crazy," he murmured, puzzled.

"What's wrong," Josh asked, alarmed. "Should I try adding the Chalycion. See if we can find him together?"

Klim shook his head. "It's like its busy," he said, looking around at the puzzled faces. "Like the link is engaged already by someone else!"

Mactire's brow narrowed in speculation. "What's so demanding of the Lute's attention that it could exclude the powerfully forged link shared by two Seeds of the Myriar?"

Klim hesitated but then replied, "If he's not back soon we'll go and find him." He looked towards Josh who nodded his agreement.

"You'll need to be careful," Danny added. "They were coming and going in legions on that island."

"We saw the news reports in the pub. They've been decimating the cities." Josh gave an account of what they had seen on the news that evening.

"In the name of Faerie," exclaimed Mactire, "I thought the world was bad enough before all this!"

"We can change it," Josh told him, his voice earnest.

"Well we can at least try," echoed Danny.

Mactire pulled a cushion under his head. "Try away my overzealous friends," he said, "and wake me up when it's over."

*

As daylight became firmly established, so too had the rain. Swollen rivers spilled over onto the roads but Suara navigated through the floodwater without stopping. The sonics that Siskin had laced into the surface of the vehicle meant his visibility was clear, despite the onslaught. Dead leaves, whipped by the wind, were shunted to either side; the raindrops re-organised their paths to bypass the windscreen. Suara was uncloaked and, at Siskin's sonic direction, was now tuned to the sound that had captured him.

The Lute followed like a lost player of a cosmic orchestra; he was inexorably pulled towards the beating drum that demanded his presence. He pulled onto a mountain road and climbed through mist shrouded villages, until the tone was at its most intense. At an abandoned farmhouse Siskin tucked Suara onto the grass verge and cloaked the vehicle.

He pulled a hooded jacket over his head and trudged along a track that ran adjacent to the old building. Climbing higher towards the summit, he was called by the ever increasing wash of sound. He had lost all idea of time when the rain abated and the sun broke through. Siskin had found the heart of the sound or was it the sound of a heart? The rhythm beat in couplets as he came nearer. The mist cleared and a rainbow arched over a pool of water ahead. On one of the three sides of the mountain was an armchair shaped hollow with what, he recalled, was known as a tarn. A circular body of water cupped high up on the mountain, that caught the light all the better for being so near to the sky. Each beat of sound stirred the pool, its centre rose and fell slightly in time to the rhythm, an arpeggio of ripples welcoming him. Siskin took off his jacket and shoes and laid them neatly by the pebbled shore. The ground fell away as he stepped into the water; his tall figure disappearing as the cold water claimed him.

*

"Why would he do that Clare?" Klim had barely slept. It showed in the sharp edge to his voice. "Why just disappear without telling you?"

Clare looked offended. "Do you think I had something to do with it?"

"Sorry," he replied, shamefaced. "It's just so unlike him."

"Well, no it's not actually, it's absolutely like him. He's been coming and going like this for the last three years. Sometimes I get a bit of notice, mostly I don't."

"Oh," Klim said lamely.

Josh, studiously ignoring the tension Klim had caused, sat opposite Clare and spread a sketch out on the kitchen table. Clare immediately recognised the mountain and lake where Tom had often taken her.

"This is where Josh has located Siskin." Klim scanned the picture with Clare.

Josh shook his head, his voice uneven, "It's all I can come up with." He looked hopefully towards Clare, "Can you take us there? Is it far?"

Clare clutched the table. "Before I tell you, I need to know what's happening. I never ask and I know his work is dangerous, but please tell me what's going on."

Josh glanced at Klim, who pulled out a chair and joined the other two around the table. Together, as succinctly as they could manage, they shared the events that had taken over their lives since, one way or another, they had all come into contact with Kier.

Siskin would have been proud, Klim thought, to see how calmly she questioned, how little she ridiculed the incredulous events they spoke of. At the end, exhausted, her eyes almost closed, she simply nodded and stood, carefully replacing the chair underneath the table.

"Thank you," she said softly. "It's called Anora Tarn and I'll drive you there."

*

Ulynyx sat on his raised seat and stared at the spot where they had, years ago, brought the body of Mwabi. Geoden, the Devouril, had seen immediately what he had failed to understand. He saw painfully and with new clarity the moment that Ulynyx had ceased to be a Mourangil. The moment he had thrust his will upon the beautiful girl, ignoring her fear and her cries. Amed's approaching footsteps were hurried but muted by the soft leather shoes. Ulynyx looked closely at the captain of his Elite, the unquestioning obedience. He felt a dull thud in his chest, what he had thought of as awe, he now recognised as fear.

"Belluvour has Toomaaris," the First in Faith told the leader of the Chunii. Ulynyx jumped up and Amed raised an involuntary arm to protect himself.

"Go," he said, calmly turning away.

Ulynyx had sought power and found it, now it choked his whole being. The Mourangil, that he had never ceased to love, had been captured by the Unbound. His eyes fell to the back of the chamber where, on the wall, remained the crysonance that Toomaaris had given him, filled with minerals and crystals linked to the Mourangils. It had been many, long human years since he had last embedded in the clean jewels that the humans saw fit to name only semi-precious. In his heart, he knew that once he had defiled the girl, the stones would not hold him. About to turn away from another painful memory Ulynyx saw a flare of green in the tourmaline and a white flash within the feldspar.

"Amed," he shouted.

The First in Faith turned at the edge of the hall, surprised and alarmed as he saw the light in his master's eyes.

"Do not disturb me," the leader of the Chunii told him. "Seal the gates!"

290

It took Josh a matter of minutes to discover the cloaked vehicle. It could only be driven by Siskin, even Klim could not attune it to movement without the presence of the Lute. Clare put out her hand and felt the solid and invisible presence of Suara. She looked paler and thinner than ever but did not speak. Klim and Josh exchanged a troubled glance as the stones of the Myriar tugged them up the hill, following the remote path that Siskin had taken the previous morning. The three sides of the mountain were dark, looming shadows gathered around a circular lake. The silence of the landscape hung heavier than the mist that rose around their leaden feet as they approached the small pile of clothes on the pebbled shore. Clare knelt down, picking up Siskin's jacket and folding it in her arms; she rocked back and forth, tears streaming silently down her face. Josh comforted her as Klim walked to the side of the lake and sat down by the water, letting his mind sink deep into its centre.

He became aware of a drumbeat of sound, in and out, rhythmic, organic, compelling. The water not only conducted the sound it seemed to be its originator. Klim searched through the dense fold of liquid matter for the presence of his friend; even if he was dead Klim was confident of uncovering Siskin's position. He concentrated his awareness in the centre, turning in each direction, reaching out towards the edge of the lake. The hours passed, as systematically he searched each part of the tarn, from centre to circumference, and found nothing. No hint that the body of Siskin lay hiding silently in the murky underbelly of this body of water.

Klim walked around the lake, trying to shake off the leaden weight of fear. Had the Devourils inflicted their cruel weapon upon their friend? Why then, would he remove his shoes and jacket? There was something, Klim was certain, that he'd missed. He splashed water on his face, settled himself, and began to scan the lake again. There, near the centre, a different texture. His heart began to quicken with excitement as he caught a thread of connection that he had previously passed over and focused his mind fully on that particular area of the lake. A tube, a kind of tunnel, yes, he could definitely feel it. There was a faint sound, the melody he associated with Siskin. Triumphant, he opened his eyes and turned towards the open aspect of the tarn.

Nothing but emptiness. Klim was sitting cross-legged; the afternoon mist replaced by a watery reflection of a dusk filled sky. Slowly, he untangled his stiff limbs and brought himself to standing. He ran to the other side of the tarn and once again let his mind sink downwards, this time with greater ease, through layers of soil and grit, the solid earth. Again, and more pronounced, he felt the melody of Siskin, felt its vibration across the land, far beneath the surface.

"Have you found something?" Josh appeared at the top of the path carrying blankets. Clare came behind him with a flask and a canvas bag.

"He's travelling," Klim said with conviction. "Alive."

"What do you mean travelling?" Her eyes flickered with hope.

"I don't know how to explain, it's like a tube underneath the ground. He's moving at speed towards the south west." He pointed in the direction he felt Siskin to be moving.

"How far?" Clare put a blanket around Klim's shoulders. he was shivering.

292

"I'm not sure, but beyond England," he said, gratefully pulling the blanket around him.

"But is he okay? Alive?" Her face was transformed with relief.

Klim nodded and smiled, impulsively he hugged the woman who accepted his words with such trust, though even to his mind they seemed fantastical. Josh joined them, laughing. Tears ran down Clare's face. "He's really alive." Josh embraced her, giving thanks that Siskin, who had become brother and friend to both himself and Klim, was still present in their lives.

"He went willingly," Klim added. "This is something he has to do. I can't explain how I know it but there's no taint of anything bad."

"But where is he? Where's he going to?" Clare pressed him.

"That's all I know, Clare." Klim's stomach growled.

"You need to eat," she told him. She rummaged through the canvas bag producing rolls and snacks and Josh spread out a second blanket. Drinking a cup of hot coffee from the flask, Klim gave them as much detail as he could of his mental foraying. He described the sense of hollowness deep underground, the strange tunnel in which Siskin travelled, encased inside some kind of bubble. He couldn't say if his friend had been conscious or not but he was sure that he was being pulled, vacuum like, towards some destination they could not know.

Eventually, when the food and drink had given them all some semblance of normality again, Clare began clearing up. "I have to get back to Juliette," she told them.

"And we to Bankside," Klim replied, trying to stifle a growing sense of urgency.

Josh gathered what was left of the food and he and Clare started down the path. Klim rolled up the blankets and turned for one last look at the eerie landscape.

"I heard you," he told the tarn. "I heard your voice this one time at least."

He was rewarded with the water at its centre suddenly spouting upwards in salute.

Chapter Thirty-four

Gabbie felt the wind press against her face as she plunged into a gallop across the field behind her mother's house. Pembicaro sounded his wild call that thrilled against the skies. She leant forward, her face pressing into his neck; it was as if they were part of the air and not on the ground at all. "Oh," she gasped and the stallion immediately slowed; his ears pricked upwards at the eerie sound that had disturbed his rider.

Gabbie peered into the gloomy shadow at the furthest point of the field. Her name, it called again from a blotch of space where the sunlight had failed to penetrate. Pembicaro neighed suspiciously but Gabbie felt as if she had been roped with a lasso and dragged towards the compelling sound. There was a shimmering shape, flashes of red. To the left of this strange figure was a tall standing stone, it's grey outline barely visible in the gloom. Gabbie could feel Arwres pulling her towards the standing stone but she turned instead towards the strange shape, there was something visceral about the whispering sound. She slid from Pembicaro's back and saw that the shape was female; the pink eyes and cloaked, crone like appearance repulsed her but she was still compelled forwards. The scream of alarm in the horse's voice was lost in the terrible fascination that drove her forward to meet Danubin.

*

Swift felt her footsteps falter, the swell of emotion at losing her grandmother had subsided. It was replaced by utter exhaustion and she sank to the ground. Lying on her back she looked down to find a lizard skittering over her legs. Her eyes flickered as the stars moved in a dance above her and she counted seven that seemed to grow in size, lulling her to sleep with their ponderous beauty. Swift woke with the touch of light upon her face but not from the sun. Thunder rolled and cracked about her and in minutes she was drenched in rain. Running for shelter she found herself heading towards a shadow that loomed solid and large in the darkness, a standing stone. Without hesitation she entered the stone, a Stozcist now almost at her full power, allowing her being to mingle with the molecules, absorbing the tiny grains of matter. A Waybearer within the Realm of Resonance, it showed her the huge grassy field, the screaming horse and Gabbie moving irresistibly towards the malignant shape that held the jewelled blade, vicious and deadly. Swift breathed in, ready to leap towards the field but stopped herself. Klim would mourn, but not forever.

*

The redwings fluttered as Kier sought for a way to follow the bloody footprints that stained the field near to the bridge. A white fog had descended and she was no longer able to see the path. The Key of Talitha held her attention as it flew ahead, breaking through the mist. She followed, finding that she now stood in front of what seemed like a huge pane of glass. Kier recognised that this was the barrier between her own and another's experiences in the Realm of Resonance. Her hand pressed against a hard surface. She stood back as indistinct shapes began to appear but moved forward again when she clearly saw the face of Gabbie. She was walking, dazed, towards a shadow that flickered with red flame.

Kier peered into the deep shadow and saw a woman who had come to her once in a dream, the true face of Danubin. She banged on the surface of the glass like material, screaming a warning as Danubin removed the weapon from her cloak. Kier cried in frustration but they did not see her, she could not enter. Gabbie looked up and then behind her, she was responding to a sound in the corner of the field. The call came from an older woman, with the same heart shaped face and sapphire blue eyes that featured in Gabbie's face. Her mother. Kier could hear the woman's voice, warning her daughter, telling her to run. Inches away from Danubin, Gabbie turned and ran for her horse.

"Run Gabbie," Kier urged, powerless behind the glassy surface. "Run!"

Gabbie was almost on the horse when Danubin's fingers reached out to grab her and brought her sprawling to the ground. The horse reared in a powerful attack but Danubin merely flicked her fingers. "Begone!" she demanded. "There is nothing that can hurt me here."

The horse vanished. A withered hand pinned Gabbie to the ground, the other holding a knife, strangely slack. Kier screamed alarm as Danubin's grasp tightened on the jewelled handle and her arm raised to deliver the blow.

"Let me through," Kier commanded Talitha.

The glassy barrier fell away as thunder banged like a drum in the sky over the field. Lightning struck the blade held by Danubin. She screamed, wringing her hands, both now blackened. Gabbie wriggled from her hold, although Danubin barely noticed. Now Candillium stood before her, The Key of Talitha glowing red in the stone around her neck.

The ground shook underneath her as Gabbie pulled away from the tight grip of the blackened hand. Shocked, her brain spinning, she watched in horrific fascination as the sky lit with flashes of lightening that spotlighted the two antagonists just feet away from her. The deformed crone cradled her newly injured hand.

"Danubin!" Gabbie recognised the murderess now, but above her stood another tall figure, a commanding presence that glowed with light. Danubin struggled gracelessly to her feet. "Candillium," she croaked, a cackle of fear and hatred. Her eyes were fixed on the red flower on the pendant that Kier wore. Unthinking, the blackened hand snatched the pendant, snapping the chain upon which it hung. Kier did not move. Triumphant, Danubin held up her prize. It was only then that the leader of the Virenmor saw that the mutilation of her hand had crept to her arm. She released the Stone of Mesa but it was too late, the whole of her left side had become blackened.

Gabble turned away as Danubin screamed, writhing on the grass as the blackness rose to encompass her whole form. In the Realm of Resonance, each despoiling life that Danubin had lived rose from her corpse and raced down to the river that had now appeared at the edge of the field. Then at last came the face of the first. "Durane!" cried Kier. Shocked, she watched in great sadness as Erion's mother rose from the ruined body of Danubin and made her way down to the river. There was a brief moment of something like humanity, when her oldest of friends wordlessly nodded her shame.

So then, all those ages ago, Belluvour had engineered the first betrayal with someone loved by Candillium.
Kier turned away, sick with horror, stumbling against the standing stone.

"Kier!" Gabbie ran to her friend and the two women embraced. "I have the key Gabbie. We need to leave. Where is Swift?"
Gabbie shook her head, dispersing the last of the clouds that had shrouded her mind. "I haven't seen her since we left the river," she replied. It seemed so long ago. There was a vibration beneath them. "Did you feel that?" Gabbie nodded. "It came from the stone." Her face, already pale, became ashen. "It's murmuring, weeping," she said feeling around the stone, searching. Gabbie stepped back in horror. At the centre of the stone was an engraving, a face. "Swift!" she cried.
Kier turned. "Come out Swift." she called. "We need to leave."
They heard the sobbing Stozcist, who appeared trapped within the stone. Kier reached out, tracing the contours of Swift's face in the stone. "She's locked in." Grimly, Kier searched the field until she found the Stone of Mesa lying in the grass, the two keys were still embedded within it. Gabbie flinched away as her friend held out her hand containing the stone.

"It's okay," Kier said, "you're a Seed of the Myriar, it belongs as much to you as it does to me."
Gabbie shook her head in disagreement but took the stone and carefully placed it within her pocket.

"Take her back," Kier instructed Talitha firmly, kissing Gabbie's forehead.

"No!" Shouted Gabbie, finally seeing what Kier intended, but it was too late. The Key of Talitha, at

299

Candillium's request, opened a doorway for Gabbie to exit the Realm of Resonance.

*

Echin watched from the metal cage as the Devourils gathered together to undertake another 'culling' as it had become known to those who served Belluvour. They filled the main body of the elaborate pavilion. He remained trapped on the platform that Belluvour had used as a stage, to remind his followers of their purpose. Echin looked towards Geoden but met the same automaton despair that he saw in the faces of all of these once illumined beings. On each such occasion Belluvour regaled them with stories of human atrocity and greed that had occurred in the cities he now sent them to destroy. He strode arrogantly across the platform. "The Alignment is almost here; the Sister Spheres will look to us to clear the surface before it can be remade. Once mankind no longer infests our planet we will create new shape and purpose." He turned to the figure sitting quietly in the suspended cage. "Where is your Myriar now Toomaaris? No one comes to save you. Candillium does not exist!"

Toomaaris sat in silence.

"What of the keys, Belluvour?" asked Geoden. "There was a report that the Key of Brunan was seen on the African continent?"

Echin saw the tightening of Belluvour's jaw before he answered.

"The keys would only emerge to make their way into our hands. We are the fate of Moura, we are the planet's only hope. The Sister Spheres will begin the new cycle and we will embed in jewelled kingdoms above the surface."

"Then," one voice called out, "why not wait until after the Alignment? We have already destroyed many major cities. Should we not preserve some of this race to serve us?"

Belluvour's mockery of a human face, perfect and expressionless, mask like, turned towards the speaker. Behind the stolen human form Echin recognised Sellonir, younger in Mourangil terms than any of the others. Rage quivered beneath the modulated voice but it had lost none of its power and seduction. Belluvour answered the challenge to his plan. "Do not forget that we kill out of mercy. Once the Sister Spheres decree their extinction, mankind will suffer long years of ruin and gradual starvation as the surface changes to befit our needs. This race will not survive, for it cannot offer any significance to either Moura or the bejewelled."

Geoden glanced at Echin. A mere flick of the sad eyes as he turned his head.

"Will you accompany us, Belluvour?" asked Geoden. "We weary of this task of killing. Your presence would light our purpose."

Belluvour came down to his followers, looking around and allocating those who needed to stay. There was a new energy in the dark crowd.

"Come then," the Unbound gathered them to him. "Let us cleanse another benighted part of our planet's surface." Echin watched the diseased flock leave the island, folded invisibly into the air. He noted that, as the solstice was almost upon them, Belluvour concerned himself little with preserving the bodies they had stolen. He retched at the thought of more human slaughter while he waited, helplessly penned in the metal cage. He was caught in an environment that made him sicker the longer he stayed within it. The presence of the Odiam above the cage had weakened him. Echin thought back to Obason when Belluvour had suspended Candillium in a metal cage above a flame. He blanched at the memory, at the suffering she had endured. He opened his mind to the possibility that Kier would not find her way back from the Realm of Resonance and he felt a sense of despair. This was of course, as Belluvour intended, part of the sickness inflicted by the Odiam and the Devourils.

Desperately weary, he could not embed in his jewelled form to escape that befouled place. Then the Mourangil found inside himself another way to free his being from the painful bonds of hopelessness, the human way. He focused on Kier, seeing her face as she had turned to him in the garden room of the Barley Field. How he had seen the starlit capacity of the love that had brought her back to Moura, to Toomaaris the Mourangil. He thought about the Seeds of the Myriar; Josh, Gabbie, Klim, Siskin and Swift. And all those gifted beings who had preceded them through the long years of Candillium's absence. He felt the flicker of joy, the love he bore for them all. He allowed himself to accept the caress of Kier's heart bound to his own. Echin knelt in the cage laughing. How could it have taken him all this time to understand?

The Devourils that had remained flicked their dead eyes towards him, thinking him to be on the edge of insanity. Already lost to them, disempowered by Belluvour, they dismissed the Mourangil and turned back to the horrendous reports that transmitted across the sky.

A soft thud sounded on the obdurate column behind, a whisper on the breeze. "Toomaaris, I come to rescue you."

Echin looked up to see an onyx jewel glimmer on one of the obdurate pillars to which the metal cage was attached.

"Ulynyx! How?" Echin directed his voice to fill only the space behind him. "Be careful, the mechanism above me holds Odiam. If the weight in the cage lessens it will expel upon me faster than I can fold into the air. Also, I am weakened."

"What if the weight in the cage is more?" asked Ulynyx.

"Any sudden change will be detected. We will both be exiled to the Secret Vaults!"

"I saw what Belluvour has made to hold the Odiam and to inject their targets so accurately. I have on my arm the same construct, made from baryte, like a gun firing a bullet. It contains crysaline." The material was prized and rare, even amongst the Mourangils. "Forgive me Toomaaris," Ulynyx continued, his voice poignant, soft as rain in that hot, eerie, unforgiving place.

Echin would have wept if the silent guards did not stand below him. "Ulynyx, you have always been my brother. Above and below the surface. There is nothing to forgive."

The rough edges of the onyx jewel softened into a smooth oval. "Thank you." The great leader of the Chunii said humbly. "You've experimented with this weapon and the crysaline?" asked Echin. There was a long silence. Echin gave a wry smile; he was reminded of a Mourangil who had leapt into the middle of human war with neither knowledge or real understanding. "You are experimenting now?"

Ulynyx made no reply. He waited until the Devourils on the platform had moved away, then changed form above the pillar and directed his aim. "Are you ready?" he warned. "I'm injecting the crysaline now."
Toomaaris felt the mildest of thuds as the crysaline covered the black Odiam above him. He waited until the attention of the nearest guard was turned and he folded into the air, sluggish for a Mourangil. Ulynyx was beside him but the touch of the obdurate stung Echin badly. It made his movement in the air, already slow, much slower. On the ground beneath them one of the guards cried alarm as he noticed the absence. "Find me in Ulyn," cried Ulynyx. His dark form appeared above the temple, mocking the Devourils below, hoping their momentary confusion would give the time he needed to escape. The guards gave chase.

Toomaaris, barely across the sea to the nearest land, swiftly embedded in a clean quartz rock that lay on a table by the beach. A young employee of the five star hotel, standing on the entrance steps, saw a dark cloud gather over the beach below. It vanished almost as soon as it was noticed. He walked down, curious, absently picking up various clutter. A light flashed within a pink quartz rock in the centre of one of the tables. He picked it up and examined it carefully, fascinated by the vein of blue within the stone. Luke felt strangely comforted by the rock as he placed it within his pocket. For some reason it made him think of Klim and Gabbie, the friends he had lost. Usually, when his mind wandered towards them he drew it back, the sadness and regret hurt too much. Today he could almost believe they were all together again, that they were still kids playing manhunt in the fields that bordered the backshore.

Chapter Thirty-five

No country had been left untouched, hysteria splashed across the internet; theories abounded about the 'necrotic plague'. Rumours of alien invasion were linked to the coming Alignment. The devastating, sudden and inexplicable disappearance of human beings seemed harder to accept than the brutal inhumanity of conflict. It seemed sinister that in areas of war and malignant cruelty, the attacks had not happened. Scientists sported a number of postulations but none could be evidenced. Fear and confusion, the base matter of aggression, burrowed their way, like ticks, into the body of man.

It was some time before Echin was able to leave the quartz stone. Slowly he made his way to the East and to Ulyn. The Devourils were still noisily mastering the art of transforming their stolen bodies in the air. He, on the other hand, having spent so long above the surface, easily moulded his human frame to join with the molecules of Mourangil being.

The elusive desert city only became visible as he entered its outer rim. Amed and the other Elite kept watch on the outskirts as he descended to the onyx palace he had visited on other occasions. The First in Faith nervously greeted the Mourangil. Echin had last come upon the elite Chunii soldier as he had attempted to carry out Elanur's execution.

"Ulynyx has not returned?" Echin began to fear the worst.

"Not as yet, Toomaaris. He asked that you wait for him in his private dwelling."

Hesitantly, the Mourangil stepped inside the sumptuous cavern. Amed, as he had been instructed, disregarded the cries he heard inside.

*

Luke sat idly on the edge of the beach and removed the quartz stone from his pocket. On inspection, he saw that the blue vein had disappeared and wondered if it had just been the play of light that had given it such a distinctive colour. Normally the hotel would be full of tourists getting ready for Christmas celebrations but, like most of the other hotels on the island, it stood practically empty. The necrotic plague had ripped through countries bringing fear, death and devastation. For most the concept of a holiday already seemed some dream of the past. Luke had no money to travel back to England, he had survived by understanding plants and how to grow food. He had created a smallholding attached to the hotel and his skill in husbandry, learnt from years on his father's farm in Bankside, kept what business they had still going.

Luke saw it again, the dark cloud over the distant island, eerie and triggering some unwanted recognition. It seemed that he was the only one to notice it, even today when it was blacker than ever. He jumped up from this rocky seat on the beach, looking around, shouting. Had no one else seen the movement in the air? The triangular cloud now headed in the direction of the hotel, as if the dark island had thrown some cannon ball towards them.

"Hurricane!" he screamed.

Others were running now, talking in fast Turkish, hurtling across the hotel frontage to the shelters below. He had almost reached the door of the nearest shelter when he saw a child running in the wrong direction, screaming for her mother. Her curls bobbed wildly as she turned her head from one direction to another in panic. Parts of the beach were already smothered in black; wind whipped loungers and signs slammed into the carefully decorated railings. A heavy, outside table whirled across to where the little girl stood transfixed. Flinging himself forward, Luke caught her and rolled onto the sand a split second before it landed. Running, he reached the steel door of the shelter that fronted onto the beach. Struggling, he yelled for help, trying to prise it open until at last the hotel owner pushed from the other side. It took all Luke's strength and attention to help hold the door open, passing the infant to his employer. He failed to see that the furious storm had lifted a yellow taxi cab, sweeping it towards where he stood. The vehicle pounded against his back, pinning him to the steel door as it banged heavily shut. The empty vehicle slid to one side and Luke fell to the ground, his final thoughts were of Gabbie, her blonde hair shining in the moonlight as she tucked her arm into his.

*

Klim had been unable to settle since their return from Stromondale. At midnight, he found himself in the 'bottom park' as they had called the play area on the back shore road. He made his way through a gap in the fence to the field beyond, pulling Siskin's black woollen hat over his ears. Clare had passed it to him, they both knew that until this time the musician had always carried it with him. Klim spotted the large oak tree where he had spent so many evenings with Gabbie and their friends. He found himself retreating into its shelter, adjusting his body into the natural hollow inside the trunk. It was different to feel the cold wood, the lack of green summer, the absence of Gabbie's warmth. In the bitter cold, amid the damp leaves, it took some time to set light to the pile of twigs and paper. Once the small flame became established however, the wind whipped it into ascending sparks. Klim's gaze followed the glimmering lights as they flew outwards to where the sea lay hidden and he watched them disintegrate across the empty field.

He remembered Swift, the first time he had seen her running, escaping across this same field. How he had known, in the pit of his belly, that their fates were intertwined. His mind fluttered to Kier, he did not yet know Candillium. Kier had touched his heart the first time she had looked through his sorrow and fear in the Seven Rivers Café. Then he reached inside to his special place that had come into being to hold Gabbie's ebullient, sometime derisive, always fierce love for him. She would have reminded him that they had sat here looking out over their fields for all those years; that it was no surprise that opening Mengebara to others, would take this form.

Klim turned his mind towards Mengebara where the ploughed field of the mind place now covered a great expanse. He sighed at its magnitude, for it now appeared as unmeasurable as the sea. The access to the field in Mengebara was through a narrow gate in a giant wall; he placed himself to the right of it. At his back, he could hear screaming, could feel the panic that stirred in them but also in turn stirred in him. Klim slowed his own charged heart beat and rapid respiration and let his mind reach out to the masses that hammered so hard against the impenetrable wall. He let his heart palpate the crowd, a desperate search for good, for truth, for purpose. He borrowed Siskin's melody and transmitted it through the wall, that now seemed to vibrate gently with song. Slowly the shouting and screaming became a calm murmur, their fear gradually muted to hope. The gate in the wall opened and one by one they entered the ploughed field.

Men, women and children stumbled through the gate, mystified and searching. Klim saw then what had been planted in the field, an individual seed for each of them. He understood that the whole field had been created on the basis of something his mother had quoted from an old woman in India, who she had revered. In the face of overwhelming need, she had told him, begin with one person, do what it is given to you to do, each to his or her own capacity.

Klim watched as each individual was drawn towards the seed that had been planted for them, the opportunity for kindness. He looked to the distant horizon; the more that entered, the greater the expanse of the field. Some found their precious seed straight away, their bodies trembling with its light. Others would have a longer search, but he was confident that he had planted for everyone, as a Reeder should. The gate had disappeared, only those who searched for truth would find this field, although Klim was happy to leave it open.

The fire sparked high in the breeze, creating a mesmerizing pattern of dancing lights against the pitch black of a moonless sky. Klim let his eyes follow the light show as his exhausted mind withdrew from Mengebara and tried to focus on his surroundings. Moments later he was alert, peering through the flames at an area of moving shadow. He threw a newspaper onto the fire and as the flames surged upwards he looked carefully, hardly able to believe what he was seeing. He launched himself upwards and ran towards the shivering figure of Gabbie, shouting her name. She turned towards him, dazed, searching his face. He waited, sensing the fog that clouded her mind and the disorientation that had left her wobbly, as if she had just come down from a theme park ride. At last a smile lit her face and she seemed to recognise him. "Klim," she whispered, reaching her hand to his face as tears streamed down her own.

*

Echin had felt their presence immediately. All three Mourangils cried out as he entered the chief dwelling place in the city of Ulyn. Faer and Tormaigh emerged from the crysonance to greet him. Tormaigh jumped backwards with shock. "Obdurate," he frowned with alarm. "And the Odiam." The two Mourangils smouldered with anger. Faer's icy glance contrasted with the candlelit comfort of the cavern. "As of old, he knows no bounds." He helped Echin to one of the many cushions strewn along the wall.

"You are sick, come," urged Faer, holding crysaline in his hands.

"No, don't waste it on me."

"But it can be reused," Tormaigh argued.

"No, it will absorb too much toxicity."

Faer replaced the crysaline that they had gathered in a container made of rock salt, about the size of a crate.

"Where did you find so much? We all but exhausted the one vein," asked Echin, confused.

"Swift," answered Tormaigh. "Beneath the island, she housed herself in crysaline and it found its way to the surface near Samuel's cottage."

"Remarkable," Echin smiled, "and the cottage still stands?"

"It still stands." Tormaigh drew the crate nearer. "There was some damage but Samuel had removed the library in time."

"But how are you here?"

Tormaigh related the story of the Waybearer stone that still remained in the hidden cavern where Candillium had first met Toomaaris the Mourangil. "She was drawn there in order to find the crossing place to the Realm of Resonance."

"I knew she would find a way into the Realm of Resonance. But it is many long years since I have thought of that cavern." Echin allowed himself to sink into the memory of their first meeting and it was as comforting to him as the pure crysaline they had recovered.

"We came to stand beside you," Faer told him. "Whatever the outcome."

Echin tried to stand but they would not let him, instead he reached for the blue stone that Elanur had given him.

"They could not touch me to search for it," he told them with a self-mocking smile.

Tormaigh sighed, even though he knew the answer, "Is it really the only way?"

*

Kier felt the weight of urgency, the threatening possibility of failure. Soon, very soon, it would be too late to recover Swift from where she was locked inside the standing stone. She thought back to Echin's words in

Stromondale, that Candillium shared some of the properties of the particular gift given to each Seed of the Myriar. Could she be part Stozcist? How had she known that this stone was a Waybearer? She placed her hand on the hard, uneven rock and closed her eyes. Kier breathed inwards, her nose curling with the stench of Danubin's death that lingered in that place. Turning away she filled her lungs with clean breath and focused her energy on the stone. Opening her eyes, she saw that the rock was no longer solid matter but a mass of molecules, trembling, parting to allow her fingers to reach into its substance and then coalescing around them. She felt the warmth of her body begin to cool as she reached into the cold stone. More and more she was drawn towards the Waybearer, until the entire length of her arm had sunk into its fabric.

Summoning her courage, she plunged her whole body inside the rock and found herself transported through the stone, that now formed a solid wall behind as she stepped onto a narrow ledge above a stream. The air brooded, the main river could be heard in the distance, raging. All was dark and Kier threw off the oppressive weight of the place as she focused entirely on the sound she could hear an agonised keening. She recognised the small bridge where she had found Martha, although it had now been transformed into an eerie crossing place. The silver birch had been uprooted and its bare skeleton choked the small stream below. As she approached the bridge she looked around for Martha but knew that her sister would not be found in this barren place.

Kier shouted for the Stozcist. The keening broke to sobbing and grew louder, echoing in the gloom. She began to fret about what was happening in the world outside and saw that the Waybearer stone behind her now flashed white at its centre. Kier went closer, placing her hand against the wall. She could hear the clink of glass, voices murmuring. "There's another way out Swift! I can feel it! We can go home!" shouted Kier. Nothing. The weeping had stopped. "Swift please, we need to go." Still nothing. Kier knew that she could walk through the Waybearer stone and out of the Realm of Resonance. She was equally certain that without her, Swift could not.

*

Echin woke to find Faer and Tormaigh had embedded and that Ulynyx had not yet returned. He hobbled over to the crysonance but the crystals were out of tune with his being. He felt despoiled, unbalanced, his whole body trembled for the effect of his proximity to the Odiam had not yet abated. He wondered how hard it must be for Ulynyx to stand there by the crysonance and know that he was no longer a Mourangil. As if his thought had called him, the leader of the Chunii strode into the hall.

"I doubled back to the island and hid amongst the obdurates." He seemed to carry the weight of the city on his strong shoulders, his eyes glittering onyx in the light of the crysonance, his head bowed.

"You took a risk indeed," Faer had materialised beside them, quickly followed by Tormaigh.

"Belluvour is returning to the volcanic power of old," Ulynyx reported. "His rage rocked the sea, crashing great waves onto the island and the shores nearby."

"More suffering and destruction," Echin's strained face turned grim.

Ulynyx nodded, "And the island itself is only held by Geoden and the others. But for Geoden the Unbound would have murdered the guards."

"What else?" Echin asked, seeing that Ulynyx had still not told him all.

"He has decimated the humans, men, women and children regardless. Geoden has estimated that almost half of the human population on the planet could now have been wiped out. Whilst the press has concentrated on the large attacks in cities, there has been an inexorable flood of Devourils across the East and into the South. Ruthlessly efficient in their silent destruction, mankind has yet to become fully aware of the extent of the atrocity."

The Mourangils paled. Hard edged, they absorbed the grim news.

"We have to find a way," muttered Echin.

"He has brought forward the next cull," Ulynyx told him.

"Where?"

"New York," he replied.

Chapter Thirty-six

Off the north west coast of Africa lies a group of islands that exploded into being with violent volcanic eruptions. A legacy of this volatile beginning is the presence of lava tubes, elongated caverns beneath the surface that sometimes open out in parts to form a cerulean blue lagoon. At dawn, two days before the Alignment, in the silent, shimmering heat, a bubble of air popped in the middle of one such idyllic lake. It was followed by another and another as the crysaline that had encased Siskin shook away from his body like a discarded garment. A reflex kick brought the Lute to the surface. Immediately, he raised an arm to shield his eyes from the sunlight. Breathing hard he was aware of the background vibration of something that he had been hearing all of his life but never identified. The white shore of the lagoon was just a short distance away. He dragged himself onto its smooth surface and saw that he was alone.

The natural habitat had been assisted by a loving artistry that caressed the plants, built wooden seats into the ascending hillside and erected signs to various parts of what was clearly a tourist attraction. Dropping down from the open lake, he came to an arched roof over a body of water, where small embellishments had been made to the natural stone to enhance the contrast of light and shade. In the darkness below, sightless white crabs milled between each other at the bottom of the pool.

Dryness constricted his throat. A wooden signpost led him to a shop that, in season, sold trinkets for tourists. There was also a fridge full of bottled water. Gratefully he slaked his thirst, reading from guide books as he did so. The cave was naturally formed but had been enhanced by the work of an island artist and hero, who had championed the local culture and the people. As a result of his influence there was only one high rise building on the whole island, all others were restricted in height so that everywhere the light fell on panoramic views across the dry, magnificently eloquent, volcanic landscape.

The vibration that Siskin had previously heard, thrummed in his veins as he returned to the lake. The water quivered. He descended steps, on the opposite side of the lagoon, into an underground auditorium. Siskin immediately recognised the melody of the place, as he saw the natural markings of the walls. As he moved downwards, through rows of wooden benches, the markings came to life in a fierce red and gold dance of colour. There was a grand piano on the stage at the bottom of the auditorium and Siskin's heart swelled with the realisation that he had been brought to this place to play his music for the heart of Moura.

*

Ulynyx stood in the centre of Times Square where huge screens reflected the destruction of city after city. And yet, he thought, they still gather like this in overcrowded places, subsumed in the business of the lives they have constructed. It seemed to him that human beings found every way to ignore the danger that was upon them. Christmas lights, masses of shoppers, baubled giant pines; Manhattan glowed like a beacon. Already he could hear the Devourils approach, undetectable by technology, moving at speed. In moments came the screams of discovery, the indiscriminate taking of human life. The shocking absence of men, women and children, with no trace left behind. Ulynyx raised himself, launching upwards into the air as a signal to those he had placed on top of the surrounding buildings as the Devourils alighted below.

Amed, First in Faith of the Chunii, began the attack. He took from his pouch an arrow tipped with the substance his master deemed so precious. Carefully he placed it within his bow. The arrows themselves were designed to disintegrate as soon as they were fired into the air. Ulynyx watched as the white rain of crysaline fell onto the stolen flesh of the Devourils, disarming the foul Odiam, forcing them to stillness. As Toomaaris had predicted the crysaline dissolved the stolen, human flesh that the Devourils had purchased by murder. Those that were not struck, quickly reverted to the skies, totally unprepared to face opposition. Where the crysaline fell on humans its touch lifted them to hope. Faer and Tormaigh weaved invisibly between the crowd, gathering the precious substance that had not been used. The necrotic plague had, for the first time, been vanquished. There was huge cheering from the crowds but they could find no sign of their rescuers or the handsome figure who had ascended into the air like Captain America.

Later that evening, the leader of the Chunii sat cross-legged on a cushion in the cavern in Ulyn. The city was already celebrating the great victory over the Devourils. Not all had yet returned. He and the Mourangils had been able to carry only some of the Chunii from New York. Others would take the roundabout routes that he had planned for them in advance. His face had been on newsfeeds all over the world, reporters and presenters each trying to surpass the other with their names for him. He was the 'unknown hero', the 'people's champion', the 'dark angel'.

The Mourangils and Ulynyx spoke together softly amid the festivities. Even with their careful husbandry, too little of the crysaline remained to defeat the Devourils. "In all these ages, has no other vein been discovered?" Ulynyx enquired.

"None," answered Echin.

Hidden within the wall of the cavern was the remaining crysaline. Toomaaris had once told Ulynyx of the rare and miraculous substance that could 'disarm harm'. He explained that they had hidden the Perfidium within crysaline as it was toxic to a Devouril. Ulynyx sighed, other than in the device he had copied from the Devourils, he dared not touch the precious substance. Instead he had directed Amed how to manufacture the arrowheads that had proved so effective in preventing a further culling.

"Is it true?" asked Ulynyx. "Has Candillium returned? Are the Seeds of the Myriar gathered?" Echin nodded but found himself evasive. He raised himself to standing and lifted his cup; all around the huge cavern the Chunii did the same.

"To Ulynyx," Echin said in a voice that echoed around the city.

"To Ulynyx," every voice joined him. "We salute you."

"We salute you," the chorus repeated.

Ulynyx lifted his cup in thanks, stood up and returned the salute to his people. He smiled as he watched them huddled together, laughing and feasting. Joy had found a way back into the eyes of his followers. He thought of Geoden, once respected and loved by the bejewelled and now committing atrocities in the name of the Unbound.

He thought of his own dark path of delusion and the fact that, had it not been for Toomaaris, he would have been responsible for the murder of Elanur.

There was activity at the entrance to the hall, where a number of the Chunii had just entered. They spoke to Amed, who reported quietly to his commander. Ulynyx, looking grave, turned to advise the Mourangils.

"You should know that the Virenmor have tracked Elanur to Ireland. My men, in turn, tracked the Virenmor. The solstice is very near and Belluvour searches for the Runeshaper."

Echin looked towards Tormaigh and Faer who immediately replaced their cups and stood to leave. They gave their thanks to Ulynyx who spoke with sadness.

"Please tell Elanur that I ask her forgiveness."

Faer nodded. A few moments later they had vanished from the hall. Echin also rose to leave.

"You are not yet well enough my friend. Stay a while," advised Ulynyx.

Echin shook his head. "I need to go," he insisted, "and as you say, the solstice is near."

Ulynyx bowed his head, his words a whisper. "Danubin was here." Echin turned in alarm. The expression on the face of the great Chunii leader told of his intimacy with Danubin. Echin turned away. "She knows that Talitha is in the Realm of Resonance." Ulynyx spat out his regret. "She seeks Candillium and the keys."

Echin wavered; he had to place his hands on the wall to stay upright.

"I am sorry," Ulynyx told him, with genuine regret. The Mourangil seemed unable to speak. He laid his cup to one side and they stood together in the chief dwelling

of Ulyn. Ulynyx answered the unasked question ."I have no knowledge that she succeeded in her purpose."
Echin nodded but remained silent and began to move away. "I have to leave," he told Ulynyx.

"May the lighted jewel shine forever in your footsteps," offered Ulynyx. Echin turned, there was an ineffable sadness in the deep blue of his eyes. "May the sacred flame forever burn in your heart," he returned.
They spoke the old salutations of those Mourangils who had left the kingdoms below, for a time, in order to aid those who breathed life on the surface. Ulynyx stood unmoving for some time after Echin's departure. Amed slowly approached him, "Can I be of service Lord?" he asked with concern.

"No Amed," his strong face turned to the crysonance he could no longer use. "It is I who must serve you."

*

The World Heritage Site in County Meath, just north of Dublin, was usually a thriving tourist attraction, particularly at the December solstice. However, the storms and necrotic plague had forced the cancellation of the annual event, where some chosen few could witness the spectacular sunrise from inside, what had become known as, a passage tomb. The narrow stone passage opened out into a chamber where each roof stone overlapped the one below, until the final capstone sealed the chamber. Inside Elanur was busy preparing for the Alignment, bringing to life the mysterious markings that had grown cold with age. As she worked each one they radiated different coloured lights according to the minerals in which they were encrusted. Already the walls

320

emitted orange, green and white flames, in which danced the markings finally brought to life in the Runeshaper's hands.

Samuel, also in the chamber, was reading quietly. Disturbed, the Riverkeeper raised his head. The River Boyne, in the valley below, had been restless all day but its rhythm suddenly ceased to be in harmony with the surrounding land. Pebbles from the riverbed flew into the air and pounded against the ancient kerbstones that circled the mound. Samuel looked towards the Runeshaper, who he had been tasked to protect but Elanur was too absorbed in her work to notice his movement. Quietly, he walked through the passage, lowering himself down behind the elaborately carved entrance stone.

Outside, three dark figures, their bodies skeleton thin, wore the ceremonial robes of the Virenmor. A blood red tunic dropped full length but did not cover the hollow faces of stolen bodies reaching the end of their use. Hastily, Samuel turned back to alert Elanur, in his mind already picking out a hiding place in one of the chamber recesses. He was only a step away from the chamber when a movement singed the air. There before him stood an expressionless Devouril. Even as the malaised creature lifted his arm to expel the Odiam, Samuel dislodged one of the passage stones with a gesture of his hand. It crushed the body that the Devouril had inhabited and threw a barrier between the chamber and the passageway. Samuel squirmed with revulsion as he felt the dark shadow try to invade his own shape. The Riverkeeper quickly transformed to become a shimmering fountain and the Devouril, stunned, diminished to a black, smoking ribbon, extinguished in the column of water.

Too far from the river's source of power, Samuel could not sustain his fluid persona and became the cleric once again. Almost immediately another two Devourils appeared, one either side of him. Again Samuel flicked his hand to bring another of the stones crashing down but this time the Devourils were too quick. There was a rush of clean air as Tormaigh and Faer materialised within the tunnel. Samuel cried out with relief but it was the last sound he was to make as the Odiam ejected from the wrist of the Devouril on his right. Faer screamed as Samuel's life was extinguished in that fleeting moment. Tormaigh fell to where the old one had been standing as he attempted to come between the Devouril and the Riverkeeper. In an instant Faer had ringed the chamber with crysaline, trapping the two Devourils and disabling their weapons. He looked behind their hollow faces to see the Mourangils they had once been. "Sellonir, Rhodon!" he cried in dismay. "You have killed an old one, a Riverkeeper."

Sellonir, distorted almost beyond recognition, replied in a hoarse, guttural voice. "He was born of the race that has plundered and despised Moura. We will destroy even you Faer, for your support of them. You were foolish to leave the jewelled realms."

Elanur wedged herself between the opening to the chamber and the stone that now lay before it. She shuffled her way forward into the passage and began to frame a smile as she saw the two Mourangils. In a second this became a look of horror as she registered the Devourils penned by a glowing ribbon of crysaline.

"Where is Samuel?" she asked, already certain of the reply.

As Elanur wept and prepared her farewell to Samuel, Faer and Tormaigh imprisoned Sellonir and Rhodon in a second passage tomb using the crysaline. After ensuring the containment of the Devourils Tormaigh followed his companion outside and across the grassy ridge. "Have you told Toomaaris?" he asked.

Faer nodded sadly. "He is already weakened, and I have delivered him a terrible blow."

They made their way down the hill to where Elanur knelt on the bank of the River Boyne. Faer and Tormaigh came either side of her and together they sang a song of grief that had not been heard in that valley for five thousand years, when the tombs had first been created.

*

Echin stumbled as he reached the towpath, a little way from the narrowboat. The crystal presence of Faer in his mind could not extinguish the news that he had conveyed. His human body was stick thin and his Mourangil heart had dulled to a joyless presence that beat only because Moura required it. The toxic presence of the Odiam, his great sorrow for the Devourils who had turned to Belluvour, had left him wasted and spent. Added to this was the possibility he had feared most, that Danubin may be the reason that the women had not returned from the Realm of Resonance. Now the news of Samuel's death finally threatened to bring even his great heart to despair. It had taken all of his strength to bring himself back to Bankside. Echin tumbled into the narrowboat; Mactire and the others came across to help him. "What day is it?" asked Echin.

"Monday," replied Danny. "December the 19th. How'd you get off that filthy island?"

"Later Danny," Mactire advised. "He can hardly stand. It's no time for questions."

"Where are the others?" asked Echin wearily, noticing the absence of all but the Tanes. Loretta took charge.

"Food and rest first," she told him, "and then we'll catch you up."

"We have lost Samuel." The words seared Echin's throat.

Mactire blanched. "How?" Echin could speak of it no more. He shook his head. They murmured in tones of distress but did not press him. He remembered the last time that he had felt this exhausted, on the rocks of Obason, when Candillium had descended to the Secret Vaults with Belluvour. Mechanically he ate the soup that Loretta put before him and made no argument when she found him a bed. He saw she had been crying.

*

Gally looked out of the window at the cruise liners standing in dock in Los Angeles. He turned back to the TV screen that was showing governments throughout the world struggling to tackle disorder and looting. Gun battles had broken out in the USA and South America; each country had a major disaster to tackle and those that hung on to some semblance of order did so only by a thread. There had been no contact with his sister for weeks and it was impossible to fly anywhere in the current destabilised weather patterns. He remembered Whistmorden and the strange beings that lived within the planet, those who inhabited the luminous jewels and changed their form to flesh and blood to walk on the surface. He silently wished that now, when despair was so prevalent, they would make their presence known.

*

It was before dawn when Echin woke in the cabin to find Klim sitting beside him. The boy had completely vanished; the accomplished man, the Reeder of the Myriar, leant over and offered him a bottle of water.

"Have you found the way to bring the army of Iridice into Mengebara?" He sat up, finding a glimmer of a smile, as Klim nodded. "Where are Siskin and Josh?

"Josh is watching the pub," Klim explained and went on to recount his story of how he had tracked Siskin's strange, apparent disappearance.

Echin gave a wan smile, "The minestraals."

Klim frowned, "I don't understand."

"They found a way to safely transport Siskin to where Moura has called him to be."

"But how did you escape from the island?" asked Klim. He gave a mocking laugh as Echin recounted his escape.

"The Chunii? Not trying to kill us, that's great!"

Echin's eyes lit as the tiny, blonde figure of Gabbie rushed into the cabin and hugged him. She glowed with power. His eyes fell to the two pendants that she now carried.

"Kier and Swift?" He looked towards the corridor as if they might materialise at any moment.

Gabbie told her story of Danubin's attempt to kill her, as the Key of Talitha left the stone and nestled into her hand as a red petalled flower.

"She tried to take it from Kier but it killed her. They'll find a way back." She patted his hand and Echin smiled, that he should look so much in despair that Gabbie sought to comfort him. "On the island, I discovered what I should have guessed a long time ago." Echin pulled himself fully upright. "The keys were the first gift of Moura and should have been planted by Belluvour during your evolutionary progress. He hid them, probably in Obason. After his exile Unethora held Brunan, and Talitha was secreted in the Realm of Resonance."

"Where no Devouril can gain access," Klim guessed.

"Nor Mourangil," Echin corrected. "Save the Prisms of Hope."

"The Tomer and Unethora?" Klim's supposition was confirmed by a nod from his friend.

"But why did he hide them?" asked Gabbie.

"In all of us, like the planet itself, there are areas of dark shadow. Belluvour allowed that shadow to grow until it coloured how he saw the human race. He could not accept that mankind should have access to the secrets of Moura. To be able to commune and learn from other worlds."

"What are they, these keys?" She looked down at the delicate flower that transformed once more into the red moon depicted on the Stone of Mesa.

"Talitha and Brunan are aspects of Moura. Like the Myriar they enhance intimacy with the universe beyond this world."

"I don't really understand," Gabbie shook her head.

"I thought there were three?" Klim noted the blue tinges at Echin's elbows and chin, the hollow indentations under his cheek bones.

"The Auric Flame is your birth right, the gift of Mesa. It found its own way back to the human race. As soon as Belluvour turned away from mankind it became toxic to him."

"But..." began Gabbie.

"No more," Echin's strained features turned away. Gabbie and Klim exchanged a fearful glance; they had never seen the Mourangil so vulnerable .Gabbie gently kissed his cheek and then they left him to rest.

*

The Glimpse of Hope was almost empty, despite the fact that it was only five days before Christmas. The group had kept watch on the place since Klim had informed them about the attunement stone. Echin had added to their concerns, as he seemed to have lost his usual grace of movement, accepting Gabbie's support as she linked her arm in his. The landlord had sullenly served Danny and then disappeared back upstairs to the flat. Gabbie, speaking softly, could tell them little else of her time in the Realm of Resonance, for she had become totally immersed in its shadowy reality. It was only when Danubin's distorting presence crept unseen into that reality, that Gabbie could recall events. "The last I saw of Kier, she had her hand on a large standing stone that held an engraving of Swift."

Troubled faces surrounded her and she shivered. "They should have been back by now," she fretted. "What will happen to them if they're still in there at the Alignment?" Echin looked towards the small stockroom that he had designed to be an exit from the Realm of Resonance for the three women.

"They will be unable to return to us," he stated.

"Then we'll have to go in after them!" Klim asserted. Gabbie recoiled at the thought even as Echin dismissed the suggestion. "It would do little good, even if we could accomplish it. You would become enmeshed in the shadows of this life."

"But Gabbie came back," Klim objected. Gabbie clung onto his sleeve. "You, of all of us, won't get back Klim," she told him. "I only returned because of Kier."

"The fact that she gave you the stones," there were worried looks around the table but Josh continued, "means that she isn't sure that she can make it back. Swift must be in some danger, just like you were." Mactire sighed, he had spent the whole night in vigil with Josh, hidden in the stock room, making their exit onto the canal before the landlord came down from the flat above. They had slept for an hour or two when Danny took over, but both still looked pale and weary. "Is this what you believe Echin?" Echin shook his head, "I don't know." He looked towards Klim, who chewed on his lip as he concentrated.

"Nothing, there's no mind print of either one. Not even a faint impression."

"Josh?" The Creta shook his head and took from his sleeve a rolled up sketch of a stone wall. Klim buried his head in his hands. "You think they're stuck in there forever?" The Mourangil sighed heavily, "I don't know but lower your voice," he warned as the landlord climbed the few steps to drop logs by the fireplace.

"Help if you lit a few," Josh muttered as the man went back to the bar. He pulled up the collar of his jacket.

"There's been a change of landlord," Klim remarked, "and it looks like he's let all the other staff go."

"Or they left anyway." Josh looked around the pub at the torn decorations and grubby seats. A grimace of distaste coloured his face, "It's not been cleaned for days."

"It's not the Mountain Inn, Josh," Echin commented.

"Keeping anywhere open now has to be applauded. But you're right," he said turning towards the bar, "something's missing."

"Maybe more than something," Josh told him as he scribbled and then passed the drawing to Echin. Josh had depicted a face on which was written long lived cruelty and avarice. Echin placed his empty glass on the table.

"Drink up, let's go," he instructed. "This landlord has the distinctive taint of the Virenmor."

Once outside Echin sent the others back to the boat, disappearing to embed in the old stone. Although it was still afternoon it was already winter dark. Moments later the landlord re-appeared, his pale face scanning the towpath and canal. He cautiously moved to the edge of the water and signalled to one of the barges moored further down from the pub. He was joined within minutes by several men, none of whom would have attracted particular attention.

"Toomaaris?" asked the first.

"And others," the landlord confirmed. "Not five minutes ago."

"You gave no sign?"

"None," said the landlord.

After further muttering the landlord quickly returned to the pub, locking the door though it was little after five.

Chapter Thirty-seven

Lapis blue edged his cheekbones as Echin reappeared on the narrowboat. The others were gathered in the saloon, spread out in twos, mugs of coffee on the tables.

"I had no choice but to close the exit in The Glimpse of Hope," he told them.

"But how will they get out?" Klim stood up in alarm.

"I need to leave a message for Elanur," was the only distracted reply. Echin reached for his pack and brought out the crysonance from Samuel's cottage. "Samuel would wish Swift to have this now, along with his cottage," he told them sadly. They each nodded in silent agreement that should the world allow, they would see it done. His fingers ran over the stones that glowed intermittently luminescent with his touch. "He wants Candillium, more than anything," he told them.

"Somehow the Virenmor have found the crossing place."

"How?" asked Klim.

"Siskin's song. It will have brought the Virenmor, those that are still left to this place."

"We could have protected them! Even if they came here." Klim was angry now, his dark eyes aflame with fear for the two women.

"It's too late Klim, we must bring them out elsewhere." Echin said quietly. "Where?" Josh asked.

"At that mound of earth, you once drew." Josh looked puzzled and then he remembered his drawing of Elanur, "Ireland?"

"Ireland," Echin confirmed. "It's time."

"And will they be ready? Can they still find a way out?"

"If we can bring Talitha to Elanur there's a chance," his voice tense as he concentrated on the crysonance.

"And what about the third key?" asked Mactire. "The Auric Flame. How important is it and where can it be found in the short time we have left?"

Echin bowed his head, when he raised it again he looked carefully at each in turn as he spoke. "Without the Auric Flame, we are indeed dry ash and hollow stone. It was only as I was penned in the cage that I at last understood. This was the planet Mesa's gift to you and it has always been yours for the taking. The Auric Flame is the true spirit of humanity. Belluvour could not deny you this, though he tried to dismantle its connection and negate its power. The Auric Flame is love, compassion, hope. All actions that feed these qualities have, over time, fed the Auric Flame."

Echin removed the blue stone from his pocket and laid it upon the table. Each of them let their gaze wander in its depths. Within the moon shaped jewel the colours lightened and darkened; one moment it seemed to show the night sky filled with stars and the next clouds filtered the surface.

"I've seen it before," said Josh. "Elanur gave it to you."

"She gave it back to me," Echin corrected. "After Candillium left, I found it by the silver stream where we first came together. It is a leaving stone."

Gabbie shuffled uncomfortably. "What do you mean, a leaving stone?"

"Moura has allowed me to seek other realms if I choose. To pass on my human life to another if it is wanted."

Mactire's eyes gleamed as they focused on the jewel.

"There have been times," Echin continued, "as I walked with human steps, that I might have taken what the stone offered. I gave it to Elanur for safe keeping but I now know that it cannot be used without the presence of the Auric Flame."

"And have you never seen," Mactire said softly, "that of us all you hold the spirit of humanity most closely in your heart?"

The Mourangil seem to gaze down through the ages.

"Only now do I see that when I passed the Myriar to Candillium, she shared with me the Auric Flame. It is this spirit that has kept me wandering and waiting across these long ages upon the surface; the same spirit that has returned Candillium to our world."

"Listen!" It was Danny's sharp ears that first caught the sound. A grand piano. The notes became louder, filling the space.

"Siskin!" Echin headed for the door and they all followed him outside. It was if the sound came from within the planet itself, seeping up from the ground to fill the sky. Siskin's rich voice sang in the language of Ordovica. The melody felt as if it had been excavated by sacred bones. Birds fluttered to the ground around them in the winter's afternoon as if recognising that the source of this music had some close connection to them. The effect on the Tanes was profound; tears streamed down Loretta's face.

"Ah, I remember," her green eyes widened in wonder. "I can fly."

Simultaneously as if the music had created a dance within them, she, Oisen and Killian changed to their elemental forms. Two great white wings spanned across the towpath, stretching from each side of the unicorn.

Mactire, Danny and Aiden were taken up on the backs of those who could fly. In minutes, they had risen into the air and disappeared towards the west.

"Loretta," called Josh, but she was already a good distance from the boat.

The song changed key as Klim sank to the ground. Siskin's melody weaved through the field that Klim had planted in Mengebara. The mind place was a vast sea of collective human thought and was gathering focus. In Siskin's voice Klim heard uncountable voices singing one song:

"We call to our hearts your promise.
We bring to our knowledge your gift."

It was only then that the Reeder noticed that the field he had planted was in virtual darkness. All those that wandered within it brought their own light source, to a greater of lesser degree. He saw them bumping into each other and blindly stumbling, each holding the precious seed that had been planted for them. Constantly criss-crossing each other's path but unable to fully see the other's face.

Klim concentrated on the sky above the field, a starless murky blanket. He reached out towards it but this body of thought weighed heavily. He breathed, ignoring the trickle of sweat at his temples. Suddenly Josh was there beside him in Mengebara. The field became picture still and Klim could now make out individual faces; Reg holding a large, round industrial looking lamp; Juliette marvelling at the glow in her fingertips. Josh reached upwards with his hand, in which he held a simple paintbrush. He moved it across the framed field, back and forth. The music changed once more, a haunting

333

daybreak of sound that washed over the planet causing the dark sky to clear. The field, planted in the starless evening, became golden in the pure light of day.

*

Ulynyx looked out at the sands that covered his invisible city, sure that the barriers he had made were all intact. The skyline darkened, a shadow in the shape of a huge, black raven descended slowly. Amed hurried towards him, the eyes that had been alight with a sense of victory were now marked with violent fear. The Raven landed in the sand, the size of a skyscraper, it towered over the underground city. In the dying sun, the shape shimmered into the human form of Belluvour. Those Devourils, who were still in human form, stood either side of the Unbound. Shocked, Ulynyx watched as Belluvour dismissed his barriers of illusion in a gesture of disdain. The alarms rang in doleful bells across the city as the Unbound breached the invisible magnetic field. With a flick of his hand, Belluvour ceased the Chunii call to arms. "You have spent too much time fighting human wars," he told Ulynyx.

The leader of the Chunii whispered reassurance to Amed. He then strode out into the desert to meet his adversary. Ulynyx, now so used to the nuances of expression in the human race, was repulsed by the tightly fixed form of Belluvour, with its lidless eyes and cruel mouth.

"It seems that we are both taken with the human form," Ulynyx mocked.

Belluvour circled him like a panther as the Chunii warrior crouched into a fighting stance. "I am curious why you want to do this," he stated calmly.

334

In the absence of any comment from Belluvour he laughed lightly, "Ah I see, you want to destroy them, their faith in me, by bringing down my physical self in a show of your mighty strength."

Belluvour snarled and lunged towards him. Ulynyx, as quick as the breeze, moved beyond his grasp. And so, it went on, both moving so fast, changing forms back and forth, so that the human onlookers could see only the shadowy outline of two human bodies wrestling in combat. At other moments, it seemed as if the air was charged with fire and black shadow. The hours went by and the Chunii waited. As instructed, Amed gave orders for the women and children to leave and find their way to hidden shelters in the city, but many refused to abandon their lord.

In the dark of the night the blurred shapes became solid as they tired. In the moonlight, the couched figure of Belluvour leant over the leader of the Chunii whose handsome face was like grey ash. Onyx showing at every bony prominence. Finally the Unbound dragged Ulynyx inside his domed dwelling place and the Devourils herded the Chunii into the main chamber.

Belluvour's obsidian face showed dull with exhaustion as he grabbed Amed. The Chunii screamed in horror, their will held by the fierce Devourils as Belluvour reached for the blade carried by the First in Faith. Slowly and deliberately he peeled the skin from the man's back, ignoring his piercing screams. He carried on removing the skin from each limb amidst the wailing of the crowd, savouring Ulynyx's impotent attempts to raise himself from the ground. Finally, he released the body and Amed fell to the ground, where the sand soaked his blood as he finally passed from his agony.

"Three of my entrusted have not returned. They left to follow rumours that Elanur had found the Myriar runes hidden in the British Isles. Rumours passed from this very camp by the female Virenmor." Ulynyx fixed his gaze on the pitiful sight of Amed's tortured body.

"You know where they are," rasped Belluvour, grabbing a young woman who stood nearby.

"You were wrong, Belluvour," Ulynyx shouted. "The Myriar awaits the Alignment, Toomaaris fulfilled his task."

Distracted, the impassioned Belluvour, threw down the girl. "You have seen Candillium?" Immediately Belluvour saw the hesitation in his opponent's face. "You have not!" he laughed crookedly in triumph.

The girl had managed to crawl a few inches from the hideous Unbound but he suddenly stepped cruelly onto her abdomen, ignoring her cries. "Tell me," he instructed coldly, "or I continue." He wiped the knife on her dress in readiness.

The defiant leader of the Chunii struggled to his feet. "Do not harm her," but he turned, defeated, to Belluvour. "The Runeshaper was traced to the old passage tombs in Meath."

Belluvour drove the knife into the girl's body amid angry screams from the Chunii. Ulynyx lunged for Belluvour who merely stepped backwards, leaving his opponent sprawled beside the bleeding body of the girl. Instantly he threw the knife with precision to reach the heart of Ulynyx. "Not one Seed will remain for the Alignment. Not one."

Belluvour looked around the faces of the soldiers in the Great Hall of Ulyn. "Destroy them all," he ordered, marching from the desert city.

336

Lying on the floor, life seeping from his human body, Ulynyx reached for the hand of the dying girl. "Forgive me Mwabi," he wept. "Forgive me."

*

A duck nipped at Klim's pants as he lay on the towpath outside the barge. He opened his eyes to meet the waddling creature's objections to the cessation of the melody. In contrast, another sound was heard in the distance. Josh pulled Klim up and together they dived into the boat, seconds before a clicking mass of shadow appeared in the sky above, travelling at speed. Echin stood unmoving in the centre of the narrowboat, his eyes closed. The boat rocked slightly with the wave of amassed discordance above them. Quietly Gabbie slipped from one of the cabins and held Klim's hand. She sniffed the burning air as Klim squeezed her hand and placed an arm around his pale faced love.

The oppressive shadow lifted and Echin opened eyes that seemed remote and grief stricken. "They gather for the Alignment." He looked towards his friends. "I've primed the barge to bring you across to the others, I'm going for Siskin."
He was gone before Josh could open his mouth to ask where Siskin might be. In seconds, the white mist filled the barge as a prelude to its transportation from Bankside.

Chapter Thirty-eight

On the eve of the twenty-first of December, beneath an indigo sky, a plume of apple smoke drifted upwards from the centre of a circle of standing stones. Sitting on a rock, in the middle of the stone ring, Elanur worked away at the clay figure she had made in Istanbul. She stared in wonder at the living beings who stood in front of the great stones around her. The Tanes had answered the summons that had been woven into their being down through the generations. At Siskin's call, the markings on the standing stones had come to life: on each stone, an emerald green light had moulded itself into the shape of an elemental being. Mactire stood before the great stone in his Adlet form, his energy tightly focused. Like his companions - the unicorn, chimera, griffin, a giant fox and a huge bear - he was ready to act on her word.

Klim, Gabbie and Josh appeared breathless on the ridge, Echin had primed the narrowboat to teleport to the river that meandered below. Gabbie hurled herself towards the two Mourangils who had just appeared from the other side of the mound. They laughed as they untangled themselves but then, to their friends' surprise, Faer and Tormaigh addressed them formally. "You are the final Seeds of the Myriar: Creta, Inscriptor and Reeder. We are bound to you. Whatever the outcome of this day, we offer you our service." The gravity of their tone echoed around the ancient site.

"We thank you," replied Josh with equal formality, repeating the greeting he had last heard spoken by Elanur. "May the lighted jewel shine forever in your footsteps." He smiled as the two Mourangils gave a nod of approval. Klim and Gabbie seemed equally impressed. The two men moved towards Elanur, who smiled as she took their hands in turn, her pipe puffing circles of smoke.

"Ah!" She looked at Gabbie in awe. "Come here little one. You are the Inscriptor, are you not?"

Gabble nodded hesitantly and went forward. Elanur placed her hand under the Stone of Mesa, with its two keys embedded within. The Key of Talitha dislodged and made a red, flowered headpiece that Elanur placed in her hair. "Quickly," she indicated that Gabbie sit with her. Klim began to walk towards the Tanes who seemed unusually still. "They will not speak now," Elanur told him. "They, like us, wait for the Sister Spheres."

Josh noticed the clay figure in her hands, "That's Kier!"

"Sssh," she scolded, closing her eyes. "I am still trying to find Candillium and the Stozcist."

Josh and Klim sat on the grass to either side, both placing a fingertip on the clay figure.

"Ah, at last," said Elanur.

*

Kier had lost all sense of time in the shadow of the huge wall. The runes had ceased to light up and the stone was forebodingly solid. Finally, she sat on the bridge in despair. "It may already be too late," she said aloud.

"It's my fault," said Swift's voice from nearby. There was a long pause when Kier said nothing.

"I could have saved Gabbie. I watched her. There was time!" Swift confessed. The keening began again. "I wanted Klim to myself!"

"And now?" Kier asked her. "What do you want now?"

"Nothing! I am a monster! I could not let Klim live with a monster." Once again, the weeping started.

"You are not a monster," Kier said evenly, "and Gabbie is still alive."

Out of the bridge emerged the Stozcist, where she had been hidden inside the stone. Her arms were torn and bleeding where she had tried to punish herself. "How?" she asked, as a child would ask a magician his secret. "How is it possible?"

"Did you sense me nearby?" asked Kier.

"I don't know," she offered. "Maybe."

"I sensed you. Some part of you knew that I would let no harm come to Gabbie. Just as I will not let harm come to you in this place. It was not your role, but mine, to face Danubin."

"Kier," Swift wept. Kier reached around the slim shoulders and tangled hair, holding her.

"So now you have faced your greatest guilt, your biggest shame. You cannot change that impulse, that action. It's in the past, borne of emotions that no longer belong to you. Do you have the courage to let it go and come with me back to a world that needs you? A world that needs the best of you?"

As Kier spoke the red weals that had appeared on Swift's body began to disappear. Her chin raised and she placed a hand over her heart and closed her eyes. Neither said a word as she breathed in slowly and deeply, gathering strength. The Stozcist stood tall, her dark eyes shimmering in the realm of shadow, fully alive. Together they walked towards the wall. Holding hands, they stepped forward, only to find that the Waybearer stone would not let them pass.

"It's my fault!" insisted Swift, plunged back into hopelessness. "Go without me."

"We go together," Kier told her. The sense of urgency was heavier than ever. She placed her hand on the wall but again it only brushed against the rough surface.

"There has to be a way out!" she cried in frustration. "Come on," she reached for Swift's hand. "Perhaps we need to go away from this place, back towards the river."

*

Echin, exhausted, had successfully carried Siskin from the island, arriving on the ancient mound an hour before dawn. "Elanur?" Echin enquired urgently as the two came inside the circle. She was sat holding the clay figure of Kier, in deep concentration. The red flower of Talitha was still in her hair. "You have set me a near impossible task, Toomaaris," she told him, opening her eyes. "Without Talitha," she continued, "I could not have found the imprint in the Realm of Resonance. I have almost completed the runes that will bring them through. But who is to say if they are waiting at the doorway or have even found it? What if they have come to find it impassable and risked everything by retreating back into the tangled web of that realm?"

"Where's Samuel?" Siskin looking dazed, scanning the strange scene around him. "Oh no!" He responded to the look in Elanur's tear filled eyes, sinking to his knees. "The others? Where's Kier and Swift?"

"We have yet to discover," Elanur told him gently, returning to her task. Klim, Josh and Gabbie, on their way to greet their friend, stopped abruptly. All those gathered on the mound stood still, looking to the air. Their nostrils were filled with a sulphurous odour as underneath their feet there was a deep rumble in the bedrock. The Tanes, in their elemental forms, moved from the standing stones. With outstretched wings, uncoiled serpent's tail and animal stealth they formed a mythical tableau. Siskin, rising from the ground, placed himself with Klim, Josh and Gabbie.

It was Gabbie who saw them first. She cried out as the dark tendrils materialised into Devourils upon the field below. Their human forms had been discarded, apart from Geoden and Belluvour. Josh had once drawn Nephragm in his natural state and now it was as if that hideous image had been copied hundreds of times and pasted evenly just beyond their circle. This was the form to which the Devourils were mostly drawn above the surface. Their coal black bodies were lined with red veins. Oversized animal limbs pawed towards the stone circle but could not make any impact upon the protective force that Elanur had evoked when she had finished shaping the last of the runes in the chamber.

"I will soon have the pattern," Geoden calmly told Belluvour, closing his eyes in concentration. Belluvour, holding a dark sack by his side, stood silent and tall beneath the purple sky, searching the faces of his enemies.

"Geoden!" Echin stepped to the edge of the circle. "Do not do this. This is Belluvour's rage, his long bitterness. It is not yours."

Belluvour, reached into the sack and brought out the severed head of the murdered Ulynyx. He thrilled with the murmur of revulsion from the Myriar Seeds. Echin, weakened and exhausted, stared with profound sadness at the mutilated corpse of his friend. Belluvour dropped his gruesome trophy onto the ground. It seemed to fall in slow motion and on contact created an explosion of soil and rock that splattered against the outer protection.

"Begone from my sight," his arrogant, croaking voice rang out. Belluvour lifted his hand and soil covered the domed barrier that Elanur had created, entombing those within.

A few minutes passed. The Devourils bayed, a strange haunting sound. They rasped out their leader's name, pounding the earth in a rhythmic drum beat, which finally fell to silence as the burial mound shook. Slowly, the heavy soil cover fell away, where on the other side of the barrier Echin lowered his arm. Inside a nearby passage tomb Faer and Tormaigh were guarding the two Devourils they had captured. A circle of crysaline pinned the prisoners at the back of the chamber. The glistening material had disarmed the cruel devices that had been constructed to dispense the Odiam. However, Belluvour's powerful strike shook the passage tomb and broke the circle of crysaline. The two Devourils now faced Faer and Tormaigh in the dark, narrow passage. Tormaigh's words echoed those of Echin, "Do not do this, Sellonir," he said, seeing the snarl of attack distort the already ragged human face. In moments, the two Devourils had discarded their human form in favour of the animalistic shape adopted by the others. Tormaigh shook his head. "That we should fight, Rhodon," he lamented.

"For Samuel," Faer said as the four became battle locked.

*

Echin faced Belluvour and looked into the limitless hollow of the eyes of the Unbound.

343

"There is still time, you can change this." Even now, the Mourangil was consumed with a sense of tragic loss for Belluvour and the Devourils. Belluvour answered with a mocking gleam. He looked to Geoden. A swathe of wind gusted between them.

"The barrier is down," Geoden told the Unbound, turning away from the oncoming slaughter. Belluvour was at Elanur's side in a flicker of movement, throwing down the clay figure upon which she had worked. He raised his arm to strike but Echin took the blow that was meant to kill the Runeshaper. The Mourangil straightened, breathless but saw his own exhaustion reflected in Belluvour. The Alignment was almost upon them. "You saw it, didn't you, when you fell together?" Echin spoke deliberately and slowly, his voice echoing across the valley. "The compassion that overwhelmed Candillium, even though you had wiped away her kind. The spirit of humanity, the Auric Flame. The gift of Mesa, one you had no power to refuse, for its source was embedded within each element that fell from the old planet. You betrayed them, you betrayed Moura. But the touch of the Auric Flame, of human love, has smarted all these human years."

The Devourils shifted restlessly. Belluvour turned sideways, his voice resonating across the fields. "Look what they have done, Toomaaris. Why do you think we have used their human form to destroy them? It is what they do best, destroy each other and all else that Moura has gifted upon the surface." His dark limbs swept around the valley. "Where is she?" he mocked, striding in front of Echin and the audience below. "She has not come. The Myriar is incomplete at the appointed hour, her promise unfulfilled. Perhaps even Candillium sees, as do I, that the human race is but a scourge upon our planet. A failed experiment between Mesa and Moura that has cost us, the children of Moura, our unity."

In the pre-dawn of the cold December day, the red veins were afire on the surface of the dark shapes below. Belluvour, his eyes reaching to the sky and then back to Echin, turned directly towards the Mourangil.

"You have lived on the surface all this time as one of them. It is not too late, come now Toomaaris, live on the new formed earth as one of us."

Echin's eyes lifted to the faces around him. Elanur disconsolately tried to gather the broken pieces of the clay figure of Kier. Klim tightened his hold on Gabbie's hand as she leaned to move towards the Mourangil.

"You are right Belluvour," replied Echin.
His friends shuffled restlessly nearby. Loretta stirred her wings in a trembling flutter.

"The Myriar is incomplete. But, as you see, the human Seeds are here, despite all that you have engineered to prevent it. You taught them to hate and destroy. Still, so many held to the gift you could not deny them. And I, Echinod Deem, stand at its centre for the one who promised to return."

"You fool Toomaaris!" hissed Belluvour.

"Arrogant and blind, eaten with jealousy," Echin returned. "You, the mighty Belluvour, could not accept that mankind could offer anything to a Mourangil." Belluvour stood back, laughing an alien cackle, ugly and discordant. "You will pass into memory from this day. You have bound your essence with theirs." He gestured to the Myriar Seeds. "And she is not even by your side at the end! Kill them," he ordered.

A chaotic melee ensued. The Tanes charged the marauding Devourils as they plunged into battle. Belluvour turned his dark, hairless body towards the Mourangil that, from the beginning, had stood between his relentless hatred and the men and women who had come so far from Ordovicia. He gathered that hate now into fists of fire, his body blazing with volcanic rage.

*

Kier, half way along the path that led back to the river, thought she heard a voice. Echin. It came and went but the further she travelled from the bridge the fainter it became. "Can you hear that?" she asked Swift who stopped to concentrate.

"No, nothing," she replied.

"Turn around," Kier instructed, heading back down the path.

"Look!" Swift shouted on her way back towards the bridge. The wall flickered with golden runes. Swift palpated the stone, "Someone has tried to make the doorway open but the connection was broken before they completed it."

"I should have waited," Kier cried in frustration, her fists pounding the stone, but the wall remained impassable. Tears pricked her eyes, she was desperate to find a way through. She felt the soft touch of Swift upon her arm. Looking over her shoulder she saw that the stream had now quickly risen into a fast flowing river and had begun to submerge the bridge. They were stranded upon the edge.

Then the words, spoken by Echin to another, came clearly to her hearing; his passion so strong that it pierced the barrier of another dimension. "The gift of Mesa shone in her the first time I saw her by the Silver Stream. I had no understanding then, of the Auric Flame that attuned her to the universe beyond. That had brought her to find the Mourangil kingdoms. But its touch of love has held me to her throughout this vast age of human existence. And it will not be broken."

Tears fell down Kier's face as she stood on the ledge of the embankment, the stone wall cold against her back. She breathed in a breath that swelled her chest and released it as the depth of her own passion erased all doubt. Her eyes glowed, she placed her hand over the flooded strip of land and the torrent ceased. There was something archaic in her voice as she spoke. "I am like a fish plucked from the river and transformed to a bird." She placed her hand against the wall. "I flap my tail through old use and choke in suffocation, for I do not recognise that I have lungs to breathe the new element." Lightly she pushed the stone. "I am Candillium," she commanded the doorway. "Open!"

*

Belluvour lunged at great speed, erupting into a fire to sweep away all opposition. Echin was not swept away, he launched his body against the burning brand of Belluvour. In a blur of movement they battled against each other, the flames smothered in fierce combat. Klim was amazed that the standing stones remained firm as the earth shook beneath. A swirling storm ringed around Echin and Belluvour. Klim felt the Iridice flare white light just as the other Myriar Stones shone against the indigo sky, wounding and blinding the Devourils, slowing their movements to a human pace. The Tanes, in their elemental forms, with augmented vision, attacked those who transformed their animal shape into the shadowy, burning strands. Oisen snapped a singed wing inward as he forced another back to the field.

Geoden scattered the Tanes as he tried to eject the Odiam against them but they were too quick and forced him back down the hill. He stumbled and lashed out with the side of the gun like weapon, knocking Gabbie to the ground. The amber fire of Arwres disappeared as the stone was thrown across the ground. The Devouril regained his footing and took aim at Klim. Gabbie flung herself against his leg, knocking his balance and the shot missed its target. Geoden kicked out to release his foot delivering a forceful blow to the side of her head. The Devouril lifted his face from the small body of Gabbie to see the fierce figure of the Reeder in the full glow of his power. The fixed impression of one who was alien to human emotion was framed in shock. And in that expression, a moment of human communion, the Reeder was able to understand what he was too far away to see. At the feet of Geoden, Gabbie's face was upturned in the still mask of death.

*

Cold air caught Kier's breath as she emerged into the December pre-dawn in Ireland. The two women emanated through the mist onto the grassy mound on top of the ancient tomb. Swift would have plunged herself into the conflict below but Kier held her back with the slightest touch. The centrepiece of the Myriar stood silently in this fraction of time. She watched the battle below and found that she was able to absorb, in that instant, all that was taking place. She saw where

Tormaigh and Faer still battled with the two Devourils in the passage tomb on the opposite ridge. Kier also perceived, beyond the field, what none of the participants of that conflict could yet see.

Echin was tiring; he felt his energy begin to yield as he fought to untangle the dark shadow of Belluvour, who had purchased a stranglehold on his being. The blind, unyielding force of the Unbound attacking his human body; a dark shadow enveloping him as the world began to fade. Inevitably he thought of Kier, the sacred flame he carried within. The gift she had freely given to the Mourangil, even as he had brought the Myriar to Candillium. The Auric Flame subsumed his human body. An overwhelming compassion for all those lost and those still present, his great love of human kind that had been transformed into long years of service. It suffused his jewelled heart and cast away the weighted shadow of the Unbound. Belluvour now gasped with pain, turning from the searing light at the heart of Echinod Deem.

Stunned, confused, Belluvour sprang to one side. Then he stopped moving, his nostrils flaring as he sensed an old presence, an old enemy. The one who had imprisoned him in the Secret Vaults. Shock mingled with rage, as he recognised Candillium standing above them.

"Once again Candillium," Belluvour spoke in a shadowy growl, "I give you the leavings of your race, such as they are, and for the fragment of time they remain. There is nothing left worth preserving, your people will shortly be extinct."

Kier did not move. She remembered their fall together deep into the Secret Vaults. Her voice, to his utter dismay, entered directly into his human consciousness.

"For all that you have destroyed Belluvour, you have also played a part in my return and the formation of the Myriar."

He tried to speak but uttered only snatched bullets of sound that were lost in the air. Kier, once the leader of Ordovicia, commanded his human form, distorted as it was. Her words flamed within him. "The atrocity of the Virenmor," her voice rang powerfully across the valley, "enabled all of us to come together. Without your lunge of vast, unthinking hatred, I could not have found the Stone of Mesa. Your rage and destruction have, in these final days, deconstructed the barriers of possession and prejudice that have divided our human race."

Candillium released him from her will and he lunged towards her in fury. Swift, who had been working a small pebble, lifted her hands and a net of crysaline descended over the Unbound. The Devourils were spread across the field beneath the mound but the eerie luminescence of their foul shapes had now dulled. They bayed with horror. Geoden slumped in horrified amazement as Belluvour bowed with pain, unmoving within the glowing net of the rare and precious substance that the human Stozcist had made from a simple rock.

Klim and Siskin seized their opportunity and plunged towards Geoden, knocking him to the ground. Siskin twisted his wrist until it pointed inward and triggered the toxic Odiam. The Devouril screamed his pain, for he had loaded the poison undiluted to use against Candillium and Toomaaris. Like so many that he had culled, he disappeared without trace. Kier whispered to Swift who went quickly to Klim's side, joining Josh in a forlorn gathering around the body of Gabbie.

Kier stood at the edge of the mound as an enchanting melody drifted to her ears. Below, across the plains of County Meath, were thousands upon thousands of people holding lights; modern and old as if shining jewels had been scattered across the pastures. They were singing the simple melody that Siskin had taught them. Above Kier, the indigo sky slowly began to change colour, as silently the planets gathered in the Alignment. Six spheres of ponderous beauty appeared and began a silent dance in a magnificent tableau. All stood still. Belluvour, beside her, was held unmoving beneath the crysaline. The Devourils covered the field below but appeared shrunken in size. They searched for obdurates in which to embed but there were none in this part of Meath. Kier understood, as their Mourangil names were revealed to her and slowly she scanned across the followers of Belluvour, seeing the jewels they once had been. Each one was held by her will as she made her way downhill to the sad group of friends who had grown to a family. Elanur reached for Echin, who was now standing. She held out her hand and he took it, moving forward to stand behind Kier.

Gabbie lay motionless on the ground with Swift kneeling beside her, weeping. Klim was prostrate, his face buried in the damp grass until Siskin coaxed him upright. Talitha released itself from Elanur's hair and floated downwards into the Stone of Mesa that Gabbie still wore around her neck. Echin looked towards Kier, his heart pleading in the lazuli of his eyes. There she saw written the long years of separation, the split being of Mourangil and man. He reached to his pocket and turned over his palm. She knew the blue stone well, for she had made it in another time and another life, to give to him with Moura's blessing. She nodded almost imperceptibly as Echin bent down towards Gabbie. Klim looked up; a face that had been ravaged by grief, now held a glimmer of hope. Swift, her long hair tangled, her skin streaked with tears, stopped weeping. Siskin and Josh placed themselves either side of the Mourangil as he knelt by Gabbie's body and gently placed the blue stone into the last moon of Mesa. He looked towards Swift and nodded. The engraving had faded to dull grey but came alive at her touch. The large circle representing Mesa glowed with silver light and the three moons radiated in gold, red and blue. In this day of the miraculous, in the dawn of remaking, the small body of Gabbie trembled as the gift of human life returned. On either side, Klim and Swift wept freely as they helped her to sit. Gabbie reached distractedly to the side of her head, where her fingers roamed unobstructed though her hair. All sign of injury had disappeared.

Another planet appeared in the sky and halted, not yet synchronised with the others. Smaller in size, it glowed pure white. Gabbie searched the grass nearby and recovered Arwres, placing it back around her neck and returning the Stone of Mesa to Kier. Kier signalled to the others to follow as they climbed the rise. The Myriar Seeds, their stones vibrating with their own particular light, formed five points around Kier who stood tall in the centre, the Stone of Mesa glowing radiant at her neck. Astonished exclamations sounded from the fields below as Kier's face appeared upon the planet that had yet to take up its position with the others in order to complete the Alignment. She spoke in the first language of the human race but Gabbie, instantly transcribed her words, into each mind that had entered Mengebara, according to their own language. "I am the voice or your first stirrings on this planet. I have been gone from you but now we are reunited for this short time. Soon the star source that first brought us to Moura, to the earth, will realign with the Sister Spheres. As I speak, the planet Mesa, remade, reads your hearts. Moura has poured her blessings, her richness upon the surface we call earth, enough for all," she continued, her expression sad. "But we have not blessed her outpouring. Instead we have looked away from the whole, to the small patch upon which we stood, where we hoarded and defended what was never ours to take and hide. Like a chick breaking the shell that has housed its world so completely, so can we break the habits of conflict, fear and greed." She paused, the face of Kier Morton, her amber eyes direct and unblinking, challenged all people across the surface of the planet. "If we are willing to do so. Our world, our humanity, now halved in number, must change or die." Kier's face disappeared from the surface of Mesa as she held out her hand for Echin, who stood on the outside of the circle. He moved towards her and stood by her side. "You are as much a part of the centrepiece as I," she told him softly. The light of the stones encompassed each Seed of the Myriar and leapt towards the centre where Echin and Kier stood entwined. The Myriar star they created dazzled; Kier could sense its reaching into every single human heart. Above them, the planet Mesa, glowing with diamond light, reached through their bodies to shine a wordless beauty upon all. The last sphere slotted into place and the seven Sister Spheres aligned with Moura. Suspended in space, shining upon a world grown quiet, the spheres glinted and mesmerised all living things.

Chapter Thirty-nine

Eclipsed in darkness, the Myriar Seeds and all life on the planet waited for the world to shift into another age. Every light was extinguished, all movement held still. Kier felt the brush of a power beyond human understanding. She held her breath. The whisper reverberated around her but there was no noise. The grief was not human but the tears flowed rich from Kier's heart. This was not sound but the essence of sound. It was not words but the sense of words. It was not new but as old as the planet and encompassed every cell of her being. The voice of Moura. Beyond language, outside of time: within the space of matter, within the matter of space.

Kier laughed, joy brimming as the darkness shifted, tilting again to the pre-dawn light. The Sister Spheres no longer showed in the sky, where the sun prepared to create another dawn; the first of a new age. Belluvour's strangled cry was lost in the echo of her laughter. One by one the Devourils disappeared from the surface, each made instantly extinct. Kier held Gabbie's hand as she stepped onto the edge of the mound, her words ringing out across the planet. "We have a new beginning and a new energy source, called crysaline. You will find it in the living rainforests, beneath the rivers but it will grow only as the rainforest grows. War will kill it, for it is sensitive to the energy of hate and destruction. But there will be enough for all of our needs if it is nurtured and harvested well."

Kier turned towards Echin, her words heard only by the Mourangil and those that were so dear to her.

"You have fulfilled your purpose here, enabled us to form the Myriar and to find the gift of Moura within us after all this long age. You knew all along what I could not know. The moment that I fully embraced the fact that I was once Candillium, my time here would be almost over. Is this why you kept yourself distant from me?" Echin nodded, "If we stay, Moura's grief for Belluvour and the Mourangils he stole from her, would feed the shadow that we have cleansed."

She buried her head in Echin's chest, his arms folding around her, as they walked towards the standing stones. Gabbie began to sob but was quickly comforted by Swift and Klim who stood to either side.

Amid the standing stones the final Seeds of the Myriar came together to embrace their centrepiece; Candillium and Toomaaris, Kier and Echin. The Tanes had given up their elemental forms and Josh reached for Loretta's hand. Swift embraced both Gabbie and Klim and found her pain had gone. She saw clearly that they were two halves of the same jewel and that she had been cut from a different crystal. The standing stones lit with the light of a thousand jewelled Mourangils. Sellonir and Rhodon had vanished from the surface with the other Devourils. Faer and Tormaigh had been unable to kill those with whom they had once embedded, the bejewelled of Moura for so many ages. Nor had Sellonir and Rhodon found that they had the will to kill the Mourangils. Faer wondered how much longer they would have fought against each other in the narrow passage had not the Alignment banished the Devouril presence from the earth.

Kier searched the intense and ever self-mocking eyes of Mactire, feeling the power and charisma of the man and

the wolf. "You have a new world where Faerie will be welcome," she told him, holding out both hands.
He kissed them. "Without you I will struggle to find the magic," he told her without any of his mock gallantry.

Tears choked her throat. She released herself from his hands and they hugged each other until Elanur walked towards her. "The runes are writ Candillium," she said gently, "and Toomaaris." She turned towards the beloved Mourangil and he bent and held her, whispering words of comfort.

"But why are you leaving?" Swift choked on the words, though in truth she, who had moulded the fabric of Moura, understood completely. Echin had given up his time here for Gabbie's life and the woman who had once been Candillium, would leave with him. Entangled within their history would always be the lost jewels of the Mourangil kingdoms, the children of Moura, removed for ever from the heart of the planet. These two beings, to whom mankind owed its continued existence, could no longer walk the surface amongst them.

Kier pointed to two figures who had climbed from the crowd. Evan came forward with his daughter Angharad. "Your family have come for you," she said softly, embracing their friends.
Gabbie held Kier for a long time. "Do you really have to leave?"
It seemed that her words were echoed by all within the standing stones for there was complete silence. It was Echin who finally answered, "We will always be embedded within the heart of man and in the heart of Moura. The power of the Myriar has passed beyond us into those who stand within this circle and those jewels who shine their light upon it."

One by one they said their goodbyes. They turned to look across the landscape at the thousands of people who had gathered with their lamps in the winter cold. Klim and Gabbie, arms around each other, wept as they said goodbye.

"You found your song, Siskin," said Kier, as she embraced the musician. "Do you have more?"
He smiled, "I have more."

"Clare and Juliette are safe in the field over there," she told him. He registered where she had pointed and then lifted her hand to kiss it. "Thank you," he said. "Thank you both."
Kier scanned the fields for the last time but her eyes were sad as they turned back.

"You're looking in the wrong place," Echin told her. Along the ridge, between the passage tombs, a tall figure strode towards the standing stones. Kier ran towards her brother, laughing, because she saw he was as always, dressed for fell walking. "Gally," she pressed herself against his broad chest.

"A Mourangil came for me," he looked around him, the shine in his eyes reflecting the lights that flickered across the vast swathe of humanity. "I saw your face in the sky," his voice was full of wonder. As she hugged him, she was his little sister again, and not the powerful, stately woman he had just witnessed. "I always thought you were destined to go beyond where I could ever follow," he whispered.

"Toomaaris!" Elanur warned, looking at the sky. Dawn was approaching.
Echin greeted Gally and took hold of Kier's hand. Gally was bereft, realising at last that he had come so far only to say goodbye.

"She's pregnant" Kier said, laughing.

"Who?" Gally stood shocked.

"Megan of course," Kier told him. The insight of the new arrival for Gally and his girlfriend had been as swift as it was accurate. "I'll never be far away really," she told him, kissing his cheek.

Kier and Echin stood for a moment in a wordless farewell, overlooking a sea of human beings shining with Mourangil light. The sparkling, jewelled Mourangils were lit with the Auric Flame of humanity. Turning from the standing stones, the couple hurried towards the ancient cave, reaching it just as the sun rose.

Tormaigh and Faer accompanied them down the narrow passage into the chamber that was now a dance of subtle colour. A tapestry of strangely shaped runes glimmered in the old stone walls. In the furthest recess Elanur, Tormaigh and Faer kissed them both in the human way and then moved to the side of the chamber. Kier reached out for Echin who took her hand. She felt she would burst with the radiant presence of him. For the first time in her earthly existence she felt complete. "All this life I have known there is another," said Kier softly. "One who was there before I breathed in this air and this time, and my heart longed to return to this other of whom I had no memory, could hear no voice and knew no name. And yet the fleeting touch of his existence in the world between worlds sustained and directed my love these living years. I was drawn to anything in this life that brought me closer to him. I was drawn to you. And now you are here. Are you truly ready Echinod Deem to greet the new planet? To journey to Mesa?"

His eyes answered her question as he nodded and pulled her close.

"And you?" he returned.

Kier glowed with the power of the Auric Flame. Her eyes were prisms of liquid light as she held close the treasure of all those she loved and who had loved her in return. Closing her eyes, she breathed in deeply and turned to Echin as she opened them again, scrutinising every aspect of his face. Straightening, tightening her hold on his hand, she gave a solemn bow towards the entrance. "Ready for home," she declared.

Outside the sun dawned on the December solstice. At that moment, a spear of light passed through the roof-box, above the entrance of the passage tomb. It travelled down the narrow stone corridor, bouncing against the dancing runes, and enfolded the two beings standing together in the recess at the back of the chamber. The shimmering sheet of light enveloped the couple so that they became part of its brightness. When the sunlight receded from the chamber Kier and Echin had vanished. After a while those left behind entered the passage. When he arrived at the chamber Klim looked around, seeing the runes as they dimmed. "You created a portal, Elanur?" he asked.

"It was already a portal," she replied. "I just gave it direction."

"And are they safe?" asked Gabbie.

"Safe?" repeated Elanur. "Safe to be free to be unsafe. Safe to find what their hearts have manifested. Safe to create a world beyond our imagining. Yes, they are safe."

"Will they come back?" asked Gabbie, tears streaming down her face as she clung onto Arwres. "Will we ever see them again?"

"That, I cannot see." Elanur rested her hand upon the young woman's shoulder.

Outside the passage, Swift reached out her arm and from the earth a strand of white glowing crysaline rose up to gather around her wrist. Her dark eyes wandered from the silken band to the fields below.

"I think it's time for the winter harvest," she observed, leading the way down to the waiting crowd.

Frion Farrell

ACKNOWLEDGEMENTS

My particular thanks to Victoria Eden, who with little
warning and great enthusiasm, accompanied me on an
eventful research trip to Istanbul. Also to Bri Hume, who
travelled with me to the amazing New Grange in Ireland.
Thanks once again to Alan Duncan for kindly stepping in
to proof this second edition of the Auric Flame and the
last of the trilogy. It has been a source of great joy for me
to be able to offer this improved version of these books.
I am very grateful to Conor Watson for his original art
work. I would have been totally lost in this first attempt
to release a novel by myself, had it not been for the kind
assistance of Jamie Sinclair to whom I am very grateful.
And finally, thanks to the A team; Claire and Veronica-
always by my side in every venture.

Printed in Great Britain
by Amazon